FILTHY KING

THE FIVE POINTS' MOB COLLECTION: SEVEN

SERENA AKEROYD

DEDICATION

TO ANYONE who has ever felt as if they're not prepared for the task ahead of them...

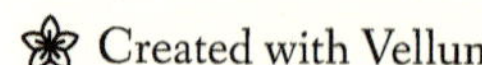 Created with Vellum

FOREWORD & TRIGGER WARNINGS

HELLO DARLINGS,

Me again!

I want to thank you for the faith you had in me with this book. I know you're waiting for Conor and Star's story, and trust me, that's going to happen. Did you meet Conor yet?

I think, once you read FILTHY KING, you'll understand why Aidan and Savvie's story had to come first.

Anyway, it's that time for me to warn you that there are GRAPHIC scenes of violence and a GRAPHIC depiction of death by hanging. This is the most violent book yet. Domestic violence—not between Savannah and Aidan!!—is also handled in the story.

But, with that being said, I think Aidan and Savannah might have scorched my fingertips with how hot they are together. Talk about burning up the pages... I hope you're ready for his ascension...

Don't forget the second FILTHY KING hits 500 reviews, I'll be dropping a bonus scene in my Diva reader group!

You can join here to read it when it happens: www.facebook.com/groups/SerenaAkeroydsDivas

Much love and happy reading to you all,

Serena

xoxo

PLAYLIST

If you'd like to hear a curated soundtrack, with songs that are featured in the book, as well as songs that inspired it, then here's the link:

https://open.spotify.com/playlist/1WhVjmXpIKJzcUKcXKHUUq?si=13195b80ec094022

THE CROSSOVER READING ORDER
WITH THE SINNERS & VALENTINIS

FILTHY
FILTHY SINNER
NYX
LINK
FILTHY RICH
SIN
STEEL
FILTHY DARK
CRUZ
MAVERICK
FILTHY SEX
HAWK
FILTHY HOT
STORM
THE DON
THE LADY
FILTHY SECRET
REX
RACHEL

<u>FILTHY KING</u>
<u>FILTHY DISCIPLE</u>
<u>THE CONSIGLIERE</u>
<u>THE ORACLE</u>
<u>LODESTAR</u>
<u>SILENCED</u>
<u>END GAME</u>
<u>FILTHY RICHER</u>

NAMES OF INTEREST:

NEW WORLD SPARROWS - often abbreviated to NWS. The members are known as Sparrows.

One of three global secret societies of criminals hidden in plain sight, mostly known for sex trafficking. Having infiltrated every aspect of US society, from the government to the courts to law enforcement agencies, they've escaped justice for their heinous crimes for decades.

Old World Sparrows - tied to the New World Sparrows. The oldest organization of the trio. Their territory is Europe.

Eastern Sparrows - the final Sparrow organization. Their territory is Asia.

Éire le chéile go deo - often abbreviated to ECD. The members are known as *cheiles*. An Irish organization dedicated to uniting Northern Ireland with the Republic and removing the British from their land.

Satan's Sinners' MC - a motorcycle club in West Orange, New Jersey. Allied to the Five Points. Led by Rex, the Prez.

Famigghia - Sicilian Mafia. Allied to the Five Points. Led by Luciu Valentini, the Don.

Russian Bratva - Allied to the Five Points. Led by Maxim Lyanov, the Pakhan.

United Brotherhood - An elite Russian version of the Masons. This far, little is known about their shady business dealings.

CONOR
THREE DECADES AGO

DREAMS - THE CORRS

I SLIPPED the candy cigarette between my lips and, when I looked in the window of the convenience store, crowed, "Look, Da, I'm just like you."

Tucking the paper bag under his arm, Da handed the clerk a twenty then peered at me, grinning as he scuffed his free hand over my hair. "Don't let your ma see. You know she don't like me smoking."

When I scrunched up my face and tried to pretend I was inhaling, Junior, smirking, muttered, "Now he really does look just like you, Da."

Da scowled at my oldest brother, and we all recognized *that* scowl. It had Junior hunching his shoulders, glancing away before he got that smirk knocked off his lips.

Quickly, he slouched over to the door.

"Why you gotta make him mad?" I grumbled as I hurried after him.

Junior sneered, "I breathe and he gives me shit for it."

I couldn't argue because he was right.

Every one of Da's boys managed to get him angry. Well, apart from Eoghan, and that was only because he was still more interested in toddling around the house than speaking. But none of us pissed Da off more than his firstborn.

"You don't know how to work around him," I mumbled. "I wish you did. He'll be all pissy on the ride home now."

"He's always pissy with me."

He sounded so miserable that I had to cheer him up.

"Not always. Today, it's 'cause you can't shoot in a straight line." I nudged him in the side. "I know you got it in you though, Aidan. I know you can do it."

"I don't want to do it, Kid. Don't you get that? I don't want to be Da's heir. I don't wanna learn how to shoot, and I don't wanna have to kill—" Before he finished that sentence, he broke off to clear his throat. "It doesn't matter. You don't know how fucking lucky you are, Con. No expectations, no standards. You can just be you." He shook his head when I made to argue. "He's coming over."

"What are you two talking about?" Da demanded, his suspicious gaze crawling over our expressions.

I reckoned we must have looked shifty because he didn't stop with the scan for a good thirty seconds. That was a *long* time, trust me.

"I was telling him about what my tutor taught me today."

Da's lips quirked up in a grin. "You learned a lot?" He scrubbed a hand over my hair again.

"I did. We were talking about this thing called the Y2K problem." I sighed wistfully. "I really hope all the computers in the world crash like the experts say they will."

Da snorted. "Destructive little fucker."

"What's the Y2K problem?" Junior questioned.

Neither my da nor my brother were all that interested in computers so I tried to figure out how to make it easy on them. "People are worried none of the computers'll be able to deal with going from 1999 to 2000 on the eve of the Millennium. They think they'll start showing 1900 instead of 2000, and that'll mess with ever-rrrrything."

"Fucking computers. They'll be the death of us," Da grouched as he opened the door to the store.

Even though I was used to him doing it, I watched him step out first, check the area, then gather nods of assent from the four guards watching us before he held it wider so we could leave too.

Da might be allowed to slap us for doing stupid shit, but no one else was permitted to hurt us. Things were tense at the moment because he was having some problems with the Italians so he was more on edge than usual.

I didn't know how you could have a problem with the people who'd invented pizza, but I was pretty sure Da'd get into a fight with a leprechaun who was offering him a massive pot of gold.

He was just ornery.

The car was waiting for us, the engine running—we never shut off cars in case there was a bomb set to explode upon triggering the ignition—and as we stepped outside into the cold night, that was when I heard it.

A soft sob.

It was barely audible over the noise from the engine, but I had good ears. Too good sometimes.

Twisting around, I blurted out, "Da, did you hear that?"

"Hear what?"

"Someone's crying," Junior mumbled, stepping away from the path toward the car and down the alleyway beside the convenience store where we'd stopped to buy some magazines for Ma.

She was in the hospital, and we were supposed to visit her tomorrow.

I'd asked what was wrong with her, and Da had called it, 'women's problems.' Brennan said she wanted a break from Da and, for some reason, Junior had laughed at that.

Either way, I didn't know which was true but I could think of nicer places than a hospital to get away from Da.

"Junior, where the fuck do you think you're going?" Da snapped when Aidan headed down the alley, his boots clicking against the wet sidewalk. Da wafted a hand to tell his men to stand down, and to me, he groused, "Stay here, Conor."

Of course, I didn't listen.

Whatever happened would end up with Junior getting a busted lip for disobeying; that was the only reason Da hadn't sent his guards after my brother—disobedience wasn't tolerated.

I shuffled after him, wanting to stop that from happening—Aidan couldn't help it that he and Da saw the world differently—and that was when I saw him, crouching on the ground in front of a lump.

The lump moved.

My eyes flared wide when I saw her boobs jiggle and she—

I reared back when it registered that she had no clothes on.

None at all.

Top or bottom.

It was freezing out here, *freezing*.

Aidan was shrugging out of his jacket and shoving it at her but she was sobbing and—

Bleeding.

She was bleeding.

From everywhere.

Her pale skin had slashes in it, and she had bruises on her face and her body, and there was blood between her legs and *everywhere*.

So much blood.

Everywhere.

Da strode over just as Aidan started dragging off his gloves to give to the woman, and when his hand went to Junior's shoulder to grab a hold of him, he stilled.

"Grainne?" He hesitated, his eyes squinting as he stared down at her. "Is that you?"

A couple things hit home. First, that was as Irish a name as was possible. Was she the daughter of a Five Pointer? Second was that Da clearly knew her. Was this beating... a punishment?

When he made no move to do anything, just stood there watching as Aidan tried to put her fingers into his gloves, I hurried over, feet thudding, and demanded, "Da, we gotta help her." My hand grabbed his and I tugged, hard.

He scowled at me. "I'm going to help, Conor."

"Oh." Clinging to him, not wanting to let go, I tightened my fingers around his. "Why is she bleeding down there?"

His jaw clenched. "Grainne, who hurt you?"

"John," she slurred.

"John, who?" I asked. Then eagerly, I explained, "My da's the scariest man in New York. He'll make sure John pays for what—"

"Kid, shut up," Aidan hissed. "John... She means *a* john. She's a... She sleeps with guys for cash."

"People do that?" I knew I sounded doubtful. Why would someone pay to sleep with another person?

"Some do." His wary gaze drifted over to our father. "How do you know her, Da?"

Rage lit up his features at Aidan's question. "Watch your mouth, boy."

"How do you know a hooker, Da?" Junior insisted, clearly angry enough that he'd lost his sense because Da looked like he was about to punch him.

"F-wank."

I blinked at the girl's slurred answer. Fwank? What the heck was fwank?

"Frank?" Aidan enunciated, his relief clear. "Our uncle? You know him? Or... did he do this to you?"

Da was silent a second before he muttered, "She used to be his side piece. He'd never hurt her."

"What's a side piece?" I questioned, but no one answered me.

Grainne began sobbing as Junior unapologetically rumbled, "I was watching out for Ma."

"You don't need to do that. That's my job," Da sniped, but he mirrored Junior by crouching in front of Grainne and asking, "You know the fucker's name?"

"Jus' lemme die. I wanna die. Lemme die—"

"No!" I cried. "You can't let her die!" It didn't register that I was sobbing, but big fat tears blurred my vision as I continued, "Da, you have to help her! You have to!"

Da hissed, "Conor, shut your mouth."

Sniffling, I obeyed, but only because he leaned forward and started to shuffle Grainne around and into a position where she was standing.

Every movement must have hurt her because she sobbed each time. Sometimes, she even screamed or cursed, and that was how I knew she was in excruciating agony because no one swore at Aidan O'Donnelly Sr.—unless they had a death wish.

Junior helped prop her up, and the three of them staggered down the alley with me darting out in front of them so I wasn't left behind.

"We need to get to Bellevue," Da groused at Jonesy, his guard, who dipped his head to tell Michael, our driver.

I watched as my brother and father helped Grainne into our car, and the second she was weeping miserably in a heap in the backseat, that was when Junior jumped in beside her, and when I should have too.

But I didn't.

I wanted to know why Da stayed back, wanted to know if I could find out what a side piece was.

"Don't say a word about this to Frank, do you hear me?"

Jonesy was shrugging. "You know me, boss. I don't say shit to no one."

"Good. Tell the others I'll have their balls if they utter a fucking word." When he saw me looking, my eyes bright with curiosity as I wiped my nose on my cuff—men didn't cry, especially not in front of the guards—he ordered, "Conor, you keep your trap shut too."

"Why would a man do that to a lady, Da?"

"She ain't no lady," Jonesy said with a snort.

I scowled. "Shut up! She is! She ain't a boy, is she?"

Da heaved a sigh and clapped a hand to my shoulder. As he squeezed, he muttered, "Women pay for the sins of man, Conor. Remember that, boy. It's why we protect and cherish them. Always."

Staring up at him wide-eyed, I nodded.

Never realizing that those words would be the only lesson I'd ever learn from the sadistic psychopath who was my father, and it was one I'd live my life by...

EXCERPT FROM AIDAN O'DONNELLY JR.'S EULOGY TO HIS FATHER

No one would say you were perfect, Da. Neither would
anyone say that you were the world's greatest father—but
I don't think you aspired to be the greatest at anything.
You taught me what it is to be a leader, and know that I'm
grateful for those life lessons even as I go my own way
when I take over your legacy.
I don't think I ever pleased you or made you proud of me
until last Christmas when I shared what truly made me a
man. As I stand here today, our family around us,
mourning your passing, I know if I'm ever blessed with a
child, you taught me how not to be a father, and I'll thank
you again for that lesson.
But for all that we never agreed on anything, for all that we
butted heads on most things, and for all that I'll forge my
own path and will never step upon the one you left
behind, know that I'll miss you, you ornery bastard.
You left a hole in our lives that none of us know how to fill.
Maybe that's fitting.

I couldn't say it in life, but I can say it in death—love you, Da. Rest in... I don't think you'd enjoy peace. So, rest in chaos.

That was always your preference.

1

____

TEXT CHAT

SAVANNAH

LODESTAR: *Vana, I want you to know something.*

Me: *About the Sparrows?*

Lodestar: *Not just about them. About us too.*

Me: *Okay, hit me with it. What have you done and who do I need to bribe?*

Lodestar: *Like old times?*

Me: *Yep. Remember when you tried to sneak off with that band who was on the starting lineup for noxxious?*

Lodestar: *I do. It didn't go down well.*

Me: *And that was with me helping you, lol.*

Me: *I watched them play at Madison Square Garden last week. They went straight to the top.*

Lodestar: *Thought Aidan Jr. would have put you on lockdown.*

Me: *No. Aidan and I were there to meet with someone.*

Lodestar: *Business?*

Me: *Always.*

Me: *Anyway, what's up?*

Lodestar: *You might not hear from me for a while.*

Me: *As long as last time?*

Lodestar: *Maybe longer.*

Me: *Shit.*

incoming call

Me: *Star, pick up the damn phone.*

Lodestar: *No. I don't want to talk. I need you to know that everything I'm doing, it's for a reason.*

Me: *This sounds like a suicide conversation.*

Lodestar: *A, what? Jesus, Vana. Can't you just let me get this down?*

Me: *No. Not if you're trying to give me an interactive suicide note via text.*

Lodestar: *I don't want to die.*

Me: *Good. That's half the battle.*

Lodestar: *That doesn't mean some people don't want me dead.*

Me: *Babe, some people want ME dead. Isn't that how we know we're doing it right?*

Lodestar: *That's your sparkling personality.*

Me: *Bitch. Why did I miss you again?*

Lodestar: *:P*

Lodestar: *You'll be receiving a package in the mail soon. There's a lot of info in it for you. You should be able to trigger hell.*

Me: *I don't hear from you in months but you always come back bearing gifts. You do know I'm always the last person who messages in our chats, don't you?*

Lodestar: *Sorry.*

Me: *No, you're not. And if I get to trigger hell, you'd better be around to see it. We always liked reigning over our personal hellscape, didn't we?*

Lodestar: *The shit our dads got up to was more like paradise than what we waded into, Vana.*

Me: *Crazy how they were hedonists and we dove deep into this batshit world, isn't it?*

Lodestar: *Typical second gen trying to prove themselves.*

Me: *Think we've proven enough?*

Lodestar: *No. I haven't.*

Me: *Then I haven't either. We're in this together.*

Lodestar: *I want you to be happy, Vana.*

Me: *I am. Aidan makes me very happy. He pisses me off too, but that's to be expected. I want you to have this, Star. I want you to be happy.*

Lodestar: *Happiness isn't for people like me.*

Me: *Bullshit. You can have this as well. We can keep on waging this war together, fighting from the trenches, and we won't stop until we win.*

Lodestar: *I love you.*

Me: *I love you too. But that's not what I needed to hear. What's going on with you?*

Me: *Star?*

Me: *Star?*

Me: *Goddammit, answer me.*

Me: *Star, you bitch, don't fucking do this.*

Me: *Damn you. Why do you always fucking leave?*

One week later

Me: *Star?*

2

———————

AIDAN JR.

MILLION YEARS AGO - ADELE

SAVVIE SNORED IN HER SLEEP.

My lips quirked up in a grin at the thought of telling her she did.

I knew it'd lead to an argument, but I didn't mind. No one argued like Savvie.

No one's eyes flashed with irritation like hers did, no one's nose tipped up just so, and no one stomped off in the perfectly adorable *and* lust-inducing way that made her tits and ass jiggle.

For all those reasons, plus a thousand more, Savannah was my wife.

She was cuddled up next to me, her thigh angled high over mine, her foot against my leg, far from my knee from habit rather than necessity.

The bum joint was no more. I wasn't as good as new but if she accidentally kicked me there, it wasn't the end of the world.

Before, I'd have preferred her to kick me in the balls rather than my knee but my new doctor had worked a fucking miracle on the replacement.

One hand behind my neck, the other hooked against her knee, I stared up at the ceiling, well aware that I should be sleeping, well aware that now wasn't the fucking time to be dealing with insomnia.

A screen flashed on, illuminating the room. I tilted my head to stare at the cluster of phones and pulled a face when I saw it was my da's.

The screen was cracked and there was blood in those cracks.

His blood.

It was fucked up but I didn't have it in me to just switch out the SIM card.

Grainne.

That was the name on the caller ID.

I frowned at the sight.

"Where the fuck do I remember that name from?" I muttered to myself as I watched the screen flash after I let it ring off.

I could have picked it up, could have just answered it to uncover why an Irishwoman was calling my da at three AM, but I didn't want to.

My hand smoothed up and down the silk that was my bride's thigh, and my gaze retreated to the ceiling once more.

It was one thing to know you were ready for more responsibility, to be tired of being treated like an untried boy, and it was another to be shoved into the fray.

I was forty-three-fucking-years-old but that was the bitch of losing your father—you were never too old to feel young when they died. Even if you were relieved, and felt guilty about that relief, that you didn't have to deal with their bullshit anymore.

The screen flashed.

Grainne.

Again.

Annoyed, I untangled myself from Savvie's clinging embrace—that wasn't a complaint—and gently shuffled her into the middle of the bed. She rolled over with a huff but didn't wake up. Since the funeral, sleep hadn't been coming easily, so when she did rest, she slept deeper than usual.

There was a majestic irony to the fact she was more grief-stricken than I was.

I grabbed the phone, eyed the blood on the glass and let my thumb swipe over the cracks that represented so much more than a fucking broken screen, then retreated from the bedroom into the living room.

I didn't stop there because I knew my wife too well to recognize that she'd pretend to sleep so she could listen in, and instead, I continued to the office at the other end of the apartment.

I'd had this room soundproofed months ago—the moment I closed the door, she couldn't hear shit from within its walls. Something she'd already bitched about.

Staring over at Manhattan at a height of a thousand feet, I trudged over to my desk, took a seat, then hit redial.

"About time you answered."

"Excuse me?" I seethed, taken aback by the attitude of this fucking stranger.

"I need you over here."

Eyes flashing, I rasped, "This isn't Aidan Sr."

She scoffed, "I know it isn't. He's dead."

"Who the fuck are you? And, if you know he's dead, why the hell are you calling my da's cellphone in the early hours?"

"Because the early hours is when I do my best business, boy." She huffed. "He didn't tell you about me?"

Dread lodged in my chest. "No. He didn't."

There was a lot of shit he hadn't told me.

A lot.

More than I could fucking handle.

God, not another girlfriend—

"I'm Grainne."

She pronounced it 'Grah-nya.' Because I preferred learning shit aurally to visually, I knew enough about Irish accents to know that was Ulster Irish. Northern Irish. From the Republic, it'd be 'Grawn-ya.'

And that, of course, was when I remembered.

The hooker.

Fuck, I'd been... what? Thirteen?

Was this the same person?

How many 'Grah-nyas' were there in the tristate area?

"Grainne," I repeated slowly.

"Your father and I were business partners."

Business, not romantic?

I seriously didn't think I could deal with Da cheating on top of all the other shit he'd been hiding.

"What kind of business?"

"Queens of Heart—"

"The strip club?" I blurted out.

The place was a landmark in a certain part of Hell's Kitchen. I knew most of the men used it for shit they needed to confess to on Sunday mornings.

I'd been there myself as a kid when Da had decided I needed my cherry popped.

That had been a fucking lesson and a half.

I just hadn't known the hooker I'd found in an alleyway that day, Grainne, might have something to do with the club.

"The strip club," she confirmed before she hissed under her breath. "He really didn't tell you about me? Goddammit, Aidan."

I knew she wasn't talking to me right then.

She called Da Aidan?

It was his fucking name, but that didn't mean a lot of people ever dared use it.

Suddenly weary, I reached up and rubbed my eyes. "What do you want, Grainne?"

"I need you to come down to Queens of Heart—"

"Why?"

"Because I have something for you, and I need you to come and make an example out of this *eejit* who thinks he can beat one of my girls."

I was on the brink of saying that was below my fucking pay grade, but her demand would only make sense if: "The *eejit's* a Five Pointer?"

"He is. Cain MacMurray."

I almost groaned.

I hated that fucking asswipe.

"What makes you think this is my job?" I rumbled, massaging my temple where another headache was starting to form.

"Because it *is* your job. Your da would come here and sort this shit out for me. We had a special relationship."

Eyes flaring, I spat, "How *special?*"

"He dealt with these problems for me."

"Every time you had an issue with a pissed off john he came down to Queens of Heart? All the way from upstate?"

"No. Every time I had a problem with a fucking Five Pointer," Grainne corrected with a sniff. "We had a mutually beneficial relationship, Junior. I'd like to continue that even if your da's dead. You'll understand when you get your ass down here and I can give you my gift."

My jaw cracked. "You weren't seeing him, were you?"

"I dated Frank," she told me coolly, incidentally confirming my supposition that the hooker in the alley back in the day and this woman were one and the same. "He was the only O'Donnelly I was interested in."

"You were his side piece." It wasn't a question.

"I was."

I rocked back in my seat. "I asked after you; Da never mentioned you and he went into business."

"No one knew."

"No one?" I asked dubiously.

"That's the definition of zero people, right? Or have I forgotten how to use the English language?"

Christ, she had a mouth on her.

I grunted. "It's hard to keep shit like that secret."

"I know it is. On paper, it's mine. But I know he's the only reason I am where I am."

Rubbing my chin, I muttered what I knew of the madam who ran Queens of Heart: "Manhattan's Divorce Maker."

She snorted. "I'm so much more than that, honey. Your wife knows it too. She's been pestering me for an interview for years. Been thinking about saying yes but knew your da wouldn't like it..."

Goddammit.

Of course, Savvie wanted an interview with her.

My wife could scent out trouble like a bloodhound.

I released a hissed breath but didn't utter a word.

Grainne hummed. "You're different than him, aren't you?"

"Than who? My da? Yeah. I am."

"I can tell. You didn't demand I don't do the interview, didn't tell me to stay away from your wife—"

"There's little fucking point. She does what she wants." Fuck me for the dumbass I was that I loved her most annoying trait of all.

Another hum sounded in my ear. "I think we'll get along well, Junior."

I wasn't particularly interested in us getting along. "Aidan," I corrected.

"Your da was that to me for a long time."

"Don't care. You want my ass down there, you'll call me Aidan."

"Okay, Aidan."

"What's the situation?"

"My security has him under control." Before I could ask what the fuck she wanted me to do if her men had the situation contained, she blurted out, "He's very high."

"On what?"

"It's that new shit on the streets—Red."

I hissed under my breath again. "Okay, I'll be there as soon as I can."

"Good."

She hung up the phone, and I immediately dialed Brennan.

"We're needed at Queens of Heart," I told him before he could ask me what the fuck I was doing ringing him at three AM.

"The strip club?"

"The strip club."

He sounded as awake as I did. "Okay, meet you there in forty-five."

I grunted, disconnected the call, then got to my feet and retreated to the bedroom.

Savvie was still sleeping.

How fucked up was it that that made me worry about her?

I'd caught her crying earlier. Fucking crying. Over my psychopath fucker of a father.

She'd hero-worshiped him though—that was still insane to me—and Da's death was hitting her hard. I didn't disturb her because she needed the rest and trudged over to the closet.

My hand automatically reached for one of my suits. One set of fingers grabbed a silk sports coat, while the other snatched a necktie from the purpose-built case that housed my collection, but then I shook myself.

This wasn't Da's city anymore.

It was mine.

I grabbed a black tee, some jeans, and a pair of shitkickers that I used to wear for wetwork. Most of it was old now because I'd been stuck in a suit since the shooting that had wrecked my knee.

Everything was too tight. I'd pumped up since then, but I determined tomorrow I'd buy some more gear. Gear that fit the new filthy fucking king of Manhattan.

I reached for a gun and holster, armed myself with two knives, then dragged on a suede field jacket. Leaving on the light for ease of movement, I headed out into the bedroom and hovered over Savvie.

Crouching down at the bedside, something my new knee permitted for short bouts, I reached over and stroked her hair away from her forehead.

She didn't stir at first, so I went to kiss her temple.

I felt her sudden wakefulness before she sighed my name. "Aidan?"

Every fucking time she did that, it got to me, shot straight to my cock and had me aching to be inside her.

Pressing another kiss to the crown of her head, I murmured, "I have to go out, little one."

Savvie yawned then stilled. Peering at me from between slitted eyes, she whispered, "Are you wearing jeans?"

Did her voice thicken or was that just my imagination?

"I am."

"Why aren't you wearing a suit?"

"Because I don't need to wear one where I'm going."

I could sense her eyes crawling over me. One hand moved to my field jacket, and her fingers stroked over the suede in a similar way as if she were stroking my cock.

My dick hardened in response, and now was not the fucking moment for that.

"It's late, isn't it?"

Yeah, her voice had thickened for real.

Fuck. My. Life.

"More like early. It's three AM. I won't be long."

Now that my dick was engaged, I sure as hell wouldn't be hanging around unnecessarily.

She started to sit up. "I'll come with you."

My wife had gotten into the habit of stunning the hell out of me, but this definitely took me by surprise.

"What? You can't; it's business, honey. You go back to sleep."

Her hand snapped around my wrist. "I-I, you, we—"

"What is it? What's wrong?" I demanded, her nervousness ramming into me with all the force of a Mack truck.

Savvie wasn't nervous.

She was confident. Bullish, even.

Her nails dug into my wrist. "How bad is it? Is it to do with your father's death?"

My shoulders sagged. "Little one, we've been through this."

"No, you went through this. I told you that you're not allowed to die. Ever."

I had to stop myself from smiling. "That's impossible."

"I don't care. You're not allowed to go—"

When she sniffled—the woman who'd faced sieges and had actively honey-trapped a producer at the TV network where she worked so she could leak the footage live on breakfast television—I knew I was a fucking goner.

I climbed onto the bed, sighing when she wriggled over to let me onto the mattress before she pretty much entangled me with her limbs as if that would keep me close.

Her face nestled into my throat, and her hands grabbed at me, holding me tightly in her embrace.

Da's passing, the death of her hero, had shaken her more than I could have anticipated, though this *was* the first time I'd been called away on business since that day.

The city was still feeling the shockwaves of Da's death, and the nation had lost their First Lady to an assassin.

In the aftermath, with police blockades in place and half of Manhattan on lockdown, shit had been quiet.

"Da lived a long life," I tried to soothe. Longer than he'd fucking deserved, that was for sure.

As I stroked my hand over her hair, holding her as tight as she held me, I tried to figure out how I could support her, but I didn't know how to help her when verbalizing my own feelings for a man whose passing I was finding hard to grieve didn't come easy.

Da had been a confusing man in life, but in death, that was magnified tenfold.

"How do I know someone isn't going to try to take you away from me too?"

The words broke me from my thoughts, sending me reeling as I hugged her harder, trying to reassure her physically as, verbally, I comforted, "You don't know that. *We* don't know that. Who was it who told me that my life, my work, is as dangerous as yours?"

Her baby sister had been kidnapped by a deranged fan, after all, because their father was Dagger Daniels—rock god extraordinaire.

"Threats are everywhere," she whispered, breaking my fucking heart with how despairing she sounded. "I don't want to lose you."

"I know you don't, sweetheart. But I don't intend on going anywhere. I have to make a name for myself. I have to prove my worth. Then I'll be untouchable like..." I broke off before I could finish the sentence.

How could I say Da was untouchable when his death proved otherwise?

That was when I realized her cheeks were wet.

My wife was weeping like her heart was breaking.

Rage spilled into me on her behalf and it made me say shit I should have kept silent about.

"Baby, Da didn't get executed because of who he was." At my words, she tensed, but ignoring that tension, I continued, "It wasn't a business rival—"

"You say that like you know who killed him."

I sighed. "I know that he framed himself. He was sick, little one. Very sick."

She swallowed. "With what?"

"ALS."

We'd only learned this yesterday after the will reading. Ma had gotten a letter from Da, and when Conor had to medicate her, he'd found that letter and had shared its contents with us.

"The person who shot him had a grudge against Ma. Da chose to sacrifice himself for her."

It was difficult to be mad at him for that, especially knowing that it had killed two birds with one stone—ALS was a fucking horrendous disease.

But ALS aside, I'd do the same for Savvie. I'd set myself up to take a bullet to protect her in a heartbeat.

It was like she heard me *think* that. Because, suddenly, she was on top of me, her legs straddling mine, her knees pinning me in place.

"Don't you dare do that for me," she growled.

"What? Protect you with my life?" I scoffed. "Bet your sweet ass I will."

She slapped my chest. "No! Aidan! NO. I don't want you to do that. I don't—"

Before she could get riled up, I shocked her by twisting us around. In a flash, she was on her back, I was between her legs, and her arms were overhead, wrists cuffed with one of my hands. The other went to her throat, and I used that hold to tilt her head back so that she was looking straight into my fucking eyes as I snarled, "There is no ending to our story where I don't sacrifice myself to protect you, Savannah. You are *my wife.* My vows weren't goddamn throwaway—"

"You didn't vow to take a bullet for me. Just like I didn't vow to *obey* you."

I hissed beneath my breath. "I never asked for you to obey. Not just because I know that'd be fucking impossible for you. I don't need you to obey. Because this is my decision. You can't control what I do, Savannah."

She burst into tears again, but before I even had the chance to sigh, her mouth was on mine, her tongue thrusting between my lips. Her hips squirmed so that her bare pussy was grinding against my denim-covered fly, and her feet dug into my ass for more pressure.

In less than thirty seconds, I went from being irrationally angry at her inability to understand what it meant when I married her to wanting to fuck her senseless.

I did *not* have time for this, but that didn't stop me from arching up, slipping a hand between us, and dragging down my zipper.

With zero hesitation, my dick was in my fist and I rubbed the tip against her clit—she was drenched and it made the passage of my shaft through her folds feel that much better.

"Goddammit, little one," I growled against her mouth, pulling back to bite her bottom lip as I ground into her. "Why are you always so wet for me?"

"Fuck," she whimpered, her head bowing back to my ravenous gaze.

I dipped down and sucked hard on the join between shoulder and throat as I started to rock my cock again.

The shit she did to me, the way she made me fucking feel—I'd never felt this alive before. *Ever*.

She was like an electric shock to my heart every day.

And I wasn't inside her yet!

As I ground my pelvis into her, the pressure from the coarse fabric had her sobbing, and when I gave her a bite that'd bruise by the morning, I moved back to stare down into her eyes.

Every single time I rubbed her clit with the tip of my cock, I punctuated each word:

"You. Are. Mine. To. Protect. Little. One."

"I don't want you to. I don't want to be without you—"

"You. Won't. Be. Without. Me."

"You don't know that," she cried out, her face burrowing under my chin as she writhed beneath me.

Which was when I stopped grinding into her.

Horror filled me when more tears collided with my skin, leaving ghostly trails to drip down my neck.

"Are you just trying to stop me from leaving?"

Her silence, followed by a sniffle, keyed me into her game immediately.

I pulled away and, ignoring her moan, snapped, "You do not control me through sex, Savannah."

That was one way to get us killed.

I could deal with many things—her being a brat, her trying to lead me around by the dick, her trying to get information out of me by asking me questions she shouldn't during pillow talk—but this was another matter entirely.

This was her fucking safety.

Our fucking safety.

And I could just see it now.

Me heading out of the building with her tailing me.

Fuck, this was another Deirdre situation all over again.

Only, Savvie wouldn't follow me because she thought I was cheating, but because she was infinitely curious about goddamn everything *and* because she was concerned for me.

The danger she would put herself in had me reacting blindly.

I reached over to the bedside table where I knew there was at least one of my neckties—

I struck gold.

Cold metal.

I grabbed the handcuffs.

Before she even knew what I was doing, her panic clear as she tried to curl her legs around my hips to draw me back down to her so I wouldn't leave, her pelvis rocking so that my dick collided with the sinful paradise she housed between her fucking thighs, I slotted one of the restraints around her wrist, looped it onto one of the rails on the headboard, then grabbed her other hand and cuffed her to the bed.

"Aidan?!" she shrieked when she registered what I'd done.

"Lights on," I commanded to the control center in the room, blinking when they illuminated the space, revealing every inch of her to me.

My dick was aching like a fucker when I pulled back, so close to heaven without getting to enter its gates, and the sight of her tied to the bed wasn't helping.

I knew she wanted sex because her cunt had been wet as fuck, but I wasn't about to let her get away with using it to distract me from the shit I had to do.

My wife's trouble was that, to me, she was exquisite. Porcelain skin, arched brows that framed her features. Amber-brown eyes that saw far too much and were topped by thick lashes. Mahogany silk bobbed around her shoulders, shielding a stubborn jaw that housed lips that were a dusky pink I wanted to lick and which were made for blowjobs. Her nose was dainty with a thin bridge, her cheeks like sharp ice picks that made her face heart-shaped.

She was the face that'd launch a thousand ships—my Helen of Troy.

"You want a guaranteed way of getting me killed, you pull stunts like this. Distractions are dangerous. For the next couple years, I have to be hot shit to make sure that no one scents any weakness from my camp, do you understand?"

Her cheeks glowed with heat and those mahogany eyes sparked with temper. "I don't deserve to be punished. I haven't done anything wrong!"

"You're trying to stop me from going out."

Need whittled away at my control as I processed the show she was providing as she tried to get loose, those luscious curves of hers making my cock ache all the more, but there was no getting free. Those weren't novelty cuffs, but the real deal because she'd broken through the last couple pairs I'd bought.

Not wanting to test my knee by sustaining my kneeling position, I swung off the bed then delved into the nightstand again.

I did *not* have time for this, but Grainne and MacMurray could goddamn wait.

I had a lesson to teach.

Uncaring that Brennan would also be cooling his heels for me, I grabbed the hemp rope and the cutter I kept there.

I'd done this very few times with Savvie, keeping it for the occasions where she really pissed me off—like on our wedding night when she'd tried to cancel the ceremony because Ma was throwing her weight around.

My wife was a grade A brat and I loved that about her, but where our safety was concerned, I had to act.

"No!" she yelped when she saw the rope.

Jesus Christ, what her position did to her tits sent bolts of lust arrowing through me.

"Yes."

"Aidan, just come back to bed. Please," she pleaded.

"Did you or did you not try to stop me from going out on business by fucking me?"

Savvie sniffled. "Maybe."

"Bullshit. Tell me the truth, Savannah."

Something about my tone had her turning her face to the side. "I don't want you to get hurt."

"If you distract me, if you try to disrupt business, people will see that as inattention to detail and they'll try to exploit that and I *will* get hurt."

"No!" she cried out, which clued me into just how distraught my wife was. Because she was smart, too fucking smart for my own good. If she didn't see that, if logic failed her, then I knew her grief and exhaustion were overwhelming her.

"Yes," I said inexorably. "I'm going to do this to teach you a lesson, little one—"

"You don't need to!"

"Yes, I do," I retorted, my tone softer. "Because, in all honesty, sweetheart, I don't trust you to keep your beautiful ass in this bed. I don't fucking trust you not to try to follow me.

"Do you know what'll happen if you do that? You'll get yourself killed, and I'm *not* about to let that happen."

She started weeping, which was further proof she was *not* herself, and I leaned over her, hands on either side of her raised arms, and I pressed my lips to hers.

As she sighed into my kiss, I pulled back, saw her tears had dried, and I rasped, "When I get back, I will fuck you and I'll make you come so hard you see stars, but until then, I want you to think about what you did.

"I want you to think about how I need you to listen to me, Savannah, and I want you to think about how you should have discussed this fear of yours with me before it got to this point."

"I need the bathroom," she said with a pout.

That pout told me she was lying.

"Do you really?"

Minutes ticked away, and I knew it was another way of her getting me to stay here, to steer me clear of whatever danger had me heading out, but I let it pass.

Eventually, I was rewarded with a garbled, "Maybe."

"Savannah."

She heard the warning. "No, I don't! Okay?"

"You're such a fucking brat, and God damn me for a fool because I love that about you, but this is something you need to resolve yourself to. Do you understand me?"

"I understand," she said sulkily.

Pulling back, pissed at the situation, pissed at having to leave, pissed because my dick made steel look soft, I grabbed the hemp rope and made short work of knots that required more time than I had.

Still, every line that I settled against her flesh, I anointed with a kiss, and as I looped bindings around her ankles that connected them to her upper thighs so she was in a kind of lotus position with her pussy bared to me, I stared down at her and rumbled, "So fucking beautiful, little one."

She swallowed. "Please don't go."

"Baby girl, I have to."

Delving into the nightstand once more, I pulled out one of the toys I'd bought a couple months ago.

Her eyes widened at the sight of it. "Aidan, no!"

I dragged the tip of the Bluetooth vibrator through her folds, getting it slick with her juices. "Little one, yes."

She wriggled as I rubbed her clit with the toy, and her breath soughed from her as, eventually, I pressed the tip to her slit.

With our gazes locked on each other's, I thrust the toy in, watching the flutter of her eyelashes as she savored the new fullness.

I didn't switch on the vibrations, just activated it then reached over to the cuffs, checking the restraints to make sure they were tight enough to hold her but not tight enough to hurt.

"There's no breaking out of these, Savannah." I eyed the head-board. "Not unless you try to destroy the frame, and if you do that, you'll hurt yourself in the process.

"I'll be monitoring this room. If you do anything to injure yourself to get free, I'll put this on full blast and I *will* spank the hell out of you when I get back."

Her eyes flared, not in fear, but interest.

The fear had faded. Thank fuck. I didn't know if I *could* leave her while she was scared.

She swallowed. "What do I get if I'm a good girl?"

This woman was going to be the fucking death of me.

I reached down and palmed my dick.

"Whatever you want."

She groaned, keying me into the fact I'd just bestowed something dangerous upon her.

Who the fuck knew what she'd come up with during her time alone, tethered to the bed, with nothing else to do but think about causing havoc...?

Another man would have second-guessed her and released her, whereas I looked forward to whatever challenge she concocted in my absence.

I pressed a kiss to her mouth, and she swept her tongue out to tempt me.

I was a weak, weak, *weak* man because I let her for a good thirty seconds before I pulled back and climbed off the bed.

My dick wasn't going to go down, nor did I want it to.

I slipped my fingers through her juices, got my palm nice and wet, spat into it for extra lube, then I started jacking off.

"No!" she cried out thickly, wriggling around in a way that'd make her wrists burn soon. "Let me! Please," she begged. "Let me."

"No. Consider this another lesson." My head arched back, sinews in my throat bulging as I forced myself to focus on not fucking her.

Quick, hard, punishing strokes got me there, faster and rougher than she'd ever touch me with, and I growled as I came, making sure that every drop of my cum landed on her milky skin.

It splatted on her stomach, some on her tits, and the stark white against her pretty pink pussy had me gritting my teeth at the sight even as I was panting with relief at getting off.

Heart pounding, I bowed my head as I let the intensity of my orgasm flood me. It wasn't as good as coming inside her cunt, but her sobs and pleas for me to fill her were like I had an angelic choir singing to me.

It got better when she cursed, "God damn you, Aidan O'Donnelly. You better not take a long time. You better get your fucking ass back here soon!"

My lips twitched as I tucked my dick away. "Two hours tops."

"Two hours!" she screeched. "You can't leave me like this for two hours."

"The bindings are tight enough to hold you but not to cut off your blood supply." I shot her a measured look as I zipped up my fly. "If you stay still and try to sleep until I get back, you'll be fine."

"You can't leave me like this!"

I arched a brow at her as I reached down and quickly fingered her clit which had her groaning.

"I think you're wetter than ever."

She hissed at me, "You bastard."

"My parents were definitely married when I was conceived," I taunted her, pulling back with a smirk.

I straightened myself and headed over to the bathroom to wash my hands. After, I veered into the closet and switched off the light.

Her shrill snarls of—"I'll get you back for this!" "You bastard! I want your dick. Give it to me now!" "I'll make you pay for this. Fuck me, baby. Please. Fuck me."—only rammed home the importance of this lesson.

As I entered the bedroom, I paused at the foot of the bed to stare down at her squirming self.

Glowering at me as she fidgeted, I studied her ripe curves, how her tits jiggled, her gleaming pussy, and I asked quietly, "Hard limit?"

She blinked at me.

Her nostrils flared.

Her head jerked to the side and away from me.

I had my answer.

Still...

"Words, little one."

"Not a hard limit," she spat at me.

Rounding the bed to get my cells, seeing a couple missed calls from Brennan, I headed over to the door, tapping out an apology about the delay to him, and said, "Lights off."

"Aidan," she screamed as if she hadn't just told me she was more than down for this. "You get back here and fuck me right this instant!"

"Love you too, little one," I called back, lips quirking as she released a roar of outrage that made my dick harden. Again.

As I opened the door, she let loose another screech, and I wanted to both laugh *and* rage because she was like fucking fire in this mood and my mind was definitely not on work.

Before I had the chance to cave in and retreat to the bedroom, I came face to face with my brother.

I immediately scowled. "The fuck are you doing here, Kid?"

He looked like shit—a combination of Lodestar, his girlfriend-but-not, doing a fucking runner and Da's death.

Savannah let me know her fury once more by shrieking, "Get your dick back here and put it inside me now, Aidan O'Donnelly Jr.!"

Conor's brows lifted as I quickly closed the door behind me. "Da owned Queens of Heart?"

Ignoring another roar from my wife who sure as hell had a set of pipes on her, I narrowed my eyes at him. "You know, you listening into our calls is getting pretty fucking tiring."

"My job."

"*Was* your job. Past tense."

"You're not my boss, Aidan. I do these things for the family's safety." His jaw tipped up. "That means I'm answerable to no one when I monitor your conversations."

"Who do you report to now Da's dead?" I jibed.

"You, of course. Wasn't that obvious?"

"Not really. What with the whole 'I'm answerable to no one and you're not my boss,' bullshit." I rolled my eyes before I repeated, "What *are* you doing here?"

"Coming with you to Queens of Heart."

"Why?"

"Because I want to go?"

"Why?"

"Because I'm curious."

I snorted. "You wanna get a lap dance? Is that it?"

He huffed. "No, fuckwit. I want to know what Grainne's going to give you. It has to be information. That's clearly the only reason Da would own a strip joint that wasn't on the books."

"You checked?"

"Of course I did. Grainne Ledger—she pays us protection money."

"She does?" Confusion had me scowling at him. "Why the fuck would Da pay protection money to himself? Why not make it known to the Points that he owns the place?"

"Secrets." Conor tapped his nose. "Hence my interest."

I grimaced. "I'm tired of those."

"I'm not. They make the world go around." He peered at the door. "Is Savannah okay?"

He timed that perfectly with a shriek louder than any of the others which was saying fucking something.

"You really want to know what I did to her?"

"She's safe?"

"She is now," I muttered, knowing point blank that she'd have found a way to follow me to the strip club. Not just because it was work, but maybe out of jealousy too.

In all honesty, knowing she was tied to the bed was like a load off my shoulders.

I didn't want to head out in the middle of the night to Queens of fucking Heart, but if I had to, at least I knew she was safe at home.

"You're right. I don't want to know."

Smirking as we headed toward the elevator, I asked, "You ain't been sleeping?"

"None of us have," he said dismissively, his gaze on the panel over the door.

I couldn't argue there.

"Any news from Lodestar?"

His Adam's apple bobbed as we boarded the elevator and I hit the button for the parking garage. "No."

Pissed at her for hurting my kid brother, I gritted my teeth. "Nothing at all?"

"I don't want to talk about this," he said coldly, his relief evident as we walked out into the garage.

Heading over to my Bugatti, I climbed behind the wheel, he jumped into the passenger seat, and we took off without another word.

It was when we reached Queens of Heart that I realized what he'd fucking done.

Outside the club, Brennan wasn't the only one standing there.

Eoghan, Declan, and Finn were too.

My brothers—by more than just blood.

I'd gotten it wrong before.

Seeing them standing there was the reminder I needed—this wasn't Da's city anymore.

It wasn't just mine.

It was ours.

3

AIDAN

GENESIS - RUELLE

"YOU CALLED THEM?" I muttered under my breath. "Or did Brennan?"

"Me." Conor's mouth tightened. "You're the leader, Aidan, but this ain't all on you. Someone dared to believe that they could take our old man out without any retaliation.

"Our family needs to reassert dominance over the fucking city. New York needs reminding who owns it."

"You're right."

"Thought you'd argue."

"No. It makes sense."

The valet looked like he was going to piss himself when I passed him the keys upon climbing out. Immediately, Brennan headed over to me as I left the guy to sort out my car.

"I didn't say shit," he started, his tone instantly telling me he was taking the offensive.

I raised a hand. "Cool your jets, I know. Kid did."

"Kid's here?" He peered over at the passenger side where Conor was just climbing out thanks to a car that had been driving past. "The fuck are you doing here? Since when do you get your hands dirty?"

From another man to a different brother, that would have been a jibe.

Not with Con.

Con got his hands plenty dirty—just rarely with blood.

"He wants to talk to the proprietress," I answered on his behalf.

"If you'd like to step this way, sirs," a smooth voice uttered from the doorway, interrupting our conversation, but I wasn't too mad about that.

I didn't want to be seen discussing business outside of Queens of Heart, anyway.

At this time of the morning, there was little to no line so, as we peered under the canopy, we were greeted by a woman standing in the entrance wearing a goddamn French maid's outfit.

Determining that I'd get Savvie in one of those ASAP, I turned to my brothers. "You know why we're here?"

"Kid filled us in," Eoghan confirmed, his hands in his pockets as he looked me up and down. "You ain't wearing a suit."

"Didn't feel like wearing one."

He dropped a 'huh' at that.

Declan cleared his throat. "You rebelling, Aidan?"

I scowled at him. "Fuck off, Declan."

His lips twitched. "Okay, bro. Calm the fuck down."

As we stepped under the canopy and began trudging toward the front door, I countered, "Not like there's anything to rebel against anymore."

That shut them the fuck up.

"You hate this shit," I said to Finn as we made it to the door.

"Plenty of shit I hate doing, doesn't mean I don't do it."

I arched a brow at him, took in the fatigue in his expression, and heaved a sigh.

This learning curve that came without ass-whoopings from our da was taking its toll on everyone.

For so long, we'd been told how high we should jump, and we'd get right to it. Now, we were making our own rules. Da made it look so easy too.

"It's been years since I came here last," Declan muttered from behind me.

I pulled a face. "Guess we know why Da discouraged us from using this place after we turned thirteen."

"So they didn't get hit up with statutory rape charges?" Finn grumbled, his distaste clear.

"You don't think he came here to use the 'services?'" Eoghan mused.

"He'd better fucking not have." Brennan cracked his knuckles. "Ma's made plenty of mistakes along the way, but if he was cheating on her as well—"

"You'll what? Kill him?" Con's laughter was a harsh bark. "Shut the fuck up, Brennan. Focus on what matters here."

Before Brennan could snap, I twisted around and hissed, "Control yourselves. You're here for a fucking reason, and it's not to start bickering like we're goddamn kids."

"Maybe it's only natural," Finn murmured. "Seeing as we *were* kids the last time we came here."

I didn't bother grimacing, just glowered at my younger brothers to get them in line.

"You're more of a miserable bastard than usual," Conor grouched.

Ignoring him, I reached for my phone. My fingers drifted over Da's, the broken glass dragging against the tips, but I shoved that aside and once I'd retrieved mine, opened the app that controlled Savvie's vibrator.

Switching it on low, I smiled to myself as I imagined her howl of outrage.

Turning my attention back to work, I saw the French maid was at the other end of the hall.

The place was a fancy bordello with *Alice in Wonderland* vibes that had creeped me out when I was a teenager and still creeped me the fuck out now.

The long hallway was all gilt and red and velvet, normal in comparison to the rest of the joint. Each doorway that led off it was decorated to the hilt, and I knew that the subsequent rooms were themed to Lewis Carroll's story which was just freaky as hell to me.

As Victorian as this part of the club was, the maid fit in with that get up, and I didn't wait for the others to follow me, just strode down the hall toward her.

She curtsied as she opened the door, another move I was totally going to steal for Savvie, and I headed in without a backward glance at her or my brothers.

As the door closed behind me, I took in the ultra-modern office with no small amount of surprise.

It was pure white, minimalist chic. Just like the woman who moved to stand from behind her glass desk.

Her suit was a stark black, the cut edgy, and her tight bun reminded me of the meanest elementary school teacher I'd had—Mrs. Parkinson. That bitch had mocked my every attempt at reading from the board.

Still, this woman was not *that* one. I'd seen Grainne in a broken pile on the floor when she was younger than I was now, but somehow, though she had to be in her fifties at least, she was pristine. Not just in comparison to the last time I'd seen her, but because she exuded the opposite of what she was.

Conor and I had been told never to talk about the hooker we'd found in the alleyway, but he'd come to me, asking questions about side pieces and why people paid to go to bed with other people, and I'd had to explain it all to him.

Nobody told you when you were the eldest that you'd end up being the one who gave your brother the birds and the fucking bees talk.

He'd also asked me why Jonesy had mocked him for calling her a 'lady.'

But that was what resonated here, now.

She *was* a lady.

I stepped forward, heading deeper into the room with my arm outstretched.

Her fingers slotted against mine and we shook hands with a briskness that was purely masculine.

Odder still.

Her gaze darted to my brothers. "You brought the cavalry?"

"No. They showed up on their own." I pursed my lips. "You'll take me to MacMurray?"

"I will. In a moment." Grainne reached for an envelope on her desk and passed it to me. "I wish to maintain the relationship I had with your father, Aidan," she reiterated.

I stared at her. "Did he use this place?"

"Your father was obsessed with your mother," she said flatly. "He could have traded her in for a newer model, but he never did. She was it for him. I'm certain that didn't change in death."

Someone cleared their throat behind me, and I knew it'd be Brennan. He was a soft touch for Ma, even if she was as much of a raving lunatic as Da was. Case in point: we'd only recently learned that she'd killed Finn's mother-in-law.

Yeah, our family was full of filthy fucking secrets.

I slipped open the envelope and pulled out a sheet of paper.

It had an address on it.

"What's this?" I asked, brow furrowed.

"I sent one of my girls to that address last night."

"And?"

"Eamonn Keegan used to be one of my regulars before his arrest and when he was in the city. He has reestablished his membership with the club."

My eyes flared. "Excuse me?"

Behind me, I felt the ice sinking into the atmosphere as we processed that name.

Eamonn Keegan had, after all, killed our father.

"You heard me. Aidan Sr. made certain I always gave Keegan what he requested."

"Because he was a *cheile?* Or for another reason?"

"Because of his affiliation with the ECD," she confirmed.

Cheiles were a bunch of despotic fuckwits who wanted Ireland to be reunited. Their brotherhood was called the ECD.

The ECD didn't give a fuck who they murdered to make that happen—my father included.

The leader, Eamonn Keegan, had spent a couple decades in prison for setting off a bomb that killed dozens of people back in London in the nineties.

Conor stormed forward and snatched the envelope from my grasp. Before he could take off with it, I grabbed his arm and kept him in place.

"How long did Da monitor the ECD?" I inquired carefully.

"For decades."

"Why?"

"He didn't trust them."

"He was fucking right not to," Declan snarled.

Grainne's gaze darted over to him and the sudden shift in her pallor had me further studying her. "The ECD were behind his death?"

"Yes." I lifted my chin. "You didn't know?"

"I didn't." She settled in her seat, heavily enough that the chair rolled back. "I thought... I thought he died of a heart attack."

That was the story we'd put out there.

No one knew that Da had been killed by a hit man in Greenwood Cemetery.

No one knew that the First Lady had been assassinated twenty or so feet away from our father.

And no one sure as fuck knew that our da was the reason the First Lady was there in the first place.

"He didn't," I said simply.

"No." She swallowed, her gaze fixed on the envelope in Conor's grasp. "What are you going to do with that information?"

For a woman who'd been calm and collected since the first words she'd spoken to me, I recognized that shaken tone.

That was something I was used to hearing.

Sick as it was, it resettled my equilibrium.

Everything about this meeting made me feel like a kid playing catch-up.

Not anymore.

"You're scared of the backlash?" I queried, taking a seat in front of her desk without asking.

"The ECD will know how Keegan's location was leaked," she rasped.

"Who are you more scared of?" Eoghan asked, his tone like silk.

"I never had reason to be scared of the Five Points," Grainne retorted, her tone stronger now.

"You know what he's asking," I rumbled, watching her mouth tighten in response.

"The Five Points' reach is further. Their goals wider. The ECD's desires are... deranged. The ECD is dangerous because of that, but the Five Points are deadlier. Does that answer your question?"

Contemplating her, I rubbed my chin. "Monitor the address, Conor. Don't infiltrate it."

Conor snapped, "You have to be shitting me. The bastard killed our father—"

I cast him a look. "Conor."

He gritted his teeth but stayed put.

"Eamonn Keegan was directly responsible for Aidan's death?" Grainne whispered.

I nodded, watching with interest as her gaze turned unfocused.

She reached up and anointed herself with the sign of the cross.

Manhattan's Madam anointing herself with the cross in her goddamn whorehouse—wonders would never fucking cease.

"Has the girl returned? Or is she still with him?"

"Meggie checked in an hour ago. My intention was to pass this information along in the morning, but circumstances dictated I move faster."

"You said MacMurray's high?" Conor queried, his tone belligerent.

"He is."

"Has he come down yet?"

"No. He only stopped behaving like a lunatic when one of my security guys pistol-whipped him." Grainne sucked in a breath. "Red is a volatile drug, especially after repeated use."

I'd heard whispers of it, but it was a rare commodity at the moment.

"You're coming across it often?" I delved, my curiosity stoked.

"Sadly." She cleared her throat. "It makes men 'last' longer. You can understand why they'd want that when we charge by the hour."

Eoghan snorted. "MacMurray can't keep it up without drugs?"

Declan and Brennan snickered, but even though I was amused too—Cain was the biggest jerk-off in Hell's Kitchen. The way he talked, you'd think he was walking around with a baseball bat for a dick—my concerns were aimed elsewhere.

"Hence Red's popularity," she murmured, her eyes still locked on mine.

"I heard that it makes users more aggressive over time?"

She nodded.

Curious.

"MacMurray's been a regular client for years. The last time he was here, his girl complained that he was getting aggressive. I fined him heavily as per your father's instructions, and he hasn't been back for at least a month."

Even curiouser.

"What did Meggie have to say about Keegan?"

She blinked at the change of topic but commented simply, "He was injured."

"How?"

"Meggie said..." She hesitated, but Grainne was clearly smart because she chose the truth, and she chose to survive tonight's meeting. "...he had a bullet wound on his shoulder."

Conor tensed. "But he was okay to fuck?"

"Maybe he was on Red too," Eoghan muttered under his breath.

"According to her, it was only a flesh wound."

"Was it fresh?"

"Unfortunately for you, I didn't send Hilary. She's pre-med," Grainne retorted. "Meggie's an art historian. The closest she's come to a bullet wound is tonight, and she doesn't have a clue about those kinds of injuries."

Keegan had gone underground in the aftermath of my father's shooting.

We'd know.

We'd had the entire city swept for him.

That had to mean he'd gotten shot either while he was in hiding—so one of his *cheile* brethren was behind it—or he'd taken a bullet in the cemetery.

Which meant someone else had been there, *watching*. Waiting for Keegan to take his shot, to wipe my father and the First Lady off the face of the planet.

Unfortunately, their aim wasn't as good as his.

Oddly buoyed by the knowledge, I straightened in my seat. "What else did you do for my father?"

"Aside from managing the club, keeping his Five Pointers under control when they decide to break their wedding vows, and acting like my little black book was his to comb through whenever he wanted?"

"Yeah, aside from that," I mocked.

She shrugged. "He was the reason I got clean. He was the reason I survived that night—"

"What night?" Declan muttered, but she ignored him.

Her gaze was fixed on me as she rasped, "He was the reason I didn't slink back into poverty, and he was the reason that I got rich and gained some power in this godforsaken city.

"As I've repeatedly said, I'm more than happy for the status quo to continue, Aidan. I have no desire for anything to change."

I studied her. "What did you take?"

"PCP. Your father had a problem with that back in the day. He knew how tough it was to get clean."

"It's not like him to help people in need," Conor said, his tone cool.

Grainne stood, marking an end to the discussion whether we liked it or not, stating, "Then you don't know your father as well as you think you do.

"Now, are you going to deal with MacMurray or am I just going to have to leave him restrained in one of my rooms until he sobers up?"

"Lead the way," was all I told her, though her words hit home.

Da had kept a lot of shit from us. Some good, most of it bad. Were we underestimating him? Or were we just desensitized to his games?

None of us spoke as she led us out of a different door than the one we'd entered. The front of the club was one thing, but the backrooms were another.

Technically, this place wasn't a whorehouse, more of a sex club, but that didn't mean that it wasn't the worst kept secret in the neighborhood.

Before my attention was snatched entirely by MacMurray, I fiddled with the app on my phone and set Savvie's vibrator onto a heavier pulsing beat. Then, tilting my screen so that no one could see, I checked the security cameras—she was still tied to the bed.

Relieved she hadn't figured out how to dismantle it—I put nothing past my wife—I tucked my phone away and returned my attention to where it should always have been: business.

Grainne led us down a hall and paused outside yet another door. This one was studded with red leather.

"I'll leave him to you."

As she passed me a small set of keys, I assured her, "I'll gladly uphold the same deal as the one you had with Da. Silent partner, protection, etc., in exchange for intel.

"We may require more information from you than he asked, especially as it's the early days of my reign. If Conor finds out you're screwing us over, all bets are off."

Before she started to drift away, her mouth twisted into a cold smile. "I've never been a threat to the O'Donnellys. You'll learn that in time."

"She'd be the fucking first," Brennan muttered in my ear.

I turned to look at him, agreeing, "She would."

Unsure of what I'd find, I gritted my teeth as I opened the door where it was rammed home just how important it was that Savannah learned to obey me in some things.

Relieved that she was angry and pouting at home because I was tormenting her with a goddamn vibrator and not here to see this, I blew out a breath.

"Jesus Christ," Finn ground out.

I'd seen more blood on a regular day at my 'job,' but knowing this came from a drug-crazed MacMurray beating a woman made it so much fucking worse.

Spinning around, I saw Grainne hadn't left the hall yet so I called out, "Grainne."

She turned back to me with a quirked brow.

"Whatever treatment the girl needs... I'll handle the bills."

Her eyes widened but slowly, she dipped her head. "Thank you, Aidan."

Dismissing her with a grunt, I graced MacMurray with my attention.

The fucker was tied with his hands around a stripper pole that took center stage in the room, head bowed, his semi-naked body loaded with bloody scratches.

The only consolation wasn't much of a fucking consolation to me —he wore his pants.

Rapist fuckers were gonna get their pricks sliced off now that I was in charge but I didn't particularly want that to be my first official act as leader of the Five Points.

Not when I could scent deeper trouble brewing.

As I stepped into the room, he lifted his head at the dull, thudding sound of my boots against the thick carpet.

MacMurray was bleeding from the temple, his eyes were bloodshot and dazed, and his gums were seeping blood too, but he was still lucid enough to greet death as, cackling like a lunatic, he slurred, "Ahh, it's the idiot who can't read. I'd bow to you, oh, great and powerful leader, but I'm afraid my hands are tied..."

4

AIDAN

BOY EPIC - SCARS

DYSLEXIA DID NOT A MORON MAKE.

But shame did.

Shame for something I couldn't help, shame for something that had affected my health, shame for something that was nothing to be ashamed of *did* make me an idiot, and it had ruled my life for too long.

Around me, my brothers surged into the room, their anger at his words clear.

However, I wasn't angry.

Not at MacMurray's deflection, not at his slur.

The blood was what infuriated me. Hell, it *enraged* me.

A hand slapped my shoulder—Conor's. "You heard of *Gerald's Game?*"

Frowning, I twisted to look at him. "Stephen King? I don't do horror. You know that."

"One of the characters ties a woman to the bed then dies before he can free her."

His pointed look had me rolling my eyes. "I'm not going to die tonight. Plus, you know where she is. Although how you know she's tied to the fucking bed is another matter entirely."

"I'm not interested in your sex life. I just know the shit you're into."

"Like you're not? Like you don't wish you could tie that Star chick to the bed?"

"If I did, she'd still be here, wouldn't she?" he intoned grimly, his jaw tightening at my bringing Star up again.

"Exactly."

Shaking off his hold on my shoulder, I moved into the room and crouched in front of one of the few guards Da had actually seemed to like.

At least, he hadn't actively disliked him.

It was, at times like these, that I was reminded why my father and I hadn't gotten along well.

Around me, my brothers settled into a loose circle.

With one hand balling into a fist, the other I used to grab MacMurray's hair so I could tip his head back to make sure that I had his full attention.

"What're you doin'? You ain't letting me go?"

"Da didn't let his guards take drugs," I mused out loud.

He tensed up.

I didn't need to be this close to him to see it either.

"Your father's dead. So's the Five Points now you're in charge," he spat, his words better articulated than before.

Without moving, I slammed his head back against the pole. I knew it wouldn't hurt, more like sting, but MacMurray sneered at me as he hissed, "Bastard."

"What drug did you take?"

"What the fuck does that have to do with anything?"

"I'm not interested in your limp dick, MacMurray."

His nostrils flared. "Fuck you."

"Got a bride who'll do it for me. Don't need you for that," I mocked. "What are you taking?"

"Got nothing to do with you—"

"It has everything to do with me," I countered, my hand tightening about his hair until he was swearing:

"Let me the fuck go!"

"What are you on?" I insisted, wanting to hear it from him, not secondhand.

"Red," he spat.

I didn't relinquish my hold on him entirely, but I gave his scalp a break. "Who sold it to you?"

"Why does it matter? Just some fucking kid—"

"On our territory?"

"No," he mumbled.

"You sure?"

His eyes slitted. "No."

"Informative," Brennan sniped.

My knee was starting to ache so I surged to a standing position, tightening my hold on his hair as I dragged him up with me.

Yelping, he scrambled to move with me, but his wrists were shackled to a spreader bar that I'd only just seen so he didn't get that far up before I let go. His legs collided with the ground, and he bit off a couple curses.

"Probably more torture devices in Queens of Heart than in your warehouse, Bren," I drawled in amusement.

"You bastard junkie," MacMurray growled. "You wanna know who my source is so you can hit him up too?"

"You're really asking for a beating, hypocrite."

Eoghan's cool tone rang around the room, but like the asswipe he was, the drugged and clearly deluded moron didn't take into account that one of the world's deadliest snipers had just uttered a warning.

Fool.

"What? It'll take all fucking six of you to deal with me?" He roared with laughter. "Sounds about fuckin' right. You'll never be like your father. Never—"

"Then we're in luck, MacMurray. I don't think any of us intend on being anything like him." I reached into the holster I'd strapped on my shoulder earlier and pressed the gun to his head. "Did a dealer come onto our turf to sell drugs or did you buy it on someone else's?"

That finally got through to him.

I burrowed the barrel into his forehead, watching his eyes cross as he stared up at the weapon.

Though he sounded more wary, he still rasped, "You won't shoot me."

"You sure you wanna take that bet?"

"Piece of shit," he rumbled before I unclicked the safety and placed my finger on the trigger. That had him blurting out, "I went onto their turf."

"Which turf?"

"Sicilian."

"You were just there for the drugs?"

"What else would I be there for?"

"That's what I'm trying to figure out, MacMurray. See, a good little soldier like you knew that my da didn't want his guards on drugs—"

"He's dead. His rules don't fucking matter anymore."

Acting as if he hadn't spoken, I continued, "And though there's been a change of leadership, we both know that Da picked his men with a purpose—you're all fucking stupid. Too stupid to live.

"So, what I'm thinking is that Red makes users more volatile and aggressive with every dose. According to the madam, the last time you were here, Da was still alive, and you beat your hooker, which means you were using then."

"Bullshit," he snarled.

"No? One junkie recognizes another," I snarled back. "Do you buy directly from the Sicilians?"

If that was the case, I was going to be pissed.

MacMurray's nostrils flared. "I don't answer to you."

"I think you'll find that you fucking do," Brennan snapped.

Swooping down, he grabbed the spreader bar, jerking it up until

MacMurray was rocking forward, his knees and wrists taking all his weight.

Brennan proceeded to grab his foot, twisting hard enough until MacMurray was screaming.

The distinct pop of a bone coming out of the socket filled the air.

MacMurray howled, "You bastard!"

"No, that's me," Finn rumbled. "And Aidan *is* your fucking leader. You *do* answer to him. If you don't like it, you can swallow a bullet because as far as I remember, this ain't a fucking democracy and you don't get to vote."

I didn't need their support, but having my brothers at my back, my left and right-hand men at my sides, sure as fuck felt good.

"Who's your dealer?"

"I buy from the source," was all MacMurray muttered, even as he was hissing with every fidgeting move he made as he tried not to put pressure on the dislocated mess of his ankle—not easy with the spreader bar supporting his weight.

Narrowing my eyes at him, I pondered his words then told Brennan, "Take him to the cement factory."

Brennan arched a brow but didn't argue. "Fine."

"*No!* What the fuck? You can't take me there! I ain't done nothing wrong," MacMurray spat, his busted ankle forgotten when he knew his life was on the line.

Under Da's rule, the cement factory had become a morgue for the living.

A tradition I was going to continue...

"I don't believe you. You had your chance to answer me, but you wasted that opportunity. I'll get my answers soon enough."

"You can't torture me," he screamed, his eyes bulging and bloodshot, his fear finally flooding the space between us. I could taste it on my tongue as he sputtered, "I'm a Five Pointer!"

"Then you're deserving of my best work," I retorted, spinning away from him and heading over to the nearest window that looked onto the hallway; perfect for voyeurs when the curtains weren't closed, I assumed.

A few minutes later, I wasn't surprised when MacMurray was silent. Not after Brennan decided to rearrange his skeleton some more by reversing his earlier move then grabbing his wrists and dragging them higher up the pole until both shoulder joints were popping out of their sockets too.

Sometimes, the simplest moves were the most effective.

Mind on more important things, I watched Brennan unfasten MacMurray's restraints with the keys I tossed him.

"Declan, Eoghan, help me with this dipshit?" Brennan requested, and I watched as they hauled my da's man out of the room.

Now sobbing with pain, MacMurray was clearly drifting in and out of consciousness. Otherwise, I figured, he'd have struggled more. Mostly he was just yelping and squealing like a pig as they carried him out.

Watching them work, Finn and Conor walked over to me.

"Don't make any sudden moves," Finn warned as I reached for my cell and connected a call with Luciu Valentini. "Or do anything you'll regret in the morning."

"Valentini isn't just an ally, Finn," I grouched. "He's fucking family now."

Finn scratched his jaw. "Jen's pregnant again."

"She is?"

Aoife, his wife, and mine shared a best friend, and we'd recently learned that Jennifer MacNeill, AKA 'pain in my ass,' was the bastard daughter of our uncle Padraig.

She'd married the new Sicilian Don this summer and had just given birth to a little girl so was more his problem than ours, thank fuck.

"She just gave birth."

Finn shrugged. "It's what Aoife told me."

"She hasn't told Savannah." My brow furrowed with concern.

They'd already had a falling out earlier this year... Had it happened again?

Was that why she was so unsettled right now? Because they'd had another argument? It'd make more sense than her being so upset about Da...

Not that that had stopped me from tying her to the fucking bed. Whether or not that made me an asshole, I'd do it again. Especially after that stunt she'd pulled tonight.

"Aidan? What's wrong?"

Luciu's cultured voice broke into my thoughts.

"Can't a cousin call his cousin-in-law for a chat?"

"Not at four in the morning." Luciu yawned, unimpressed by my mockery. "What's wrong?"

"Are you manufacturing Red?"

Silence greeted me, but slowly, Luciu admitted, "Yes. It's my brother's creation."

I stared around the blood-spattered walls, the unintended aftereffects of the drug. "Some creation."

He grunted.

"You don't approve?"

"No. I don't. But Custanzu is a grown man. He can do as he wishes with his free time."

"I didn't realize he had a background in chemistry."

"We all had a background before our father was killed," Luciu said before he released a brisk laugh. "Mine was history. Has the drug caused an issue in your territory?"

"You could say that." I pursed my lips as I placed the call on speaker. "Got one of my men saying that your brother's directly selling it to him. Now, we're fucking allies, Luciu, so I'm going to ask you nicely if that's a lie."

Apparently, he heard the warning in my inquiry because he rumbled, "Custanzu sells to no one directly."

"Luc? Who is that?"

The sound of Jen's voice had me offering, "I hear more congratulations are in order."

"That had better not be a fucking threat, O'Donnelly."

"How quickly I went from Aidan to O'Donnelly," I mocked. "I want to speak with your brother."

"Is that Aidan?" Jen snapped in the background. "Tell him to fuck off. Some of us have a baby who doesn't sleep to deal with."

I didn't bother rolling my eyes.

Was it any fucking wonder she was friends with Savannah?

Both of them had bigger balls than Cain MacMurray.

"He isn't directly selling the drug to anyone," Luciu repeated, ignoring his wife.

"You know this for sure?"

"I do."

"Then what happened? Why is my man saying that your brother sold him the stash?"

"He's a fucking liar. Stan is more interested in the creation of the drug than the selling of it."

"That's your domain?"

"Partly," he answered. "And I can tell you now that my dealers know not to distribute on territory other than our own.

"We struck up the deal together, Aidan. I have no intention of rupturing our alliance over a couple million dollars."

My lips pursed as I shot my brothers a look.

It was obvious that, like me, they believed him.

"So what happened?"

"I don't know, but it isn't my problem if my product landed in one of your men's bloodstreams. It's something for *him* to justify. Not me."

"I don't disagree," I stated calmly. "But I needed confirmation."

Luciu grunted, then before either of us could cut the call, Jen was on the line. "Aidan, are you and Savannah still coming over for brunch this weekend?"

I rubbed my brow. "I didn't realize we were."

She snorted. "She must have been intending on shanghaiing you into it."

"Congrats, Jen. Luciu," Finn murmured.

"*Grazii,*" Luciu intoned, but he still sounded like he had a stick shoved up his ass.

"Aoife squealed?" Jen was complaining. "Goddammit. Aidan, don't say a word to Savvie about the baby, okay? She'll get jealous that I told Aoife first."

"I won't say anything. See you on Sunday."

"Saturday," she corrected.

"Whenever."

"Pussywhipped," Conor muttered, earning himself a glower he batted away with a smirk.

As I hung up, Finn cleared his throat. "That's the problem when your women cross factions."

"No shit," I retorted, palming my cell before I pocketed it.

"That's not going to be awkward," Conor derided.

I reached up and tested my neck, sighing with relief when I got it to crack. "Luciu will get over his snit by then."

Eying me, Conor queried, "What are you thinking, Aidan?"

"I'm thinking that MacMurray was taking drugs when Da was alive. Da might have been deteriorating, but his mind seemed like it was all there—"

Finn grimaced. "As much as he was ever in possession of his faculties."

Conceding that with a nod, I continued, "—so, I'm wondering if Da knew his man was on drugs. If he didn't, I'm wondering what kind of headcase MacMurray is to risk it by taking drugs when Da was alive."

Conor winced. "Remember when Da found out Peter Kelly was on coke?"

"His nose still ain't right."

"Right?" Finn hooted. "He looks like a fucking pig, and he's had about five reconstruction surgeries since then because he can't breathe through it."

"If MacMurray *was* hooked, then sourcing his pills wouldn't have been easy," Conor remarked. "Not with the threat of Da finding out."

Finn scratched his jaw. "You're thinking he's a spy?"

Staring around the room, I mused, "Maybe."

"Sparrows?" Conor asked.

"Likely." I heaved a sigh. "Look at the fucking mess here. What the hell did he do to that woman?"

Conor shoved his hands into his pockets. "Hookers aren't people to bastards like MacMurray."

I knew he was right and was sickened by that truth.

"I'll be surprised if she survives," I said softly. "The blood..."

"Grainne didn't mention she was at death's door. And she said she had a medical student on staff. Maybe she saved the girl?" Conor asked, his tone hopeful.

"Maybe," was all I said, but I doubted it.

"How do you know Grainne?" Finn asked after a couple minutes of looking at the spatter pattern on the wall.

"Long story," I rumbled. "Conor can tell you later. We have shit to do."

Conor grabbed my arm. "What's the plan?"

"I'm going home."

"What?" Finn demanded, his surprise clear.

I didn't answer, just took a final glance around the room before I told him, "Twelve o'clock sharp, arrange for every Five Pointer to be waiting for me at the cement factory."

"You mean just the lieutenants, surely?" Finn sputtered.

I shook my head. "Every single one. It's time I introduced myself to them."

"They know who you fucking are, Aidan," Conor argued.

"No. They know me as Junior, Kid. They..." Hesitating, I considered MacMurray's defiance. "*Most* of them were terrified of Da, and rightfully so." Dragging my arm out of his hold, I cracked my knuckles. "He was insane, but it's time they realize that a sane leader comes with benefits—and pitfalls too."

5

____

SAVANNAH

DREAMS - CRANBERRIES

WAS I pissed at being tied up?

No.

Was I pissed at being left trussed up like a turkey?

Yes.

Unequivocally, yes.

But...

I prided myself on being able to read the room—even if, technically, it was empty right now—and I had to accept the truth.

Manipulating a man through sex was not something to be proud of.

In fact, hadn't my producer done that at TVGM? Hadn't Wintersen used sex as a tool until I'd honey-trapped and exposed him live on TV?

Guilt hit me, followed by mortification, which made me squirm. My wrists were already sore from tugging though, so I needed to minimize the wriggling, and I was starting to feel the strain in my thighs. Although, *that* felt good.

Really fucking good.

Better than I deserved after I tried to lead Aidan around by his dick.

I blew out a breath as I stared up at the ceiling.

"God damn, Aidan, and God damn him for knowing me too well."

This was going to end one of two ways—one: me killing him by making him suffocate via my pussy. Two: me getting a cramp in my thigh which would suck.

Because I really didn't want that to happen, I tried to relax. But the more I relaxed, the more I became aware of the vibrator. My pussy clutched at the stuffing it wanted to be thrusting inside it, not staying still like this.

As well as Aidan knew me, I knew him though. I was just *waiting* for him to switch the damn thing on. I knew he'd do it. Knew it'd happen just when he thought I'd fallen asleep or something.

The weird anticipation stopped me from getting bored and made me hyperaware of my body in a way I'd never experienced before— and we'd been together nearly ten months now. It wasn't right that he could make me feel like this, especially when he wasn't here!

Every inch of me was exposed, though, my cunt spread wide, pussy lips parted, tits hypersensitive, nipples budded—

Ugh.

I swallowed.

My heart started pounding.

"Fuck," I rasped, aware that I was making myself wetter. "How is it he can get me like this?"

My pussy flooded with slickness, making it harder to clutch the vibrator and keep it in place. The more gravity worked against the solid weight, the harder my inner muscles had to strive to keep it inside me. Thank God I was an expert at Kegel exercises.

Eyes long adjusted to the play of shadows in here, I wriggled against the bed, twisting until I was sitting taller, my legs folded for real now as if I were practicing yoga. My arms were at an awkward position, but it eased the pressure inside my pussy. The trouble was that the new position let me see how he'd restrained me and it made me wish I could rub my clit.

"Just one little orgasm," I panted, arms working as I twisted some more. The cuffs clinked as I moved, forcing me into stillness.

If he was watching me, he could misinterpret my actions—

That was when the bastard struck.

"Shit!"

The vibrator turned on.

I screamed in surprise then groaned.

"You fucker!" I hissed.

But knowing that he was somewhere in the goddamn city and was thinking of me when he was doing his mobstery stuff—that was hotter than the vibrations.

This was a special toy—it had a slight thrusting action to it—but nothing compared to Aidan's cock.

Fifteen minutes later, it sped up even more, and I had to riffle through the Declaration of Independence to keep myself under control.

Spoiler alert: it didn't work.

My breath started soughing from my lungs, and I knew I could get off from this. Knew it wouldn't be awesome. Knew it would be mediocre. The standard orgasm I'd had before I'd fallen into Aidan's life.

"Wait, wait, wait, wait," I chanted under my breath, well aware that I was flushed and overheated and totally unsure if I could stop the inevitable from happening.

Of course, that was when he struck again.

The toy *stopped* vibrating.

Thanking God that I hadn't tried to get off, that the cessation of movement came as a relief, I nevertheless narrowed my eyes at the door, just waiting for the bastard to come home.

Where he'd be safe.

My mind was a whir of confusing emotions, none of which was

helped by the fact that both Aidan and I had been sleeping terribly since his father's death.

Which meant that this lesson came at a really bad time.

But he was right.

Even though I hated that he was.

If he took his eye off the ball, that could get him killed.

And because my husband was too smart when it came to me, he knew how to ram home a lesson so I didn't forget it.

Following him was something I'd tried to do after he'd ghosted me five years ago. I was ashamed to admit to that, but it was the truth, nonetheless. I'd never told him, and I was grateful I hadn't.

If Aidan was going to survive, if he was going to live as long as his father, then I needed to be at his back, supporting him. I didn't need to be whiny and a wuss. I had to help, not detract from what needed to be done.

That didn't stop me from grinding out, "I'll get you back, Aidan Jr.," when a low throb settled in my core and the vibrator got to work again.

Mind splintered between ways I could support him, how I could get loose to throw something at him when he came home, and which Kegels would help me not get off—I forgot where I was. What I was. *Who* I was.

Until, ten minutes of agony later, the outer door opened and the vibrator turned off.

My thoughts elsewhere, on anything other than the state of my pussy, the sound, as well as the sudden silence in here, were triggers back to last Christmas when I'd dealt with a home invasion in this very apartment.

That I was tied to the bed, unable to defend myself, made fear shudder through my bones, rattling me from the inside out.

It could be anyone.

Aidan was a target now, so was I—maybe someone had broken in? A Sparrow? An enemy?

My heart began pounding just as a shiver rattled down my spine.

My mom said that was when someone walked over your grave, but that didn't ease my anxiety any.

Silence was imperative if it *was* a home invader, but I needed to know so I screamed, "Aidan! Please tell me that's you!"

"Who else did you expect?" He walked through the door as calm and as collected as you like and turned on the lights. The instant relief I felt got me riled up. "Jen?"

His mockery had me squinting at him and blowing out a puff of breath to get the hair off my forehead.

In comparison to my discomposure, he was so put together it was annoying. He'd always been hot, but this year, some of the strain had begun to ease from his features.

His cheeks were no longer gaunt; the creases around his eyes and at the bridge of his nose hadn't disappeared, but they were easing up as if he weren't scowling so much anymore.

Salt and pepper flecks blurred in the tangled dark hair that always made my fingers itch with the need to stroke it, and his bright green eyes were no longer muted, but bright with life. Even after the last couple weeks of stress and strain, of grief, they hadn't reverted to how they'd been last December.

There were makings of a beard on that jaw of his that was forged from cast iron... God, he was beautiful.

"Little one?" he rumbled, making me realize I'd just been gawking at him.

Heart beginning to slow now he was in my sights, the shock slowly leaching out of my system, I whispered, "I thought you could be a home invader."

"Shit!" His jaw tensed, and his anger, self-aimed, had him storming over to me. "I am so fucking sorry, sweetheart. I never thought—"

"No. I didn't either," I admitted gruffly. "Until you opened the door."

His hands stroked down my arms before he pressed a kiss to my mouth. "Let's get you loose."

His reaction was so immediate that it calmed me down. "No. I don't want that. I don't need that. I just need you."

"You have me." He wrapped his arms around my waist which was pretty awkward in my current position, but I'd take it.

Pushing my face under his chin, I forced myself to calm down and slowed my breathing by sucking in air that scented of him.

His arms tightened. "Are you okay?"

I firmed my mouth to still a quiver. "I'm fine. I just freaked myself out."

"No one will get into our home again, Savannah," he told me, his voice a strange combination of smooth and rough that had all the hairs on the back of my neck standing to attention. "Tell me you trust me to keep you safe."

"I trust you to keep me safe," I whispered, joining our mouths together in a silent reunion.

I breathed into that kiss and he swallowed it, took a hold of me and my fears and turned them the right side up.

When he pulled back, I murmured, "I want you to be safe too, Aidan. *I need that.* I won't do anything to jeopardize that."

Slowly, he pulled back, dipping his chin to allow his slippery gaze to drift along my body.

Something about how he looked at me always set me on fire.

"Look at that pussy," he mused, making me bite my bottom lip in response. "Bright red and wet. Need my dick, little one? Even after the scare?"

Swallowing, I nodded.

His smile was a surprising combination of tender and cocky—it looked good on him.

Seeing him stand looked better, so did watching him walk over to the vanity table.

Not for the first time, relief filled me that he'd listened to me and had gone to the doctor my dad had used for the knee replacement surgery.

He was stronger. Not just because of that, but because he'd been working out too.

I didn't think he was unstoppable, but he was a damn sight less of a target than he'd been before, now that his knee was at almost total functionality.

Watching him shrug off his jacket and lay it over the chair in front of my vanity table, I stayed silent as he went to drag off his tee shirt.

His arms bulged, his pecs did too, and his abs—sweet, merciful, beautiful, kind Mother Mary—they were just... I couldn't begin to describe them without getting overheated.

"Leave the jeans on," I requested, aware my voice had turned guttural.

His lips quirked up at the corners. "Like them, do you?"

My man lived in suits. Something else I wasn't going to complain about. But jeans?

"You have the ass for them," was all I said.

Understatement.

He moved over to the bed after he bent down and unknotted the ties on his shitkickers. Toeing out of them as well as his socks and, walking over to me barefoot, I tried not to melt into the mattress but it wasn't easy.

"I'm an intelligent woman."

He paused on his walk toward me. "I know you are."

"How can your feet be sexy? Why do you do this to me? It isn't fair."

I had to credit him with being smart because he didn't smirk at my whining, just reached down and unzipped his fly.

Was it getting hot in here?

He pulled his cock out and I watched him roll his hand along his shaft, murmuring, "Is this fair? Me driving around Manhattan with a boner because I know you're here, waiting for me, when I have business to attend to?"

A deep sigh drifted from my lips. "I need you," I whispered, unable to say anything other than the truth.

"I know, little one."

"I hate your lessons," I sniped, squirming against the restraints.

"The state of your pussy tells me differently. I should probably punish you for lying to me all the time."

I hissed. "I don't lie."

"You manufacture the truth?"

Despite my agitation, I had to smile. "Something like that."

He stepped over to the bed. "When were you going to tell me about us having brunch with Jen and Valentini this weekend?"

I blinked. "Huh?"

"Brunch. With your best friend. My cousin."

"Umm." Was it just me or had his hand sped up as he jacked off?

He clicked the fingers of his other hand together, and when that didn't stop me from drooling over his dick, I saw him grab something from his pocket.

A second later, the vibrations started.

"You bastard," I roared but it tapered off into a whimper.

"Concentrate, Savannah," Aidan intoned.

My pussy clamped down around the vibrating dildo and I writhed against the bed, trying to offset the arrhythmic tempo he'd picked. I liked strong and steady. One consistent pulse. This was all over the place.

"What do you want me to concentrate on, Aidan?" I snapped at him, outrage and annoyance spewing from the words.

"Brunch."

Nostrils flaring in annoyance, eyes clenching as a vibration hit one of my sweet spots, I ground out, "Brunch, I forgot. We arranged it before your father's death." A breath whistled from between my teeth as the vibrations doubled down.

"How about you tell me what you learned from tonight?"

"Oh, my GOD!" I shrieked, my legs slamming together, restraints be damned, as I felt that buzz deep in my core. Tireless, ceaseless. It wouldn't stop before it broke me— "It was... I was... You were... We were, I'm nottousesextocontrolyoubecauseyou'reacontrol FREAK!"

The buzzing stopped.

A harsh breath escaped me, and through the blur that came from the tears leaking from my eyes, I turned my face to the side as he stepped over to the bed.

His fingers were slick—oh God, from his pre-cum?—as they gently traced over my wrists.

"I didn't think this would get you so hot," he mused as I winced at where the skin had rubbed raw from my movements. "Short-sighted of me," he continued, that same musing tone still lacing his goddamn words. "Brats like boundaries."

Outrage had me retorting, "I'm not a brat."

"You're the dictionary definition of a brat," he disregarded with a hum. "Luckily for you, I like a side of discipline with my fucking—"

"All you Catholics are the same," I jibed, but he ignored me.

"—so if you move your wrists one more time, if I hear the cuffs rattle against the frame, I will stop whatever I'm doing, do you hear me? *Whatever* I'm doing, little one."

I heard the warning, and knowing that he was a bastard who would leave me in the lurch, one quite capable of tying his wife to the bed to go and do mobster stuff all while said wife creamed herself silly in their marital bed, I quickly promised, "I won't move my hands."

And not only because I didn't want him to stop whatever he had in mind but because they were fucking hurting as well.

Gracing me with a smile, he let his fingers trail over my arm, down my chest. He rubbed them around my nipple then pinched, making me jerk in response. He moved over my stomach, the caress almost ticklish enough that my belly turned concave—fuck, that almost made me move my upper body.

He switched gears by letting the tips drift through the landing strip that was the welcome beacon to my pussy.

Slowly, he retrieved the vibrator and pulled it out, tossing it onto the bed at my side.

With the flat of his hand, he tapped my pussy. Once. Twice. It gave off a weird thudding sound because I was dripping wet.

I didn't have it in me to be embarrassed because he found my slit with two fingers and thrust inside.

Heat.

Him.

Not silicone.

My pussy knew the difference just as well as my brain did.

The butt of his hand ground into my clit as he speared them into me, driving them deep. I shrieked as, in a pathetically short amount of time, my overeager body soared high, exploding as he graced me with the smallest amount of attention.

I screamed when the orgasm blasted me between the eyes, and it just made it so much better when he said, "You're so fucking beautiful when you come for me, Savannah. So fucking beautiful. So perfect. This cunt was made for me, wasn't it?" Amid the whirring praise that spiraled in my brain, he suddenly paused. "Did I hear a rattle?"

Amid the glut of pleasure hitting me in the face, within that chaos, I knew to freeze.

"No! It wasn't! I didn't move my hands!" I whined, but his fingers were already leaving me.

The orgasm wasn't broken, but fuck if I hated that he moved away...

Of course, when he lifted that hand to his mouth and sucked on the digits, I released a guttural groan.

This was the tiniest of examples, but Aidan proved himself to me again—he was *nasty*.

And I was here for it. Even if this was only a small display of how deep and dirty sex with him was.

Once he'd sucked down on his fingers, he curled them around his cock. "Tell me why I should put my dick inside you?"

I was so going to load his oatmeal with salt tomorrow.

Well, today.

Later on.

Whenever.

I hissed out a breath as impatience exploded inside me. If I gave him what he wanted, he'd give me his dick. If I didn't, he'd make me watch him jack off again.

God damn him.

He probably wouldn't let me shower either.

I'd walk around covered in his cum all day—fuck, that shouldn't make the core in my belly light up.

Every feminist fiber in my being decided that I couldn't roll over on this one.

I *could* fight fire with fire, and it was time to use his words against him: "Because my pussy was made for you. Because I want to feel you come inside me."

As he gritted his teeth, I felt like howling with triumph, and when he clambered onto the bed and finally settled between my thighs, I *did* howl.

With a growl, his mouth was on mine, and he fucked me there much as he'd fuck my pussy. Another growl escaped him as our tongues collided, and I didn't back down; I fought him inch for inch.

Maybe he was right. Maybe I *was* a brat. He could tie me up and restrain me, could fill my cunt full of silicone and torment me into an orgasm; I'd let him do anything he wanted to me, but when it came down to the wire, I'd always fight back.

When his dick was there, rubbing against my slickness, I bit his tongue as he thrust into me.

No warning whatsoever.

This time, I realized that my last howl wasn't a howl at all.

I jerked my mouth away from his and screamed with just how fucking perfect his cock was inside me.

"Who does this pussy belong to?"

I sagged into the mattress—I couldn't stop myself.

"You," I whispered on a cry, then my feminist core wailed as I begged, "It's yours, it's yours. Please, please, please."

His guttural, "Fuck," was like music to my ears, and he sped up, powering into me, fucking me hard and fast all while our gazes were connected.

A sense of empowerment filled me because I was restrained to the bed like a naughty brat, my legs were tied open, and my pussy belonged to him, sure, but I owned him as much as he owned me.

Then, as if he knew that, like his mind read mine, his lips quirked into a smirk before he united our mouths again.

With no clitoral stimulation, with no other touch apart from his penetration, he took me to the stars.

Only this man could do that.

Only *my* man.

I shuddered underneath him as the orgasm struck me again. Detonating behind my eyes, inflaming every nerve ending until my cries echoed around the bedroom, entwined with his low grunts, his raspy groans.

As he came inside me, I could feel the new slickness that was a result of our mutual pleasure, and I felt like fucking purring.

This pussy had gotten the cream.

Yum.

6

———

AIDAN

COLORBLIND - COUNTING CROWS

I SHOULD HAVE TAKEN the restraints off sooner.

As I unlocked them, that was my initial thought, but Savvie didn't give me much time for many thought processes to form. Not that she ever did.

With her thighs freed from the simple bindings and now her hands, she snatched at me, locking both her arms and legs around me before I even had the chance to rub them to ease any lingering soreness.

I smiled as she burrowed her face in my throat, her slick cunt settling against my lower abs while I placed my hand on her back and let it drift up and down her spine.

Having never permitted this kind of intimacy before Savannah, I was finding that I was a sucker for this too.

And it had nothing to do with aftercare.

Just appreciation.

The quiet relaxation of our bodies as we came back to ourselves.

As the physical and the mental halves rejoined within this, the safest of spaces.

She sighed as she sank into me, her bones melting against me, and with her mouth pressed into my throat, she mumbled, "Where did you go?"

My ease died. "You know I can't talk about business with you," I chided, but my hand didn't still its soothing motions.

"Why not? Maybe I'd help you make wiser decisions."

"You'd be too busy fangirling."

She pshawed. "I've gotten better about that."

That had me snorting. "Since when?"

"I've met some crime bosses. Once you meet them, you can't get excited about regular joes."

My lips twitched at her serious tone. I didn't even have it in me to be jealous. "You haven't met the Bratva Pakhan yet." We'd made arrangements but he'd canceled unexpectedly.

"I'm reserving judgment on him."

I arched a brow. "Why?"

"You ever spoken about him with Inessa?"

My youngest sister-in-law and I weren't exactly firm friends. For no other reason than the fact that she was so fucking young she made me feel ancient.

"No, little one," I said wryly, "I haven't talked about the leader of the Bratva with my youngest sister-in-law. She's nineteen. I have nothing in common with her."

She harrumphed. "Well, you should make time. She's family too."

"I once asked her if she'd seen *Casablanca*. Know what she said?"

"No, but she'd like to visit?"

I laughed at her. "Right on the money."

"She's kind though. Just has shitty taste in movies. She's never seen *Silence of the Lambs*. Can you imagine? I asked her if she'd seen *Sleeping with the Enemy* too—"

"You're so fucking funny," I joked.

I felt her lips curving against my throat. "I couldn't resist. It was too perfect. But it was wasted on her."

"Maybe Camille would know it?"

She hummed. "I'll give it a shot the next time I see her. But that doesn't help this situation with Inessa."

"There isn't a situation with Inessa. We don't have to be BFFs. She knows I'll kill for her; that's enough of a relationship. She isn't like you, Savvie," I pointed out. "She was raised to know—"

"If you say, 'her place,' I'll put more than salt in your oatmeal when we have breakfast."

My grin flashed into being. "I like salt in my oatmeal."

"Not this much salt."

"And I didn't mean it that way. I meant that she was raised not wanting to make waves. I think it'll be a miracle if she takes a stand with Eoghan, never mind with me, before she's at least thirty."

"She's just started college. That'll toughen her up."

"It'll be good for her," I agreed as my fingers gently stroked her hair. "What did she say about Lyanov?"

"She caught him having anal sex with a woman."

"Poor Eoghan."

She stilled. "Huh?"

"If she's traumatized by anal sex—"

Savvie reared up to slap my chest. "Shut up, you. She wasn't traumatized by anal sex. She's nineteen in the new millennium, not the last," she scoffed. "The woman was bleeding and he carried on fucking her anyway."

"Do you know how easy it is for the anus to tear?"

"It scared her," she said mulishly.

"Well, I understand that, but I'm assuming the elephant in the room is that Inessa thought Lyanov was raping the woman?"

She pursed her lips. "Yes."

I shrugged. "Asses bleed when you stick nine inches of cock into them and apply friction."

"How do you know it's nine inches?"

Rolling my eyes at her when she stuck her tongue in her cheek, I said, "I was referring to my dick, brat. That's nine inches."

"My ass doesn't bleed."

"Does sometimes. I use more lube—"

"We need to not talk about that right now."

"Fucking hell, Savvie. You just got off. Twice."

"Are you bitching at me for getting turned on when we talk about this stuff?"

"Yeah, seeing as you're the one who brought up my sister-in-law." I grunted. "When did you even talk about this shit with her?"

"After he canceled that dinner we'd scheduled. She warned me that he might be beautiful, but he was a nasty piece of work."

"Why was she warning you about that?" I grumbled.

She patted my chest. "Don't be jealous. You know how I am."

I rolled my eyes. "Would you like it if I started drooling over models?"

"I keep your dick too busy to worry about that."

She had a point.

When I huffed, she smirked knowingly at me.

"Tell me what happened." Her smirk twitched into a pretty pout. "Please."

"Savannah," I warned.

"Come on, Aidan. I'm not going to get involved. You and I work well together, don't we? We bounce great ideas off each other."

Another point struck.

"Plus, now that I'm here, maybe we can keep your mind on track. Seeing as, you know, you were messing with the vibrator when you should have been focused on work... Which was kind of the whole point about me not controlling you through sex, no?"

Yet another point struck.

Sighing at her sass, I just said, "Let me clean up your wrists."

"I can do that myself."

Temper flashed in my eyes. "That's my job."

She bit her lip. "Okay."

"Stop getting turned on."

"I can't help it. You're wearing jeans, my thighs are killing me, we just talked about you fucking me in the ass, and I had to lie here and think about your dick for at least eight hours—"

"An hour and fifty-six minutes to be precise."

She blinked. "Huh?"

"I was away for an hour fifty-six minutes."

Thank God traffic had been quiet and the club was on our territory.

"Well, it felt like eight hours."

Hiding a smile, I shuffled us so that we were closer to the edge of the bed, and I hauled her onto her feet. She hobbled from maintaining her earlier position for so long and winced until I grabbed her in a fireman's hold and hauled her over my shoulder.

She yelped but moaned when I slapped her ass.

My little sex fiend.

Striding into the bathroom, I kept us tilted toward the mirror as I stared at a droolworthy sight. "Look at that pussy."

She shuddered. "If you want me to stop thinking about sex—"

"Work of fucking art," I mumbled, eying the cum that was seeping from between the lips, the little dots of dried semen that I'd coated her in earlier.

Sex with Savannah was nasty—in the best of ways.

She brought out the beast in me, and I fucking loved that she did.

In the sack, with us drawing out the worst in each other, it let me burn off some of the crap that was going on in my head.

Working it off on her ass and knowing that she'd take whatever I had to give, and would *love* it, made it so much fucking better.

She twisted up and back to look at where I was studying, and the moment she started squirming, I choked out a laugh.

Savvie was so fucking predictable sometimes.

Because my dick wasn't ready to be pounced on yet, I carefully set her down on the counter.

"Stay there," I grumbled at her, knowing she'd hop down the moment my back was turned.

She huffed but did as I asked when I pulled out some alcohol wipes and antibiotic cream from the first aid kit.

"That's not necessary," she grumbled back. "That's how bacteria is getting too dependent and resistant to some forms of antibiotics."

"I'm annoyed about this, Savannah," I chided as I carefully cleaned her wrists. "How the fuck am I supposed to tie you to the bed if you wreck your wrists every time?"

She perked up at that. "Minimize movement. Or... ya know, use nicer cuffs."

"I don't always have time for that," I groused with a sigh, pissed when she hissed as the alcohol went to work on the wounds, causing a sting that I knew too well. "Plus, the last time I used those fake cuffs, you got free."

Her smile made my dick ache. "I forgot about that."

"I didn't."

"You can't just expect me to lie there and stay still when you turn that vibrator on."

"Yes, I can. In fact, I'm going to spank you for that later."

"That isn't fair—"

"Who said I had to be fair?" I rumbled, staring deep into her eyes, watching her pupils bloat in response to my words and tone.

She swallowed. "Aidan?"

I hummed.

"I'd really like it if you could fuck me right now."

"That would be rewarding bad behavior so why would I do that?"

"Bad behavior!" she croaked out.

I ran my thumb over the alcohol wipe along the pink, tender flesh on her wrist where the cuffs had left a mark.

"Yeah. *Bad.* The opposite of good."

She sniffed.

Savvie never failed to astonish me, but as ridiculous as it was to make this threat, I knew it'd ram home with her.

"No sex until you figure out a way to apologize."

Her lips parted. "No sex until I apologize for hurting my wrists which were only hurting because *you* tied me to the bed?"

I shrugged. "Yup. How else are you going to learn that sex can't be weaponized and that your safety is my priority?"

She gaped at me. "You're mean."

I shot her a grin and reached for a roll of bandage. "I know."

"That's overkill, Aidan. It's not like they're bleeding," she argued. "They only started stinging when you prodded them."

"*Cleaned* them."

"If you say so."

"I do."

"Okay, come on then. If you won't fuck me, tell me what happened tonight."

I scowled at her.

She scowled back.

I'd totally left myself wide open for that attack. Moron.

"We're married now. The Feds can't make me testify against you."

"I'm not worried about the Feds. I've never been worried about them," I sneered. "I'm worried about my enemies."

"I have guards."

"So did Camille, Inessa, and Victoria. They were attacked. Aela and Shay were in the line of fire. Aoife—"

"You need better guards," she interrupted.

"Better guards—" I rubbed my eyes. "You're right."

"My dad got these guys who are ex-Israeli special forces after Aspen was kidnapped. They're like ghosts."

"I'm sure the men will love me bringing a bunch of Israelis in."

She shrugged. "You wouldn't need to if they were better at their jobs, would you?"

She had a point.

Again.

Goddammit.

Resting my hands at either side of her thighs on the vanity, I stared at her.

She stared back.

"Da would—"

"Your father's dead." Savvie swallowed as if saying the words was hard. Her bottom lip quivered, but my little one pushed through her grief to ask, "You're not going to rule like him, are you? Just because I was a fan doesn't mean I didn't see his faults. He was short-sighted to the point of stupidity, believing everything that's Irish is intrinsically better than anything else."

A breath whistled from between my teeth. "You're right."

"It happens," she said, but she wasn't smug about it.

Savvie was more than capable of being a smug pain in my ass. That made her words pack more of a punch than usual.

"Your father—I miss him—"

Before she could continue, I rasped, "How can you? He was a monster."

"He wasn't perfect—"

"Damn straight he wasn't."

"—and he fucked with his sons' heads, but—"

"But, what, Savvie? What's to miss? The guy who'd crucify people in his warehouse? Who spent half his life beating on his kids to try to make men out of them? Who—"

She pressed a hand to my shoulder. "Aidan, your father wasn't a monster. He was an animal. I judge him as an animal, and not as a man."

A choked laugh escaped me. "What the hell?"

"Think about it. He acted without thought, reacting purely on instinct. He was the top of the food chain, and he had to stay up there. He'd do whatever it took, kill whoever it took, to maintain that standing.

"Lions will kill their own sons, did you know that? If the sons challenge them, I mean. Your father would never have done that. Lions also have a harem of women, and we both know that Senior was cured of that mentality a long time ago.

"In everything that was related to the Five Points, he was an animal. But where it counted, he wasn't. I respect that, and I understand what it took to stay at the top amid the turmoil of the seventies, eighties, and nineties. It was a brutal place, but he did it."

"I was there for most of it," I grumbled, not liking her stance but somehow able to understand where she was coming from.

My wife had a way of doing that—tilting my perspective.

"You were, but you weren't. You'll never know what it took for him to remain top dog during those decades because he lived that, not you.

"Your reign will be different. Difficult in some matters, but it won't be the same."

"How do you know? There are still drug wars and—"

"There are, yes, but he consolidated your position. He left you the city, and you can do with it what you will. What you eventually do to it is down to you."

Her eyes were soft and compassionate as she stared into mine.

I didn't understand why.

Until she reached up and stroked her thumb over my cheek.

It was then that I realized I'd been crying.

What a fucking pussy.

"He made me hate him," I rasped.

"You loved him too," she countered. "It wasn't an easy love, but it was love, nonetheless. That shone through in your eulogy." Her lips twisted. "I thought Lena was going to have a heart attack when you started thanking him for teaching you how not to do stuff, but, and I know you've been struggling with this, Aidan, there's a reason they say there's a fine line between love and hate."

I gritted my teeth. "He was a bastard. He treated us like toy soldiers."

"He wanted you to survive. He wanted you to have the tools that would allow you to live a long life.

"Do you know how many mob bosses lived to his age?"

"Not many."

"Exactly. You don't have to like him to love him, Aidan. And you don't have to agree with him to know that he reared you in his image. He had to learn the hard way, and so did you."

"I won't do that to our kid."

She arched a brow at me. "Kid?"

"Yeah. Kid." I grunted. "Not putting you through that more than once."

"My vagina appreciates your sacrifice, but don't I get a say in this?"

"I overheard you talking with Aela a couple Saturdays before he died."

"You did?" Her voice had turned wary.

"You were talking about how you didn't know how to tell me that you didn't really want to start a family now. That, even if you did, you couldn't cope with lots of kids like your mom." I shoved a hand through my hair. "It made me think about why I wanted a big family, and I realized that isn't for us."

"Why not?"

"Because it isn't what you want," I rumbled, watching her eyes flare wide. "And what you want matters to me. More than what I need, and that got me to thinking about *why* I'd need a big family anyway. To be like my own?" I shook my head. "I don't want what I had. If we're blessed with a child, they'll have cousins. Lots of the fuckers. That can be enough for them."

Her lips had formed a perfect 'O.' "Thank you, Aidan."

"You don't have to thank me," I said gruffly. "I want a kid for them to be their own person. Not to have future Five Pointers.

"Maybe I wouldn't have pieced that together without Da's passing, but he *did* die. And I *did* realize that.

"I want a little boy or a little girl because they're a part of you, not because they'll reign over the Five Points when I'm dead and gone."

A gentle breath escaped her, and as I stared deep in her eyes, I knew my words resonated.

I thought she'd talk more about that, but she didn't. Instead, softly, she asked me, "Is that the first time you cried for him?"

"Since that day, yes. Didn't fucking know I was crying. Fucking puss—"

"Don't you even think about finishing that sentence," she snarled, her hands slamming into my shoulders. "You are *not* a pussy for grieving your father, especially not with me. If you're my safe space, then I'm yours too."

Reaching up, I rubbed at my forehead. "Seems like two minutes ago I was heading over to West Orange to attend the funeral of the ex-Prez of the Satan's Sinners' MC, never thinking Da would be next—"

"You went to that?"

"I did."

"You didn't tell me," she said with a pout.

"I didn't want you to know. I knew you'd demand to come."

"What was it like?"

"Why?"

"They say bikers' funerals are impactful."

My jaw worked. "It was better than that fucking shitshow of Da's. Somber and miserable when half the city was grateful that he's dead, and that wake was more of an excuse for a party than anything else.

"Catholic funerals are miserable affairs. Bear's was a celebration of his life, not commemorative of his death." Because I knew she wanted details, I kept going, "They made a fucking racket. There was a funeral procession and they drove around the town then headed back to the compound. There was music and the council danced. It was..." I shrugged. "It was touching, I guess."

"Very un-MC."

"They raised hell too. Blasted their horns for at least ten minutes." My lips quirked up in a grin. "The song they played, I heard someone say that it was Bear and his Old Lady's song."

"That's so sweet," she whispered.

I nodded. "Was better than 'The Lord is my Shepherd,' that's for goddamn sure."

"You sound angry."

"I am," I muttered. "I didn't realize it, but I am. You're right. He was an animal, and there was shit he put us through that I'll never forgive him for, but mostly, I'll never fucking forgive him for dying like that. For choosing *that* end.

"Even though I know it was to protect Ma, even though I know he was sick, he could have..." I sucked in a breath. "He could have said goodbye."

She cupped my chin again, and just when I thought she was going to argue, she placed her mouth against mine and graced me with a single kiss.

"Men like Aidan O'Donnelly Sr. don't say goodbye, Aidan."

And the bitch of it was, I knew she was right.

7

SAVANNAH

AFTER THAT CONVERSATION, he took me back to bed and we both napped. I awoke to an empty apartment, which pissed me off, but I found a note on the refrigerator after I'd showered, changed and had gone to make coffee.

> *No one will ever understand me like you do, Savannah. I'm grateful for you.*
> *Jr.*

I STROKED my fingers over the note, wondering if he knew what he'd done by choosing to sign off with 'Jr.' and not just Aidan.

The son was leaving me the note, not my husband.

It got me thinking about how many roles we played on a day-to-day basis and how we juggled them. Sometimes doing a good job of it, sometimes doing the opposite.

As I set the machine to brew me a double shot of espresso, I grabbed my cell and rang my mom.

"Hey, baby," she chirped, sounding cheerful.

I used to think she was on medicinal pot she was so cheerful, but now, I just knew that she was at her most merry when she was stressed.

Considering where my mind had drifted before I'd called her, I told her, "You sound stressed."

"How can you infer that from two words?"

"Because I know you as well as you know me? What's going on?"

Lorelei Daniels was many things, but she was not a liar. Not even if it made it easier on her family.

When she was silent, I mused, "Remember that time when you told Camden, Paris, Aspen, and I that you and Daddy were divorcing because he'd cheated during a tour?"

"I do *not* sound like I did then."

"You were cheerful then," was all I said. "You chirped out the explanation as if you were telling us how many gifts Santa had brought us."

"I made a mistake. You know that," she grumbled.

"I'm not arguing. That fan was a whack job. She made everyone believe that they were in a relationship together."

The psycho had gone so far as to make deep fake sex tapes of them together. They'd gone viral in a heartbeat until Daddy had gotten an injunction against her and they'd been taken down.

Not that anything was truly deleted from the internet.

"I'm just saying that you sound like you did then. That's all."

I refused to freak out until I knew what was going on.

"I have to have surgery."

"What kind of surgery?" I asked cautiously.

"A hysterectomy." She swallowed. "I-I had cancer there, baby, but I beat it and I was in remission, and now they're saying that it's wise to have the whole... area... removed."

It took a lot to rob me of speech. A hell of a lot, in fact.

But Mom's news had me unplugging the coffee machine so it'd stop hissing at me and backing away to the nearest wall so I could slide down it.

"Baby? You still there?"

"You had cancer and you didn't tell us?"

That was the one part my brain was sticking fast on.

"Your father and I agreed that it would only freak you all out, and it wasn't necessary."

"Wasn't necessary?" I shrieked. "Okay, are you still in New York because I need to come and kick yours and Daddy's asses."

"Savvie!" Mom chided. "Don't say that. We were looking out for you. Aspen and Paris aren't in a good place right now. Your sister's night terrors have come back, and you know what one feels the other does too.

"Then there's the fact that Camden's gambling addiction is going crazy seeing as the anniversary of Locke's death is coming up, and you just lost your father-in-law—"

"So? All of that shit is shit. It's life. So is you being sick and your kids not being there to support you. I can't believe I'm only just hearing about this.

"Do you seriously think we care so little that we wouldn't have been there for you?"

"Of course not," she said with a sniff, sounding more like the mom who'd raised me to be an independent woman who took no shit from any man.

Or woman.

Or mother.

As the case might be.

"Then?"

"I wanted to deal with it alone, Savannah."

"Why?" I sputtered.

"Because it was my right to. I didn't even want to tell your father, but it's impossible to keep anything from him." She huffed. "He's all up in my business."

"Thank God he is!" I ground out. "Why wouldn't you want us there?"

"Because being sick is undignified, child. For God's sake, can't you see that?" She blew out a breath. "The only reason I said anything now is because I just got off the phone with the damn doctor and you took me by surprise."

My brow furrowed. "You wouldn't have told us about the surgery, either?"

She was silent long enough that I knew her answer was no but that she didn't want to say it out loud.

For a second, I let that silence between us settle.

I thought about Aidan's bitterness at his father's lack of a good-bye; I thought about how Aidan Sr. had kept *his* illness a secret from everyone too.

The parallels were many, and they hurt.

But... Mom, more than anyone else, had taught me about consent and the right I had over my body: a dominion no one else had over it.

It pained me to see this from her perspective, but wasn't this just another type of consent? Of control over oneself?

I licked my lips and, slowly, whispered, "I want you to tell me if you need me for anything. I want you to tell me if you need me to come to the hospital. I want you to know that I'll be there in an instant the moment you message or phone. I want you to know that I'll respect your privacy, even if—" I sucked in a breath, withholding the 'even if it hurts me' because that wasn't something to burden her with. So I just swallowed and rasped, "—even if... just... know that I love you, Mom. Okay?"

A sniffle sounded down the line. "Thank you, baby. I'll bear all that in mind." There were a couple more sniffles before she cleared her throat and, sounding cheerful again, queried, "Now, why did you call?"

"Does there have to be a reason?" I argued, needing to be my usual snarky self before I burst into tears.

If she could be cheerful then I could be snarky.

"Well, no, but there usually is with you."

Was that true?

"I need to get better at checking in with you if I only call when I need something," I groused.

"It isn't like that. Sometimes, you just want me to agree with you." Her soft, tinkling laughter hurt my heart and healed it at the same time. "I like knowing that you're working out your best arguments on me. Makes me feel useful and relevant."

"You *are* useful and relevant," I said grouchily, and suddenly feeling really old, I rolled onto my knees and staggered upright.

Mom had cancer.

I exhaled.

No, she was in remission.

But she needed a hysterectomy.

Preventative, by the sounds of it.

Which meant there was a chance it could come back.

Oh, who the hell was I kidding? That was as much cancer's MO as Aidan Sr.'s preference for crucifying his victims!

Fear tightened my throat like a hand was choking me.

"Is the cancer why you retired?" Mom had been a sex therapist for over twenty years.

She sighed. "Yes. The chemotherapy was aggressive, and it drained me."

Hesitantly, I asked, "Did you lose your hair?"

Her abrupt answer told me she didn't want to talk about it: "Yes."

She and Daddy had attended Aidan Sr.'s funeral, but I hadn't realized she was wearing a wig *or* that she'd been sick—that I called myself an investigative journalist was embarrassing.

"You don't want to go back to your practice?" I asked to change the subject.

"Not particularly."

"Why not?"

"I decided I'm going to take a leaf out of your book."

"You are?" If I sounded wary, that was because I damn well was.

"I am. I'm going to write my memoirs."

My brows lifted. "Jesus."

She chuckled. "It's not that bad."

I thought about what I knew of my parents' relationship, and I cleared my throat. "Please tell me you're not going to talk about the threesomes you and Daddy had—"

"That's between me and my manuscript."

I cringed. "Paris and Aspen won't like it."

"They're prudes. And you don't sound particularly pleased by it, Savannah," she chided.

"Do you think the world is ready to know that before he died, you, Daddy, and Gerard Sullivan were an item? Heck, I don't think Star even knew you were back together."

Star—the bane of my existence—hadn't approved of her father's relationship with my parents and had taken off.

She did that a lot.

I put the call on speaker so I could check my messages. The bitch hadn't replied to my last texts after she'd given me her SMS version of a suicide note.

I was so going to smack her for that when she eventually rolled back into town.

Which she would.

She had to.

"Don't talk to me about Star," Mom was saying, her tone having turned sour. "Why shouldn't people know that we all loved each other very much?"

"It'll break Star's heart." The 'again' went unsaid.

"She broke her father's first."

"That isn't fair—"

"Really? She's a selfish girl. Always has been. Taking off how she did practically killed Sully until we brought him back to life, and every time she disappears, it hurts you too."

She had a point.

But Star was... God, no one had ever understood her. Sometimes,

I didn't, but I knew what she'd gone through. Intimately. I knew the details. Mom didn't. And it wasn't my story to share.

"Star feels too much," was all I could say.

"That's no excuse."

"I don't understand why you're being such a hard ass about Star," I complained on a huff. "You haven't seen the woman in years. How can you judge her when you don't know her anymore?"

"I'm judging her actions."

"The reasons for which you're clueless about."

"And you're not?"

"No. Some days, I wish I were."

"That... bad?"

"Makes what Aspen went through look like a walk in the park."

When she let loose a shocked gasp, and without breaking Star's privacy and right to share her own history with whomever she chose —be that my mother or no one—I knew I'd gotten my point across.

"What happened?"

"Not my place to tell you. I just know that she's made a lot of sacrifices, Mom, and I won't let you judge her unfairly. I know you loved Sully—" God knew that I'd *seen* that love once when I'd walked in on them. "—and I know Star hurt him, but haven't we all hurt you and Daddy at some point? Isn't that just life?"

"When did you get to be so wise?"

"Had a good teacher," was my rejoinder, and I was surprised that she'd ceded to that argument so quickly.

Still, her staunch anger at Star had surprised me too.

This whole goddamn conversation was one big dose of bewildering.

"You won't tell your brother and sisters, will you?"

"About the cancer or the book?" Before she could answer, I muttered, "Whichever. No. Just like Star has the right to share her truth, you do too. And while I understand why you want your privacy regarding your health, I think you're foolish to cut us out when we could support you. Still, I won't preach or lecture you. I have to get going, but I'll call later."

"Why?"

"Because I take you for granted and I shouldn't. Every day is precious."

"This is what I didn't want to change, dammit. Savvie, you have your own life, and I have no desire to infringe upon that."

"You're not infringing. My husband and his father had a shitty relationship, and yet, I'm living with the fact he misses him and can't even comprehend that he misses him because he didn't particularly like him.

"I'm seeing how confusing that is with my own eyes. And I don't dislike you, Mom. We get along great. Maybe you always were more on Camden's wavelength, but that doesn't mean we shouldn't appreciate every day we have together because nothing is guaranteed. Especially not in our world."

"You really feel that Camden and I are on the same wavelength?" Her tone was laced with her shock.

I found comfort in that.

"I'm the odd duck. I'm fine with that. I never wanted to ride off Daddy's coat tails, whereas Camden and the twins were fine with that."

"I'm sure they'd disagree with that character assassination."

"I'm sure they would," I said smoothly. "That's why we argue a lot."

Her laughter was gentle. "Okay, Savvie. I'll look forward to your call."

"Later, Mom."

Wishing I could slam my phone down, instead, I just disconnected the line then stared blankly at the island in front of me.

Hands tightening around the kitchen counter, I bowed my head as my eyes started leaking. I tried to process the fact that Mom had been sick and hadn't told any of her kids, but it wasn't easy.

My temper swiftly got the better of me and I rang Dad, greeting him with, "You should have told us."

His silence wasn't because of the words, but my tone.

He wasn't used to me being angry with him.

I was, after all, a daddy's girl.

Always had been.

As his eldest daughter, I knew I'd seen a side of him that Aspen and Paris never had.

I'd known him before he was *the* Dagger Daniels. *noxxious's* fame had exploded when I was a kid, and there'd been a time when it had definitely gone to his head, ego, *and* dick.

The latter I wished I knew nothing about.

Eventually, a deep sigh sounded in my ear. "It was her choice. What was I supposed to do? Go behind her back to tell you?"

I huffed out a breath. "I don't know. Sent it to us via smoke signal? Given us a hint?"

"She didn't want that, honey. I didn't think she wanted that now, to be honest. She really told you?"

"I broke into her file at the hospital and read it all."

"What?!"

"I'm joking," I groused. "Yes, she told me. But I don't think she meant to. It was more like I surprised her."

"You can't surprise your mother."

"You can when she gets a phone call from her doctor telling her she needs surgery."

"Shit. I need to go to her—"

"I know you do, but Daddy, before you go, is she going to be okay?"

I knew he couldn't answer that question, knew he couldn't reassure me, but goddamn, I felt like I was back to being eight and we were losing Locke all over again.

The thought had me knuckling at my eyes.

So many secrets...

Things the public didn't know about, would *never* know about. God, even Aidan didn't know about Locke.

Daddy heaved another sigh. "She has the best of the best oncologists, sweetheart. We had her treated in Switzerland, and I've flown in guys to deal with her treatment stateside. She has more second opinions than the Queen of England would."

I bit my lip. "O-Okay."

"I'll call you later, all right? I need to speak with your mom and find out what's going on."

"Yeah. Thank you, Dad."

He paused. "What for?"

"Loving her so much."

His laughter was brisk. "You don't have to thank me for that."

He couldn't see my shrug. "Maybe I don't, maybe I do. Maybe it's because of you that I know how a man *should* love his woman."

His pause was loaded. "Everything all right with you and Aidan?"

"Things are perfect with us," I told him honestly.

He hummed. "Good. Tell him I know people who aren't scared of him and who will break his kneecaps if he hurts you."

"Leave his knees alone. They've been through enough strife." When he sniffed, I retorted, "I thought you and he got along?"

"We do. But that doesn't mean I shouldn't remind him who he's messing with from time to time."

"If you say so," I said with a laugh. "Okay, go. Love you."

"Love you too, baby."

With dead air buzzing in my ear for the second time in as many minutes, I dug my fingers into my eyes in an effort not to start blubbering. That'd get me nowhere. One thing I'd learned in my life was that tears didn't fix the past.

Plugging the coffee machine back in, I let it finish up my espresso. This time, I decided against shots and, steaming some milk, I tossed in the espresso to make a latte.

Throwing in some cinnamon syrup, I chucked in a couple ice

cubes after that was stirred in, and as I took a deep, bracing sip, I decided what my plan of action was.

I'd inadvertently discovered that my mom was sick and that she was keeping it from her kids, but Dad had that handled, and she didn't want me to do anything anyway.

Even if I wanted to go over there and read her fucking case notes, it wasn't like she wanted to get me involved.

God, that hurt.

I rubbed at my side where I felt like I'd been stabbed, and when that didn't work, I decided that distraction was the aim of the game.

We'd moved into Aidan's place in the city for a while after our wedding, but even though I had bad memories in mine, I preferred my apartment: the building itself and the layout.

It had undergone extensive renovations so Aidan was comfortable here, but I knew he liked it too—mostly because he was close to Conor. That was handy for me as it made it easier to snoop and, as of right now, would be the perfect distraction.

Coffee in hand, cellphone tucked into the waistband of my yoga pants, I headed toward the front door and made my way to the security door that had led to me meeting my soul mate all those months ago.

Back then, Lodestar had helped me break into Conor's apartment. Now, I had a direct line to the man himself.

"'Sup?"

"It's me, Conor."

"So?"

"So, I want to come in."

He heaved a sigh. "Why?"

"Because I want to talk to you."

"We're talking now."

"I want to speak to you face to face."

Silently, he released the lock on the door so that I could push it open.

Most people wouldn't use this entrance, but most people didn't have a weirdo for a brother-in-law. Or, in his case, a sister-in-law.

Poor Aidan had to deal with both of us on a daily basis.

Standing on the helicopter pad as I overlooked the city, it'd be easy for some to get an attack of vertigo at this height, but ignoring the view, I strode over to the stairs.

Before Christmas, I'd been in such a rush, bleeding and injured from a home invasion, brain clearly not working and frazzled from, ya know, the murder attempt, that I'd fallen down the steps.

Now, I took them carefully, sipping my coffee as I made my way down onto Conor's terrace.

He was standing there, one arm braced against the door, feet bare, a brooding expression gracing his handsome features.

If Aidan didn't make my body sizzle, I swore Conor would be the one who got me locked and loaded.

He had that whole intense genius aura, and his eyes, whenever you looked into them, you just knew he'd been to hell and, for the right person, would go straight back there to save them from themselves.

I figured that was pretty apt considering he had feelings for Star.

If anyone's crib was next door to Lucifer's, it was Lodestar.

"You heard from her?"

That that was his first question, when my thoughts had just taken me there too, had me jolting in surprise.

But this was Conor.

He read between the lines with an accuracy that was enviable.

"No. You?"

His mouth tightened. That was all the answer I got before he turned around and headed inside without another word.

I followed him from the terrace and into his living room.

Conor had the weirdest taste.

Star Trek meets Captain America.

Still, his couch was comfortable.

I joined him in the seating area, and because I'd been here often in the last couple months, I felt at enough ease to slip off my sandals and to tuck my feet under my butt.

He eyed me all the while with an intensity that would be unnerving if Aidan weren't my husband.

"I showed you our text chat," I complained because I knew why he was glowering. "You didn't show me yours."

"Yours was different than mine."

"How so?"

"Yours was a goodbye. Mine wasn't."

I studied him. "Maybe she wasn't saying goodbye to you."

Anger flashed across his expression. "Maybe."

"Whoa," I sputtered halfway through a sip of my iced latte. "What was that about?"

"What was what about?"

I wafted a hand at him. "You got angry."

"I *am* angry. If you haven't figured that out by now, Savannah, you're not as intelligent as I thought."

Ignoring the insult, I told him, "I know you're angry at her disappearing, but that was different." How did I verbalize what I'd seen? "That was a response to a specific train of thought."

He scowled at me. "Bullshit."

"It isn't," I sniped. "I've seen you get fired up about her leaving since she pulled her disappearing act. But that was specific. What is it? What's happened?"

I was used to Star going quiet. Conor clearly wasn't. It was a shitty habit of hers, so I could understand why he was restless.

He surged to his feet and stormed over to his office.

At first, I just thought he was avoiding the conversation entirely, but when he hovered by the door, scowl darker than ever, and demanded, "Well?" I scurried over too.

I peered inside the office that never seemed to change apart from what was on the screens, and I whistled under my breath when I found a couple interesting things on the monitors.

He plunked himself down behind one desk that I knew was his

'main' desk, and he beckoned me over, pointing at the screen when I made it to his side.

A video was playing on repeat.

Had he been watching this before my call?

Lodestar was sitting in the very seat he was using now. She wrote something on a note, took a photo of it, placed it in the trash, looked straight at the camera as she did, got to her feet before...

I sighed.

Her hand clutched at the head rest of his desk chair, and upon closing her eyes, the sweetest, purest misery flashed onto her expression.

Grief.

"She has feelings for you," I choked out.

His jaw clenched. "Would she have run away if she did?"

"I think we both know that's bullshit." I cast him a look. "Just like it would be bullshit for you to hide from the fact that you have feelings for her too."

"I'm not hiding from the fact. I know I do. I fucking love her," he grated out. "And she fucking runs off like I'm a part of the problem too."

"Star isn't..." I blew out a breath. "Star's always been complicated. Even as a kid, she could never take the easy path when the tough path looked more interesting."

He studied me a second. "*noxxious* formed a couple years before your birth, didn't it?"

I nodded. "And Star's. Camden's too. We were around for the early days. Not that any of us remember all that much."

"You know how her mom died?"

Tension hit me. "Why?"

"Why not?" He narrowed his eyes. "Did you know her mom's file at Langley is redacted?"

I pursed my lips. "That's none of my business."

"You knew she worked for the intelligence services?"

"I know that when Sully met her, my parents didn't think it would last," I said carefully.

"Why didn't they?"

"Because they came from two different worlds." Cautiously, I asked, "How much do you know about *noxxious?*"

"A lot."

"I know you're a 'super' fan, but did you just obsess over the music or the musicians too?"

"More over the music. But knowing my brother's father-in-law is Dagger fucking Daniels still blows my mind. Does that answer your question?"

"Mom, Dad, and Sully lived together for a long time."

He blinked. "Lived together?"

I cleared my throat. "Mom was raised by hippies. Rich ones. They left Ireland where it was prejudiced and uber-religious and women had to be married if they were pregnant or they'd be dumped in a 'home for unwed mothers' and enjoyed the sixties in the States."

"So?"

"So she believed in free love." I blinked back at him. "You know what I mean?"

"Are you trying to tell me that Gerard Sullivan and Dagger Daniels were living in a threesome with your mother?"

I grimaced. "It's something the record label tried to keep under wraps."

"I'll just bet they goddamn did." He frowned. "So, your mom was with both of them until he got with Star's mom?"

"Camden's the eldest, so he was the only one who technically lived within that dynamic."

"How do you know this?"

"After Star's mom passed, Sully nearly killed himself with booze and drugs. They reverted to that relationship to keep him alive." I took a deep sip of coffee, choking out the next half-truth. "When Camden was a kid, he was in this accident. It was the first time my parents had confirmation that Camden was Dad's and not

Sully's. Dad has a rare blood type, and all his kids are AB negative too."

Conor's mouth rounded.

When he stayed silent, I winced. "I've done the impossible—shut you the hell up."

He wheezed a second. "Your dad—Mom—Sully—"

"It was unorthodox but they never pretended to be freakin' choir boys."

"Does Star know?"

"It's why she ran away from home. Well, the first of many times." I stared at the video that was playing on an endless loop. "What was she doing to your computer?"

"Uploading a folder onto it."

"Malware?"

"No." He scraped a hand over his head. "The father of the Prez of the Satan's Sinners' MC... They were the brothers who we called in for clean-up duty at the compound after the Sparrows came for you—"

"Dude, I know who they are. I'm buds with Star, remember? She's been living with them for ages. *And* she and that Old Lady, Amara, are my sources for all the exposés!"

"Just checking that Aidan hasn't frazzled your synapses."

I sniffed. "Sexist, much? If anyone's synapses are on the fritz, it's his."

"Good to know. I'll check in with him."

"Please make sure I'm there when you have that conversation," I drawled.

Aidan would totally slap him across the head for that.

Well-deserved in my opinion.

"*Anyway,* Bear died last Christmas."

"I know. Star told me."

"He left behind a lot of information pertinent to the Sparrows' case. She was giving me an info dump to end all info dumps. There are terabytes' worth of data to process."

My throat closed as fear hit me. "She gave you all that?"

"She did."

We shared a look.

"I don't think I was wrong about that last text chat being a kind of suicide note," I whispered.

His nod was sharp. "Wherever she is, whatever she's doing, she thinks she's going to die. The question is why the fuck didn't she involve me? Why did she keep me out of the loop?"

"Honestly?"

"When have I ever come across as the type of guy who likes being lied to?" he growled, giving me another flash of that temper.

It made sense—he was an O'Donnelly. They all had a temper. But Conor was usually so fucking affable you forgot that he was bred from the same stock.

"Firstly, Star hasn't trusted anyone in years. Secondly, she never expects people to fight her battles for her. That's the God's honest truth. Her war is not your war, and she'd never put you in a position where you had to choose sides."

Conor studied me for so goddamn long I wondered if I had dirt on my face.

"What you're saying is," he said slowly, "that she's doing something that is against the O'Donnellys?"

"I'm not saying that," I dismissed immediately, not wanting to put my sister from another mister in the line of O'Donnelly fire.

Although, it *would* make sense.

Why else would she disconnect from him?

They clearly talked a lot. Conor wasn't the type of guy who wore his heart on his sleeve and who'd catch feelings easily. Yet he'd just told me that he loved her. And her expression on the video... just thinking about it made my heart squeeze.

"You are. You just don't want to get her in trouble." He wasn't wrong. "Was she involved in Da's shooting?"

On edge, I folded my arms against my chest. "How the hell would I know?"

His gaze turned thoughtful. Somehow, I knew he was changing the topic as he informed me, "I went to West Orange."

Curiosity pricked, I let him divert my attention. "To see Star? When?"

"The day Da was shot." His chin tipped up. "Impeccable timing as always."

"Don't be hard on yourself," I said gruffly, wanting so badly to reach out and hug him, to comfort him, but he had a wall around him that might as well have been a mile thick.

He merely shrugged. "I spoke with Lily Lancaster."

Star had been living with Lily and her partner in Jersey. I knew Lily. Not well, but some. Her father had once been the Sparrows' chief money man.

"You talked with her about Star? What did she have to say?"

"That the only person who knew where she'd gone was Katina."

I didn't know Star's foster daughter well, but I knew that she was devoted to the little girl.

"I'm guessing Lily didn't let you interrogate the preteen child?" I drawled.

"No. But maybe she'd let you."

"I'm not going to traumatize a little girl, Conor."

"Who said anything about traumatizing her?" He grunted. "Do you know what Star would do to me if I upset her kid?"

My lips twitched. "True."

"If you go there, speak with her, maybe—"

"Katina doesn't know me. She has no reason to share secrets with me." I raised a hand when he started to argue. "But I'll go. Okay? Not today, I have some shit to do, but I'll head over to Jersey and speak with her when I've got a moment." I leaned a hip against his desk. "What was in this info dump that Star left you?"

Not unsurprisingly, he didn't answer, just asked, "Did she send you that parcel she promised?"

I shrugged. "More bank statements. Some other info on how

Sparrows were chosen and inducted into the ranks. Mostly lists of banking transactions.

"Boring shit, but it's evidence the AG's office will like. Some forensic accountant is about to get a boner from all the numbers she sent me."

"Disappointed?"

"Maybe. You can't write exposés on crap like that."

"Running out of people to write about?"

"With Star away, yeah." Trying a different tactic to get info out of him, I asked, "You got anything I can write about to spread the word?"

"I'll transfer you some files over that I think might be of interest to you."

Barely hiding my glee, I nodded. "Thanks."

"The induction process was in the info dump. It's curious she included that in the package she had delivered to you."

"Why?"

"Of all the shit she sent over, why did she focus on that?"

I blinked. "Good point. I'll start digging."

"I'll send you anything I think is pertinent."

"Great. Appreciate that."

Though I thought he was about to dismiss me, he asked, "What made you come up here this morning?"

"I was thinking about Star. I had a conversation with my mom about her, and it kind of pissed me off, but I also get why she's angry. I get why you're angry too."

"You're not though, are you?"

"With Star?" I shook my head. "When she came back into my life, and I realized that everything my family had dismissed as 'make believe' was actually true, I promised myself that I'd never let her down again.

"I wish she could confide in me, but I understand why she can't. I think, if you really do care for her, you need to accept that she isn't a woman you'll ever be able to be comfortable around."

His brow puckered. "What's that supposed to mean?"

"It means she isn't the little woman. It means that you can't leave for the office and expect her to always be in the kitchen when you get home with dinner waiting for you."

"I don't expect that. What about my life makes you think I would?"

I didn't answer that last part. "Good thing... if you still want her."

He gritted his teeth but gave me a similar answer as before—a question.

"What about the men in my family made you think that when we want a woman, we don't go after them with everything we've fucking got?"

I shot him a smirk. "Then she's in for one hell of a ride when you get your hands on her, isn't she?"

"Damn straight," he growled.

8

____

TEXT CHAT
AIDAN

GRAINNE: *My girl died.*

Me: *From the blood spatter, I didn't think she'd survive.*

Grainne: *She was a good girl.*

Me: *I'm sure she was. I'm sorry, Grainne.*

Grainne: *Your sorry doesn't bring her back.*

Me: *Like I said last night, we'll handle any bills she may have incurred.*

Grainne: *Funeral as well as the hospital?*

Me: *Yes. Does she have any dependants?*

Grainne: *No.*

Me: *Family?*

Grainne: *We were her family.*

Me: *I'm sorry, Grainne. Truly.*

Grainne: *Your sorry won't bring her back. Your father would punish him. Make sure you do too. I expect justice for her, Aidan.*

Me: *She'll get it.*

9

AIDAN

THE CEMENT FACTORY was a working front.

That meant cement was fabricated on-site, but its production was mostly there as a cover.

Didn't mean that we didn't provide our construction sites with cement from this place, just that most of the factory was used for Five Points' business.

With Grainne's texts reverberating around my head, my temper was spiking at what MacMurray had done, but also at how she'd tried to manipulate me with that whole, 'Your father would punish him,' bullshit.

From the looks I got as I walked into the warehouse at the back of the factory, I figured my displeasure was etched into the lines of my face.

Good.

It was time to prove that the apple might have fallen far from the fucking tree, but that didn't mean the same worm wasn't crawling in it.

I didn't know where he'd gotten all the chairs from, but Brennan had lined up hundreds of them and had created an aisle for me to walk down.

I'd have felt like a bride walking to my doom if, at the end of it, MacMurray wasn't lying on the floor, taped up with enough duct tape that there was barely any of his flesh peeping through the bindings.

There'd been hushed mutterings before I showed up but, upon my arrival, the chatter reached a fever pitch.

It prolonged the adrenaline boost that my short text conversation with Grainne had triggered.

Despite my annoyance at her attempt to manipulate me, even before Savannah, I'd hated it when women were mistreated.

My da used to say that it was women who paid for the sins of men, and I knew that to be the truth.

Most of these fuckers in here hadn't had their mom kidnapped and brutally gang-raped. They hadn't almost lost her several times over the years as the past ate her alive.

No, women were supposed to be safe in the Five Points' world.

So why had an innocent woman died on my goddamn watch?

I kept my gaze straight ahead, but from the periphery, I saw that Brennan had used his brain and had grouped men together by crew and by rank.

When I made it to the end of the room, Brennan approached, informing me, "I confiscated their cellphones."

"Good job, *dearthair*," I said approvingly.

He wriggled his shoulders. "Took their guns too. Not their knives though."

"You're gonna have a blast handing them back."

He shot me a grin. "That's for my crew to sort out."

I snorted. "Lucky them. Do the men know why they're here?"

"I think if they did, when they saw MacMurray, they quickly recalculated shit."

"They know it's MacMurray because he's missing?"

"Yup. And these fuckers are bigger gossipers than teenage girls."

Nodding my understanding, I turned around to find Finn standing there.

"You need to keep your cool," he warned me.

"What makes you think I'm going to lose my shit over a piece of trash like MacMurray?"

"You forget that I know you as well as I know myself," he grumbled.

I shot him a smirk before I strode over to MacMurray.

My back to the crowd, I called out, "I'm sure that being gathered together with such short notice has come as a surprise to you." Turning to face my men, I dug my foot under MacMurray's shoulder and tipped him on his side. "I'm running a risk, after all, having you grouped in this one space, but I figure it's worth it."

"No one would betray the Points, sir," someone shouted.

I peered over in the direction from which it came, but I didn't bother getting the guy to stand up.

"You'd be surprised who'd betray us," was my reply.

I figured I kept it cool enough because, from the corner of my eye, I watched Finn's shoulders relax some.

Finn tended to know what I was going to do before I fucking thought of it thanks to decades of friendship.

It was obvious that I was going off script at the moment.

Maybe that wasn't a bad thing.

Especially with how easy it had been for MacMurray to talk smack about me to my face.

My words triggered whispers.

"You'd be surprised who'd betray us," I repeated. "*Our family...* Because that's what you are, are you not? My people?"

A low wave of murmured agreements greeted me.

After I unfastened the buttons on my sports coat, I shoved my hands into my pockets and peered over at them, ensuring that I was talking to no one in particular but to the collective.

Not even at Da's funeral had every Five Pointer been in attendance, with only the top brass joining the inner circle there and at the wake.

For the runners, I'd made sure there was an open tab at one of their bars—the unimaginatively named *Flanagan's*.

"When my father died, I inherited you. You might not see it that way, but I do. I inherited this position, I inherited the men, and I inherited the problems and the enemies as well as the allies.

"But it's come to my attention that some of you think I'm a pussy." Ignoring the grumbles of disagreement as the bullshit they likely were, I waved a hand down at MacMurray. "A secret Cain let me in on."

My knee was at eighty-five percent strength. It had to be at a hundred for this, but if they needed proof that I was a changed man, here, *now*, was where I had to show them.

I stood on my weak leg, used the other to rear back, and kicked Cain in the ass.

He yelped around his gag as he tumbled five or so feet away.

"Do you agree with him?" I queried, staring at them with a forbidding expression as I followed Cain. In response, the men in the front row angled back and away from me. "Feel free to speak your mind. Like Cain also said, I'm not my da."

Darragh, the father of my cousin, Mary Catherine, got to his feet. "You're not Senior, Aidan, but that doesn't mean you're not formidable in your own way."

I pursed my lips when I heard someone snarl, "Ass kisser."

"The second I inherited this bullshit was the second I knew someone would think they could try to take it from me.

"You can try, you will fail, but I understand that a man has aspirations. Give it your best fucking shot," I intoned calmly. "But what you will *not* do is what Cain did."

Jonesy, one of Da's guards like MacMurray, stood. "What did he do, Aidan? Why you got him taped up like that? He's one of us, not an enemy."

"Cain was detained after he beat a hooker to death—"

"She died?" Brennan, who'd been leaning against a wall, straightened up.

"She did," I confirmed, shooting him a look that conveyed my displeasure at being interrupted.

My eye caught on Finn and I saw his tension had risen again.

"What hooker?" Jonesy questioned, his brow puckered. "We left him at Queens of Heart last night—"

"I think you just answered your own question," Declan rasped. "She worked at Queens of Heart."

Jonesy's nostrils flared. "He killed that girl he was with? Fuck, she was only a baby."

I knew my distaste flickered onto my expression.

Jonesy was in his late fifties, but he'd thought nothing of using a hooker who was in her early twenties.

Sick fuck.

I watched as the older man scrubbed a hand over his face. "What do you know about this new street drug making the rounds, Jonesy?"

When his throat bobbed, I knew he was going to lie to me. "Not heard much about Red, Aidan."

I barked out a laugh. "Bullshit if ever I heard it. How do you know its goddamn name if you haven't heard much about it?"

His cheeks turned pale. "I ain't lying. Just know the name."

"You sure you ain't lying?" I mocked. "Feel like getting some of what's coming to Cain?"

Jonesy's mouth bobbed open and closed in response.

"Cat got your tongue, Jonesy?" I snarled.

Lucas jerked to his feet. My captain—the formal title for the leader of the crew I needed to start utilizing as more than guards— confirmed his usefulness by informing me, "The Sicilians are selling it out of a warehouse in Queens, Aidan."

"Now, was that so complicated, Jonesy?" I reached into my shoulder holster, drew out my gun, and pointed it at him. "You fucking lie to me again, I'll have your tongue before I blow out your brains. Do you understand me?"

He swallowed, his gaze drifting from the gun and back to me. "You don't mean that, Aidan."

"You really wanna take that bet, Jonesy? Your loyalty was to my father. You need to prove your loyalty to me. That isn't something that gets passed down as easily as the business. And that ain't on me either. It's on you fuckers to prove that you're trustworthy."

"Our loyalty is to the O'Donnellys," Jonesy argued.

I studied him a second. "See, this is what interests me about all of you. You know I'm not like my father. You know he was insane. You know that was why he scared the *bejesus* out of everyone.

"But isn't it far more terrifying to have a man who's completely rational slice out your tongue for lying to him?

"Nothing I do can be excused away with an insanity plea. Everything I do will be undertaken with me in complete *compos mentis*, so you'd better watch yourselves and you'd better stop fucking bullshitting me."

Blanching for the first time, Jonesy stuttered, "I-I-I don't know much about what he was taking."

"You and Cain were Da's guards," I pointed out.

"Yeah," he agreed.

"So what you're telling me is that this motherfucker has managed to get addicted to it and that's happened without you or any of Da's other men realizing it?"

"Well, we—he—"

"We—he—" I jeered. "Is that another fucking lie I see you trying to come up with, Jonesy?" I pointed my gun at Anthony, another of Da's guards. "Stand up."

He bolted upright, blurting, "Cain's been addicted to Red for the past two months."

I narrowed my eyes at him. "So, he got hooked when my father was still alive?"

"Yeah, he did."

"Where's he buying it from?"

Anthony cleared his throat. "I'm not sure. I just know that he always has plenty. It started out where he was using it only on the nights we went to the brothel, but then he started taking it more regularly."

Mind racing, I pondered that. "So, Anthony, what you mean to tell me is that though my da specifically told you that he wouldn't accept any of his guards taking drugs, you knowingly covered up for Cain?"

"It wasn't knowingly at first."

"Key words being 'at first.'" I slowly nodded. "I'm starting to see that you fuckers weren't as terrified of my father as I initially suspected if you thought you could hide that from him."

"He was sick at the end," Jonesy excused. "We all saw it—"

"So you took advantage of my sick old man?"

He turned impossibly paler. "N-No, I didn't mean that."

Finn ground out, "I'd sit my ass down if I were you, Jonesy, before your widow finds herself joining the Old Wives' Club."

Throat bobbing, Jonesy plunked his ass on his seat. When he swiped at his forehead, I realized he'd been sweating.

Over something else he was potentially lying about?

Filing that likelihood away, I asked Anthony, "Did you take Red?"

"Most of us did," he muttered. "Only on nights we went to Queens of Heart."

"Fuck you, Anthony," Jamie, Ma's guard, snarled, leaping to his feet. "I never went with this bunch of perverts, Aidan, and I didn't take any-fucking-thing."

I slipped off the safety. "That true, Anthony?"

"S-Sorry, yeah. It's true. I forget about Jamie. He's with your ma so much that it's easy to forget he's one of us."

"That's because I ain't one of you," Jamie spat. "Neither's Fenris."

"Sean ain't either," Declan inserted. "He was mine until I transferred him to Ma's guards."

Nodding at him, I ordered Jamie, "Sit down."

After he begrudgingly complied, I studied Sean, Fenris, and Jamie, taking note of their expressions. They were relieved I believed them, but they were angry too. Angry at being lumped in with these treacherous fuckers.

"Those on my father's security detail expecting reassignment will no longer be transferred to my or my brothers' crews, but they will be demoted. Apart from Ma's detail. You're your own crew now."

"You're demoting us over some two-bit whore?" Jonesy yelled.

"Thought she was just a baby," Eoghan rumbled, his disgust clear.

"She was a fucking hooker," Jonesy grated out. "It's part of the job."

"Getting their asses killed? Thought it was just to lie on their backs and spread their thighs instead of processing the fact they're fucking old creeps like *you* to pay their bills," Declan sniped.

The color had made a reappearance in Jonesy's face, and I welcomed it with open arms.

"You took drugs when that was one of Da's few golden rules. You protected Cain over obeying those rules. Then you compounded that by lying.

"What makes you think you should be reassigned to any of our crews? How the fuck can any of us trust you to obey *us* when you've proven that you're lying sacks of shit?"

Anthony protested weakly, "Your da cultivated that—"

"He cultivated you lying to him?"

"No. He wanted us to be like family. To have each other's backs."

"There's having each other's backs, and there's hiding shit like a drug addiction from him. There's hiding shit like the fact Cain was buying product from another faction." I waved the gun in my hand. "No, you're all fucking runners again. Don't care if you're too old and too fucking fat to run, Jonesy. You made your bed, and you're going to lie in it."

Reaching into my pocket, I pulled out a slip knife before I crouched down in front of Cain.

Resting my gun on the floor beside his shoulder, I sliced through the duct tape on his face, ignoring his screams as I slit his flesh open at the same time, deep enough to cut into the bone.

When his features were free, I saw that Brennan had worked him over in my absence because he was pummeled to fuck.

Watching the blood oozing from the deep wound, I questioned, "Where did you buy the drugs?"

"Why's it matter?" Cain slurred.

"Because I don't fucking trust you, that's why. I know what it takes to maintain a habit, and I know that you make good money, but you don't earn enough for that. Especially some chemical that's 'exclusive.' That means you were getting the money or the drugs from somewhere else. Where?"

"Fuck you." He went to spit at me, but I shifted out of the way, surging to my feet before I kicked him in the head.

"Where did you get the drugs?"

"Fuck you," he slurred again, so I kicked him *again.*

To my audience, I declared, "Disobedience—when I'm your leader and you're supposed to be so fucking loyal to me."

I dropped to my knees once more, hiding a grimace at the force of the collision, and I grabbed Cain's nose with one hand and my gun with the other. Squeezing the nostrils closed until his mouth dropped open, I shoved the butt of the revolver between his lips.

Pushing it down his throat until he was gagging and choking on it, I looked up at the men, spying what I'd intended from this gathering.

Fear.

Respect.

I wasn't going to lead them like Da did—but that didn't mean I shouldn't cultivate both at the start.

"Cain's obviously not understanding his position," I drawled, watching as guys at the back stood up for a better view.

When the bastard spewed, vomit speckling his jaw, chin, and chest, some chunks even landing on his forehead, I pulled the gun away.

As he retched, rolling onto his side to get his breath back, I asked, "Where did you get the fucking drugs from?" At his silence, something broken only by his sputtering, I seethed, "Don't make me fucking kick you—"

"Stepanov!" he cried out.

I stilled.

"Stepanov is against Maxim Lyanov," Lucas informed me, jumping to his feet again.

Bratva.

But we were goddamn allies.

Jesus fuck.

"There's infighting in the Bratva?"

"Yes. They keep it on the down-low mostly."

"How?"

He shrugged. "I don't know. But if you head over to Brighton Beach, there are a shit ton of bar brawls—one of my informants keeps me looped in.

"Lyanov's new blood. Stepanov is the only one left of the old guard who was high up the ranks. Lyanov eradicated the rest."

Which meant the Pakhan thought he could trust Stepanov...

You just couldn't get the fucking staff anymore.

I cracked my knuckles as I processed that, then, well aware I had an audience which was frozen with anticipation, and quite comfortable in living up to their nightmares for the moment, I pulled out a set of tweezers from my pocket.

They were longer than the ones Savvie used to pluck her eyebrows, and they had a kind of downward-angled tip with pointed ends. I'd bought them this morning with this task in mind.

The vomit made his face slimy, but I still managed to pinch Cain's nostrils. His mouth gasped open, and I snatched his tongue with the tweezers.

"My father's day is done. In the past. It's my time to rule over you, and I do shit differently than him." I scanned the crowd, putting pressure on the tweezers when Cain started to struggle until he was yelping in agony at my hold on the slippery muscle. "Get on my bad side and I'll fuck you over. Get on my good side and I'll reward you. But if you fucking lie to me, that's it—game over."

And with those words imparted, that warning tossed down like the gauntlet it was, I sliced through Cain's tongue.

As he choked and gagged on his own blood, I let him drown, ramming home the visual, forcing them to accept that I could more than live up to my father's reputation if I chose to.

The sounds of his death graced the room with all the splendor of an aria sung by a soprano at the Met.

As they rang around the high ceilings, Finn rasped, "If you kill him, you can't question him further."

He had a point so I hurled the bloodied mass that had been Cain's tongue into the crowd, dug my foot under his shoulder, and shoved him over.

Around an agonized wail, he sucked in deep, gulping breaths as blood poured from his mouth.

That sure as fuck had ripped away his attitude.

I glanced at Brennan who, understanding my silent order, barked, "Morrison, Port, get him out of here. Eoghan, cauterize the wound."

The two runners jumped to their feet, and Eoghan, the only field medic with in-depth training, strolled after them as they dragged him along to a backroom.

Upon snatching the handkerchief Brennan tossed me, I wiped my hands. "Don't mistake sanity for weakness. Liars will be treated the same way as MacMurray. Traitors will be executed.

"If you have any information about Red, about the Bratva disagreements, about any-fucking-thing suspicious, you go to your captain, and they will relay that information back to me, Lucas, or any of my brothers. Understood?"

When I didn't get a response, I snarled, "UNDERSTOOD?"

"Yes, sir!"

"Yeah."

"Yes, of course."

"Sure."

Affirmations—a cacophony of them.

And when they came from hundreds of men, it sounded like a song written just for me. Maybe not an aria like what Cain had serenaded me with, but it sure as fuck sounded sweet, nonetheless.

I turned to Brennan again and waved a hand this time. He surged forward, shouting, "Leave the room in an orderly fashion. I don't want to have to recruit more brothers because you have about as much sense as fucking lemmings. Your cells and pieces will be returned to you by one of my crew." He directed a look at Forrest who heaved a sigh.

When Bren didn't head off with them but stuck to my side, I wasn't altogether surprised when Finn and Declan did the same.

A strong front.

The O'Donnellys against the fucking world.

Well...

Fuck's sake.

"Where the hell's Conor?" I demanded amid the furor from the crowd.

"Where do you think?" Declan rolled his eyes. "I'm sure he'll watch this back later."

"Fucking snoop," I groused. "He was supposed to be here."

"That bitch has got him riled up," Declan excused.

"Don't let Savannah hear you call her that. She'll slice and dice you a new one."

"No one ghosts our brother," Declan mumbled.

Warning delivered, I ignored him. "Does anyone have any hand sanitizer?"

Brennan tossed me some and I liberally applied it. The stench of alcohol was preferable to the pervasive sourness of vomit.

The four of us watched as the men formed an orderly line, gossiping all the while, and managed to leave the room without causing a stampede.

Only when we were left alone did Finn murmur, "Thought you weren't going to be like your... *our* da."

"What did you expect me to do, Finn? Hold his hand and tell him he was a naughty boy?"

"The road to hell is paved with good intentions," Brennan intoned, but he didn't sound disapproving, more jaded.

I knew how he fucking felt.

"I can't do anything unless they respect me and, after Cain's behavior last night, it seems as if I'm going to have to work hard for that respect."

"You went down in people's estimations after the shit with your knee," Brennan told me. "Not everyone knew about the drugs, but they knew to come to me instead of you if they needed something. It fucked with your rep."

Brennan wasn't the kind of guy who'd soften a blow to make me feel better. I didn't need hot smoke blowing up my ass, just the truth, so I nodded. "Saw that for myself."

"If he'd gone about this differently, Finn, they'd have thought he was weak," Declan concurred. "Aidan might be the natural heir, but that doesn't mean there isn't a snake in the ranks looking to exploit a weakness."

"You looked good out there too," Brennan complimented. "Your knee not giving you any trouble?"

"Not unless I overexert myself." It was twinging now. "I'll need to rest it tonight."

"How about the drugs?" Declan prodded.

I couldn't be annoyed that we were having this conversation beside a puddle of vomit and blood in a cement factory. Even if it was demeaning.

"I'm okay."

It wasn't a lie. Nor was it the truth.

When Declan quirked a brow at me, I shrugged. "What do you want me to say, Dec? It's fucking rough. Some mornings, it's difficult to get out of bed. Some nights, I crave them worse than I could ever crave sleep.

"I'm a recovering addict. That's what I'll always be. But I'm strong right now, and I just need to keep it that way."

"Do you really think there are men who'd exploit Da's death to take over the Points?" Finn rumbled, his mind on business like usual.

"I don't see why not. Especially if they think they can take out the weakest link early on," I replied before I changed the subject too. "The Russians are our allies. Why would they bribe one of Da's guards?"

"You just sliced off the tongue of the only man who could tell you," Finn grumbled.

"He's got a hand still," Brennan drawled. "He can write his answers down."

Finn let loose an impatient sigh.

"How did you know something was going on with him, Aidan?" Declan inquired.

"There's an advantage to being an ex-junkie. I know how to spot the signs in other people, and I know how fucking low they'll sink to feed their habit." To Brennan, I said, "I want answers."

He cracked his knuckles. "Leave it with me."

10

———————

TEXT CHAT

SAVANNAH

ME: *I need you to kiss me when you get in tonight and then take me to bed.*

Aidan: *No. Did you forget about last night?!*

Me: *I deserve a kiss after the day from hell.*

Aidan: *Why? What's happened, little one?*

Me: *My mom did what your da did.*

Aidan: *You might need to narrow that down, baby. My father did a lot of shit. Three-quarters of which I can't even begin to imagine Lorelei doing.*

Me: *She got sick and didn't tell us.*

Aidan: *Oh. Fuck. Is she okay? I'll be home in around forty minutes.*

Me: *You don't have to come back if you're not ready to.*

Aidan: *Little one, if you need me, I'm there.*

Me: *Don't make me cry.*

Aidan: *I wasn't trying to, sweetheart. Why do you never say what I think you'll say?*

Me: *It's an art form.*

Me: *I don't understand why they think it's okay to keep this shit from us.*

Aidan: *Because outside of being our parents, they're people too?*

Me: *Don't you dare be reasonable about this!! You can't tell me you weren't pissed at your da for hiding his illness from you.*

Aidan: *I can't tell you that, no.*

Me: *Well, then.*

Aidan: *Your relationship with your mother is less complex than mine.*

Aidan: *What's her diagnosis?*

Me: *I think she's okay, but she's having preventative surgery to make sure it doesn't come back.*

Aidan: *Cancer?*

Me: *Yes. Ovarian, or uterine. I'm not sure which. She was cagey.*

Aidan: *Now I know where you get it from.*

Me: *Pfft.*

Me: *I don't know how they hid it.*

Aidan: *They were away all summer. They left for Europe after our wedding, didn't they?*

Me: *Shit, you're right. Daddy said she had her treatment in Switzerland. Some vacation.*

Me: *You know, I used to get grounded for lying?*

Aidan: *Lol. That sounds about right too. Anyway, I'm not sure you can ground your parents. Can you imagine Da on the naughty step?*

Me: *Lol. Don't make me laugh.*

Me: *I hate that she went through this without us.*

Aidan: *She told your father, baby. She wasn't alone. Maybe he was who she needed to get her through.*

Aidan: *Maybe she needed to be Lorelei during her treatment, not 'Mom.'*

Me: *I hate that that makes sense. Stop being logical.*

Aidan: *I can't help it. :P*

Me: *I guess if we'd been there, we'd have hovered over her, and* she'd have wasted energy she didn't have trying to spare our feelings when she was the one who needed the attention.

Aidan: *I'm thinking so, yes.*

Me: *Being a mom sucks.*

Aidan: *Another reason why I'm only going to put you through it once.*

Me: *What if I change my mind?*

Aidan: *And want two? Lol. That'll never happen. Stop being ornery.*

Me: *¯_(ツ)_/¯ If the shoe fits. ¯_(ツ)_/¯*

Aidan: *Do you need me to come home, little one?*

Me: *No. I'm fine. Well, I'm not but I have work to do, and I know you're busy. Thank you though. I just needed to tell you but if I say it out loud it makes me cry. I hate fucking crying.*

Aidan: *I know, baby. But you can always cry in front of me. No shame between us. Ever.*

Me: *Hey.*

Aidan: *What?*

Me: *I love you.*

Aidan: *Love you too.*

Aidan: *You never have to thank me for being there, Savannah. You're my wife. My fucking everything.*

Me: **swoons**

Aidan: *Dork. Lol.*

11

———

AIDAN

THE DRUGS DON'T WORK - THE VERVE

THREE NIGHTS LATER

"WHAT?" I snarled.

"What's with the road rage, dude?"

I gritted my teeth as Savannah started riding me, her nails digging into my chest as she ground that sweet, sweet, *sweet* fucking pussy into me, doing shit that a magician couldn't do for my cock.

"I answered the phone because you somehow set my ringtone to 'Crazy Frog' and now was not the fucking time for that soundtrack, Conor."

"Jesus, are you having sex?"

"You're the one who didn't take a hint after the sixth time I cut the goddamn call!"

He made a gagging sound. "Ring me when you're finished."

"I'm going to kill him," I rasped, reaching up to grab her tits.

With one hand, I shaped the globe, and with the other, I tweaked the nipple.

Pinching it, I watched her wriggle closer so that I could take it into my mouth. I bit down until I elicited a moan from her and her pussy was clutching at my cock even more than before.

Bound with silk, knotted above the bandages I was making her wear, her wrists were tethered to the headboard again via the zip tie I'd looped around the silk bindings—no more cuffs for my wife. She couldn't be trusted with them.

Sucking her nipple, I dragged her deeper into me by wrapping my arms around her and used pressure to make her ride me slower so that every cosseting inch of her cunt enveloped my shaft.

Moving a hand, I grabbed one of her ass cheeks and swiped my fingers along her slit from behind.

We'd made a fucking mess together, and I was here for that.

"Such a good fucking girl for me, Savannah."

Her moan lit me up inside and out.

"Only in bed, of course," I drawled, choking off a laugh when she clamped down on my dick.

I reached up and toyed with the necktie we were using as a gag. It was drenched with saliva, and while she could still make sounds and mumble words, it kept her quiet for the most part.

"This pussy," I rumbled, swiping my slick fingers over her upper lip. "Can you smell it? Can you smell us?"

The room stank of us, and I fucking loved that too.

She groaned, *"Yethhhh."*

"So fucking wet for me, little one. Only me." I reached for my knife on the nightstand and sliced through the zip tie that tethered her to the headboard. "Straighten back up, baby. I wanna see those tits jiggle some more."

She squirmed into sitting up and I grabbed her ass cheeks to help steady her.

Her torso was flushed with heat and arousal, and even though her face was just as sweaty, her forehead dotted with perspiration, hair sticking to her, she'd never looked more beautiful than she did right now.

"You feeling better, baby," I taunted her as I started to finger her clit.

Another bob of her head.

"Tell me."

Her tongue prodded the necktie but, *"Bedder,"* was the only word she could get out.

All these months of marriage, of strain and strife, and I'd come to learn that my wife did *not* handle her emotions in a healthy way—she hid her true feelings through snark. Grieving my father's passing, exhausted from lack of sleep, and then the news about her mom meant that she'd been sassing me ever since her phone call with Lorelei—this wasn't the first time I'd fucked her out of her mad, and it wouldn't be the last either.

I spanked her ass. "Get off."

Her brow furrowed and she shook her head.

I spanked her again. "Do it, Savvie," I growled, using the tone I knew she'd respond to.

She wriggled off my dick, releasing a sobbing gasp before she toppled onto her side next to me.

I scampered upright then headed directly into the closet. Ignoring her yelp of annoyance, I found the item I'd purchased earlier today.

Sure, MacMurray had inspired said purchase, but she didn't need to know that.

Her eyes widened at the sight of the spreader bar before the lids lowered into slits.

Watching her breathing change, I warned, "If you kick me, I will make you pay for it."

"Won't," she garbled around the silk.

"Good girl," I praised as I reached for one foot and set the cuff around the ankle.

Lifting it, I nipped her big toe, smirking when she squealed. Sucking the digit between my lips had her eyes flaring ever wider, and when she squirmed to get free, I released it before I smoothed my tongue over the arch.

Her shudder was *not* from revulsion.

She groaned and mumbled, *"Feelth good."*

"I know it does, little one."

I let go of that foot so I could snag the other and wrap the cuff around it too. With that done, I fastened the spreader bar to the cuffs then yanked it apart, tutting when I saw it barely parted her legs.

With every inch I spread them, her moans changed, getting progressively deeper.

When the muscles of her inner thighs were straining, I eyed her soaked cunt with satisfaction.

It was on display, but... not enough.

Reaching down, I clenched my fist around my balls and gave them a rough squeeze before I grabbed the bar and lifted her legs until the front of her thighs were resting against her chest.

"I'm going to put the bar beneath your head. Nod if you think you can manage it."

Her nod was eager.

I hummed as I worked, positioning a pillow between the bar and her head as I settled it there so that the cold metal wouldn't hurt her neck or dig into her too much.

Now, she was totally on display, her cunt leaking juices that were a mixture of both of us, and my mouth watered for a taste.

Sitting on the edge of the bed, I reached over and dragged my nails down the flat of her left sole. She screeched then squirmed as I proceeded to tickle that same sensitive flesh.

"I'm not going to fuck you until you leave a puddle of cum on the sheets beneath your ass, baby girl."

Her eyes bugged wide at that.

Shooting her a smirk, I let my nails drag over the length of her calf and down the back of her thigh before I moved to the other leg and gave it the same treatment.

A tremor whispered through her, and I watched as her bound body responded to a stimulus I rarely gave her.

When my hand struck her sit spot, she yowled.

"That's for sassing me this morning," I told her calmly.

She scowled at me.

Gracing her with another spank, I watched as her nostrils flared as she sucked down a breath.

"Did you know there's something infinitely satisfying about mussing you up?" She swallowed at my words. "You're always so fucking put together. I could parade you on a catwalk—that's how pristine you are. And whenever you're at your most beautiful, I think of you like this. Gagging on my dick, your eyes wet. Your cunt dripping." I sucked in a breath that I released noisily. "Your face and chest bright pink, sweaty, eyes glazed, pussy lips spread wide around my cock.

"Your ass gaping as I pull out of it to jack off over your back, thighs trembling from the position I put you in...

"Yeah, this is how I picture you. Not all neat and beautiful. That's the woman on my arm. This is you in my fucking bedroom.

"This is where I'd keep you all the time if I could, but where would the fun be in that? How could you sass me by telling me to go fuck myself when I say that you need to take a nap and *not* work yourself ragged, hmm?"

Her words were too garbled to understand.

"Too late for words, baby. Action's what's required." I patted her pussy, dragging my fingers against her slit then pumping two into her. "You thought I'd fuck you to help you sleep without showing you how wrong you were to sass me?" I tutted. "Oh, ye of little faith, Savannah."

She released a screech that sounded through the gag as I twisted my hand and raked down against her happy spot.

The spongy flesh beckoned me and I rubbed it until her thighs were quaking much as I'd described, her eyes were both glazed *and* wet, and she was one big quake as I took her close to the edge.

"Aidan," she mangled. "Please."

It was somehow hotter that it came out as 'pease.'

My fingers slowed down as I pulled them out, flicking them so that her cum flecked the backs of her thighs.

"Still no puddle."

I leaned down over her and set my tongue to work. She howled, her ass tipping high as she tried to knock me off, but she was pinned down and the only place she could wriggle was left or right.

I grabbed her hips and held her firmly as I tongued her slit then focused on her clit.

Sucking down, I alternated between soft flicks of my tongue and fast ones that had her mewling behind her gag.

I didn't stop until the moans she released went from intermittent to one long, low groan and that was when I slid my fingers into her slit again.

They returned to the earlier scene of the crime—her G-spot—and this time, I doubled down on my efforts until I pulled back.

The short, intense burst of her cum squirted forth, landing on the sheets. My fingers moved faster, raked harder. Another burst. Then one more.

And throughout it, she screamed and pleaded and begged and squirmed until she was panting from exhaustion.

That was when I slipped my cock into her.

Her pussy fought me inch for fucking inch, but goddammit, it felt good.

I leaned over her, resting my weight on her thighs, and I circled her lips with my tongue. Her eyes were so pretty, pleading with me to stop, to start, to fuck her, to leave her alone, that I stared straight into them as I took what I wanted.

Her cunt clamped down around me every time, and sweat soon beaded my temples as I reached up and did something I'd never done before...

Placing a hand over her nose and mouth, I whispered, "You are mine, Savvie. I will protect you. I will watch out for you. I will make sure you're safe and well. I will check you sleep enough and that you eat." Her head rocked back as she tried to breathe. "I will always give you what you need. Even air..."

Fucking her faster, I maintained that connected glance, watching her pupils turn to pinpricks, and I held it.

And held it.

Her eyes flared wider as she strained for oxygen.

But the trust...

It floored me.

She didn't panic.

She held it.

And held it.

Before I let go.

As the air penetrated her lungs after it whistled in down her nose, her pussy rebelled.

This time, she came around me, and I felt her slickness drench me as she screeched with her pleasure.

I rode her through it, not stopping now until I was biting off curses as I exploded inside her.

Only when I was done did I pull away.

Only then did I realize she was sleeping.

Grinning sheepishly, I shook my head as I pulled out of her, hissing at the release of pressure.

I stared at our mutual mess, smiling in delight, then began to unravel her from the bindings I'd put her in.

She didn't even make a murmur. Not when I released her legs and settled them on the bed. Not when I unfastened her hands or untied the gag.

Once she was free, she rolled onto her side with a sigh and continued sleeping.

I pressed a kiss to her temple and told her, "Baby girl, you need to go pee."

She mumbled under her breath and flopped a hand on the sheet. "Later."

"Savannah," I warned, smiling as she huffed and trudged off to the bathroom.

Swiping my boxers over my abs to clean up some, I dragged them on then, heading into the closet, tossed the necktie and the silk ties into the laundry basket.

After, I doused the spreader bar with some spray alcohol and stored it in the drawer that used to house my watches but was now starting to overflow with the toys I'd been buying for Savvie—I still needed to add the French maid's costume to it. Maybe I'd get her that for Christmas?

Only once everything was put to rights did I grab my cell phone from where I'd tossed it on the mattress earlier, taking note that she was still in the bathroom.

All I really fucking wanted was to get into bed with her and sleep for six hours, but Conor was waiting for my call, and I knew he wouldn't let me rest until I'd talked to him.

The moment the door to my office was closed behind me, I dialed his number and snapped, "What?"

"You're doing sex wrong if you're this fucking grouchy afterward."

"I don't need a critique on how I 'do' sex, Conor. What the hell are you calling me for at this time of the night?"

"Thought you'd want to know Jonesy is with the ECD. But if that's not as interesting as—"

Though my brain screeched to a halt, I still snarled, "Nothing's more interesting than Savannah's pussy. Just FYI."

"TMI."

"Shouldn't have gone there," I dismissed. "You saw him speaking with Eamonn Keegan?"

"Yes. I've been monitoring him nonstop since Grainne gave us the address."

I sucked in a breath. "Jonesy's really a *cheile*?"

"He is. I haven't been able to get inside his apartment to plant bugs yet, but the visuals are impossible to deny. I'll send them over to you now."

My phone buzzed so I placed it on speaker and sought out the photos he'd sent.

"Unless he has a twin brother—" He didn't. "—that's him," I agreed.

The camera was clearly a CCTV device that Conor had hacked into because I could see Jonesy standing in the hallway, shaking hands with an unknown person. The stranger's fingers were literally the only parts of him that were visible.

Another photo showed me the same scene from a different angle —this one from the street side.

Eamonn Keegan's face was barely on show, but I was still able to make out that he was the one greeting Jonesy.

"What do you want to do?"

"You send these to anyone else?"

"Nope. Not yet."

I zoomed in on Keegan's hands—the wrists were badly scarred.

Filing that away, I told him, "Share the photos with family only. I want eyes and ears on Jonesy. I want to know where he goes, what he eats, when he takes a fucking piss—I want to know it all."

"You don't want to bring him in?"

"No. I want to know what the ECD is planning. I want to know why Keegan is still in New York."

"He's lying low."

"Hardly," I mocked. "The man's got hookers on speed dial, and his apartment building is nothing to be sniffed at."

"It's not impossible to lie low in style," Conor retorted.

"I doubt it."

Conor was silent for a little too long, enough to raise my suspicions.

"What is it?"

"As much as it pains me to say this, I have it on good authority that the ECD are allied with us against the Sparrows."

Brow puckering, I demanded, "What do you mean?"

"I mean they're anti-Sparrows. How the hell can I reword that?" he sniped.

"Are you defending the guy who shot and killed our father?!"

"No." He sighed. "Well, not really. I'm not defending that. I'm just telling you what I know."

"Which is?"

"That last bombing Keegan was sent up for—it wasn't for the ECD cause. He blew up a building where a bunch of Sparrows were having a meeting. Some of their top brass got slaughtered."

"Jesus," I rasped.

"Yeah."

"The source is solid?"

"Beyond solid."

Only this week, he'd shared with me some of the treasure trove of information that Lodestar had gifted him via the ex-Prez of the Sinners' MC—Bear. But I knew it was so extensive that intel came in slow bursts as he was going through it on top of his other duties.

"Bear? Or someone else?"

"Bear," he confirmed.

"I don't know what to do with that information."

"Me either, in all honesty," he admitted. "It doesn't take away from what he did to Da, but..."

"But what?"

"In Keegan's eyes, Da *did* kill his sister."

Moving over to the sofa in front of my desk, I took a seat, plunking down heavily as fatigue settled like a lead weight on my shoulders.

"What a fucking mess," I muttered as I raked a hand over my head.

"No shit. I'll get eyes and ears on Jonesy. I'll also have his car tagged so I can see where he goes."

"Tap into his cell, Conor. I want to know everything."

"I understand, *dearthái*." His gruff endearment resonated. "Might do the same with the rest of Da's guards too. Just to be on the safe side."

"Do it."

"Been looking into this guy Stepanov as well."

"What have you learned?"

"He was one of Denis Abramovicz's underlings."

Before his death, Abramovicz had been the Bratva's version of Finn. "He's in finance?"

"Yeah. Pretty good at it too. For the most part. He's invested millions in NFTs, the dipshit."

I frowned. "Why would he be in-fighting with Lyanov?"

"He was definitely higher in the ranks than Lyanov was before the takeover. I don't think it's surprising that becoming Pakhan was easier than holding the position."

"True." Pondering that and what it meant for me and my new role, I instructed, "Thanks, bro. Okay, make sure you get some rest."

"After the to-do list from hell?"

"You're the one who decided we needed to have this fucking conversation at two AM."

Conor just grunted then cut the call.

It was times like these that the desire for oblivion crawled up my ass.

Times like these where I was reminded that I would always be a fucking addict.

That was when there was a tap on my door.

I blinked in surprise but called out, "Come in, baby."

Savannah peeped through the crack as she sleepily asked, "Why aren't you in bed?"

"I was about to come join you."

She opened the door wider and held out a hand.

I released a heavy breath as I got to my feet, strode over to her, and entwined our fingers.

It didn't release me from the chokehold of need that was clawing at my throat, but it took some of the load off...

I raised her hand to my mouth in thanks, pressing a kiss to the knuckles as we returned to our bedroom.

Only when we were back in bed, her all up in my space to avoid the wet spot—I wasn't going to complain—did I take another deep breath and force myself to relax.

Sleep didn't come easily, but it graced me eventually. That, in my current predicament, was something I considered to be a blessing.

12

MAXIM

VEGAS - DOJA CAT

THE SECOND I stepped inside the elevator, I dragged off my necktie. The doors closed as the receptionist watched me. With barely an inch of a gap remaining, I saw him reach for the phone.

Eyes were on me everywhere here.

As I unbuttoned my shirt collar, I heaved a sigh. Giving myself some breathing room, I watched the numbers while I surged toward the penthouse in one of Moskva's tallest buildings.

I did not want to be in Moskva.

It didn't matter that I was staying on Pozharskiy Pereulok—an expensive street that I'd have killed to live on when I was a starving boy—it was still the last fucking place I wanted to be.

When Stepanov and the few remaining Old Guard pieces of shit I hadn't killed had started making waves, however, I knew I could only consolidate power by getting approval from the homeland—a move I'd been avoiding since the new year.

So here I was.

And here I'd been for the past three weeks.

I hated Moskva.

Americans thought they had it so fucking bad with their cities that were a capitalist's idea of heaven, but Moskva was hell.

I'd dragged my ass away from the streets and into a multimillion-ruble property, but it didn't matter.

Whenever I came back to the city of my childhood, I always felt hungry. Always remembered what it was like to feel myself starving to death.

For a second, I ran my fingers along my collarbone, remembering what they'd felt like when they were brittle bones poking out through my flesh. Now, even there, I was muscled. Strong. So unlike the boy I'd once been when the motherland was my home and not somewhere I avoided at all costs.

My cell rang, and I eyed the caller ID warily.

Though I'd just arrived at my building, that wouldn't stop the leaders from dragging me out again. The *Krestniy Otets,* the head of the Bratva in Russia, the man who kept each individual gang in line, was putting me through my paces.

Though I was relieved his name didn't light up my screen, I gritted my teeth when I saw VICTORIA there instead.

She'd been calling me more often than I was comfortable with. Because she was still a child, I knew she was scoping me out, and I had to keep it clean.

My life was *not* clean.

But if I didn't want to terrify her, then I knew this was how I gentled her to me.

Of course, that made me feel like a fucking pedophile, and no way in hell was I one of those *izvrashchenets.* I'd dealt with those bastards on the streets.

Patiently impatient, my voice was gruff as I answered, "*Katyonok,* you know I'm in Moskva."

"I'm sorry, Maxim," she said miserably. "I-I didn't know who else to call."

My brow furrowed because I heard genuine tears clogging the words.

"What's happened?" I barked in concern. She remained silent, then she sniffled. "Tell me, Victoria. Now."

I didn't realize I'd slipped into Russian until, in our mother tongue, though hers was heavily accented, she whispered, "He touched me."

Rage flushed through me. "Who touched you?"

"It was only a small touch," she corrected with a sniff. "Just my boob, but he said I was a whore. He said I was just like Mama."

As the fury settled in my gut, I rasped out, "Who touched you? O'Donnelly?"

"NO! OMG," she sputtered, back in English this time. "Never! Brennan would never hurt me. *Ever*. I can't believe you'd think that—"

"Then, who?" I growled, my other hand balling into a fist that I clenched so hard, my knuckles popped.

"A boy in my class."

"He's one of us?"

She sniffled. "Yes. That's why I didn't go to Brennan. He wouldn't... couldn't... Not without starting—"

I gritted my teeth. "Who?"

"His name's Timofai Stepanov."

Of course it was.

Stepanov.

The bane of my fucking life.

I'd been ruling over my men in a way that was politically wise until this point, but that had just shifted a gear.

Seething, I growled, "No one will ever call you a whore or touch you against your will, Victoria, not while I'm alive."

She swallowed. "He's only sixteen, Maxim. You can't cut off his head too."

"Watch me," I snapped.

"No! He's just a boy. H-He's no one. It was stupid. I should never have called you."

"You *should* have called me. This is the only reason we should be talking, Victoria. I know you're curious about me, *katyonok*, but you're too young to speak with me unless it's about something important like this."

A breathy sigh escaped her and she admitted, "I like your voice."

Whatever the fuck I thought she'd say, it wasn't that.

"My voice?"

"Mama was from Moskva. You have the same accent."

Skotina, I was comforting to her?

Suddenly exhausted, I scrubbed a hand over my face. "I'll deal with the boy, Victoria."

"Please, don't kill him."

That she pleaded for his life pissed me off more than it should.

Through gritted teeth, I demanded, "Which hand did he use to touch you?"

"It was just a little touch," she tried to wheedle.

"So little that you decided to call your personal boogeyman in to make it right?" I half-taunted. "You knew what would happen when you called me, Victoria. Which hand?"

Rage throttling me, my fist shot out, and before I even realized what I was doing, it collided with the mirror to the side.

As the glass shattered, she yelped, "The left one. What was that noise?"

"Nothing. Ignore it. The left one. Your breast, nowhere else?" I demanded as I studied my bleeding knuckles and the shattered glass. She went quiet again. "Victoria," I rasped. "Tell me, *katyonok*."

"H-He tried to put his hand up my skirt when I smacked him."

"Left one?"

"*Da.*"

Yes.

Her voice had turned into the softest of whispers.

She knew what she'd started by calling me. She knew what was going to happen.

"I thought O'Donnelly was teaching you self-defense."

"He is. Timofai took me by surprise," she muttered.

"If O'Donnelly is a useless instructor, I'll teach you myself when I'm back in the city."

"You will?" she demanded sharply.

I closed my eyes, immediately regretting the stupid words that had fallen from my lips.

"It will cause trouble if I do," I warned her, deciding that playing to her cautious nature would be smart.

"Oh."

Thank fuck, she sounded disappointed. I knew that meant she wouldn't ask me to help teach her.

For a young woman, she had a brain inside that beautiful head of hers.

"I'll try harder with Brennan," she vowed.

The elevator finally arrived at my floor, and as I stepped out, leaving the mess I'd made, I told her, "Good. You might not be the Pakhan's daughter anymore, but that doesn't mean you didn't inherit his enemies. Don't you have guards on you?"

"I do, but not in school."

"That's where it happened?"

"Yes."

"Where?"

"Gym class."

"You didn't report it to the faculty?"

She sucked in a breath. "I could have."

"But you didn't. Why?"

"H-He said I'd be your whore, Maxim—"

"He mentioned me by name?" That little *mudila*.

"*Da.*"

"You were born a Bratva princess. Princesses do not become whores. He was trying to shit stir, *katyonok*. He wanted to know if you were in contact with me, and he'll find out the answer when I return. Do you understand?"

"I-I do."

"You are not a whore. Say it. I want to hear you say it. You are not, and never will be, a whore."

She swallowed. "I'm not, and never will be, a whore."

I gave her an approving grunt before I stated, "Victoria?"

"Yes, Maxim?"

"Never speak his name again. He is not Timofai to you. He is *nothing*. Do you understand?"

"I understand," she whispered. "Thank you, Maxim."

She cut the call, and I was grateful because I didn't know if I could.

She was mine. I protected what was mine. But I couldn't have her yet. Didn't want her at the age she was, but she represented so fucking much.

Stepanov clearly knew of my intentions—the question was *how*.

After pondering the situation, I called Misha over Nikolai. Nikolai was better with a knife, but unfortunately he was in Miami. Misha's preference was death by asphyxiation, but he was at home.

Misha wasn't my Sovietnik or my Obschak, but I trusted him more than Kirill or Tima in this matter—maybe that said a lot, or maybe it just meant that old habits died hard.

The three of us had come up together from these godawful streets, after all.

With the dial tone in my ear, I moved straight for the bar.

This place was a white-on-white nightmare. I fucking loathed it, but it was minimalist and the best the Bratva had to offer a visiting Pakhan.

I grabbed the vodka from the fridge that sat on the bar, and I jerked at the screw cap one-handed before I gulped some down and then splashed a glug onto my busted knuckles.

"It's a travesty to waste a twenty-four-hundred-dollar bottle of vodka by using it to clean a wound."

I froze then moved my cell to the counter and laid it on the marble.

Bottle still in hand, I twisted around and stared at the woman seated on the sofa, perched there as smartly as the hookers the *Krestniy Otets* had sent me that first night as a welcome gift.

I'd returned them without sampling the merchandise—fucking spies, the lot of them.

"I know you," I said warily.

She shot me a smile as she sipped at the vodka she'd poured herself. "You do."

My mind raced as I scoured my memory for her identity. When it hit me, I frowned. "Star Sullivan."

"Ten points to you," she rasped.

"What are you doing here?" Not just in Moskva, but in my goddamn apartment.

"I'm not here to kill you," she said, her tone amused as she eyed how I was holding the bottle by the neck, just ready to slam it against the bar and use it as a weapon. "I could have done that before you entered the building. I want a favor."

Her words had me grabbing my cell and disconnecting the call so that Misha wouldn't hear the conversation. She didn't make any moves to stop me, just studied me with that same annoying smile—as if she knew she was the most dangerous creature in the room.

Maybe she fucking was.

Lock Star Sullivan in a padded cell with five armed men and she'd kill them blindfolded.

I tipped up my chin. "What do you want?"

She got to her feet and strode over to me with the grace of a catwalk model. In a shift dress with a high split, she looked the part. Everything about her spoke of money. From the cut of her hair to the style of that dress.

Red nails drifted down the lapel on my jacket as my cell buzzed: Misha, most likely.

Ignoring the call, I stared down at those claws and studied the peculiar silver tips that adorned her little fingers.

I'd seen women wear crazy designs on their nails, but these came with the sharpest of points on them. More weapon than decoration...

Maybe that was fitting for a woman of her reputation.

"I need you to lend me your arm," she murmured, breaking into my thoughts.

"What?" I demanded, confused.

"You can get me into places that I can't access alone. At least, not without raised brows."

"What do I get in return? Sex?" I sneered.

Her top lip curled at that. "No. You get to live." Her hand was suddenly at my throat. It was brittle, shaped differently to the rest—the silver tip on her pinkie. "I scratch you with this and a neurotoxin enters your bloodstream. I'm sure you've heard of novichok."

I didn't bother tensing up.

This wasn't my first death threat of the day.

She pressed her mouth to my cheek so that her words were whispered into my ear—she clearly knew the place was bugged to the hilt. "I'll also help you with the *Krestniy Otets*. I know the brotherhood aren't certain if they want a street rat leading their most lucrative gang in the States. I can be a very, very good friend if you play nicely with me." She pulled back to look me in the eye as she asked, "Do we have a deal?"

13

AIDAN

"YOU OWE ME FOR THIS."

When a woman could make you think about oral sex just by how she could peep at you through her lashes, you knew you'd found yourself a keeper.

Unfortunately for me, Savannah decided to grace me with that look when we were in the elevator on our way up to Luciu and Jen's penthouse.

It was bound to be awkward, but I was hoping to discuss business with the Don before we sat down for brunch.

"I know I do. I'll gladly pay up though," she teased.

Not only had traffic been hell thanks to all the extra security measures New York had implemented since the First Lady's assassination, but: "I fucking hate brunch."

"Don't be a big baby."

"I'm not! Next time, if you're going to make me suffer through social niceties, make it breakfast or lunch."

"How can you hate brunch? It's literally a combination of the two. You should love it."

"Well, I don't."

"And you say I'm the brat," she retorted with a sniff.

Lips twitching, I curved an arm around her shoulders and rested my hand on her chest. As the doors started to open, I squeezed her tit, grinning as she laughed at me before she clamped her fingers over mine so that Jen could witness me copping a feel.

Jen being Jen, i.e., impossible to embarrass, muttered, "I guess I should be grateful I didn't catch you sucking him off."

"If the building were taller, I'd have given it my best goddamn shot," Savannah sniped, to which Jen rolled her eyes. "Where's my namesake, anyway?"

"She isn't your namesake."

"She's Savvie, isn't she?"

"*Saverina*," Jen corrected.

"Her name will totally get abbreviated to Savvie. I'll make sure of it," she drawled. "You let Aoife be godmother, so I get the perks of naming rights. Don't take it away from me."

"Saverina," Jen enunciated, "is sleeping at long last and I'm not about to wake her up when it took me ages to put her down for a nap."

Grousing, Savvie twisted to give me a kiss before she strode off, dragging Jen away and onward to the room her friend had claimed as her office after her marriage to the new Don of New York.

I'd been here many times before, so I knew the layout well.

Still, with no Luciu in sight, I hovered awkwardly, not as comfortable with being here as Savannah was.

She, after all, was friends with Jen. I wasn't friends with Luciu. Plus, after the debacle with Cain MacMurray, I didn't want to push my luck.

I knew Luciu was making me pay because he had me waiting a good five fucking minutes in the hallway before he appeared in the doorway, intoning, "Would you like something to drink?"

Bet his fucking ass I did.

Still, it was eleven AM.

I sucked in a breath. "Coffee would be great."

He waved a hand to encourage me to follow him, and I did, stepping deeper into the apartment that seemed to me to meld a hybrid of cultures together.

Luciu had told Savannah that their apartment represented Sicily perfectly.

Having never been there, I couldn't agree or disagree, but it was comfortable. Warm. Homely.

Not what I'd imagine of the Sicilian, to be frank. Minimalism suited him more than this place. Especially when I thought of the precise method he had of slicing up his enemies' faces.

I half-expected to be guided into the kitchen, but I was led into the dining room. Luciu had already taken a seat and he was murmuring something to the woman I recognized as his housekeeper.

She nodded at him, barked something in a language I didn't understand, then bustled away after gracing me with a grim look.

I'd clearly been found wanting.

A sentiment she never failed to silently transmit whenever I was here.

"Take a seat," Luciu invited, slouching back in the chair at the head of the table.

Places had been set, and I appreciated that he hadn't pulled a power move and made me sit at his side.

Settling opposite him, I reached for the glass of orange juice and took a deep sip.

"I need to apologize for that business earlier this week," I murmured, eyes on my glass before I focused on him.

"Apology accepted," he said easily. So easily, in fact, that I blinked. "You did not think I would accept your apology?"

"I didn't," I confirmed, my tone stiff.

"I understand that a man in your position is pulled in many ways. I understand that more than most considering I, too, am new to my role.

"We must present a strong front to our allies and enemies alike. It is hard to strike the right balance, is it not?"

I grimaced. "It is."

"I heard about Cain MacMurray."

"How?" I snapped in outrage.

He shot me a wry grin. "You just told me half the story. He is dead now?"

"He is," I said grimly, not amused by that stunt.

"Did you uncover his source?"

"I did. Russians."

Luciu's brow furrowed. "I do not sell to the Russians. Things are too fractious with them right now to distribute to them."

"They are? Why?"

"In-fighting, mostly. Lyanov is trying to court Moscow as far as I'm aware."

"He's not in the city?"

Jesus, how had I been so blind?

"At the moment, no."

Taking all of that into account, I mused, "One of your dealers must be making the sale for you."

He didn't argue with me, just said, "We're friendly with the Russians. Has Lyanov given you cause to suspect that friendship has been dissolved?"

I thought about my sister-in-law, the one Lyanov wanted to marry when she turned eighteen, and I shook my head.

Whether he wanted to 'dissolve our friendship,' as Luciu had phrased it, or not, I got the feeling Lyanov wanted a wife who'd authenticate him as leader.

As the last Bratva princess in Manhattan, Victoria Vasov would do that in spades.

"Stepanov is the Russian purchasing Red from you," I told him.

"Never heard of him."

"Me either until this week," I drawled. "Now I know what size shoe he is and which type of vodka he prefers."

"Is that information pertinent?"

"Know your enemy," I said with a shrug.

Da hadn't agreed with my obsessive need to nitpick. Regardless, this was my time, not his, and I could rule how ever the fuck I wanted to.

Da thought everything was for gain. Every slice of information was something that could be leveraged.

Knowing Stepanov's shoe size wouldn't help me long-term, but being aware that he had a bunion, that he required hand-tailoring, that he specifically visited a certain shoemaker in Manhattan to purchase his hand-tooled leather shoes...

That was helpful.

"Be aware that I don't disagree. Knowing the minutiae can help when attempting to dissect an enemy, but I'm hoping you learned more than whether he prefers his vodka plain or flavored."

His words tripped me into silence. Not because he was right or wrong, not because he'd angered me, but because here I was, about to break bread with a Sicilian all while discussing business.

Here we were, our women, best friends, gossiping in the background, one of them about to share the news that she was going to become a mom again.

It was likely that Savannah would be this child's godmother...

Times were changing.

This wasn't the nineties.

Hadn't Savannah told me that the night this whole shitshow with MacMurray started?

I reached for my orange juice, but before I could take another sip, Luciu's housekeeper appeared with tiny cups loaded down with the good stuff.

Caffeine, sugar, and an infrequent whiskey were about as much of a fix as I was allowed nowadays, so I took mine expensive and strong—and where coffee was concerned, as sweet as Savvie's pussy.

"Thank you," I told her as she placed the cup in front of me on a saucer.

She dipped her chin, muttered something at me, delivered Luciu's coffee to him, then disappeared.

He eyed me. "The sugar is there."

"I can see it." I arched a brow at him as I dumped a couple teaspoons of sugar into the muddy drink, querying dryly, "Minutiae?"

His smile was shark-like. "As I said, it helps to know this information about people. However, in my instance, it is inbred."

"Why?"

"My mother is a British aristocrat. Teaching her children to be good hosts was important to her."

I knew his mother was alive still so the past tense wasn't about her in particular. "It isn't anymore?"

"Many things changed when my father died."

"I know how that feels."

His smile was more of a grimace. "I'm sorry for your loss, Aidan. Truly."

Raising my cup to my lips, I took a sip and nodded. "I believe you."

And I did.

We shared a glance.

"We are not our grandfathers or our fathers," Luciu mused. "You sit at my table, about to share brunch with my wife and me, who is best friends with yours... You came to our wedding. You were there for Saverina's baptism, and you'll be there for our secondborn's.

"We are no longer simply Sicilian and Irish, Aidan."

Hadn't I just been thinking the same thing?

"I know." I mused before I slowly murmured, "We are family."

He dipped his chin in satisfaction, seemingly aware I'd had to choke the words out.

Because it was easier to discuss business, I informed him, "Stepanov has set his sights on taking Maxim Lyanov down. He wasn't high in the ranks when Vasov was Pakhan, though he *was* a trusted financier. He believes he is more suitable for the role of leader.

"Before MacMurray died, he shared with us every piece of information he'd given to Stepanov."

Interest lit up Luciu's eyes. "Anything... dangerous?"

"Depends on what Stepanov does with it," I dismissed.

"What information did he share?"

"Trade routes, mostly."

"Drugs?"

"Guns, other shipments. Our partnership with the Satan's Sinners' MC over in New Jersey was of particular interest to Stepanov."

"Think he'll try to poach the MC?"

I shrugged. "Perhaps."

"You don't sound worried."

"The Russians don't do business like we do so I can't see it happening."

"Every leader does things his own way."

"Of this I'm aware," I drawled. "I'll touch base with the Prez of the Sinners. We met earlier this year at a funeral."

"A cheerful reunion."

"It's a year for death," I agreed, taking a deeper sip of my drink. "What's going on with the production of Red?"

Lines of tension bracketed Luciu's mouth, but he answered easily enough, "My brother is tweaking his creation."

"I saw what his creation did," I said darkly. "The only reason I knew MacMurray was up to something is because he beat a hooker to death." Luciu's moue of displeasure had a lightbulb shining over my head. "You don't like that he's making the drug, do you?"

"Would you?" he bit off waspishly. "It's one thing to trade in the misery of others, another to create it from scratch. But Custanzu is Custanzu and he'll do what he wants until he tires of it."

"Production is limited?"

Luciu nodded. "Very."

"I'd heard it was exclusive but didn't realize the extent. We both know how that works in these circumstances."

"We do. I originally sold a tab of Red for twenty-five dollars. Now I can sell them for two hundred bucks and people are buying it." He shrugged at my low whistle. "First and foremost, I'm a businessman."

"Are there plans to widen distribution?"

"Why? Do you want in on the game?"

I shot him a grin. "With those kinds of profit margins? Of course."

He snorted. "Custanzu will not be pushed. He keeps his production low."

"To spike the price?"

"No, because the high is not what he seeks." He took a sip of coffee, and before I could ask him about that cryptic comment, he stated, "He also handles each batch with all the care of a baker making pastries." Luciu rolled his eyes, his impatience and love for his brother clashing. "He has played his part well in our rise to power, so the least I can do is support him in this."

"You're more generous than I am."

"Our struggles are not your struggles," he dismissed. "I will keep my ear to the ground for more information on Stepanov and will investigate who among my people is distributing to him."

"I appreciate that."

He bowed his head. "All those months ago, I meant it when I told you that you and I are the next generation, Aidan.

"I never imagined the ways in which we would ultimately be tied, not just through blood but by our wives' friendship too, and while we have very different methods of handling our respective businesses, that doesn't mean we can't be more open with one another."

"Information holds more power than a gun," I murmured.

"Precisely. Sharing it would be beneficial to us both."

I didn't argue. I couldn't.

Not when he was right.

"So," I asked, deciding now was a good time to change the subject, "how's fatherhood treating you?"

His dopey grin, I figured, said it all.

14

TEXT CHAT

AIDAN

ME: *Caught a rat in my midst.*

Rex: *Dead rodents are the worst.*

Me: *Aren't they though?*

Rex: *Anything leaked?*

Me: *Trade routes.*

Rex: *With the Feds?*

Me: *No. With the Russians.*

Rex: *What?!*

Me: *Yes. A faction within the Bratva is gunning for Lyanov's position.*

Rex: *Are we at risk?*

Me: *No. Not yet. If that changes, I'll tell you.*

Rex: *How did they make the rat talk?*

Me: *Drugs.*

Rex: *Fuck.*

Me: *Yes. Annoying.*

Rex: *Very. I appreciate you keeping me in the loop.*

Me: *Watch out for a similar approach by them. I think they're* *aware that if they take the faction by force and oust Lyanov, we'll break ties.*

Rex: *So they're trying to find ways to stabilize their income by using established trade routes?*

Me: *I think so.*

Me: *Lyanov won't give up his throne, so this is a dead-end conversation, but I wanted to keep you apprised of the situation.*

Rex: *Thanks. Any rats crop up here, I'll swing the info your way.*

15

SAVANNAH

"HAVEN'T you seen those moms on social media who are totally strung out after having kids so close together?" I screeched the second Jen told me she was pregnant *again* after having Saverina, like, five minutes ago.

Immediately huffing, she stacked her hands on her hips and sniped, "What use is that now? Do you and Aidan use social media as a contraceptive?"

"No. We use clever things like the shot to make sure we don't get pregnant. You hate kids. Why do you want another one?" When a weird smile curved her lips, I gasped, "You're happy about this!"

She grumbled, "This is why I didn't tell you right away. I knew you'd be like this."

"You knew I'd be the voice of reason," I retorted, refusing to feel hurt because I knew what that meant—Aoife had found out about Jen's pregnancy first.

This wasn't fourth grade, however, so I didn't let it get to me.

"What voice of reason? Telling me to watch videos of strung-out moms *after* I pissed on a stick and found out I'm pregnant?"

"Yes! Anyway, you're the one who told me that if you ever

decided to get pregnant, I was to drag you to a psychiatrist first. I didn't do it with Saverina, but maybe I should have."

"That was before. I didn't exactly have a great role model, Savvie. Now, I have a family."

I folded my arms across my chest before I grouched, "I'll bet Luciu's happy."

"He is. We both are."

Sniffing, I strolled over to the window and leaned against it as I peered onto the city ahead.

"Aren't you going to congratulate me at all?" she groused.

"Since when did we do things like that?" I countered.

"You mean, since when did we act like regular human beings? Oh, I don't know when that started."

"I do. When we got married. That's when everything changed," I said glumly.

"Is Aidan pressuring you to have kids? Is that why you're spewing anti-children propaganda at me? You said it yourself, you're not the one who hates them."

I didn't particularly like them but my new nieces and nephews were cute. And Shay was the only O'Donnelly who knew how to debate so that was always a fun time.

I scowled. "No. If anything, he said he wanted a battalion of kids but he's changed his mind."

Jen shook her head. "Are you pouting?"

"No. I don't want a battalion of kids." I glowered at her. "Did he pressure you into having sex early or something? Savvie's a newborn!"

"Feminism 101, babe. Doctor gave me permission at six weeks, and I jumped back on that saddle the second I could."

Her cheerful tone had me demanding, "I know you love being anally probed, but I just had proof that Luciu is from Mars because his dick has clearly fucked with your mind. What the hell has he done with my best friend?"

She smirked. "You said it yourself... Made me fall for his cock."

I pshawed at her until she sidled up to me and tucked her arm around my waist. "I'm happy, Savvie."

My nose crinkled. "I'm glad you are."

A laugh escaped her. "You're feeling chirpy today, aren't you?"

"Sorry," I said on a sigh. "I don't mean to be a bitch."

"Sure you do. That's who we are. Don't change now," she teased, which made me pull a face. That, in turn, had her frowning. "Hey, what's going on with you?"

"Everything's changing," I said softly, my gaze on the city skyline again. "I-I was okay with that, but it's just shifting too fast."

"Tell me. A problem shared is a problem halved."

My eyes flared at that. "You seriously have been kidnapped by aliens!"

"No, but Luc's mom comes out with those kinds of sayings all the time." She shot me a sheepish grin. "I like it. She's nice."

Jen had low expectations for parents, and after how she'd been raised, I couldn't blame her.

I hoped Luc's mom was kinder than his sister.

I still wanted to stomp on Aurora's tits for the way she'd acted at Saverina's christening.

"Anyway, out with it. What's changing?"

"You know Star?"

"The hacker friend of yours who's a headcase?"

"Yeah. She's gone missing. Aidan's father died. Your dad did a Jesus at Easter act. Mom's sick and she kept it from us. You're pregnant again—"

"Whoa! Lorelei's sick?"

"Yeah. 'C' word. And I'm not talking cunt. Although, maybe it is. It's in that region. Can you catch cancer of the cunt?"

"I don't think so. Why don't you know which 'region?'"

"Because she didn't want to tell me."

"I guess that's her right," Jen said softly.

"I'm not saying it isn't." After talking about this with Aidan, who'd made me understand things from my mom's point of view, I got it. It didn't mean it hurt any less though. "I'm just saying everything is changing, and I still feel like I'm twenty-one and have a lot to prove to the world."

"Is this because you're going to be thirty-six next year?"

"No. Maybe. I guess? I don't even know."

"How are things with you and Aidan?" I shot her a dopey grin which had her laughing. "So, one thing's right in your world at least."

I chuckled. "Yeah. Oh, my God, he tied me to the bed and left me, Jen. He actually left me to go out on business. I've never been more pissed off and turned on at the same time."

Snickering, she shook her head. "You're crazy."

"About him," I agreed with a wink, but I mirrored her actions and looped my arm around her waist too. Hugging her, I pressed a kiss to her cheek and whispered, "If you're happy about the baby, then I'm happy too."

"I'm beyond happy. Luc is such a great dad. It's perfect how close in age these two will be to each other." She beamed a grin at me, one that was infused with so much contentment that I had to sigh.

"You're growing up," I said pitifully. "I guess that means I have to as well."

Snorting, she told me, "You'll be eighty and will still act like a thirteen-year-old, Savannah. Aidan'll be in luck though."

"Why?"

She stuck her tongue in her cheek. "Because you'll keep his prostate nice and young."

"Ew," I joked, shoving her in the side, but I was laughing at the same time.

Over the next hour or so, as we eventually joined our guys in the dining room, I came to realize that she was right.

Sure, she was going to be a mom again, but another kid wouldn't change the fact that Jen was a snippety, exacting pain in the ass. Saverina sure as shit hadn't changed her sparking personality. Nor did my turning thirty-six change the fact that I was a bossy bitch who got on people's nerves.

Aidan liked me. Jen did too.

I just had to make sure her kids did as well.

It looked like I was going to be spending a fortune at toy stores the country over because, even if Jen made Aoife this kid's godmother too, that wasn't going to stop me from being the best aunt in the universe.

16

SAVANNAH

RELEASING A DEEP YAWN, I watched Aoife as she cooked our Saturday night meal.

This was a new ritual, one that I enjoyed.

There'd been an unofficial divorce within the O'Donnelly clan, and we were the kids who weren't taking sides and were appeasing both 'parents.'

Sundays used to be a family day. We went to the compound upstate and we ate together.

Now, after this past year and all the secrets that had come to the fore, the family went to Aoife and Finn's on Saturdays, and Sundays were for Aidan's parents.

The last couple Sundays since Aidan Sr.'s death, however, there'd been no Sunday get-together. Lena had called each of her sons earlier this afternoon, though, and informed them that the meal was back on, and that she expected everyone to attend.

'Everyone' didn't include Finn, Aoife, and Jacob, their son, and I was actually jealous.

I figured most of the other wives were too because Aela was

grumbling, "I didn't expect her to go into purdah, but I'd have liked if she did it for a couple months. Just to let the dust settle."

Aoife studied her then surprised me by standing up for the woman who'd freakin' killed her mom: "She needs her family around her. Couples who are as symbiotic as Aidan and Lena were rarely do well after one of them dies."

"Do I smell your brownies?" Camille chirped, making me hide a smile behind my glass of wine.

"It's okay, Camille. You don't need to change the subject. I can talk about the old bitch without wanting to cry," Aoife said wryly. "I can even pity her. I just won't break bread with her."

"Did Finn tell you if she called him or not?" Aela queried.

"He'd have told me if she had because he knows that if he keeps any more secrets from me, we're done."

The words, combined with how she was carving up the roasted chicken in front of her, packed a hell of a punch.

Aoife had, before her marriage, attended culinary school and had been taught how to properly butcher animals... Finn would be a fool to forget that fact.

"You wouldn't leave him," Inessa said, tone scandalized. It blurred the lines between a statement and a question, but Inessa's ingrained obedience won out in the end.

Raised the way she'd been, much as Aidan had declared, it was no wonder really.

"I would," she said grimly. "I love him. I want to be with him. But I won't deal with any more of his secrets. If they're big enough to tear us apart, then I'll let them."

I whistled under my breath. "You've gone hardcore, Aoife. I didn't know you had it in you."

"There's plenty you still don't know about me," was her cool retort, but she softened it by saying, "Plenty I still don't know about myself either." To Camille, she said, "No, you can't smell brownies. I'm making blondies for dessert."

Taken aback by the change of subject, Camille blinked. "Oh. Okay. Great!"

"Have you stopped weeping into your water about the old bastard croaking?"

I frowned at Aela. "That's mean."

"Do you know what he did to Declan?" she grated out. "He's lucky I'm only calling him an old bastard. I have plenty other words I can use to describe him."

"Aela," Aoife chided. "Savannah's grieving him."

"I don't get it," she said flatly.

I didn't either so it wasn't like I could judge.

Shrugging, I murmured, "It's just a sad, sad day, you know?"

"I did a happy dance," Aela groused before she grabbed some nuts from the dish Aoife had set on the breakfast counter where we were all perched, watching her cook.

"You would," was my rejoinder. "I'm not even sure what's going on with me right now. I'm... I think I'm just worried about Aidan."

"About losing him?" Aoife asked me, her voice soft.

Nodding, I took another sip of wine, feeling more brittle than I wanted to admit.

"It's a fear we share," Camille said solemnly.

"I just got him back."

Inessa curved her arm around my shoulder. "They're untouchable, Savvie."

I faked a smile and pressed a kiss to her cheek. "They are," I said brightly, but as my gaze tangled with Aela's, I knew she was worried too.

Transitional periods were always dangerous, and the city had never been more volatile.

As I drank some more wine, my phone buzzed. Seeing who'd texted, in desperate need of liquid sustenance, I took a larger sip.

Paris: *I'm in New York.*

Me: *So?*

Paris: *So?!*

Me: *SO.*

Paris: *You're not still mad at me?*

Me: *Clearly, I am.*

Paris: *Sigh.*

Me: *So boring, isn't it? Screwing your sister over when she made plans THREE times to have lunch with you and you ditched her for your latest squeeze.*

Paris: *Content is king. This reality TV show is sucking the life out of me.*

Me: *Boohoo.*

Paris: *I'm here now.*

Me: *So?*

Paris: *So. We can catch up. I'm worried about Mom.*

Me: *Why?*

Paris: *She's being cheerful. You know what that means.*

Me: *That she's stressed.*

So, Paris wasn't utterly self-obsessed. That came almost as a relief.

When *noxxious* had announced a few tour dates for this December—something I was suspicious of because I thought they'd twisted Daddy's arm for this exact reason—combined with my recent surge in fame, *and* Camden winning four Grammys, some of the TV networks had suddenly been interested in my sisters' pitch for a reality show.

It was ludicrous seeing as all they did for a living was spend Dad's cash.

Paris: *Do you know why she's stressed?*

Me: *No. When do you want to do lunch?*

Paris: *Are you not talking to Aspen either?*

Me: *Is she in the city?*

Paris: *She is. Duh.*

Me: *Tweedle Dum and Tweedle Dee.*

Paris: *Yeah, yeah.*

Me: *She pissed me off more than you did.*

Paris: *Why do you think I'm the one texting you?*

Me: *I can see you sometime this week. Tuesday? 1pm?*

Paris: *Great. 12 would be better.*

Me: *Didn't think you'd be awake in time.*

Paris: *I have a couple meetings before.*

Me: *My sisters are growing up. It's enough to make me teary-eyed.*

Paris: *Yeah, yeah.*

Me: *Paris, no cameras.*

Paris: *You're such a fucking killjoy.*

Me: *I live my truth.*

Smirking when she shot me a couple emojis of the bird, I input the lunch date into my datebook and asked Aoife, "How are you liking the new house?"

The brownstone was practically palatial, and far too big for two adults and a kid to roam around in. Still, that was the perk of wealth. You could have more space than sense, and enough bathrooms that a housekeeper could curse you every time she had to clean a different toilet.

"It's weird being beside the road," she mused. "I like the traffic sounds though. It reminds me of when I was younger. Jake likes it too."

"Not Finn?" Camille teased.

"Nah. He's being bougie. He soundproofed our bedroom!"

"Aidan soundproofed his office," I said with a pout.

"That's because he knows you'll try to eavesdrop," Aela pointed out.

"And he's right," Inessa teased. "You totally would, wouldn't you?"

"Duh. Doesn't mean his lack of faith doesn't sting," I grumbled until Aela elbowed me in the side.

"Don't be a baby. I have enough of that living with all these men."

"One of whom is still in diapers."

"Cam's the quietest. Trust me." Aela snatched another handful of nuts. "Surprised you're not baking a little O'Donnelly by now."

Aoife tensed, and while I knew Aela noticed, she eyed me pointedly, not letting me back down from the conversation.

Inessa saved me by arguing, "If anyone should be pregnant, it's me. I've been married the longest after Aoife."

"You don't want kids yet," Aela argued. "Plus, you're like a baby yourself."

"I'm not a baby. I'm nearly twenty."

Aela snorted. "You're a baby. Eoghan's a pervert."

"He is not," Inessa complained.

"The age gap makes it hotter," I countered. "You're missing out, Aela, and you don't even know it."

She flipped me the bird then peered around her sisters-in-law. "The O'Donnellys clearly like child brides. Only Declan had the good sense to marry someone his own age."

As the others booed her, I retorted, "I'm long since past the age of being a child bride, but I appreciate the compliment about my youthful glow, Aela."

She started laughing, and like it was infectious, most of us joined in. Aoife did as well, though it was a tad strained.

I knew Aela meant well, but she had about as much subtlety as a kick to the head administered via a steel-toed-boot-shod foot.

Aoife's miscarriage earlier this year was the elephant in the room. We didn't speak of it unless she brought it up, which she didn't.

Ever.

Same went with Lena.

With the news that we'd be joining our mother-in-law for lunch tomorrow, it was only natural that she was a hot topic of conversation. One that fudged the unspoken rule of things we were and weren't supposed to discuss.

"It still surprises me that you coordinated the funeral, Aoife," I said softly. "I don't think I thanked you for that."

Her gaze on the carrots which she was cutting into fancy shapes, she said, "I was better prepared than most of you in knowing what to do."

Therein laid the rub.

"I should have helped more," I said apologetically.

"I didn't expect you to."

Aoife's authority over us came in sharp relief to the fact that I was married to the head of the Five Points, and went deeper than the fact that she'd been a part of the family the longest.

Clans like the O'Donnellys had things like matriarchs and patriarchs, but for all that Aidan and I were technically the heirs to those roles, I didn't think we settled in them naturally.

I was A-okay in letting Aoife be the one who took the position off my hands.

I thought Aidan would be okay with letting Finn take that mantel too. At least, on a personal front.

He was far too bossy to let Finn replace him as head of the Five Points.

As was often the way with so many women clustered together, side-conversations sprung up.

Inessa and Camille started arguing about a show they were watching together, and Aela joined in the bickering because she'd DNFed the series.

With Aoife still chopping veggies, and me just downing my glass of wine, I decided to take the bull by the horns.

"How are you, Aoife?"

She cast me a glance. "I'm fine."

"Are you? Jen told me she was pregnant again today," I said, my tone careful though I was aware that Jen had shared the news with her already.

I was right to be cautious.

For all that I'd anticipated that she wasn't as bright and breezy as she was attempting to portray, it still made me jump when she accidentally sliced into her finger.

Jolting back, she grabbed a dish towel and wrapped it around the cut.

"No blood on the carrots," she pronounced, making me realize she'd been scanning the platter for droplets.

"Like that matters," Inessa scoffed, bustling around the counter in an effort to drag Aoife over to our side of the breakfast bar. "Take a seat. I'll tape up your finger."

"It's just a scratch," Aoife dismissed.

I eyed the bloodstain that was spreading on the cotton fabric. "Hardly." Straightening up, I held out a hand for the first aid kit Camille had dug out of a drawer somewhere. "This is one thing I can do. I took a class."

Aela snorted. "You took a class to learn how to fix a Band-Aid onto a boo-boo?"

I blew her a raspberry. "Feeling hormonal today, are we, Aela?"

She flipped me the bird. Again. She did that a lot.

Digging around the box, I grabbed the things I needed, and while she huffed through it, Aoife finally let go of the dishcloth.

The cut went deep.

"That'll need stitches," Camille murmured softly.

"I know. I can handle it." I looked at Aoife. "I promise."

She wafted her other hand. "Go for it."

"Put pressure on it again until I'm ready?"

"Fine," she agreed.

Not unsurprisingly for a trained chef, her first aid kit was extensive. I dosed her up with numbing spray after I cleaned the area and made quick work of suturing the site.

"You'll need a tetanus shot."

She shook her head. "Got one a few years ago."

When I'd finished, she peered at the neat stitches as I bandaged up her finger.

"Seems like there's plenty I don't know about you too, Savannah."

"My dad had us attend these survival camps when we were younger," I said grumpily. "It was insane. He was convinced if we got kidnapped, we'd be taken to the jungle."

"Was he on LSD?" Aela drawled, making me laugh.

"He was on many, many things at the time. I'm pretty damn sure LSD was one of them. Did you know Pink Floyd wrote a lot of their stuff during acid trips?"

Aela chuckled. "I didn't know that, but it makes sense."

"They say that if you listen when you're tripping, it *does* make sense," I said wryly as I finished my quick repair job on Aoife's finger and began clearing up the mess I'd made on the counter. "That rumor got *noxxious* into acid. *Lucifer's Daughter* was written when they were stoned."

"They won Grammys for that album, didn't they?"

I nodded at Inessa. "Five or six. Surprised you know that."

"Conor got Shay into them, and he got Victoria in on it too. For heavy metal rock, it's quite catchy."

"I'll make sure to tell my dad that."

She laughed. "Catchy wasn't what they were going for, huh?"

"Nope," I said with a grin.

"I've never actually done drugs," Aela admitted sheepishly.

"Me either," said Aoife.

"I almost tried coke in school but I was scared Papa would find out," Inessa confessed.

"I've smoked weed," Camille said. "But I never went deeper than that. It's dangerous territory even if they say it isn't a gateway drug."

I snorted. "You're all prudes."

"Oh, and you're Pablo Escobar in your spare time, I suppose?" Aela jibed.

"No," I retorted with a sniff. "But when I was a teenager, there was so much shit floating around backstage, I experimented."

Aoife frowned at me, and her hand tightened around my wrist. "Were you safe?"

"Probably not. Some of the roadies were grade A creeps; their intentions made the coke they were sniffing look pure. But Camden and I got along back then. We used to try shit out together."

"You never got hooked?"

"No." There'd been a couple times when I'd tried to get to sleep with pot, but the aftermath wasn't pretty. I didn't react well to cannabis. "Neither of us did, actually. His vices lie with cards."

"What are yours?"

"I didn't really have any until recently."

A bubble of laughter escaped Aoife. "Oh, my God." She released my wrist and clapped her hand to her mouth. "It's sex, isn't it? That's your vice?"

My nose crinkled. "Specifically with Aidan. I'm living my teenaged self's best life."

Camille derided, "Like sex isn't a vice we all share."

Aela reached for some more nuts. "She has a point. Have you seen our husbands?"

"I have." The smooth tone had us twisting around to face the intruder. Declan strolled over with Cameron against his chest. "What about us? Should our ears be burning?"

"No, but your dicks probably should," I drawled.

"Sounds painful."

"It does actually... I meant it to be the opposite," I admitted.

Aela chuckled. "You should see your face."

Declan arched a brow. "So, we shouldn't have STD-like symptoms but boners is what you're saying?"

"Is this a conversation you want to be having with your sisters-in-law?" Aoife countered smoothly.

Declan leaned against the breakfast bar, and it didn't escape my attention that he'd taken note of the bandage on her finger. He only retorted, "Smart ass."

"Why are you interrupting girl talk anyway?" Aela complained.

"Cam wants food, and I can do many things, but grow tits ain't one of them."

"Vulgar," Aela grumbled, but she shut up when Declan swooped in and graced her with a kiss that had her slotting against her husband like two jigsaw pieces.

It was low, low enough that I shouldn't have heard him say it, when he rumbled, "Don't pretend as if you don't like me just as I am."

Pretty accustomed to these blatant PDAs by this point, not just with Aela and Declan but with the whole family, the rest of us gave them a wide berth until Declan was strolling out of the room, child-free, and with a cocky swagger to his step.

Aela's cheeks were burnished with heat, her pupils were like pinpricks, and kiddo was nursing.

"I think if you could catch pregnancy, you'd be pregnant again," Camille teased the second he was out of the kitchen for real.

That was how we knew how far gone Aela was because she just hummed in response...

So me being me, I changed the topic. "Camille, have you ever watched *Sleeping with the Enemy?*"

17

CONOR

WAIT - M83

"WHAT ARE YOU DOING?"

As Cameron fussed on his chest, I peered at Shay.

I didn't mind that babies cried.

That came as a shock to me too.

I didn't *like* that they cried—I wasn't a fucking monster. But I'd grown used to Cameron's fussing. I could even work through it. Of course, I'd mastered the fine art of working through noise because my brothers made more chaos by heading to the can than Cameron did by demanding to be fed.

"I'm about to start a DDoS attack."

His eyes bugged. "Isn't that illegal?"

My lips twitched. "You going to call the cops?"

"No." Brow furrowed, he stared at my computer. "Why are you doing that?"

"Because I want to."

"Helpful." He huffed but relinquished control of Cameron to Declan who offered to take the kid to Aela to be nursed. With the kid gone, he peered at my computer. "Go on then."

"I don't like an audience."

Shay chuckled. "I'm not an audience."

I cast him a look. "You don't approve, so why would you want to watch?"

"Be more interesting than talking to anyone else tonight."

"Surprised you came. Victoria stayed home."

"Didn't feel like being alone."

His admission had me switching gears. "You doing okay, Shay?"

His jaw worked. "I should be okay."

The inference being that he wasn't.

"What's wrong?"

"Don't you miss him?" he whispered, almost as if he were admitting to a crime.

"Of course. You're allowed to miss Da," I pointed out when he fell silent.

"Mom hates him. Dad doesn't like to talk about him, and I get it—Grandda wasn't exactly nice to him. I can't imagine being called names just because I like art and going to the ballet. He was a bigot and mean and he had zero taste, but..."

"He was your grandfather." I said it flatly, my tone judgment-free. "You don't have to like someone to love them. You don't have to like someone for them to make an impression on you.

"To be frank, Shay, you were the only one he ever tried to impress. They say shit changes for a man when he becomes a grandfather. I saw more changes in my da with you around than I did in all the years of my life."

"Do you think they made him a better person?"

I snorted. "No. Da wasn't a good person to start with, so he couldn't be better, but he tried, Shay. With you, he tried. And isn't that something?

"That nasty old bigot who *was* mean to your dad, who didn't understand or accept him, tried to get *you* to accept *him* even though you were just a miniature version of your father.

"Your mom won't get it, neither will your dad, but I do. You're allowed to miss him. You're allowed to grieve. That's your right. They can't take that away from you."

"It's not like they're trying. It's just... They don't talk about him. I didn't think I'd want to, but I guess I do. Mostly they're talking about Cameron and what's going on with him—"

"You jealous?" I asked. "I know how it feels to get a baby brother, and I was a lot younger than you and used to having siblings."

He shrugged. "Maybe. Maybe not. It's tough when I want to talk about stuff and I can't because Cameron needs to be nursed or something and that takes precedent, but no, mostly, it's okay. And he's cool, you know?"

He was.

As much as a baby could be dope, Cameron was.

"Tell you what, Shay. You ever need to talk, you come to me. I know you're still training with Brennan; well, you can talk to him too. We've all got complicated relationships with our da. None of them were healthy. But Bren and I aren't afraid to say the hard shit, and we're not afraid to listen."

"Thanks, Uncle Con."

"Don't have to thank me. It's what I'm here for."

His grin was sheepish as he said, "I'll leave you to your DDoS attack."

"That's *so* kind of you. Where you going?"

"Finn's game room. Bren got him a new arcade game as a housewarming gift."

"Sounds good. Might come in later and try to beat your score."

His eyes gleamed. "I'll make sure you can't."

As he darted off, my lips curved into a grin, but I wasn't gifted with much peace as Declan returned to Finn's new man cave, declaring, "They're talking about us."

Rolling my eyes as I began the DDoS attack on the exchange I needed more info from, I murmured, "Yeah, because that's all they have to talk about, Declan. Your dicks and asses.

"Not that Aela's got a massive exhibition coming up or that she's finished Finn's portrait. Not that Inessa's started school, or that Aoife's thinking about opening three more storefronts on the island—"

Finn turned to look at me. "How the fuck did you know about that?"

I sniffed. "It's my job."

"She only talked about that with me yesterday, Conor," Finn growled. "Goddammit, I thought you weren't listening into our conversations anymore... Da's dead."

There was always a hesitation when he used that label.

I got it.

I did.

He'd used it more since the man had died than in our da's life, but it was getting easier.

Time always made shit like that easier.

"Gotta keep my eyes on you all."

"No, you don't," Brennan rumbled.

"Aoife cut her finger, Finn," Declan said in an aside.

Finn, because he was overprotective as fuck, jerked to his feet and made to storm into the kitchen like he was an ER doc.

Declan, snickering, grabbed his arm. "Savannah's already doctored it."

"You couldn't have led with that, dipshit?" Finn snapped.

"Nah. Wanted to see if you'd go running after her."

"Like you're not as whipped for Aela," he jibed.

While they bickered, Brennan demanded, "What about Camille?"

As my six thousand bots went to work on freezing the website, leaving me a window of time to hack into a back door I was racing to uncover, I asked, "What about her?"

"What do you mean, 'what about her?'"

"Brennan, are you fucking complaining that Conor ain't spying enough on her?" Declan drawled. "Dude, we get it, you're the second kid. You got issues—"

Brennan flipped him the bird—didn't need to take my eyes off the screen to know that he did either. "Well?"

"Well, what? I know you bought her those stables, and she's taking over some of the tour rides for kids."

"Which stables?" Eoghan queried.

"Camille likes horses?" Finn asked.

"I bought that under a dummy corp's name, Conor," Brennan complained.

"Brennan, make up your fucking mind. Do you want him spying on you or not?" Aidan snapped.

Brennan huffed. "I don't want him leaving Camille out is all."

"Out of being spied on?" Eoghan chided. "You're fucked in the head."

My lips twitched. "He's something in the head. Maybe Ma dropped you on it when you were a baby, Bren."

"Or rocked you too close to the wall," Declan jeered.

"Nah, he's her favorite," Aidan retorted. "If she dropped anyone, it's you."

While my brothers hooted, I just sniffed as, with a few flourishing attacks, I got into the website and started snooping around.

"What about Savannah?" Eoghan asked me.

"Ain't it Aidan's job to be worried about Conor not spying enough on his wife?" Finn mocked.

Aidan just shrugged. "Everyone fucking knows what my wife's been up to."

"Sucks about her mom," was all I said.

Aidan scowled. "You know about that?"

I hummed as I found my way into the site's server, creating an access point for myself so that I could visit later on without needing to arm six thousand bots.

Sure, I'd David and Goliathed the hell out of the elite crypto exchange's website, but I didn't have time to mess around anymore.

My woman was on the fucking loose—and I needed her back here. Yesterday.

It hit me on the raw that she was the only person in my family I didn't know the whereabouts of. It hurt like Aidan had stripped a couple slices of flesh off my back and had packed it with salt.

With my access point found, I tucked it behind a bunch of code that would shadow the security breach and turned my attention to my family.

They were all watching me.

Frowning, I asked, "What?"

"Aidan won't tell us what's going on with Savannah's mom."

"Probably because it's private?"

Eoghan scoffed, "You don't know the meaning of the word."

I placed a hand to my chest. "Little brother, you wound me."

"Take more than words to wound you," he retorted with a squint as he sank back a couple fingers of Aidan's best scotch—a house-warming present to Finn.

Shit had been tense between Eoghan and me since he'd found out about the sniper attack Star and I had subverted.

Snipers around the globe had been targeted by various governments in a game of cat and mouse as they tried *and failed* to uncover the plot to assassinate the bitch we'd once saluted as our First Lady.

Eoghan, AKA 'The Whistler,' had found himself in those crosshairs, and Lodestar via one of her friends had learned about the job. Together, we'd saved his butt and all he was pissed about was that I hadn't cleared Inessa out of the building first.

But I'd had to make it look authentic.

My ass had been the one on the line, not hers, for fuck's sake.

She'd been in the kitchen making goddamn smoothies. A fucking freight train could have rolled through their living room and she wouldn't have noticed. I was pretty sure that she *still* didn't know what had almost gone down that day Lodestar had picked off the man hunting Eoghan like he was a stag in a forest.

I arched a brow at him, well aware that it fell into a staring contest.

Sometimes, because my mind was always focused on work, they forgot that I was as much Da's son as they were.

Eoghan grunted when I didn't back down and finished his glass, shoving it at Finn to pour him another one.

"Hey, fuck off. That's forty-thousand-dollars a bottle and as rare as a pink unicorn, Eoghan. You wanna get wasted, drink some of the shit that I serve to guests."

Finn's complaint had me smirking, but all I said was, "You can't hack me. I won't tell you everyone's secrets if they shouldn't be shared."

"King Solomon has spoken," Aidan retorted as he swirled his own scotch in his glass.

I knew he limited himself now. His tastes had gotten more expensive and more rare, as if that were a method of curbing how much he imbibed.

A different man stood before me than the one who'd come to my penthouse last year, strung out on heroin and prescription meds.

I was fucking proud of this one.

The other had earned my loyalty and respect, but this one was worthy of being my leader.

Seeing him take a tiny sip, I watched his eyes close as he sank it back. "Where's your head at?"

His eyes drifted open again. "What do you mean?"

"I know you're plotting something," I told him. "Just don't know what. Yet."

"Aren't you the one who said you can't hack a brain, Con?"

"I know," I groused.

Brennan mused, "So, if we want to keep shit private, we have to think about it?"

Aidan dipped his chin at Brennan. "Until fuckface over there figures out how to read minds."

"I'm closer to that breakthrough than you think," I mocked, but my tone was pious enough that they all glanced at each other.

Hiding my laughter because they didn't know if I was lying or not, I watched as Aidan headed over to the chair in front of me and took a seat.

I couldn't imagine how much better he felt for not being in constant pain; I owed Savannah everything for taking that away from him. Maybe his doctor had done the surgery, but it was Savvie who'd gotten through to him, who'd forced him to get a second opinion.

"You got a plan?" Brennan queried, getting shit back on track.

"How long until dinner?" Finn asked Declan.

He shrugged. "Aoife was slicing carrots."

"Good. We have time to talk, then." To Aidan, he prompted, "Let us in, Aidan. Don't be like... Da. Keeping all this shit back."

Aidan pursed his lips. "I ain't keeping shit back. It's not like that. I don't know if what I'm thinking is attainable."

"Let us be your sounding board," Eoghan murmured.

I cracked my knuckles. "You been thinking about what I sent you the other day?"

Aidan nodded, but Finn demanded, "What did you send him the other day? And why the fuck weren't we CC'ed on the conversation?"

My eyes ached with how hard I rolled them. "Finn, calm down, dude. Seriously, you're getting to the age where we have to watch your heart."

He gaped at me before he seethed, "You're only a couple years younger than me, oh, wise one."

I grinned at him. "It's about time you knew I was from a different time and age."

"Feels like some creepy backstory for a comic book hero," Dec drawled, planting his cheek on his fist as he got comfortable on the sofa.

We were too used to the bickering not to take our comforts where we could find them.

Aidan snorted. "Shut the fuck up you two."

I snorted right back. "But it's so much fun."

"I got a fucking migraine," he groused, taking another sip. His features relaxed for a couple seconds, as if the alcohol were all it took to calm him. "Tell 'em."

"When Lodestar broke into my apartment—" I was gonna spank her for that. Especially when my brothers started snickering. "—she left something for me."

"A turd on the bed?" Declan joked.

I huffed. "No. Information. Bear—"

"The Old Satan's Sinners' Prez?" Brennan questioned.

"Yup. He'd uncovered a fountain of information about the Sparrows. Good and bad shit. Things that help us, things that don't."

"I should have been included in this conversation," Finn snapped, bristling.

Aidan rubbed his eyes. "I told him to give me a head start."

"Why?"

His jaw worked. "Because I take longer to read than you do."

Silence fell among us.

"Think that's the first time he ever admitted that out loud?" Declan whispered to Eoghan.

"I think so," Eoghan agreed as he kicked up his feet and settled them on the coffee table. "You accepted you're not stupid just dyslexic?"

Aidan scowled at him but, to me, said, "Send the files over to these asswipes."

A couple taps later, and the information was in their inboxes.

Well, *some* of it.

"What's going on with you, Aidan?" Finn rasped. "You've been acting weird since MacMurray."

"Nah, since before then," Brennan argued. "But that slicing off the tongue shit rammed the message home nice and clean."

Aidan cast him a look. "No complaints in the ranks?"

Brennan shook his head. "None. Aside from with Da's detail. But we knew they'd be a problem."

Aidan clamped his hand down around his glass. "Anything Da touched is a fucking problem. It ain't going to be enough to keep them under our thumb through fear. We've got too many potential leaks. They'll sink us if we ain't careful."

Finn's nod came slow as his brain raced to follow Aidan's when he was in the dark about a lot of shit. "You're talking Sparrows?"

"I'm talking Sparrows, and I'm talking ECD, and I'm talking just plain old Bratva. Da got too fucking big for his boots, and instead of letting us in when he got sick, and allowing us to manage the leaks before they spread, now I'm the one who has to consolidate everything before it comes tumbling down on our heads."

The words settled around us like nuclear fallout.

The bitch of it was, I couldn't argue.

"*Deartháir*," Brennan rasped, "talk to us."

But Aidan just sighed. "Ain't it obvious what I need to do?"

I frowned. "You're shitting me."

Finn scowled. "No. You can't do that."

Eoghan, Declan, and Brennan shared glances, their confusion clear, but Aidan didn't let them speak, just rumbled, "I'm the filthy king, ain't I? I can do whatever I fucking want."

18

———

AIDAN

"DECLAN SAID you fixed up Aoife's finger."

"Do you have a boo-boo too?" Savannah taunted, making me smirk as I braked at the stoplight up ahead.

"I've got plenty of other things you can kiss better," I murmured, smirk deepening at her grin.

"Oh, really?" Her hand drifted from where she'd rested it on my lap and shifted higher toward my dick.

As she cupped me, I drawled, "Not sure Midtown's the best place for oral."

"I think it sounds like the best place," she rasped, her fingers unbuttoning my fly and tugging at my zipper. "You just concentrate on driving us around, and I'll handle the rest."

I bit down on the inside of my cheek as her hand drifted inside the space she'd made, her fingers tugging at my cock and balls until she had full access.

A hiss burst from me when she thumbed the tip and dipped her head low enough to slide her tongue through the pre-cum that had already started gathering there.

Savannah shot straight to my dick faster than a dose of Viagra ever could.

I sat up so she could get better access and pressed the button that would move the seat back further. She took advantage by gathering spit in her mouth and coating my cock in it.

"Goddammit, no one gets to me like you do, little one."

Her moan told me she enjoyed hearing that.

The only thing I needed now was a fucking auto-pilot button on my ride so that I could just focus on her sinful mouth getting me off.

One hand on the wheel, I drove off as the lights flashed green, and rather than head to our apartment building, I aimed for the outskirts of the city because I fully intended on enjoying every moment of this.

"Fuck, you take me so well, baby girl."

Eyes engaged on the road, I didn't get the visual of her mouth around my cock, but it sure as fuck felt like heaven.

She sucked the tip, hard and long until I was gritting my teeth, then she gathered more spit that slid down my shaft. Her lips followed those trails, and she made slurping noises as she bobbed her head. Faster, faster. Deeper, deeper. She choked at the end, cushioning the glans in the muscles of her throat.

"Your mouth was made for my cock," I snarled and, unable to stop myself, I grabbed her ponytail and used it to control her movements.

Tugging at it, I slowed her down. A sharp sigh escaped her at the burst of pain, and I knew, just fucking knew, she'd be getting wet.

Savannah hadn't been raised in a convent, but she sure as hell acted like she'd been reared by nuns—the craziest, unsexiest shit turned her on.

She pulled free from my shaft and shot teasing licks along the back of it, pressing sucking bites to the veins that roped my dick. That tongue of hers poked and prodded all while her hand delved between my thighs to cup my balls.

Rolling them together, she twisted gently then gasped as I dragged her head up and back.

"Stop teasing me, Savannah."

She only had the chance to release a soft mewl before I stuffed her mouth full of my cock again.

"The next time we go out, I'm making you wear a vibrator," I grumbled. "Maybe I shouldn't let you out of the house without one."

A stuttered, "P-Please, Aidan, please," had me thanking Christ that there was a stoplight. I rocked my head back against the rest and gritted my teeth as that vibration went to work on me.

"Fuck," I snarled, jacking my hips up until my cock was sailing toward the back of her throat.

She groaned, shooting more of those vibrations around the length of me.

My eyes slitted as I reveled in the ecstasy throttling through my body thanks to my wife's filthy mouth. It was only *because* of that filthy mouth of hers, however, that I noticed the red SUV behind us.

Had I seen that before? Back in Midtown?

I must have tensed because Savannah's efforts doubled down, and, as I set off once the lights changed, I knew there was no point in trying to hold back.

Using my grip on her ponytail to keep my cock deep in her throat, I growled as cum slalomed into her mouth.

She mumbled words I didn't understand, sounds that made me think she was the one getting off, not the reverse, and I grunted as she swallowed every drop I had to fucking give.

When, finally, I was finished, I gently eased her head off my dick, and though it was awkward, I wasn't altogether surprised that she rested her face on my lap and got her breathing back under control.

I stroked her hair back from her sweaty temple. "Thank you, little one."

"I'm so wet," she rasped.

"I want you to hold onto that arousal." I knew my tone had darkened. "No squirming or touching yourself until we get home."

"No fair," she pouted.

"I think we're being tailed, baby. I don't want anyone seeing that expression of yours when you get off. That's for me alone."

"Don't say things like that," she hissed. "Unless you want to make me miserable on the ride home."

That she was more miserable at the prospect of being horny for the ride home than being tailed told me how close she was to climaxing. Ordinarily, I knew she'd be thrilled at being tailed.

My wife was weird like that.

"Trust you to focus on that part."

She sniffed then slowly rose, wincing because of the uncomfortable position she'd been in.

As she settled in her seat, she asked, "Which car?"

"Don't look—"

"I'm not going to look," she scoffed. "What do you take me for? An amateur?"

My lips twitched. "You a full-time criminal now?"

"I live with one," she retorted. "I know how these things work."

Though I rolled my eyes, I told her, "Red SUV. Two cars behind us in the right lane."

She fell silent as she lowered the visor. On the pretense of applying lipstick—because that was what every woman did in the dark and in the glow from the streetlamps—she tilted the mirror just so.

As she smoothed the stain onto her lips, she said, "I see it. But it's more maroon than red. Do you have any clue who it is?"

"No."

Savvie was quiet again. "You mean that, don't you?"

"I do."

I wasn't surprised she could tell the difference.

All week, I'd been avoiding speaking about the reason I'd been dragged out of bed in the early hours of the morning to deal with MacMurray.

Her curiosity was justified but that didn't make it any easier to hide the truth.

"Why don't you tell me what's going on?" she questioned. "Maybe I can help."

"It ain't your place, baby."

"I'm getting pretty fucking tired of being told where my place is or isn't, Aidan," she drawled, her tone cooling. "I'm not an idiot. Nor am I like Inessa or Camille. I'll worship that cock of yours and I might fangirl like crazy, but a docile and obedient wife I am not."

"You think you're telling me something I don't know?" I snapped.

"So just tell me the rest. Is it an issue with the Sparrows? I know you and Luc were discussing business earlier. Is there a problem with the Sicilians?"

"I told you at Christmas that if you don't tell me what's going on, I'll go hunting for answers on my own."

That was only part of the problem.

When she'd told me that, like the moron I was, I'd immediately fucking lied to her about how many Sparrows were in the ranks.

I scraped a hand over my jaw.

What to do, what to do.

I knew she was more than capable of getting her ass handed to her as she went investigating shit on her own.

Last time she'd done that, she'd come to my da's fucking attention. Which was what brought us to this point in the here and now...

I released a breath and went for broke: "You heard of Red?"

"The drug?"

Heaving a sigh, I muttered, "Of course, you know what that is."

"Is that a complaint?" she retorted sweetly. "What about it? I know it's more popular with men than women, but I think that's an urban legend."

"Urban legend? It's a new drug. How the fuck has it started an urban legend?"

"They say this guy had a boner for seventeen hours with it," she said around a chuckle. "He had to go to the ER to get it to come down."

"What's the urban legend? That he got the boner?"

"Nah, that it fell off."

I had to snicker at that and, as both of us chuckled, I shook my head. "One of Da's men got his hands on some Red. He visited a club that I found out Da owned on the side, and the hooker whose services he purchased, he beat to death."

"That's so sad," she murmured, twisting in her seat as she turned to look at me.

Traffic was bad again so I couldn't glance at her, but I felt her sorrow.

That was half the reason I didn't want to share shit like this with her, dammit.

"Yeah, it is."

"That's the problem?"

"No. Da had a rule for his detail—no drugs."

"Because of you?"

"No. Da had a problem himself back in the day, not that I knew that until recently. But I think that's why. He was always the same with the guys that were his or Mom's guards.

"Anyway, Red makes users progressively more violent."

"Yeah, I heard that too. I don't know what the compound is, but it has a similar trajectory of anabolic steroids, except for the erection thing, of course."

I nodded. "I realized that the guy, Cain, had to have been taking drugs when Da was alive. He'd have had to be careful about how he got his fix. No going to the usual sources. It made me realize something was going on, and I found out—"

"Told you just like that, huh? Sang like a canary?"

Another stoplight was upon us. "What do you want to hear, Savvie? That Brennan beat the shit out of him? That I cut out his tongue for lying to me?"

Her mouth rounded. "You cut out his tongue?" She edged forward. "How did you do that?"

"How do you think? A fucking knife."

"That's so Old Testament," she drawled. "I like it."

"Of course you would." I shook my head. "Will there come a day where you don't surprise me, Savvie?"

"Doubt it." She hooted. "Oh, damn, I bet that set the tone well with your men."

"What do you mean?"

"I mean there are always teething issues when there's a new leader. Always some dipshit who thinks he can upset the apple cart. You dealing with this Cain guy with fire and brimstone will definitely have made them realize you're not to be messed with."

My hands tightened around the wheel. "You told me that you'd studied our kills from your informant at the morgue."

Her fingers moved to my lap again and gently, she squeezed. "I did. And I also told you that your father's enjoyment in his kills was clear, whereas it wasn't in yours. This is different, Aidan. You have to see that.

"If you don't make a stand now, they'll think you're weak and your position will be undermined.

"I understand that you're going to have to do some not-so-nice things to secure your place as the head of the Five Points."

At first, I wasn't sure why her compassionate understanding robbed me of my tension, but as I processed it, it became glaringly obvious.

It had made me hopeful when she told me I wasn't like my father. I'd never aspired to be like him, and following in his footsteps wasn't something I'd ever particularly craved—perhaps because it was something I'd automatically inherited whether I wanted it or not.

Choice had never been an option for me.

Her faith in me had buoyed me, and...

God.

Did she know what she brought to my life?

My hand dropped to hers and I drew our fingers together, entwining them as I squeezed. "Thank you for understanding, Savannah."

"Has this been bothering you?"

"Maybe."

"You should have talked to me about this sooner. You never have to thank me for being an open ear—"

"What I did was heinous, Savvie. It's not something you can talk about with your wife over dinner."

"I'm not a regular wife, remember? I was a news reporter. I'm exposing all these Sparrows to the world, and the shit they do is horrific, Aidan. Did you know they were trafficking kids?"

My hand clenched around hers. "I didn't. Not specifically. But it makes sense. They sold every fucking thing else, why not that too?"

She clucked her tongue. "It's disgusting."

"You won't hear me arguing. Remember who you're talking to."

The brother who'd butchered a priest for daring to rape his little brother.

She released a soothing sound. "Sorry, baby. I didn't mean to make you think about the past. I was just saying, there isn't much you could do that would disgust me. Piss me off, sure. Just don't lie to me, Aidan, and you never have to worry about me going anywhere."

"That's your hard limit?" I rasped.

"Yeah. It is. I don't want to be in the dark, Aidan. I never have. Becoming what I am, becoming *me*, has all been about never being in the dark again." Before I could answer, she murmured, "Oh! The SUV just took the exit to Brooklyn."

I blinked.

Crap, I should have seen that before she did.

Peering behind me, I confirmed she was right and released a soft breath.

"You were nervous?" Savvie asked, her surprise clear.

"You're in the car with me. Of course I am."

"If you were alone, you wouldn't be?"

"No. I'd have forced a confrontation."

A squeak escaped her. "You had better be joking."

I just snorted.

"Oh, my God, you're not. You do know I'll make the damage that bullet did to your knee look like small potatoes if you get hurt, don't you?"

"I do." I smirked. "Did I ever tell you how fucking hot it is that you're as psychotic as you are?"

She huffed. "Don't you dare get turned on when I'm mad at you."

"Like you don't get turned on when I'm mad at you?!"

"That's different."

I shot her a bewildered look. "How is it?"

"Because you're Aidan O'Donnelly Jr. You're my crush."

"You're my wife."

"Don't play dirty," she retorted. "Especially if you're not going to fuck me when we get home."

Shaking my head, I had to laugh. "You might not want to fuck me by the time we get back."

"I always want to fuck you," she said, her confusion clear.

"Jesus, Savvie."

"What? I do. I can't help it. Do you know how much bad sex I've had in my life? Aidan, you are literally walking proof that the male gender is not completely useless in bed.

"I'm pretty damn sure that men had to subjugate women because they were so crap in the sack that that was the only way to control them!"

"Please, if you have that argument with Aela, I need to be there to watch the show."

"Bring popcorn because I bet her feminist ass would agree with me."

"Have the discussion with Declan in the room too. He'll growl and get pissed off that you're talking about her exes."

"Like you're not jealous?"

"I might have been if you hadn't just told me that I'm the best you've ever had." I straightened my shoulders as we approached the turn that'd take us onto our block. Deciding to bite the bullet, to get this off my chest once and for all, I stated, "Okay, I need to tell you that I lied to you. It happened once, and I've regretted it ever since."

She stilled at my admission. "What did you lie to me about?"

"St. Stephen's Day. After the party at the compound."

"You mean during that conversation where I told you not to lie to me?"

"Yeah."

"And you lied to me anyway?"

"Yeah."

"You're right. I don't want to fuck you now." She blew out a breath. "What did you lie about? How many Sparrows infiltrated the Five Points?"

That she remembered that conversation at all told me I was fucked.

"Yes."

"Why?"

"I was..." I sighed. It seemed so dumb now. "We were new," I tried to reason. "So fucking new, and you're so goddamn fast to write these articles and shit."

Her voice was dangerously calm and it set me on edge as she mused, "You thought I'd drop that information into one of my exposés?"

"I wasn't sure. You'd just helped Mary Catherine run away, for God's sake. You were a loose cannon. I wanted to claw back some control."

"You didn't trust me."

"I didn't wholly trust you," I corrected, somewhat relieved that I'd decided to come clean in the car. At least she couldn't run off. She was stilted enough that I thought she might do exactly that.

Then, because I realized my wife was crazy enough to do the unthinkable, I cast a glance at her and saw her hands were fisted on her lap and not on the handle so she could hurl herself out of the moving vehicle.

"Little one—"

"No, you don't have the right to call me that now."

My temper surged to life, but I sucked it up and blew it out.

She was correct.

I didn't get to use her pet name against her when I'd fucked up.

It didn't stop my mood from souring as, with every minute that passed as we journeyed closer to home, the quietness seemed to thicken between us.

I was used to her asking questions, peppering the silence with conversations that varied from wonder at Aoife's recent concoction in the kitchen to aggravation when a source let her down in her work against the Sparrows.

She might throw in how she thought the mayor was a jerk or that the country was going to hell in a handbasket because most people weren't embracing pure matcha tea like they did matcha lattes.

Simple shit.

Complicated shit.

Crazy shit.

Savannah shit.

We made it back without a single goddamn word passing between us.

I tried, Lord, I did, but it was a losing battle.

When she headed into the bedroom and returned a couple minutes later in gym clothes, I decided that leaving her to work out her frustrations might be the wisest option.

Tempted to push things along, I almost changed into workout gear myself, but something told me that giving her some room to breathe was the smartest choice.

I headed to bed, well aware that tomorrow was going to be a long one though, technically, it was a 'rest' day.

So I tried to relax, but I didn't sleep until she showered in our bathroom and got into bed beside me.

For the first time in our marriage, her ass didn't rub up against me. She didn't come anywhere near me.

Even when she had her period, she was all over me because Savannah didn't see why I shouldn't have to deal with a little period blood if she was horny.

It was then, with the chasm on the mattress separating us, that I realized I might have done the unthinkable.

Five years of ghosting her hadn't done it, but *this* could...

Had her fangirl obsession with me died?

Had I fucked this up like I'd fucked up everything in my life before her?

And Christ, that only included these past ten months because I'd fucked things up before then too.

My mind raced with hideous thoughts that had the sickness that was addiction rearing its ugly head.

I passed out around dawn, not realizing that she didn't sleep in all that time either.

When I eventually did fall asleep, the cravings shredding my soul apart, I didn't even register when she climbed out of bed and left me...

19

SAVANNAH

WRECKING BALL - MILEY CYRUS

I'D BEEN LET DOWN BEFORE.

I was a thirty-plus-year-old woman living in New York City.

Of course I had.

I'd been mugged—that mugger had regretted such a foolish act—I'd gone to a shitty Broadway play, and I'd taken part in some of the recent marches protesting the new antiquated laws that were crippling gay and trans people in this country.

Then I'd shoved those pictures under Aidan Sr.'s nose and had watched his mouth tighten as he flicked a look at Shay—the only boy in his family he didn't seem to want to upset.

So, sure, I'd been let down, but never by my husband.

Not since we'd married.

We weren't idyllic. We argued. *A lot.* I got in his face because he seemed to forget that my way wasn't the Five Points' way, but this?

He'd goddamn lied to me.

I could deal with silence, could deal with non-answers, but an outright fucking lie was beyond my limits. Especially where the Sparrows were concerned.

Not only did it not bode well for our relationship, but if he could feed me wrong intel and let me use it in an article, what did that say about his faith in *me*?

Which led to the worse question of all—what did that say about his faith in *us*?

As I passed the New Jersey Turnpike, I registered that my temper was still as spitting hot as it had been last night. That didn't, however, make me a moron. Behind me, some of my guards followed but I didn't take any notice.

Since my marriage, I'd adapted to having shadows drifting in and out of my awareness as they worked to protect me. They could tell Aidan where I was—I wasn't about to endanger my ass so I could get back at my stupid husband—he just wasn't entitled to know *why*.

For that reason, I stopped off at a gas station a couple miles away from Lily Lancaster's house.

Me: *Don't tell Aidan anything about why I'm heading to Jersey.*

Silence.

I was about to set off again when I received a message.

Conor: *You two had an argument?*

Me: *Yes.*

Conor: *Had to happen eventually.*

Did it? Really?

I scowled.

Me: *This is different.*

Conor: *Sure it is.*

Me: *He lied to me.*

Conor: *Pretty sure you've lied to him a time or two.*

Me: *This is different.*

Conor: *You said that already.*

Me: *This was important to me.*

Conor: *Did he think he was doing it to protect you?*

Me: *No. He was testing me.*

Conor: *Oh. This is about the Sparrows in the Points, right?*

Me: *You knew?!*

Conor: *I bug all your phones, Savannah. What do you think?*

Me: *That you need to get a life. And if you listened to us having sex, then I'm going to kick you in the dick the moment I'm home.*

Conor: *I'm trying to get a life. Ain't that a part of the reason why you've gone to Jersey?*

I huffed out a breath, well aware that he'd skipped over the part about him listening to Aidan and I having sex.

I was pretty goddamn sure Aidan had told me how many Sparrows were in the Five Points while he'd been inside me.

Or maybe *after* we'd come...

The orgasms tended to blur together, dammit to hell, so my memory was shot.

Me: *You don't get a life by being with someone you love. You have to make your own life.*

Conor: *That's the title of your new self-help book, right?*

Me: *No. I'm being serious here, Conor.*

Me: *You really knew he was lying to me and didn't tell me?*

Conor: *Savannah, I gotta ask you a question. I need you to think long and hard about this one...*

Me: *What is it?*

Conor: *What about my brother didn't key you into the fact he's a chronic self-sabotager?*

Before I could wince, he continued:

Conor: *Don't answer yet. I just hacked your car's GPS and know you're on the outskirts of West Orange.*

Conor: *Let me know what your answer is when you arrive at the Lancaster place.*

As he suggested, I didn't reply, just started up the car again, and as I rolled down the highway toward Thomas Edison's hometown— he was a total fraud as well. *Men.* I was just destined to be surrounded by the treacherous fuckers today—I thought about Conor's question.

"He has a point," I muttered to myself as I turned up the music so loud that it made my ears ache.

Trust me, when you grew up backstage at concerts, it took a *lot* to make my ears twinge.

Screaming along with Miley Cyrus about wrecking balls and adding a few choice lyrics about the balls I was going to wreck when the day was done, I made my way to the address Conor had given me.

I'd meant to head here earlier, but that hadn't worked out.

Researching the Sparrows' induction process had been fascinating and had taken pretty much all of my spare time.

Well, spare time that wasn't spent worrying about my mom or fucking my husband.

Lily's mansion was as glorious as could be.

I expected nothing less for someone who was born into old money.

As I gave my name at the intercom to the gates, I anticipated not being permitted entry, then someone pressed the button and they folded inward, allowing me to creep along the driveway that was a perfect foil for the grand house while also showcasing the beginning of the season's passage from fall to winter.

It was a little early for the Halloween displays, but I dug the hell out of it as I took in a pumpkin that had to weigh over four hundred pounds and had been carved into a dragon.

At least, I thought it was a dragon.

Squinting at it as I pulled up, I reached for my cellphone and tapped out:

Me: *Just because he self-sabotages doesn't take away my right to be furious with him. I self-sabotage all the time and he gives me shit for it.*

Conor: *I never said that it took away your right to be angry.*

No, I had to concede. He hadn't said that.

Conor: *But you have to ask yourself is love so fickle that you can forget all about it when he fucks up?*

Me: *That isn't fair.*

Conor: *The truth rarely is.*

Me: *If you love Star, then you should forgive her too.*

Conor: *Who said I won't?*

Me: *You're angry with her.*

Conor: *I'll spank her ass when I catch up with her, but catch up I will...*

Conor: *That's what happens when someone belongs to you.*

Conor: *You go after them.*

When he didn't continue the conversation, I bit my lip as I stared at my cell.

I knew what he was implying—he thought Aidan would come after me.

Was it bad that I didn't think he would? That I thought he'd go running to his mother's house because she'd summoned all her sons to her?

The notion that he'd go to her, and not come after me, hurt.

It had no right to. She was grieving, her sons were—even if it was a weird grief—and they should be together.

But he *was* mine, wasn't he?

He *should* come after me, shouldn't he?

Feeling uncertain, which pissed me off more than him lying to me, I got out of my car.

Whatever Aidan decided today, I was here for a purpose. With that purpose in mind, I headed over to my guards' SUV and waited for the driver to open the window.

I ordered Lucas, Aidan's captain, "Stay here."

"That isn't safe—"

"Might not be safe, but it's what you're going to do," I retorted. "We're on allied territory, Lucas. Who's going to hurt me?"

"Enemies?" he countered waspishly.

My lips twitched despite my bad mood.

He'd be cute if he didn't always fucking frown.

"It's okay, ma'am, I'll keep him contained to the car."

I flicked a glance at the guy in the passenger seat.

Not unlike Lucas, he had dark blond hair that flopped onto his forehead, and what he did to a suit should have been illegal.

"Who are you?" I queried, not unaware that he was eying me up in my own tailored suit.

I couldn't be mad at him—I looked hot.

Aidan, if he did pick his mom over me, was really fucking unlucky that he didn't get to see me be this hot today. I was rocking a skin-tight turtleneck that did epic things for my tits too.

Lucas elbowed him in the side. "He's my brother. Cade's newly promoted."

Pursing my lips, I shrugged. "I don't know how long I'll be, but don't disturb me."

Lucas frowned. "Ma'am, you're supposed to be heading upstate—"

"No, I'm not," I told him sweetly. "You can pass that message onto my husband if you'd like."

Lucas's eyes widened. "You mean he doesn't know you're here?"

"No."

"But you said—"

"I lied," was my calm reply.

"I got his message—"

"I used his phone to contact you." I pulled a face at him. "Would you ask Aidan this many questions?"

"To be fair, he *is* our boss," Cade inserted.

"Well, I'm the boss's wife and I don't like being questioned either. Now, keep your asses out of trouble. I don't want to start a fight with anyone today."

With that, I swiveled on my heel and headed to the door.

It opened before I could knock on it, and I was greeted by the scowl that could launch a thousand ships.

Honest to God, Amara was a beautiful woman even when she scowled. I figured the world wasn't ready for her smiles yet.

"Cat."

"No. Savannah. You remember me, don't you?"

Amara was the reason I was the face of the 'Die Motherfucking Sparrows' movement that was sweeping the US.

"I do not forget faces, remember?" Amara scoffed. "Bird."

"Dog?" I replied, wondering why the hell she was spitting out random animals at me.

A chuckle sounded behind her and a kid, not much more than Inessa's age, strolled out from one of the many doorways that lined the foyer.

"Hedgehog."

Annoyed, I stacked my hand on my hips. "Look, I don't know what's going on here—"

"Good. Is not your business," Amara said with a sniff before she stepped back and grabbed the guy's hand. "Mine," she told me before she stuck up her nose.

"AKA Quin," the kid drawled, holding out his other hand as easily as he grinned at Amara's declaration.

"Can I touch you or will she bite me?"

Amara snapped her teeth. "I do bite. But only bitches. You bitch, but you help. I like."

Quin whistled as I shook hands with him. "First, she talks about animals, and then there's an admission of liking. You *are* blessed."

This was a warm welcome?

Now I knew why Lodestar had just passed along the information Amara had helped her uncover without letting me talk too much to her.

Mostly, I'd listened in on their conversations over Skype, typing out questions that I didn't think Lodestar was covering.

Amara was as prickly as the aforementioned hedgehog and clearly nuttier than a pecan pie.

"What is hedgehog?" Amara demanded after she purposely grabbed my hand and Quin's and separated them.

Quin just rolled his eyes, evidently accustomed to her possessiveness.

"I'm married, you know?" I refused to wince as her fingers had dug into my tennis bracelet as she disconnected our hands.

She shrugged. "Married women, single women, they all have eyes. Look at his face."

Quin shot me a sheepish glance. "You'd think we were Michelangelo's creations the way she goes on."

'We.'

That was right. Amara lived with two guys.

An unusual living situation for many, but more so considering Amara's traumatic past.

Trafficked from Ukraine, sold into sexual slavery, and left to die in a pit that would have been an atrocity to cage animals there, never mind humans...

"Prettier than statue," was all Amara had to say to that before she asked, "What is hedgehog?"

"Hamster with spikes. Remember?"

I snorted at the description.

"Spikes," she repeated. "Points. Little. Goes to ball when scary."

"When it's scared," Quin corrected easily, curving his arm around her shoulders. "What do you think?"

It took me a couple seconds to realize he was asking me that question, not Amara.

"About what?"

"Hedgehog or cat?"

"What about them?" I demanded impatiently.

What the hell was going on here?

"Which is your spirit animal?"

I blinked at them both. "I don't have one."

Amara sniffed then mumbled something in Ukrainian.

Quin appeared to understand some of what she was saying because his lips twitched.

"Are you here to see anyone in particular?"

"Lily, I guess." I tugged on my lapels. "Have I interrupted something?"

"Just a BBQ." He beckoned me inside. "Come in. There's plenty of food to go around." He peered at the car idling in the driveway. "You can invite them in too. They won't come to any harm. It's a family day."

I blinked again. "MCs have family days?"

"They do now."

That was as much information as I got about that.

But, if it was a picnic, that meant Katina would be around somewhere. Hopefully playing so I could potentially talk to her about Lodestar...

That didn't sound at all predatory, did it?

Grimacing at the thought, I twisted back and stared at Lucas until he opened the window.

"You're invited in," I called out before I stepped inside, grateful for the relatively warm welcome, waiting only for my guards who scampered in, their surprise clear.

As Amara closed the door behind us all, I muttered to them, "Behave. Or I'll have your balls on a platter."

"She means it," Lucas drawled.

Cade snorted. "What if that's what I'm into?"

"Shut the fuck up," Lucas ground out, low enough that I shouldn't have been able to hear...

If I'd needed confirmation, I had it—Lucas was definitely the older brother.

I left them to it, reasoning that Lucas was Aidan's captain and my main guard because he had some brains and knew not to piss off an MC on home turf. And if Cade fucked up, well, that was on us both.

I had a double-pronged mission.

Well, multiple prongs in all honesty.

The house was as luxuriously appointed on the inside as the outside suggested.

There were some installations in one room that I just *knew* were Aela's work. The intricate glass baubles gave me the idea that I'd like those in my apartment.

Hey, I was family. She'd give my commission priority, right?

Knowing Aela, she wouldn't.

I smirked at the thought as we crossed the room that I'd seen through a camera, but not in person.

This was the first time I'd come here, though I knew Lodestar had been living with Lily and her partner, Link, ever since there'd been a blast at the MC's compound.

Katina's older sister, Alessa, also lived on the grounds somewhere, in a pool house I thought Star had once told me. She had a partner too—Maverick.

Not that they called their significant others that here. Old Man and Old Lady were the correct vernacular.

Only problem with that was that not a single goddamn woman in the back yard was old enough to be called an *Old Lady*.

Still, I'd watched *Sons of Anarchy* like the next woman.

Before Aidan, on my bang list was Charlie Hunnam.

He might have even surged higher up my list after last night's debacle.

I swept into the crowd with all the confidence of someone who'd never actually met anyone here but who'd been on breakfast television for years.

The men scowled at me mostly, especially one with a kid in a carrier that had skulls and crossbones on it, but another one, with the girliest carrier ever made—hot pink with flowers on it—stepped over to me with a wary look in his eye.

"You're Aidan O'Donnelly's wife."

I sniffed. "That might be a temporary label."

"You're getting divorced?" he questioned.

A snort sounded from behind him. "Sounds more like that time when Nyx told me it was just one more push and there were at least ten to get his kid's big head out of my cooch."

"Jesus, Giulia," another woman groused. "Do you have to talk like that in front of strangers?"

"She isn't a stranger, Rachel," Giulia groused back. "We've met."

"We have." Albeit virtually. "I should have brought gifts for the babies. I'm sorry."

Giulia shrugged. "Have enough of your own shit to deal with. I can forgive you this once."

She held out her hand, I clasped hers in mine, and we shook on it.

"That's right. I was sorry to hear about your father-in-law," the woman Giulia had called Rachel told me. She held out her hand too. "I'm Rachel. Rex's Old Lady. Welcome."

People started to gather around us, and I recognized most of them from the time Star had introduced us to each other before I'd taken all my exposés public and had begun hitting the Sparrows where it hurt.

"If you *are* divorcing Aidan O'Donnelly, we can't offer you a safe haven."

"Shut up, Nyx," Giulia hissed, stacking her hands on her hips. "Is he beating you?"

"Aidan? Jeez, no!"

"Treating you like shit? I bet those fucking O'Donnellys think their crap is made of gold—"

"Giulia," Rachel snapped.

"What? I'll bet it's true."

My lips curved. "It is. Partially. But no, he isn't abusing me. That's not why I'm here."

"No? You look pissed to me. Sound pissed too if divorce is in the cards."

"I am pissed, but I won't divorce him yet." I straightened my shoulders. "He lied to me."

Giulia grunted. "Men are dipshits like that."

"Agreed," Rachel muttered.

A bright blonde head—Lily, I recognized—bobbed. "They never realize we always know when they're lying."

"We are here, you know?" Rex drawled, but his lips were twitching.

"What did he lie about?" Giulia inquired, ignoring him.

I almost told her it was none of her business, but... I'd inadvertently stirred camaraderie among us.

That was unexpected, but helpful.

"That's none of your business," Rachel slotted in on my behalf, but her head had angled to the side as if she were just as curious.

She'd given me an out but I decided not to take it.

"He tried to entrap me," I told them simply.

Rachel frowned. "I'm an attorney—"

"Not like that. He fed me information because he wanted to know if I'd use it in an article."

"That's it?" Nyx's scowl told me he was unimpressed by my logic.

Giulia pinched his arm. "Shut up, you. If you did that to me, when writing shit for newspapers was my job, you'd have ten more piercings, Mr. Frankendick."

Nyx stunned the hell out of me by grinning. "You make that sound like a punishment."

Jesus...were they going to kiss?

All of a sudden, the air had electricity zipping through the atmosphere. It was so fierce and so ferocious that it was like the onset of a storm.

Someone let loose a piercing whistle, loud enough and close enough to make my ears ring.

"Back it up, you two. There are minors present."

Lily beamed, her hand outstretched as she declared, "Link, meet Savannah."

The blond guy ambled over to me, curling his arm over Lily's shoulder as he said, "Pleasure to meet you. You're the chick from TVGM, aren't you?"

"I am."

"Can I just say, on behalf of men everywhere, my dick ached on that jackass's behalf. It was fucking awesome. Asswipe deserved worse."

My old workplace had had a toxic environment, one that I'd taken it upon myself to cleanse.

I had a feeling my ex-boss had gotten worse than a sprained dick when I'd honey-trapped him. The bastard used a casting couch in exchange for promotions... *Not anymore.*

Maybe Aidan wasn't all bad.

Suddenly feeling more cheerful at the prospect of Aidan

torturing my rapist fuck of an ex-boss, I had to grin at Link. "There was a lot of built-up annoyance in that hit."

"I could tell." He tipped his head to the side. "Your other half here?"

"No."

"He lied to her, Link."

Link arched a brow at his Old Lady. "How bad of a lie? Fifteen-to-life or a white one?"

"He gave her the wrong intel and wanted to see if she'd publish it," Rex murmured, soothing his daughter who started fussing.

Did these uber masculine guys with all this baby paraphernalia realize how cute they looked?

And it was just wrong for bikers to look cute, but they did. *Hella cute.*

Maybe this was why Jen was okay with being pregnant all over again.

Would Aidan wear something ridiculous like Rex if we had a daughter?

I bit my lip at the thought because I'd bet that he would.

What had he said the other night?

That he wanted a son or a daughter not to have an heir or an heiress, but to have a child. Someone that was a part of us both.

I straightened up my shoulders as my ovaries started to melt. "I found out last night about his lie."

"Is that why you're here?" Giulia asked.

"No."

"But the salt in the wound is still raw." Link gave me a commiserative nod. "Well, there are ribs and burgers on the grill, steaks too, but you wanna ask Giulia to prep you those because she's the only one who'll make it taste good—"

Giulia grinned. "Thanks, Link."

"My pleasure, hellcat," he retorted with a laugh. To me, he said, "Make yourself at home."

"Feel free to have something to drink," Lily offered. "There are all kinds of cocktails because Tiff is making those, and we have a dessert bar if you feel like drowning your sorrows in carbs."

Was it really as easy as that?

I figured it must be because the guys started to drift away, but the women didn't.

"I didn't expect you to be so welcoming," I admitted, not making a move toward the barbecue, bar, or dessert table. "I figured you'd be suspicious."

"Oh, we are," Giulia chirped. "But you're Star's friend, you helped Amara out, and you're an ally. You might bring some chaos to our family day, but I like chaos with my burger. Makes it digest better."

I immediately picked up on what she meant. "Aidan won't come," I told her even though, after the conversation with Conor, I hoped he did. "He's going to his family home for Sunday lunch."

Rachel cleared her throat. "I've met your husband."

"At your father-in-law's funeral, I know. My condolences, Rachel."

She hitched a shoulder. "Your grief is fresher than mine."

"Grief doesn't work like that, does it?" I mused, seeing warmth flicker into her cool eyes at my words.

"No," she concurred.

"Maybe that's how it's supposed to be. The more impact someone has on us, the more we feel their loss when they're gone."

When the prickle of tears inadvertently struck me, I gnawed on the inside of my cheek to offset them. I hadn't meant to get maudlin. Especially not after the news about my mom this week.

I needed PMA, not to be a negative Nancy.

Changing the subject, I repeated, "Aidan won't come."

Giulia smirked. "Wanna bet?"

"What would you bet?"

Rachel warned, "Giulia, no gambling with guests."

"You're such a drag, Rach," the other woman grouched, which made Lily chuckle until her laughter died off, her gaze drifting from us.

Giulia's attention wandered to a point behind me as well.

"Oh, fuck," Giulia said on a sigh. "You met Amara on the way in?" At my nod, she huffed. "Did she ask you about animals?"

Rachel also sighed, and that had me twisting around to see what was going on.

Amara, Quin, and another guy, one who reminded me of Giulia with the dark coloring and strong features—Hawk, I thought his name was—were each holding an animal.

"It's like the Dr. Doolittle version of *Jeopardy*," Lily grumbled.

I noticed then that the guys who'd stuck close enough to their women to make their presence felt, all while giving us privacy to talk, moved further out as if the trio were contagious.

Lily grimaced. "Might as well get it over with."

"Get what over with?" I questioned in surprise.

"You're about to become a pet owner."

My mouth dropped open. "What?! I don't want a pet."

"You came to West Orange like a naive, naive fool," Giulia mocked. "That means you're going away with one of Quin's shadows."

"They're following Amara now too," Lily muttered. "Have you noticed?"

Giulia nodded. "It's freaky as hell."

The trio stopped in front of me. Quin's cheerfulness hadn't abated, Amara looked as if she were going to try to beat me in a staring competition, and only Hawk seemed not to want to be here.

"Before you give me shit, Giulia," Hawk mumbled, "we're running out of room at the bunkhouse."

"I don't want a pet," I blurted out.

"After our place is built," Giulia said, speaking over me, "we need to focus on getting you some land. You need somewhere to put them all."

"Hey! We're next on the list," a woman I recognized from the papers groused.

"Shut up, Stone, do you want another dog?"

Stone pulled a face, and that was, of course, when I remembered her.

She'd helped bring down an Angel of Death at the hospital where she used to work in Manhattan. The murderer had tried to capture and kill her, but Stone had freed herself—not without getting grievously injured in the process.

"Okay, you can get the next house," Stone agreed quickly. "I can't deal with more animals roaming around our place. Mrs. Biggins is wicked pissed at us getting some dogs. I don't think she'd cope with anymore."

"Mrs. Biggins?" I inquired.

Giulia smiled. "Stone's ancient cat."

"Less talk, more decide," Amara broke in. "Which you take?"

"I don't want a pet. I live in an apartment in the city!" I retorted, but Amara demanded, "You pick!"

Rachel's tone was sympathetic as she informed me, "That's more choice than we got."

"She just turns up and expects you to take them," Lily agreed.

"Decide," Amara intoned with enough authority that I considered the animals in the trio's hands.

There were two cats and, in Quin's grasp, a hedgehog. It was curled up in a ball until Quin stroked its nose. Then, it scampered up his arm and settled on his shoulder, making him chuckle and me almost bolt out of my skin.

What had he called it earlier...? A hamster with spikes?

That felt unerringly close to the truth.

"Cat, then," Amara said with a decisive tone as she took in my reaction to the small creature.

I stared at the remaining animals, wondering what the hell was happening here.

Was this a joke?

But it was a rhetorical question because I knew it definitely wasn't.

None of the Old Ladies were laughing, the men had disappeared as though they were sick of being given animals to adopt, and I was, I realized, quite, quite alone.

Unless...

"My guards would probably appreciate a pet," I remarked, not caring that I was totally selling them out.

Amara pursed her lips. "We bring more. There plenty in our house."

Fuck.

Giulia chuckled. "Nice try, Savannah."

"Is this for real?" I muttered.

"Oh, it's for real," Hawk said on a sigh. "Just pick one. Trust me, it's easier to surrender."

Quin snorted, but he didn't argue.

It was clear that this was Amara's show.

I scowled at her, unafraid when she scowled back. Then, she stunned me. That mean frown of hers softened. "Is gift. Make happy. You smile more with animal."

"She'd be happier if her husband didn't lie to her," Giulia mocked.

"Cat no lie," Amara retorted. "Cat loyal."

Stone chimed in, "Cats are loyal to themselves. I know if I died in my bedroom, Mrs. Biggins would eat me to save herself."

"Steel chose Mrs. Biggins for you. Not Quin," Amara dismissed. "Pick, Savannah. My thank you. For all help. *Tak?*"

Rejecting that offer of thanks would have not only been rude, it would also have been selfish.

I really didn't want a goddamn cat, but I could see she meant well, and...

Was I truly considering this?

Jesus on a cracker.

"Where did they even come from?" I mumbled.

"We bring from clubhouse," Amara informed me and her tone turned more unyielding as she said, "You need one. Pick."

I'd done a segment on native cats for TVGM so I recognized the breeds.

One was fully grown—that was the one in Amara's arms. The creature was large with a bushy tail, and it kept on butting Amara's chin. A Maine Coon, I thought it was called.

Hawk held a kitten. Well, I thought it might be a teenager.

Teabag, my last cat, had died years ago and I was still grieving. I didn't particularly want another animal that could break my heart. Not when I barely kept myself alive most days.

But... the one Hawk held had spots on its back and big pointed ears.

I bit my lip as the desire to stroke those ears had my fingers curling in on themselves.

"That's a Savannah cat, isn't it?" I asked softly.

Quin nodded. "She came when I called."

I frowned. "Huh?"

"Quin's got this, like, Dr. Doolittle thing going on," Giulia explained, as if that made any sense. "Animals come to him. If they're sick or don't have a home, they trail around and then, when they run out of space, Amara dumps them on us. She's better than the SPCA at fostering pets out."

Quin smiled at me. "She's been out of sorts since she came here."

"Who has?" I asked with a frown.

"The cat," he said with a laugh, kind eyes twinkling. "But when I whistled, these three were the ones who showed interest."

This had to be a joke.

It wasn't the first time I'd thought that, but only Amara's tapping foot declared an impatience that belied any humor in the situation.

Was I seriously about to be forced into selecting a pet?

I took a step back, but as I did, the teenaged kitten yowled at me.

I jerked in surprise at the insistent sound—the fur ball was far more adamant than Amara.

I looked at it in the eye.

Swallowed.

And melted.

20

AIDAN

MY HANDS ACHED from how hard they were curled around the steering wheel as I drove toward Jersey.

Furious wasn't the word about having to cancel lunch plans with Ma who was back to popping pills like they were jellybeans. Throw in my worries about the Russians, the fact that I'd fucked up majorly with my wife and that there was no one to blame but myself, and I wasn't in the best of moods.

There was one consolation—she hadn't tried to escape her guards.

I knew that wasn't out of deference to me and my position though. Savannah had been raised by a rockstar whose fans would and could turn mean. She'd experienced the nastier side of life as she'd told me so often back in the early days, so while I knew escaping her guards was something she might have done before our marriage, becoming a Fecker bride had made her more security conscious.

Thank fuck.

With shit up in the air, I didn't need her going off half-cocked without any security measures in place.

Lucas was on her too. I didn't know the man as well as I should, but I knew he was conscientious. I knew he'd keep Savannah safe until I could.

My cell buzzed as I made it to West Orange.

I growled when I saw it was Conor.

Definitely not in the mood for a *chat* with him, I hit the button on my steering wheel and snarled, "Conor, I don't give a damn if the Five Points' empire is about to sink into quicksand. I've got more important shit to do today than talk about Russians, ECD, or the fucking Sparrows."

"You should start with that when you suck up to Savannah."

"Excuse me?" I demanded, mouth gaping at his statement.

"Start with that when you suck up to Savannah," he repeated.

There was a slurping sound, and I hissed, "Are you eating ice cream?"

"I am."

I knew what that meant.

Ma never allowed dessert before we ate.

And if that didn't make me feel about five fucking years old, I didn't know what would.

Jesus H. Christ.

"Why aren't you at the house?" I snapped.

"I didn't want to go."

"You have to be there. Ma'll lose her shit if I'm not there and you ain't either."

"She'll just have to lose her shit then, won't she?" Conor drawled nonchalantly. "Anyway, Uncle Paddy said he'll go instead of me. You know he'll cheer her up. I wouldn't be surprised if he had a crush on her—"

"Don't be so disgusting," I spat.

"What's disgusting if they make each other happy? You know, that nice feeling that you experience when you're with a person who gets you? Until *you* fuck it up, of course."

There it was.

The pointed barb.

'Until *you* fuck it up.'

I vowed, "I'm going to make it up to her."

"You'd better," Conor rasped. "I like her, Aidan. She's good for you. She won't take any of your shit, *but* you're a rockstar to her so she'll cut you slack where other women wouldn't.

"I still can't believe you managed to fuck this up."

"It was one lie—"

Conor sounded unimpressed. "Definitely don't start with that."

My shoulders hunched. "I don't know why I said that. I *know* I fucked up."

"You're a man. We do stuff like that." He hummed, and I knew his attention had drifted a second. "But," he said slowly, his fingers tapping something on his keyboard, "you're in luck. She loves you. When women love you, they'll let you get away with shit if the apology is big enough."

I rubbed the back of my neck. "I don't even know how to apologize for this."

"Well, let's face it, you didn't fuck another woman or lie about sexting some broad. This is about pride. Not betrayal."

"I don't think she'd agree," I said on a deep sigh.

"Nah, maybe not, but I figure information will get her to come around."

"What kind of information?"

"Tell her what's going on with the ECD. That'll fascinate her, and with her contacts, she might find out some shit that we haven't uncovered."

My brow furrowed. "You being serious?"

"Yup. She's your wife, Aidan. She's not Ma. She's strong and capable and she's got a fucking brain on her that won't be happy peeling carrots in the kitchen on Sundays to feed the family.

"No disrespect to Ma, or Aoife for that matter. That shit makes *them* happy, but your wife ain't like that. She ain't like them."

No.

She wasn't.

And I didn't want her to be either.

I loved that she was independent and headstrong.

I adored the way she challenged me. In bed and out.

I didn't want her to change. Ever.

Rubbing my brow, I muttered, "If I get her involved with that, there's no getting her out again."

"No need to. She's your bride, Aidan. She'll be that until both of you die because, for some fucking reason, she loves your dumbfuck ass. Be grateful for that, show gratitude by opening up to her. She won't be happy being left out in the dark.

"Do this, *dearthàir*, and you'll have a happy wife."

"And a happy life?" I choked out, hands gripping the wheel again, this time enough for the leather to creak.

"If you're lucky," he drawled. "Don't fuck this up. I expect to see her next Sunday at lunch."

He cut the call before I could answer, and I sucked in a breath.

With women in the past, I hadn't given a fuck if they'd walked off. Whether it was in annoyance or hurt. I'd been an asswipe back then...

Still was, apparently.

Was he right?

Was being open with her the key to earning her forgiveness?

I knew she craved information, understood why too, but...

It seemed so clinical.

Savannah was, though, wasn't she? Not with me, but in her working life, she was hard as nails. Arrogant. Severe.

Through my stupidity, she'd proven that if I told her she couldn't use the information I gave her, she wouldn't. So she could be trusted to obey me...

Unless she wanted her own back.

I knew, more than most, that she was capable of long-term, thoroughly detailed revenge...

Thoughts whirring, I followed the GPS link that Lucas had sent me earlier to the fancy neighborhood where Lily Lancaster lived with the MC brother who'd claimed her as his own.

We were tied more intrinsically to the Satan's Sinners' MC than the Five Points would ever know.

It went deeper than Mary Catherine and Digger's marriage and their son.

Brennan's Camille had found a dubious sort of sanctuary here, my father had concocted some fucked-up plan to eradicate the earth of pedophiles with the club's VP, their Reaper had cleared away dead bodies for us, and together, we'd brought down the *Famiglia.*

Then there was the old Prez: dead for close to a year now, yet somehow still the Gordian knot that tangled so many loose filaments together.

Every day, more information came to light.

Every day, more conspiracy theories became truth.

Savannah said that my reign would be different than my da's. That there wouldn't be the wars like he'd led the Points through, but I was waging a different kind of battle.

This one threatened us all.

Not just those living in the underworld, but those in regular society too.

No one was safe.

Not from the ECD or the Sparrows.

If *we* weren't untouchable, then they could get to everyone and anyone.

Like poisoned blood that necrotized the tissue it touched, we were all slowly dying.

And it had nothing to do with global warming.

I made it to the Lancaster mansion with few issues aside from a call from Finn, undoubtedly wanting to know where the fuck I was.

I ignored it and hit the intercom on the gates, fully expecting not to be allowed inside.

The second I mentioned my name, however, the gates immediately opened.

I drove in and, at the end of the driveway, saw Savannah's sporty little coupe.

Thinking strategically, I blocked her in by parking beside her guards' SUV, feeling more comfortable now that I knew she couldn't run away.

At least, not by car.

Hoping she was wearing heels so I didn't have to run her down on foot—I put nothing past my wife—I headed for the door.

It opened to reveal the Prez of the Sinners.

Rex stared at me, his hand on the door handle, an ease in his stance that put me on edge.

We were allies, after all. Not friends. Still, from how he was looking at me, you wouldn't think we'd been texting each other yesterday.

"I thought Catholics believed Sundays were the day of rest."

"They do, but I'm not Catholic."

Christ, that felt good to say.

His eyes narrowed. "Your father was. The last time I saw him, he was preaching fire and brimstone."

"That was what he did best," I rasped.

Rex bowed his head slightly. "The pain doesn't go. Grief twists with time. But you know that already. Our fathers aren't the only family we've lost."

I studied him, and I had no idea where the words came from, but I asked them nonetheless, "Does forgiveness come with time?"

Our gazes collided.

Eons passed as we took the other's measure.

Then, he said, "Acceptance does. That they're only men. That they made no promises to be perfect."

"That isn't the same as forgiveness."

"No," he agreed, keeping it at that.

I gritted my teeth. "Shame."

"Isn't it?" He sighed. "What are you doing here, Aidan? Savannah will leave at the end of the day. You had no reason to come here."

"I had every reason. Wouldn't you follow your woman to the ends of the fucking earth?"

"I have."

"What's goddamn Jersey by comparison?"

He conceded that with a snort, but he moved aside and said, "You're welcome."

I frowned. "For letting me in?"

"No. The kitten."

"The fuck?"

His lips twitched. "You'll see soon enough."

21

SAVANNAH

LOVE YOU LIKE THAT - DAGNY

I'D FELT the electricity in the air when Nyx and Giulia stared at each other and Link had broken them up.

Nyx was mean, moody, a bear with a paw full of blisters that shielded the broken glass lodged in his flesh. I'd gathered, from the whispers of gossip that spread among my sisters-in-law, that he was the one who'd broken Camille's heart.

But I knew a love like his and Giulia's.

It didn't excuse cruelty, nor did it permit negligence.

Yet when I thought of Camille and her Brennan, and of Inessa and her Eoghan, Aela and her Declan, Aoife and her Finn, I knew that each of us shared that same ability to make magic happen.

You could only do that with the right person.

Before Aidan, I'd been half-convinced that love was a con. More than that, a conspiracy. That men used it to control women, to oppress them.

Hadn't I seen it with my own eyes?

Jen hadn't helped. She was more convinced that love was a losing game than I was.

After him, I'd learned love was like you were keyed into some *verboten* part of the universe. Something that only unlocked when you felt this deeply for another person, when you trusted this wholly.

The songs made sense.

The poems resonated.

That was why the second he stepped out into the yard, I knew he was here.

Relief almost made me sag, but my cat dug its claws into my arm. The damn thing was heavy, but whenever I put it down on the ground, it wouldn't leave me alone, had almost tripped me up three times, so I'd taken to carrying it.

At that moment, I was grateful.

The pain gave me an edge.

It let me turn around, let me face the crowd as I saw him standing in the French doors that led to the garden.

Rex was beside him. The Prez murmured something in his ear then stepped into the yard too. Was I surprised when he found his Rachel? No. He immediately collected their baby, Lisandra Sommer, Sommer for short, and hugged her to his chest.

That was the power of love.

It brought strong men to their knees, and they didn't mind. They embraced that weakness because it made them even more formidable.

He saw me then.

At that exact moment.

His glance darted over the yard on the hunt for me until, finally, our gazes clashed and held.

That was when I felt it.

My skin tingled.

My heart pounded.

My lungs burned.

This was what he could do to me.

No other man could make me feel this way. No other man could hurt me with such a simple deception.

I straightened my shoulders, lengthened my spine, and braced myself for the powerhouse that was my husband who was walking toward me.

In a three-thousand-dollar suit or a thousand-dollar leather jacket with jeans, he exuded power. The bitch of it was, I already wanted to melt in the face of that.

God, those fucking jeans were going to be the death of me.

"Let him come to you."

The whisper came from Stone.

I dipped my head slightly.

"Make him work for it."

Giulia.

"Words mean nothing without action."

Lily.

As they drifted away, leaving me alone apart from my new kitten, I tucked one of my hands into the small creature's fur. There was a surprising amount of comfort to be found there, and I drew from it as I watched him.

Much like the Five Points, blood and money were at the foundations of the MC. But for all that, Aidan had these daunting men veering out of his path. They didn't know they were doing it, but they edged aside nonetheless, allowing him to walk toward me without stopping.

Nearer.

Nearer.

Then, he was there.

Right in front of me.

"You left."

His first words.

It was like a knife punctured my lungs and air leached from them.

Words mean nothing without action.

That was what Lily had said.

"I needed space, and I needed help. Both things the MC could provide."

His gaze never left mine as he growled, "You don't need space from me."

"Don't tell me what I need," I grated out, uncaring that half the club was probably listening in to the conversation.

He gritted his teeth. "What help do you need from the MC?"

"Lodestar has gone missing. I was hoping for some information on her whereabouts."

His nostrils flared. "They won't help you run from me. You're mine, Savannah. I told you—you belong to me. It didn't take a wedding ring to cement that."

His words triggered an explosion inside me.

Want and need combined with fury and outrage.

Five years, he'd ghosted me before we'd gotten together. Five years, I'd longed to hear those goddamn words spilling from his lips.

A hiss escaped the cat who pounced at Aidan. I didn't have a clue how I stopped it, but I did. I grabbed it around the belly and hauled it into me. It spat and snarled until I rubbed its ears and it settled down with a purr.

"What the fuck is with the cat?" Aidan blurted out, his shock clear.

"It's our new pet," I snapped.

"Pet?" He blinked. "I'm a fucking mobster, Savannah. We don't have pets."

"These are fucking bikers, Aidan," I sniped. "If they have pets, we can have a pet. Anyway, I didn't have a choice. This was a gift."

"You don't even like animals."

"Don't tell me what I like or don't like," I groused. "I had a cat before. Teabag, remember?"

"You haven't had one since."

"The cat's cool. It stays."

His temper flashed in his eyes but I ignored it. Then he rasped, "*Our* pet?"

"What's mine is yours, isn't it?" I rejoindered calmly.

The tension in his shoulders lessened. Not by more than a fraction of an inch. I still saw it though.

He released a soft breath. "I'm sorry, little one."

"For lying? For trying to entrap me? For not trusting me? For having no faith in me? Which one, Aidan? Take your fucking pick."

His jaw clenched. "All of them."

"Not good enough."

"I should have told you the truth," he conceded.

"Damn straight."

"I shouldn't keep you in the dark."

Interest spiked inside me.

Curious, I tilted toward him without realizing it until he rested his hand on my arm.

I didn't shrug his hold off, just asked, "You shouldn't keep me in the dark about what?"

"Anything. Everything."

My interest flatlined. "Not good enough."

"I need to be more open with you," he conceded.

I was back in the game.

"You do. But will you? Is that how you're going to buy my forgiveness, Aidan?"

"I'm not buying anything. I'm not bribing you or coercing you.

"I know I fucked up, Savannah. I know I'll fuck up again. You can't leave every time I do that."

"I didn't leave," I snapped. "I chose not to argue with you. I chose to get some space. I chose not to hang out with your family today. I chose to come to people who know where someone in *my* family might have gone underground.

"I'm your wife. You're my husband. We have similar concerns, but that doesn't mean my priorities are your priorities and vice versa.

"I didn't leave. I retreated. I'd have said stupid shit to you in haste that would have prolonged the antagonism between us.

"I know myself too well, Aidan, not to react accordingly. You fucked up. You could have ruined my credibility by giving me false intel—"

"I needed to know that I could trust you."

I scoffed, "Me not publishing that information proved you can?"

"No. I've always trusted you on a personal level, Savannah. Even when I shouldn't have. Even when I didn't know you.

"If you were anyone else, after how you uncovered that Uncle Paddy faked his own death, I'd have had you killed," he rasped. "But I didn't. I protected you. I watched over you. I killed to keep you safe, and I made sure that your enemies paid with their lives—"

A shudder whispered down my spine.

"I've always trusted you when I shouldn't. But business is different. Business is dangerous. I was short-sighted and didn't realize that I already blurred those lines with you.

"My family is business. *We* are business. That's why I told you last night, Savannah. I wanted this bullshit out of the way. I didn't want it to fester overlong like it did with Finn and Aoife." He released a deep sigh. "I really am sorry, little one."

I pursed my lips at him, but Conor's words resonated in my head.

He'd come for me.

He was here for me.

"If you want a steak, get Lily to make it for you."

Hope flashed into being in his eyes.

He wasn't to know that Lily could burn hot water.

Forgiveness *could* taste like charred beef...

22

———

AIDAN

"HELLO."

For a second, I thought I'd drunk more than the two beers I'd allotted for myself, then I realized why I couldn't see the person who'd greeted me—she was short.

I stared down at the kid and shot her a wary smile. "Hello."

She peered up at me expectantly.

I peered down at her expectantly.

"I'm Katina," she prompted.

"I'm—"

"Oh, I know who you are."

"You do? One of the brothers told you who I am?"

"Nope. Star told me you're Aidan Jr. She says you're Conor's brother."

Star?

I cleared my throat. "She talked about us, huh?"

"Yep," was Katina's cheerful retort. "She says that not all monsters that hide under the bed are ugly."

My eyes flared. "Meaning that I'm a monster that hides under the bed?"

"That's Star's way of saying you're hot. It's her version of a compliment."

I twisted around to find that Savannah had come to my aid, which wasn't confirmation she'd forgiven me. That goddamn cat was still tucked in her arms, though: 'our' new pet.

Forgiveness felt as if it were incoming.

Her wry rejoinder had me rolling my eyes. "You think that's a compliment? Good thing I'm the one who praises *you*."

This conversation was worth it the second she blushed.

God, Savvie did that so rarely that it was a fucking treat when she did. Her cheeks could turn faintly pink, but when she blushed, she blossomed like a tomato.

It was both hilarious and endearing.

She shoved my arm. "Hush, you." To Katina, she beamed a smile. "Does Star talk about me?"

Katina nodded. "She told me about the time you ran away to L.A. together."

I choked on my sip of beer. "You ran away to L.A.?"

Savannah smirked. "Our dads told us we weren't allowed to join the circus."

"You tried to join the circus?!"

"Nah, they didn't get in," Katina answered me, her tone placid. "Star says that even in the Stone Age when she was a kid, adults didn't let twelve-year-olds work in the circus."

"You were twelve?!" I boomed.

Savannah laughed. "You look just like my dad did when we got home."

"I think I might spank you for that anyway. Jesus, Savannah."

"I was twelve! You can't spank me for something I did before I knew boys didn't have cooties. Just Camden."

Katina, apparently in the dark about spanking and its 'medicinal' purposes, giggled. "I like Camden." She twisted her hands together. "Star said that if I asked nicely, you'd get an autograph for me."

Savannah took a seat on the picnic bench behind us and plunked her face into her hand. The cat meowed but snatched at the opportunity to stalk off.

Peering through her fingers once the feline from hell had disappeared, she mumbled, "You know that if I do that, he'll never let me live it down, don't you?"

Katina seemed to recognize Savvie was teasing her.

"Star said that's why I had to ask you to ask him. She said that he's a pain in the ass, but I can't see how he'd be a pain in the ass." She sighed. "He's so pretty."

Savvie's lips curled inwards before she said, "I'll be sure to let him know that."

"You will? Do you think he's too old for me?" she queried wistfully.

"I really do. He's older than Star, and you said it yourself—she's from the Stone Age."

Considering Star, Savvie, and Camden were younger than me, I didn't appreciate the distinction.

"True."

"I tell you what. When Camden's in town, I'll get tickets for you, hmm?"

Her eyes blew wide. "You will?"

"Sure."

"For Alessa too?"

"Why not?"

Katina's face puckered. "Oh. Maverick wouldn't be able to go and I don't think Alessa would leave him."

"Why not?" I asked in surprise. It wasn't like Savvie had mentioned a specific date.

"He gets super bad headaches. When he has one, I have to be really quiet in the garden or it makes it worse, so I don't think he'd be able to go to a concert."

Savvie shrugged. "Alessa doesn't know me but Star and I are practically sisters. I tell you what—I'll get permission from her to take you. We can go ourselves."

Though I frowned at her, I didn't say anything. Just took a sip of beer.

"Thank you so much!" Katina cried. "That would be awesome,"

"You're welcome; I'm glad you think so. It'll be something you can tell Star too."

Katina hooted. "Star will be really happy. I wanted to go see him when he was in Cincinnati, but she said that she'd prefer to stick pins under her nails." She leaned in and whispered, "Anyone else, I'd say she was being melodramatic. But not Star."

When my lips twitched, I didn't have to worry about hiding my smile for long because she took off on a screech, shouting, "ALESSA! WHERE ARE YOU?! I NEED PERMISSION TO GO TO A CONCERT."

Over Led Zeppelin, the rowdy crowd, and a couple babies crying, she was audible.

Watching her race over to a woman who had a remarkable likeness to her, I happened to catch a glimpse of Cade vomiting into some chrysanthemums.

I hated those fucking flowers—they always reminded me of funerals. It was a Five Point tradition to have a casket covered in the damn things. White for truth.

Ha.

I arched a brow at Lucas who just rolled his eyes in dismissal.

Ah, the joys of being the eldest—a burden both of us bore.

Maybe we had more in common than I fucking thought.

Taking a seat beside Savvie, I asked, "What was that about with Katina?"

"What was what about?"

"Now I know you're trying to bullshit me."

Her sniff was another clue. "What are you talking about?"

"Why would you take her to Camden's concert?"

A smile danced on her lips. "You know I love his music."

"Yeah, love to hate," I mocked, even more suspicious now.

Her soft smile turned into a moue. "The way she talked about Star, it was like she's still talking to her. Don't you think?"

I dissected the short conversation and nodded. "It was like that, yes." I considered her. "That's why you're here? You want to know if she knows where Star is?"

"A little bit of this. A little bit of that."

"Helpful."

"Now you know how annoying it is to be given half the damn story."

"My story could get your sexy ass killed," I remarked.

"Yeah, sucks to be you that you fucked up and as an apology, you have to be truthful with me," she retorted smugly.

"I bet you're glad I lied, aren't you?"

"It's going to prove useful," she agreed, but her nail dug into my tee as she prodded me with her finger. "Don't do it again. I wasn't glad last night. I was fucking furious. And hurt." Her brow furrowed. "You hurt me, Aidan. I had five years of that when you made Casper look like a stalker. No more."

Sighing, I snagged her hand and raised it to my lips. "I'm sorry, little one."

"I don't want apologies," she dismissed, swallowing thickly. "I just want us to be honest with each other. I know that you think that isn't possible because of what you do, but you know I'll never go to the cops. You know I won't report anything that you don't want to be made public. You can trust me."

"I know I can, and you know that my concern is our enemies—" Agony splintered in my chest. "The idea of something happening to you like what happened to Ma, Savannah—" My mouth worked, and when our eyes met, hers widened as I rasped, "I'd make what Da did look *sane*.

"You don't understand what I feel for you, baby girl. You don't know what I will do to keep you safe, and this world ain't safe." I released a breath. "Last December... it was a stupid test, and I regretted it almost as soon as I fucking started it." I pressed my forehead against hers. "Shit got real with *everything* shortly afterward, and it just got pushed aside."

With our foreheads still connected, she tipped her chin up so she could kiss me. Her lips lingered on mine for a couple seconds.

"You trust me now?"

"I trusted you then," I said with no small degree of annoyance. That small degree was totally aimed at myself. I reached up and cupped her nape, keeping her in place as, against her mouth, I rasped, "I won't just kill for you, Savannah. I will *decimate* New York City for you. I will tear it apart and I won't put it back together again.

"I'll make Da's retaliation look like child's play. Do you understand? Do you know what's at stake if I share what you want me to share with you?"

Though she released a shaky breath, she whispered, "We can go to war together."

My jaw clenched at her words as I accepted that there was no going back.

She was all in.

I just hoped neither of us lived to regret it.

23

SAVANNAH

THIS TIME YESTERDAY, I'd predicted I'd be eating roasted beef or chicken with two types of potatoes, gravy so thick you could stand a spoon in it, green bean casserole, and cauliflower au gratin, not BBQ in the cold.

But I was glad to be here.

We stayed until it started getting dark and the brothers and their Old Ladies with kids began their short journeys home.

We could have stuck around longer—the party definitely wasn't stopping—but I really needed my husband's dick in a part of my body, *and* Cade, one of my guards, had had some kind of allergic reaction to a bite. He said he didn't need to head to the ER, but he kept on puking.

For both reasons, it was time to leave, but I was grateful for the escape. It was a brief prelude to a change in mine and Aidan's relationship. More than that, I'd gotten to know the women Star considered family.

Before we left, I headed to the restroom. That was when Katina popped up.

"Do you want to see Star's office?"

Surprise had me pausing in the hall. "I thought you'd gone to bed."

She snorted. "It's, like, nine PM. Star lets me stay up later."

Because I could imagine Star and boundaries weren't really a thing, I let it go. I wanted to see Star's office, after all. I just didn't feel like starting a turf war as I went snooping around Lily Lancaster's home on the hunt for her rooms.

"You don't mind showing me?" I asked softly.

"No. She said if you turned up then I had to take you in there."

I stilled. "She did?"

What fucking game are you playing, Star Sullivan?

"She did." Katina squinted at me. "Do you really mean it about taking me to that concert?"

"I do. Alessa said yes."

"Alessa thinks you don't mean it."

"Well, I do. I'm like Star—we don't break our promises."

That had her biting her lip. "I don't like it that she had to leave."

"I really don't like it either," I concurred with a pout that teased a small smile out of her. "So I bet you don't, honey. But you talk to her, don't you?"

She dipped her chin. "Almost every other day."

I tried to hide the fact that my heart started racing at her admission. "Do you know where she is?"

"I know where I can reach her if I need to," she hedged with all the suspicion of a kid who'd been in a foster home.

Squatting down in front of her so that she stood taller than me, I murmured, "When I was your age, I was the only person who used to get Star out of trouble."

"She said *she* got *you* out of trouble." She beamed a grin at me. "I think you were both bad."

"You'd be right," I said sheepishly. "But she was definitely worse."

Kat's grin widened before, abruptly, it sank. "She's not in the US right now."

"She isn't? Where is she?"

"I think Russia. I heard something the last time we talked and it reminded me of when Alessa and Amara are together. But it wasn't Ukrainian. I'd have recognized some of the words if it was."

Why the fuck would Star be in Russia?

I sucked in a breath. "I want to bring her home."

"You do?"

"I do. I want her to be happy, Kat."

"Me too." She peered down at her feet. "After my mom and dad died, I went to live with some really bad people."

Reaching over, I gently cupped her hand. "Did they hurt you?"

"No. Star got there before they did. She saved me." She angled her head back and, tugging on my hand, said, "I want to help bring her home. I want her to be back here where she belongs. With me."

Releasing a shuddery breath, I nodded. "I'll help do that. Don't worry."

"Come with me?"

"Of course."

She took me down some stairs then up some and along a few walkways that told me if I *had* tried to find it, I wouldn't have managed on my own.

Star's room was much like it had been when she was a kid—computers fucking everywhere. These were sleeker, of course. Newer. And, weirder still, they weren't running.

I had no idea why that choked me up more than anything.

Dead air.

Star never saw a computer that she didn't leave switched on at all times with some stupid program running.

Kat had pulled away to turn on the light, so I took that moment to lean against the doorjamb to catch my breath at the sight.

When Kat faced me again, her mouth turned down at the corners. "It's strange, isn't it? It used to have this weird smell in here, and it was always hot. Noisy, too. A constant soft, low hum," she whispered. "This isn't right. I don't like it."

"I agree. I don't either." I stepped into the room. "What did Star want you to show me?"

Silently, she moved over to one of several desks in here that had a laptop on it. "She wanted you to take this."

"Take it?" I asked warily.

"Yes." She picked it up and carried it over to me. "Here."

If that laptop had any security information from the MC on it, then my taking it was a declaration of fucking war.

My hands balled into fists.

But if I didn't accept it, then Conor couldn't have it. That had to be Star's end game—for Conor to have it.

I released a breath and took it from her. It wasn't a large laptop, more like a mini, and I knew I could smuggle it back with me under my shirt.

With the chilled metallic frame against my heated palms, I tucked it under my arm and reached into my purse. Drawing out a card and a pen, I jotted down my address on the back of it and handed it to her.

"If you need anything, Kat, *anything*, you can come to me, okay?"

She peered down at the address. "Conor lives in this building, doesn't he?"

"You know who Conor is?"

"Sure. Star talks about him all the time." She released a sniff. "She says I talk about Camden too much, but she's just as bad. It's aCooooig this and aCooooig that."

Her words rammed home my belief that whatever Star was doing went against the Five Points.

If she had feelings for Conor like I suspected, then cutting ties in this way was how she could justify it.

What the fuck had she done?

The only thing I could imagine that Conor wouldn't forgive her for was—

The rush of blood to my head almost had me stumbling back into the door again.

Aidan Sr.

She…

No.

She couldn't have pulled that hit, could she?

"Savannah?" Kat questioned, her voice sharper than I'd heard it so far. "What is it? What's wrong?"

I shook my head. "N-Nothing."

"Are you sure?" she asked dubiously.

"I'm sure," I rasped. "I-I'd better go, Kat. Aidan will be waiting for me."

She tucked the card I'd given her into her pocket. "Do you know how to make it back downstairs?"

"I think so. Did you stay awake to speak with me?"

"No, but I hung around to catch you on your own. I hope you bring her home soon. I miss her," she said simply, nearly fucking breaking my heart with the admission.

Star had left her behind.

She'd left me behind.

She'd left Conor behind.

Whatever she was doing, it was a thousand times worse than I could imagine.

I'd come here chasing answers, and now that I almost had them, I was terrified of what I was going to uncover.

Kat and I parted with a soft farewell, and I scurried back toward the party, still on the hunt for a restroom.

I used it, then I grabbed my cellphone, and I called Conor.

He answered immediately. "'Sup?"

"I spoke with Katina."

A harsh breath escaped him. "Any news?"

"She says she thinks Star's in Russia. They're talking every other night, and Star left me something."

"What?" he demanded, his tone harder than I'd ever heard from him before.

Star's leaving, Senior's death—they'd been rough on Conor. I didn't take offense because I felt his pain.

"A laptop. Can you access it remotely?"

"Maybe. Have you turned it on?"

"Not yet. I haven't even opened the lid."

"Do it now."

"Okay. I don't have long. Aidan will come looking for me soon. I just wanted you to have this information now."

"You've no idea how much I appreciate that, Savannah."

Oh, I did, and I didn't need him to tell me how much.

The second I opened the lid, a piece of paper fluttered with the movement.

A note.

Star's scrawl was there in black and white.

"She left a note."

"What does it say?"

"*Savannah, this computer has never been hooked up to the internet. I need you to go online by piggybacking off your cellular data. If you don't know how to do that, Conor will help. BUT you must connect it to your phone first.*

I hope I see you again.

Star."

I let out a ragged sob before I could stop myself.

"Everything she sends me feels like a goodbye."

"I know," he snarled. "Goddamn her for doing this alone when she isn't anymore."

His words hit home because I genuinely didn't know if Star knew that.

Even when she'd been surrounded by the *noxxious* family, not just the relatives but the extended members, the non-creep roadies who had traveled with us all our lives, the backup singers who'd been around since we were kids... she'd been alone.

She was that kind of person.

"Are you hooking it up to your phone?"

"I'm going to now."

Switching on the hotspot function on my cell, I turned on the laptop. There was no password which was weird for Star, but it let me connect to my cell easily enough.

"Now what?" I groused.

"What's going on with your phone?"

"Noth—" I peered at it in surprise. "Oh!"

"What?!" he barked.

"It powered down."

"Turn it back on."

I did as he said, then I heard clicking on the other end of the line. "What are you doing?"

"Remotely accessing your phone to see what she's up to." He let out a triumphant snarl a couple minutes later. "I'm in."

"Into what?"

He didn't need to answer.

The laptop wasn't showing a regular desktop anymore. It had gone black, but not like with my phone. There was a glow to it, and a command made an appearance.

'Permit remote access from external IP address?'

"Hit 'Y.'"

I hit 'Y.'

Nothing happened.

My heart sank.

"Did I do something wrong?"

"No."

His fingers went wild then. Endless tapping in my ear that I swore was going to give me PTSD the next time I heard it. Not exactly helpful considering I was a fucking writer.

I didn't interrupt, just stayed on the line because I knew he'd have cut the call otherwise.

Another couple sounds rattled in my ear as I took a seat on the toilet and stared blankly around the swanky bathroom.

Then, finally, he hissed, "Got it. When you can get to my apartment, come and bring the laptop with you."

He cut the line, leaving me swearing at the vanity. That was, of course, when a knock sounded on the door.

"Savvie?"

Aidan.

I surged off the seat, opened the door, grabbed his hand, and hauled him inside.

A smirk danced on his lips until he saw that I wasn't pulling him in here for a quickie.

"What is it?" he demanded, his urgent tone in response to my expression.

I slammed the computer against his chest. "I need you to hide this."

"Who does it belong to?"

Standing on tiptoe, I pressed my lips to his ear. "Star. She told Katina to give it to me."

"Are you fucking kidding me?"

"No. I'm not."

His nostrils flared as he tugged on the hem of his tee, dragged it up—it was a testament to my state of mind that I didn't ogle his abs—and then hooked it against his waistband, grimacing at the sudden cold.

"I guess I should be grateful you're wearing boxer briefs for once," I drawled as I watched him zip up his jacket to cover the new 'smoothness' of his abdomen.

"Not funny," he sniped.

"I think it's hilarious actually." Shooting him a quick grin, I murmured, "I'll explain in the car."

His dark stare told me without a word that *damn straight* I'd be explaining in the car.

"Good thing it's a long ride home," I mused. "We've got some sharing to do."

Though he snorted, he just curved his hand around my arm and guided me out of the restroom.

Thankfully, no one was there to witness us departing together. I wouldn't have minded normally, but because we were smuggling something out that the MC might not be happy about, I was grateful for the reprieve.

We said farewell to the hosts, Link shaking Aidan's hand while I kissed Lily on the cheek. She'd talked to me about her new position working for the foundations Rachel, Rex's Old Lady, had started, and I'd offered to help out where I could.

We parted as friends, but that didn't stop me from releasing a heavy sigh as soon as we were heading for my car.

Except...

"You boxed me in," I groused the second I saw how he'd parked his goddamn tank of an SUV. The new model of 'city-chic armored vehicle' made his old car look swank.

"Bet your ass I did," Aidan retorted. "We'll ride home in mine. Lucas will arrange for someone to collect your car tomorrow."

"Cade's still too sick to drive?"

"Let's put it this way, Lucas will need to sanitize the interior once they get back to the city."

My nose crinkled, but all I asked was, "Do Lily and Link mind if we leave the car here?"

"No. I squared it with them earlier. Whichever guard Lucas sends will collect your cat too."

My mouth rounded. "Shit, I forgot about the cat."

Aidan rolled his eyes. "This is a disaster waiting to happen. I bet I end up feeding the little fucker."

"I managed not to kill Teabag."

Though that was a long ass time ago.

My lips curved as we rounded the SUV with my elbow in his grip, and after he opened the door and helped me up then leaned in and fastened my seatbelt for me, I watched him head back to the driver's seat.

It was ridiculously archaic to have him open doors and fasten my seatbelt for me, but I loved every fucking moment of his chivalry.

I was as much of a feminist as any woman—hell, I went above and beyond in some instances—but we really were missing out with all this BS.

No, I didn't need a man to do anything for me, but that he was foreshadowing my movements, his complete and utter attention aimed at me, the only one suffering from inequality there was him.

Not me.

The thought sent a shiver rushing down my spine.

Power. Not just any power though—an intrinsically feminine power over a man who'd told me he'd destroy New York City for me.

Goddammit, who needed porn when you had a man who'd promise you *that?*

He opened the door, bringing with him the scent of gas from the driveway where a couple of bikers had just driven off, lingering notes from the bonfire out back, and then him.

Aidan.

My husband.

The mobster who was going to tell me all the Points' dirty little secrets.

At least, he'd better.

I wasn't above milking this situation for everything I could get.

"Don't look at me like that," he rumbled.

"Like what?"

"Like you want me to fuck you in the driveway."

"We don't lie to each other, do we?"

He gritted his teeth at my taunt; I watched the cording of his muscles in the light above the dash as he sneakily pulled out the laptop and handed it to me so I could stow it away behind his seat.

"No lies, but I'll accept half-truths about sex because I can't fuck you with my guards behind us and a bunch of goddamn bikers a few hundred feet away, Savvie."

My lips twisted into a smile. "Shame. Although... I never was into exhibitionism. Unless you're the one I'm showing off for."

The growl he released had my heart pumping, but he ignored me, climbed behind the wheel, and triggered the button that started the engine.

Only once we'd headed down the meandering driveway and made it onto the open road did he say, "I bought a flogger last week."

My pussy clenched. "Interesting."

"Isn't it? You're lucky that I still feel like a piece of shit for letting you down or you'd have earned a flogging."

I smirked into the darkness. "Earn—meaning you'll reward bad behavior?"

"Savvie," he snarled.

"What, Aidan?" I jeered. "Tell me you don't fucking love that I answer back. That I don't just let you roll over me."

His hand shot out to grab mine. His hold was firm and steady as he bridged our fingers together and placed them on his knee.

"Now isn't the time for this conversation." I huffed at his words, but he snapped, "You just had me smuggle a computer out of a Sinner's house, Savannah. That's guaranteed to make an enemy out of an ally. What the hell's on there that she needs you to have?"

"I don't know, but Star really did want me to have it. There was a note for me and everything."

"Just because she gave you permission to have its contents doesn't mean the Sinners feel the same."

"No," I conceded. "I know."

"What's going on with Star?"

For the first time, my confidence was shaken.

Not for myself, but for her.

Star—my sister from another mister.

I had to protect her, but protecting her meant lying to Aidan, and after our falling out, I couldn't play him false like that. Not without there being repercussions.

Trust, after all, was a two-way street.

Damn, Mom would be proud of me for thinking that.

"It's hard to explain," I said, reaching up to rub at my tired eyes.

"When Rex's father died, he left behind a treasure trove of information. She sent that to Conor before she left."

"What kind of information in particular?"

His phrasing had me frowning. "About the Sparrows. Conor hasn't discussed this with you?"

"I know there's a lot of information, and I know that unless I ask for specifics, it'd be like asking Siri to recount the dictionary. Tell me what's pertinent."

He had a point. "I can explain what I know. I don't have all the facts. That's how Star works. You never know everything. Sometimes it's so she has the upper hand, and sometimes it's because she wants to keep you safe."

"What is it in this instance?"

"Neither," I admitted softly. "I think she's in so deep that she doesn't know how to get back out. I think she's gotten mixed up in something so fucking crazy that she knows she's going to die."

"Jesus. Conor knows that? He loves her, Savannah."

"I know he does. I've seen it with my own eyes. Why do you think I'm helping him?"

He raised our joined hands to his lips to kiss my knuckles. "Thank you on his behalf."

Heat flushed through me. "I'm not doing it for you."

"No, you're doing it for your family. He's your family now."

God, he was right.

Conor *was* family.

The O'Donnellys weren't just mobsters that I drooled over from afar. That I kept obsessive tabs on like a stalker because they were my idea of a celebrity.

They were my kin.

I sucked in a breath. "I think she was involved in your father's death, Aidan."

While I expected him to lose his shit, he didn't.

Instead, he shook his head. "She can't have had anything to do with Da's death. I know who killed him, Savannah, and it wasn't Star."

I twisted in my seat. "You told me that he framed himself, but... You know who killed him?"

"I even know where the bastard is right now."

"What?! He's still alive?"

"He is. But only by the skin of his teeth."

"I don't understand."

"What do you know about the ECD?"

"The Irish freedom fighters? What about them? Are the Points involved with the ECD?"

He grunted. "More than we'd like. My grandfather was the leader."

"Which parent?"

"Ma's."

"Makes sense." Years of genealogical research on his family, both sides, came to my aid. "Was your father?"

"He was inveigled with them, and I know he supported the idea of a unified Ireland, but as per fucking usual, he was all smoke and hot air.

"Aoife's uncle, Savannah, is the current leader of the ECD."

In the light from the dash, I saw that he'd turned to flash me a glance, but he didn't have to bother because I wasn't looking at him.

I was piecing together the roots of what made humans human.

Lena had killed Aoife's mother.

Yet Lena lived.

Aidan Sr. had been shot by Aoife's uncle.

A, B... C.

"I know that he sacrificed himself for her," I whispered. "But this is unprecedented."

The tangled web was so knotted that I couldn't figure out if he was right or not—was Star involved in Senior's death like I suspected?

There were too many ways in which a woman like Star could dig her own grave.

"Why haven't you repaid the favor?" It was all I could think to ask.

"Because I found out his location through sheer luck, and if he uncovers my source, she's in danger."

"She?"

"Remember I told you that Da had a stake in a club? Well, it's a brothel. Aoife's uncle, Eamonn Keegan, is a client."

"That's why you left in the early hours the other night, isn't it?" I demanded, every possessive bone in my body not appreciating that he'd gone to a brothel—for business or not.

"Partially. A Five Pointer had killed one of her girls, and she wanted me to make him pay."

I blinked. "MacMurray?"

"Yes."

"He's the one involved with the Russians—"

"Yes. I learned Jonesy is with the ECD too."

"God, he *is*—?" I broke off. "Who the fuck can we trust, Aidan?"

"Family, Savannah. Family. That's who we trust." His hand tightened around mine. "It'll be all right, little one."

"I don't need you to coddle me, Aidan," I retorted calmly, but I clutched at his hand so he'd know I wasn't being contrary. "What's the plan?" When he stayed silent, I tugged on his fingers. "Aidan, talk to me."

"What was your gut instinct when I told you that Keegan had killed Da?"

"I asked why he was still alive."

"Da sacrificed himself, but the blood of Keegan's sister rests on the hands of my family. My father, for all his fucking sins, believed in an eye for an eye. That's why he accepted his fate and was even pleased to have found a way out.

"We're talking Aoife's mom, Savannah. Not just Keegan's sister."

"Where does an eye for an eye end?" I whispered, seeing where he was going with this.

"Exactly. I kill Keegan, so Finn has the right to kill me on his wife's behalf? And then Brennan takes out Finn for coming after me?"

"That'd never happen."

"I'm not saying it would, but it could. That's how revenge works."

"What are you thinking?"

"I'm thinking crazy shit, Savannah. The worst."

"Explain."

"The Sparrows are dying, but cancer doesn't quit without leaving a mark on every cell in a body.

"There are more than just the NWS, did you know that?"

"I did. A European faction and an Asian one."

He nodded. "Then there's the ECD. They're intrinsically linked to us. Our cause used to be their cause before Da found capitalism and became its whore.

"And then we have the Points. Diversifying into real estate while still dealing with the worst of the worst."

"Aidan," I rasped, watching his hand tighten around the wheel. "Tell me what you're thinking. I already know all this. Where are you going with it?"

We pulled up at an intersection, and with his face tilted toward me once more, and with that ethereal glow from the dash on his features, a glow that seemed to grow more intense with every word he uttered, he intoned, "There's only one solution, Savannah. Three factions, one head."

That was when the twin lights glowed even brighter than before.

As I squinted against it, it came tunneling into us. Barreling closer until Aidan slammed his foot on the accelerator to try to get away, making both of us buck forward.

But it was too late.

I screamed.

The collision was already in motion.

Our fate was in someone else's hands.

24

CONOR

HEAD ON COLLISION - NEW FOUND GLORY

ME: *Jonesy's left Manhattan. Any idea why he'd be heading in your direction?*

Me: *Aidan?*

Today had been hell.

Literal hell, and I already knew it wasn't anywhere near over. Not just because of what I'd uncovered, not only because of what Savannah had sent to me via Star, but because I'd gotten an alert that Jonesy had left Manhattan and was approaching Jersey.

Suspicious in itself when we had no business that way and our territory was definitely not in the Garden State, but once I sent the message to Aidan, I allowed my attention to shift to what I'd been working on for months.

Something that had culminated in my DDoS attack yesterday—the security breach in the elite crypto exchange where I was currently rifling through blockchain after blockchain in an attempt to match addresses to identities.

Star's gift was helping.

The powerful worm she'd allowed me to access was tearing through the exchange at an unprecedented rate, making connection after connection that would save me hours of time; essential as the exchange was working on locking me out.

Annoyingly, my zero-day exploit had a half-life of thirty hours.

Celebrities and criminals alike were exposed as the worm went to work, linking IDs to payments, putting faces to anonymous bits of code that enabled me to see the extent of the Sparrows' clientele.

My hands curled into fists just thinking about what I'd discovered.

A shopping website—*for people.*

Transactions made as if those people were simply objects.

And this was only in the dawn of the crypto era.

What about before, when crypto was a glint in Satoshi Nakamoto's pseudonymous eye?

How many financial transactions had been deleted when paper pushers could fudge the numbers?

I existed on the dark web. It was my playground. I knew what went on, was aware that the seedy side was so much worse than the Feds would ever realize, but Star had been on that site.

I'd seen her fucking listing.

Like she was a bottle of shower gel or a goddamn tee shirt.

I knew what they'd trained her to do. I knew what she'd been forced to learn. I'd seen pictures I wanted to scour from my brain.

The men and women who'd bought her...

I wanted to kill them all.

Tear them apart.

So fucking many had tried to break my woman, but she was still standing. Still strong. Still somewhere not here, but fuck.

Fuck.

I let my forehead connect with the glass surface of my desk—a new one I'd had shipped in overnight because I'd shattered the other when I'd first come across her listing—and the cold chilled my heated flesh.

No wonder she was so afraid to trust.

No wonder she preferred to do this shit alone.

She'd been sold out by our government.

By her bosses.

She'd learned that the only person she could trust was herself.

I needed to prove her wrong.

I was here now. She had me. I'd slit my throat before I ever betrayed her how she'd been betrayed in the past.

We had issues; she was somehow involved in my da's hit—though I had a feeling she was the reason Keegan had a GSW—and she'd decided to leave when we could have joined forces, but none of that mattered now.

Perfect for the individual who likes non-consensual interactions with a slave who will respond aggressively.

Just remembering her listing made me want to kill someone.

No, nothing mattered but getting her back home.

Safe. Sound. No longer alone. No longer dealing with her past on her own.

My cell rang, the vibration hitting me differently because of how my face was connected with the desk, and I blindly picked it up. Shoving it beneath the surface, I stared at the caller ID through the glass and frowned.

Lucas Frasier.

I frowned and hit the connect button. "Lucas?"

"They're fucking gone, Conor. They're gone."

Surprise at his tone had me jerking upright, querying, "Who's gone?"

"Aidan and Savannah. Their car's a fucking wreck. We're at the Clinton Avenue and Union Street intersection in West Orange. It's here, but they aren't."

My brain took too many seconds to compute what the hell was going on, but as his words registered, I shoved against the desk and used the momentum to wheel over to the other where my Five Points' work was open on three different desktops.

"Kidnapped?"

"That has to be what happened. The doors are wide open—"

"Give me a moment," I interrupted, hacking into the satellite Star had given me access to before she left and using it to find static images of him standing beside a SUV that was veered to the side, skewed against the traffic lights.

There was no traffic around, however; probably because it was close to ten at night on a Sunday.

"T-boned?" I demanded as I zoomed in.

"Yeah."

That was when the part of my brain that was dedicated to family switched off.

I couldn't think about my brother and sister-in-law, about what they were enduring, where they were. I just had to get them out of wherever *there* was. And had to figure out the who.

"Signs of blood?" I rapped out.

"No. The airbags were deployed though."

"The windshield held firm?"

"Of course, it's bulletproof. It's an armored vehicle, Conor. Most of the damage is purely external. I don't understand how the fuck they got them out of there unless—"

Unless they had a key.

Neither of us said that out loud.

Jonesy had been heading into Jersey... He was a common denominator that was easy to scratch off the list of potential suspects.

Even as a part of me was hoping it was him so I'd know who was behind this, the other part that was tired of being betrayed by men who were supposed to be loyal to us was thoroughly on edge as my fingers raced across the keyboard while I pinpointed Jonesy's location.

Of the thousands of traces I was running, his was the only one that wasn't black. His was red so I could see that little fucking flea from every vantage point.

Getting rid of the other trackers to make it easier on my fatigued eyes, I watched as said flea crossed through Mid Island as I zoomed in to watch his trajectory.

A coincidence that he was avoiding Five Point territory?

Nope.

Coincidences didn't exist in my world.

"I'm so fucking sorry, Conor. Cade started puking again, and I had to pull over. He needs to go to the goddamn ER, but—"

I didn't let him finish. "I need you to get that SUV off the road, Lucas. Can you do that?"

His rambling stalled. "Yeah. Of course."

"Leave Cade in your vehicle. I'm going to get some EMTs out to see to him. I need you to take that SUV back to Sinners' territory. There should be a laptop somewhere in there. Bring that to me when you can. Can you do that?"

A breath escaped him, but his tone was back to its usual cold rasp as he stated, "Affirmative."

I hit up 911 and had an ambulance sent to Lucas and Cade's location.

"Stay on the line," I ordered, listening in the background as he quickly explained to Cade what was happening, then I heard the sound of running and an engine starting.

"How did they get a key?"

"Someone on your crew must have sold him out."

A sharp breath sounded in my ear. "Conor, it wasn't—"

"Never said it was you or Cade. Doubt you'd have called this in if it was." Never say never, though. People did crazier shit in an effort to look innocent. But Lucas, I knew, was proud to be Aidan's captain. He wouldn't fuck that up. Not for anything. "Aidan's earned no loyalty with his men. You can't deny that."

Lucas fell silent before he sighed. "No. I can't."

Any other time, my lips would have curved. "I appreciate your candor."

"Will it earn me a bullet to the skull?"

"Only if you're the one who gave them the key to copy," I dismissed.

"I didn't. Neither did Cade."

"He's making waves. It was bound to piss people off."

"Wait. You don't just think someone on his crew sold him out, you also think a Five Pointer kidnapped them?" he bit off, his bewilderment clear.

That was what I liked about the Frasiers—they were soldiers through and through.

"I think it was Jonesy. He left Manhattan tonight and entered Jersey for no good reason."

I needed to check the old bastard's location history but first, I needed to get my shit in line.

"I don't understand," Lucas mumbled.

"You don't have to. Mickey, Jamie, Connolly—anyone there have a friendship with MacMurray? To Jonesy?" He went quiet, letting me know that he was thinking, so I told him, "I'm calling Rex, the Sinners' Prez, to get him to let you on his compound. Stay on the phone."

"Okay."

The engine shifted gear and I could hear the sound of a dirt track as I pulled up another line.

"What?"

I didn't blame Rex for being pissed, not considering the time of night when he had a newborn daughter to care for.

"This is Conor O'Donnelly, Rex. One of my men is heading for your compound with my brother's SUV—"

"What? Why?"

"I need you to let him park the vehicle there," I continued as if he hadn't interrupted. "It's been involved in a crash."

"A crash? Aidan Jr. crashed his car?"

I could have lied.

I could have.

I didn't like sharing Five Points' weaknesses—even with an ally— but Star considered the Sinners family.

If I expected her to have faith in me, in my people, then I had to have faith in her people too.

"He and his wife have been kidnapped." I stunned myself with how clinical my voice sounded, but panic had no place here. Not when I fully intended for Aidan and Savannah to be home before the night was over. "I'm going to need that information to stay between us."

"Understood," was Rex's cool retort. "You need any help?"

"No." I paused. "Maybe. I think we have it covered. I just need you to shelter the vehicle so the cops don't come sniffing around."

"I can hear a car racing up the road. That's one of your guys?"

"It's Aidan's captain—Lucas. If you could give him a ride back to his SUV, I'd appreciate it. It's at the Clinton Avenue and Union Street intersection."

"Fine. His brother still sick?"

"Apparently. I just called an ambulance for him."

A hum sounded in my ear. "I'll get the Prospect to open the gates." He paused a second. "Call me in if you need back up."

"Star trusts you," I rasped, aware that this was the first time the pitch of my voice changed.

"You can too."

"I hope so," I rumbled. "Thank you for your help. The favor will be extended in turn."

"Appreciate that."

He cut the call first, allowing me to say to Lucas, "The gates will be opening and you can park the car there. They'll take you to your vehicle. Get your ass back to Manhattan ASAP and if I don't send you a new address before then, head for my building. Don't forget that goddamn laptop."

I didn't wait for a reply, just ended our conversation before I watched the little red dot that was Jonesy's car.

With some breathing room now the SUV was off the road and out of the line of sight of the authorities, I pulled up the location history on Jonesy's tracker.

His vehicle had come to a stop at the Clinton Avenue and Union Street intersection where the collision had occurred.

Occam's Razor never let me fucking down.

That didn't mean the confirmation sat right with me. Not because I doubted my eyes, but because Jonesy had been around longer than I fucking had.

How could he betray us like this?

How the fuck could he have done this?

I needed to get my brothers involved, I knew that, but I had nothing concrete.

You didn't arm a nuke without setting a location for said nuke to land.

I shifted the GPS tracker onto my phone so I could watch out for Jonesy's end destination. As he drove through Mid Island, then crossed the Verrazzano-Narrows Bridge into fucking Brooklyn, my heart sank lower and lower.

When he continued onto the I-278 E, rage replaced dread.

The second he hit the Belt Parkway, I knew where he was heading—fucking Bratva territory.

Brighton Beach.

Because I had the worst luck, that was when my other computer notified me that the search on the crypto transactions I'd been tracing was complete.

Attention split because I could be thrown out of the exchange at any given moment, I didn't text my brothers as had been my intention. I triggered a group call instead so that I could work and talk at the same time.

"Conor?" Finn grumbled around a yawn.

Eoghan sniped, "What's going on?"

My fingers clacked against the keys as I raced to withdraw as much information as I could from the site while Declan groused, "Some of us have a baby and appreciate all the Zs we can get."

"Shut up," Brennan snapped. "Conor wouldn't have called us unless there's a problem. Why isn't Aidan in the group call, Kid?"

I had no idea why, but his use of their stupid nickname for me helped me breathe.

I inhaled noisily and released it just as fiercely, but the blast of oxygen helped clear my head.

"Because Jonesy fucking kidnapped him," I rasped. With the clock running down on me, I tried to explain as clearly as I could, "Got a call from Lucas saying his vehicle was found abandoned at an intersection in Jersey—"

"Jersey? What the fuck was Junior doing in Jersey? Is that why he wasn't at Ma's today?" Eoghan questioned.

"Savannah went to speak with the Sinners. He was going after her. Look, this isn't what matters. Their car was T-boned and they weren't at the scene—"

"Jonesy wouldn't fucking dare kidnap Aidan," Brennan growled.

"Aidan's been kidnapped?" I heard Camille shriek in the background, but I couldn't deal with her emotions on top of the fuck ton of tabs I had open in my brain.

Shutting her out, I cast a glance at the download bar as I pulled out every ounce of data I could from the exchange and rasped, "Jonesy's tracker says otherwise, Brennan. And he's heading into Bratva territory as we fucking speak."

"Those pieces of shit—"

"Fucking bastards."

As they spoke over each other, a quick look at the GPS tracker revealed that the vehicle had finally veered off the parkway and was heading into the city—that was when I accepted I had to make my retreat from the crypto exchange.

With only seventy-five percent of the information I'd hoped to attain.

Dammit to hell.

Shoving that disappointment aside, I wheeled over to the main computer where Jonesy's tracker was running and I had a more detailed map at my disposal.

"You know of any place in Brighton Beach where they could take him and lie low?" I asked them.

"There are a couple warehouses near the wastewater treatment plant," Declan grated out.

"Is he driving past Sheepshead Bay?" Brennan demanded.

Though he couldn't see me, I nodded.

"Words, Kid, words," Finn rasped, as if he knew where my head was at.

I swallowed, inhaled. "Yeah, he's slowing down—" I used my satellite access to try and pin down any photos I could find of him.

"How are you tracking him?"

"Gave him and the rest of Da's detail a gift," I told Eoghan absentmindedly.

"What kind of gift?" was his suspicious reply.

"Knicks keychains."

"They were bugged?"

"Yup."

Finn grunted. "Those assholes deserve to get their nuts nailed to the ground. Who the fuck'd think you were giving them gifts?"

"I think I should be offended. I give great gifts."

"Now's not the time for this argument," Brennan groused.

"Because I wasn't at the warehouse," I admitted, "I think they think I don't agree with Aidan."

Silence fell at my words, until, "Is that true?"

Eoghan.

I snorted.

"No. I wasn't there because I had bigger fish to fry."

"Like what?" Declan asked warily.

"My woman."

"You want to fry her?" Eoghan mocked.

"Not the time," Brennan snapped out the warning, and while I didn't need him to defend me, I appreciated him cutting me some slack.

Rustling sounded that made me realize Finn was getting dressed as he queried, "How did you give them keychains and they didn't suspect you?"

"Fuck, let it go, Finn. Let's be grateful they did—"

"Brennan, this could be a goddamn trap!"

He had a point.

"It could be, but I don't think so. I got them made up special."

Declan mumbled, "You did?"

"You remember that Easter game Da took his guards to back in 2012? Knicks vs. Bulls?"

"How the fuck do you remember that?" Brennan rumbled, but in the background, I heard the undeniable sound of a gun being loaded.

"Had to listen to him crow about it for months. You forget, he used to talk to me not just beat me up like he did with the rest of you."

The unmissable click of a flick knife sounded in my ear before Declan hissed under his breath. "No arguing with that."

"Anyway, the Knicks were playing to make sure they had a chance at getting into the playoffs. The Bulls were conference leaders, and they were making it known. Melo drained three and took them to OT. They beat their asses with one point to spare. It was a big deal." Jonesy was circling around the wastewater treatment plant. Attention on that, I muttered, "I got them tickets made of brass to commemorate the night. Told 'em how much Da appreciated them, and how much I appreciated them. Told them the story, and that was that."

"They believed you?" Finn asked.

"Yup." I thought they had, anyway.

Time would tell.

The pinhead that was Jonesy stopped pulsing and my heart almost fucking did too.

Zooming in on him via satellite, I saw he was driving a pick-up truck.

Thanking God that I hadn't tracked their vehicles but the men themselves, I started taking photos, trying to see if I could get a look inside.

No dice.

"What are you doing, Kid? Send us a location. We'll be on our way," Brennan ordered.

"I don't want to send you the wrong address," I mumbled, switching from the satellite as I hacked into the traffic cams, thanking God for the asshole mayors who'd made East New York the most surveilled neighborhood in all three boroughs.

Watching him drive down Knapp Street, I chanted, "Come on, come on."

A couple minutes later, he turned left into a driveway.

"Gotcha," I rasped and, as the gates opened and he drove onto the compound, I sent them all the coordinates then mused out loud, "I think it's a fishing dock. Or the front is that. It's near the marina.

"Eoghan, do you know the area?"

"I do. I'll get into the wastewater plant. That's the tallest building around there. I'll hit you up for security passes when I'm at the gates, Conor."

"I'll work on it," I concurred, my fingers sliding over the keyboard again as I worked to get him the 'key' he'd need.

"Game plan?" Declan demanded as the whirring of elevator doors sounded in the background.

I heard a kiss, then an unhappily whispered, "Be safe, Brennan. I love you," from Camille.

Finn said, "Aidan's friendlier with the Russians than us—"

"You spoke with Maxim at Christmas, Brennan," I pointed out.

"I watched as Aidan spoke with them," he disregarded. "But I'll contact the Pakhan. Aidan told me the Don said he's in fucking Moscow though."

"We wade in there and cause shit, we're starting a war with the Russians," Finn warned, his feet clicking against what sounded like concrete. I heard the squeal of tires a few minutes later.

"I'll deal with that," Brennan muttered. "By the time we're at the dock, I'll have it cleared."

"We get in and we get out," Declan stated.

"Agreed. I'll pick out anyone who tries to fuck with that," Eoghan vowed.

"What about Jonesy?" Finn questioned.

"What about him?" I mumbled.

"Dead or alive?"

"Can't question a dead man." Brennan ground out, "And don't cut out his tongue until we get him to talk because that was a fucking nightmare with MacMurray."

My lips twitched at his aggrieved tone. "It rammed the point home with the firm."

"It rammed something fucking home," Brennan growled as his engine started. "Okay, leave it with me. I'll see you on the other side, *dearthāirs.*"

That was the cue for everyone to cut the call. That didn't mean I didn't listen to the dead air for a couple seconds.

My brain raced ahead, trying to figure out how to get them what they'd need before they needed it, planning to help them keep their asses out of the line of fire.

As I sent them security footage from the nearby buildings of the lay of the land, I switched gears onto the wastewater plant and its piss poor security.

Cracking my knuckles, I got to work on gaining access so my baby bro could set up a sniper's nest there.

It was easier to think about that than to think that the last thing I'd said to my oldest brother was an order not to fuck up his marriage...

25

SAVANNAH

CINDERELLA'S DEAD - EMELINE

I CAME AROUND in the truck.

Consciousness wasn't like an on and off switch but a slow, grating awakening that involved a headache that was worse than the hangover from a three-night bender Star, Camden, and I had enjoyed when we were kids in Vegas.

I knew *this* wasn't Vegas, was well aware that Camden was in L.A. right now getting his ass handed to him in a private casino and that Star was only the fuck knew where in Russia.

Someone had T-boned us.

The airbags—something had gone wrong. I could feel the burns on my throat and cheeks.

We'd been kidnapped.

Fucking kidnapped.

I remembered the locks clicking as the car doors opened from the outside and we were dragged out onto the road. I'd passed out when my head had collided with the asphalt.

Goddammit, that's why my skull ached like a motherfucker!

Aware that I couldn't groan, that I couldn't even rub my forehead, that I couldn't do anything, I tried to stay as still as was possible within my current position, but the urge to see if I was with Aidan or not was overwhelming.

As was the need to vomit.

Was Aidan alive? Dead?

He'd been quiet in the aftermath of the crash. Too quiet. I remembered that much. Had he passed out from the pain of whatever the air bags did to him, or did he have internal injuries from the crash? Was he dying as I lay here trying not to move?

Everything was fixable, but you couldn't fix death. So he wasn't allowed to be dead. It just wasn't happening.

My lips trembled at the thought.

We had so much to do!

So many things still to accomplish together.

He could *not* be dead. I refused to believe it.

Point blank.

He was dead only when someone forced me to stare into a set of blank eyes that didn't crinkle at the corners when he looked at me.

They always crinkled.

Even when I'd done something to piss him off.

It was as if, deep down, something about me always made his soul smile.

I bit my lip to stop that train of thought—it'd get me nowhere fast and would only lead to sobbing that'd let our kidnappers know that I was awake.

Instead, I did something useful—I took stock of my situation.

Something covered me, something like a blanket but it didn't warm me through. A tarp? Could be. It had shifted off my face with movement from the road.

My hands were taped together, my feet too—tight enough that it dug into my flesh. Not in the nice way that happened when Aidan was mad at me, either.

Still, I was used to being tied up, and I was beyond accustomed to wriggling around when restrained, but I didn't dare until I knew where we were.

Behind my closed eyes, something changed—it went from a darker light to a more intense kind. The traffic noises shifted too.

Staying as still as possible, I allowed my eyes to open into slits. Peering through the one that wasn't covered by the tarp, mostly, I saw streetlights, and I had to slither my eyelids into slits because the bright glare tore my retinas into shreds, burning them as if it were an acid.

My ears picked up some of the slack, and the amount of traffic made me think...

Were we crossing a bridge?

My woozy mind tried to imagine a map from Jersey to Manhattan, but it'd make no sense to drive us straight through Five Points' territory.

Maybe Mid Island?

My anxiety wouldn't let me rest. It became imperative that I figure out where the hell I was.

Expansion joints—the truck rattled every time we crossed one. We were definitely on a bridge.

Struggling to find a sign, I squinted and strained, finally seeing one for 'Verrazzano-Narrows Bridge - Staten Island.'

So, he *had* taken us through Mid Island. We *were* in Brooklyn.

Russian territory.

But the Russians were our allies.

Amid the chaos of information plaguing my brain, I recognized that it was the current Pakhan who was an ally, and that he was having trouble holding onto his throne. That was... My mind struggled to remember the name of the Five Pointer who was involved with the Russians.

Conceding defeat, I asked myself if a pretender to the Bratva leadership would trigger a war with the Irish?

Wasn't that an insane move to make?

The Irish had cleaned up after the Italians and Russians went to war. The Five Points had never been this powerful. A declaration of war against the Irish was like requesting, *nicely*, to get a bullet between the eyes.

I heard a beep which set my nerves on edge.

Then I realized it was the toll.

We were getting off the bridge.

I spent the next twenty minutes trying not to puke from the pain in my head, but the ache was only compounded once I started to panic as I felt the vehicle slow down. I tilted my head more as we turned, using that as an excuse for movement.

The migraine from Hades made my vision dance, but when I caught a sight of the bulge a few feet from me, I felt like weeping.

Aidan.

It had to be.

He wasn't moving.

Oh, God.

Tears pricked my eyes again, but I couldn't let them fall.

For years, I'd studied the moves the mafia pulled. There had to be some advantage to that.

They weren't like serial killers, where stopping them from moving you to an alternate location was imperative. With them, it was about information. That meant torture. That meant they'd want us awake, so pretending to be unconscious was the way forward.

The vehicle—from the size of the cargo bed where we were lying, I figured we were in a covered pickup truck—slowed and the texture of the road changed.

I heard a squeaking noise that reminded me of the gates at our estate near the O'Donnelly compound where Aidan's parents lived.

Well, parent.

I forced myself not to think about Senior.

This could have happened if he was alive. There'd never been any guarantees for our safety, none whatsoever, and I couldn't pretend otherwise—I'd known exactly what I was getting into when I'd said, 'I do,' to Aidan.

Forcing myself to go slack again, aware that we'd be moved soon, I knew that the toughest part would be not revealing myself through any grunts of pain as they hauled me around.

I was right.

Pretending was a nightmare.

Pain splintered through my brain as the truck jostled as one—no, *two*—people jumped out of the front, and then again when the trunk opened.

When someone dragged off the tarp then hauled me over their shoulder like I was a bag of potatoes, I would never know how I didn't scream as the agony in my head and the rest of my body clamored for supremacy.

It was then that I knew I was as much of a badass bitch as I'd always told myself—this was Star-grade acting.

The more pain I was in, the limper I became until I began taking pleasure in the man's panting breaths as he moved me wherever he wanted me.

The sudden stench of fish hit me just as he muttered, "Fat bitch," and dumped me on a pile of—nets?

Ewww.

I was more offended about that than the goddamn 'fat bitch.'

I clearly needed more curves because when they said that eating a cake made it harder on potential kidnappers to snatch you, they weren't fucking wrong.

A couple seconds later, I heard a weird dragging noise, and then someone was pretty much dropped next to me a few feet away.

A door slammed closed and a locking sound was audible next. I waited a couple seconds but it was silent in here, so silent.

The stench was putrefying, and not gagging was another thing to award myself for.

When noises sounded from outside—an engine starting, a car

moving, and then, in the distance, voices—I released a breath and dared open my eyes to pitch black darkness.

It didn't come as a surprise, but fuck, it made it more grueling to move around, especially as I kept getting caught on the netting below me.

"Bastards," I hissed as I wriggled and writhed, shuffling over to where the weight had shifted earlier.

I felt like a snake slithering amid a pile of shit as I managed to get myself on my knees and awkwardly shuffled forward in a crawl that would win me no prizes in the grace department.

That was when I smelled him.

The relief of him hit me like a sack of bricks to the temple.

I was blind, in the dark, restrained, my life in danger, but all I knew was that he was here, that he smelled like home, and I knew we'd get through this.

Like we got through everything.

Together.

For a handful of seconds, we weren't here. Instead, we were eating omelets in the kitchen at home while he bitched at me for downing my third triple espresso.

He'd shaved and I was sniffing that delicious aftershave I could bathe in.

We were in bed, safe and protected from this horrible, horrible world.

The normalcy of it spurred me on.

I wanted it back.

I wanted my life back.

It let me suck in a deep breath I regretted which was when it hit me—they hadn't taped my mouth or blindfolded me.

Confusion struck, but I didn't let it stop me. Instead, I half fell on Aidan when the netting shifted beneath me.

With my face, I nuzzled into him, whispering, "Aidan, baby? Please wake up."

I pressed my forehead to his mouth, nearly sobbing when I felt duct tape there and not his lips. But air from his nose brushed over my skin, making me close my eyes with joy.

Inhaling his scent again, I put my mouth to his ear. "Aidan, I need you to wake up. We need to get out of here. Please. Please. Please."

It didn't work.

It didn't fucking work.

What had they done to him?

Those bastards.

I'd make it out of here just so I could skewer them. I'd seen enough autopsy reports from Aidan and his da's kills to know exactly where to make people hurt.

Then, a worst-case scenario hit me.

What if they had jacked him up on heroin?

As night followed day, I knew that'd be the easiest way to incapacitate Aidan. To bring him to his fucking knees.

I planted my head against his chest to see if I could sense his heart rate. With the migraine still clouding my judgment, I tried to think about the physiological responses to a dose of heroin, but it took a few minutes to remember what they'd be.

Slowed heart rate and slowed breathing—thank God, but Aidan was showing neither of those signs. His heart wasn't racing or didn't seem too slow. If I held my breath, I could feel the faintest vibration and that felt normal too.

I couldn't check his pupils—

Okay, I needed to think practically.

Bindings—I needed my liberty so I could properly check his pulse.

Empowered just by his presence, I twisted onto my back and raised my arms to my mouth. With my lips, I found the binding and let loose a sob of thanks as I uncovered the edge of the tape with my teeth and started to drag it off, but every time I did, it made a noise. A loud one. Too loud.

In increments, I managed to work it off, wondering if a fucking zip tie would have been easier to escape from.

Shoulders beginning to ache, I forced myself to continue. It took what felt like a lifetime, but with that done, I got to work on my ankles. That was easier, faster too because I wasn't in an awkward position.

Once I'd freed myself, I moved over to Aidan and I took his pulse—*normal*. His temperature felt normal too. Still unsure, but knowing my limits, I started working on releasing him, which was when I realized he'd been zip tied. Only his mouth had been duct-taped.

"The motherfucking audacity," I rasped under my breath, determined now to crush some skulls. "How dare they underestimate me!"

Aidan was a threat but I wasn't?

The goddamn nerve.

"So fucking sexist," I sniped as I patted my inside jacket pockets to see if they'd been dumbfuck enough to leave me with my phone.

They hadn't.

Huffing, I shuffled onto my knees and started crawling around the place, hoping there'd be something sharp I could use to free him.

I froze.

The floor was slimy.

"Oh, God," I whispered, literally forcing myself not to retch.

Fish had been in here recently.

The stench told me that.

But the slime...

If I was crawling around in fish guts in a Prada suit, someone was going to pay for that too.

There was nothing sharp or pointy. Nothing that would let me cut him loose, but there *was* a flashlight.

I found it by chance when my face collided with a wall—faces were useful sometimes. I hissed, though, because the burn on my cheek from, I assumed, the deployment of the air bag stung as the tender flesh grazed what felt like a roughly hewn plank of wood.

My head connected with the flashlight next, making it worth the duel for supremacy between the burns on my cheeks and throat, the pain in my skull, and the stench in my nostrils over which would make me vomit first.

Fumbling, I switched it on, wincing at the bright gleam, wincing even more when my supposition was right.

Fish guts.

The floor was bright red.

I gagged for real this time before I clenched my eyes closed and focused on my priorities—don't look down.

"Do not look at the goddamn floor, Savannah," I told myself, trying hard not to retch again.

It was easier to walk around with the flashlight, and I quickly studied our surroundings. It was a fifteen-by-fifteen shed, clearly used for gutting fish. Or something. I mean, it had to be fish, didn't it? In a place like this, with a smell like this?

Didn't they have nice clinical places for that now? They did. Fish markets!

Something wasn't right.

This wasn't the forties.

So what were they gutting here that smelled of fish but wasn't for food?

Or were they using the fish to—

"Of course," I muttered grimly.

Trafficking came in many forms.

I'd heard of heroin being transported inside the bellies of cattle which were shipped from Afghanistan, which then traveled across the continent to the West.

But...

"I thought it was a joke," I whispered to myself.

There'd been a rumor that someone was bringing in blood diamonds in Atlantic halibut trawls...

Dismissing that for the moment as I was *not* researching a story but trying to save mine and my husband's lives, I quickly realized that the room had no windows or doors. And I'd yet to find anything sharp or pointy either.

Squinting at the flashlight, I saw it was an older model, not a newer one. It not only weighed a ton, but it had a glass cover on the front, not a plastic one.

Removing a shoe, I stood on the disgustingly filthy floor. "Aidan, this is proof of how much I love you."

Standing on the net, my sole squished against the blood. I preferred to wear those torture devices I called stilettos rather than feel the gross texture against my toes. These heels were a half-size too small and I figured that was the only reason they were still on my feet —because they were lodged on.

What could I say? I hadn't been able to resist them.

"No impulse control comes in useful sometimes," I muttered to no one in particular as I slammed the heel into the glass shielding the flashlight's bulb.

The noise was jarring, and it hurt my entire body to jostle myself, but I did it again and again until, finally, it worked.

The glass shattered, tumbling inward. The pieces were too small but I didn't damage the lightbulb. It meant I had to hold the flashlight in a vertical position like an uplighter—considering the state of the floor, I didn't think that was such a bad thing.

Hooking my shoe back on because no way was I walking in this gunk again, I shuffled over to the door and put my ear to it to make sure that no one was incoming because they'd heard me fumbling around.

The flashlight was hefty enough to do some damage to a skull, so I tightened my grip around it as I waited for something.

Anything.

But there was nothing.

Not even a single sound.

What the hell?

Had they just dumped us and left for the night? Or had they gone to collect someone?

Confused and angry and in pain and grossed out by our location, I strode back to Aidan.

Without any care, I dragged off the duct tape from his mouth. I felt like a bitch, but I hoped it'd wake him up.

It didn't.

Huffing, I pressed the back of my hand to his mouth—more confirmation of normal breathing. Then, I carefully lifted an eyelid and shone the light into it—that provided me with no clue as the pupils constricted, and I had no way of knowing if that was from the intense light in such a dark space *or* a dose of heroin.

Desperate, I shoved his sleeves up and checked for track marks— there were none.

Finally free from the specter that he'd been doped, my relief took a chokehold on me. Tears pricked my eyes, and I had to shake them off because I didn't have time to cry.

Later, I'd sob.

Now, I grabbed the largest glass shard that had collected around the bulb and rested the flashlight on his lower abdomen so that I could get to work on cutting the zip tie.

It was finicky and sweaty and I cut myself with the glass and blood got everywhere but finally, I made a nick in the plastic.

Buoyed by that, when my hand slipped, I grimaced as it sliced into his arm.

"Shit, sorry, my love," I whispered, not expecting a response, but when I got one, I froze.

"Sa-vv-ieee?"

It was more of a slur than I'd like, but I'd take it.

I'd fucking take it.

On the brink of yet more pathetic tears, I murmured, "Aidan, I need you to stay quiet, baby. I'm trying to free us."

His entire body tensed then as if he'd been shocked with a taser.

His voice immediately changed. "Where are we?"

It was thick from whatever they'd done to him, but the level of self-control that took to shift from unconscious to an angry *bark* would have impressed me if I weren't just relieved to hear him. Alive. Not well. But awake. Awake and hurting was better than dead.

"I think we're in Brooklyn. I heard voices but nothing loud enough to know who was talking."

Well, to hear any accents if I was being precise.

"Brooklyn?" he rasped.

"Yes. I woke up as we drove off the island. They brought us here—it stinks of fish. We're clearly at a dock somewhere."

"Russians own all the docks in Brooklyn," he rumbled, his pitch changing. "Lyanov is dealing with in-fighting; that means we're in no man's land."

Trying not to panic, I carried on rubbing at the nylon tie with the glass. When I cut him again, he jerked in surprise then groaned under his breath. "My fucking shoulder's dislocated."

I swallowed. "Want me to pop it back in?"

His scowl told me he wanted that as much as I did. "You sure you can do it?"

"I told you before that Dad sent us off to Jungle Jane camps to figure out how to survive a kidnapping. I just never frickin' thought I'd have to survive one in Brooklyn!"

In the glare of the flashlight, I saw his lips curve. Mine, however, thinned.

"It's all right for you," I groused. "They at least zip-tied you. They just duct-taped me."

"You have to appreciate sexism sometimes," Aidan drawled as, finally, I got his hands free. "They underestimated you."

"Damn straight they did," I said with a sniff. "The audacity."

I ignored his snort of amusement at my temper and took stock of myself.

My fingers were slick with my blood, his, and some poor Atlantic halibut's. The cuts on the tips were stinging like mad. When this was over, because it *would* be over, I wouldn't be able to write for a few days, that was for sure.

My head ached less, but the stark glare from the flashlight made my eyes burn. My stomach was still the most vulnerable part of me—I was going to vomit if I accidentally looked at the floor again. That meant I had to be cautious.

"Savvie?"

"I think I'm going to be sick."

He straightened then hissed as that clearly affected his shoulder. "Do you have a concussion?"

"No. Maybe. I don't know. I just think we're sitting in a pile of fish guts." I swallowed. "It's on my hands too."

Our blood and a bunch of dead fishes' blood were probably having a bacteria party.

Shoving those thoughts aside, I shuffled around the netting to reach his other side.

"Are you sure you're good to do this?" he asked me.

"I wouldn't do it if I couldn't."

"I don't mean that—are you in too much pain?"

"No. And if I was, I'd still do it because this is not how we go out for good. I want Lady Gaga singing at my funeral, Aidan. I will not be fish food; do you hear me?"

"I hear you, little one," he soothed. I didn't need soothing, dammit. His hand cupped my jaw. Well, maybe just a tad. "Shoulder first, Savvie, then once that's back online, I'll take over trying to liberate my feet."

"What do you want me to do while you're handling that?"

"I need you to see if you can pick the lock on the door."

My brows lifted. "How did you know that I could do that?"

"I read every single article you've ever written, Savannah," he drawled, his voice cool and calm like we were back in our bedroom and not, ya know, *here.*

God, that he knew me so well was more comforting than he could have imagined. Acceptance—was there anything more beautiful than knowing you had it from the man you loved?

"You have the repertoire of a cat burglar," he was saying as I maneuvered my hands into position. "It's never boring with you around, Savvie."

As he teased me, I popped his shoulder back into position.

And dear Lord, he didn't make even a gasp of a sound.

I blew out a breath as I watched the veins in his temple pulse and his skin turn red as his face flushed with blood, but aside from that, not a peep.

"You'll need the flashlight," he rasped as he dumped the glass onto his stomach and began piecing through the shards to find something better than the one I'd used.

"I don't have anything long enough to pick a lock with," I mumbled as I straightened up. The blood rushed to my head, making it pound, but I heard the faintest noise. "They took my—" It took me a second to register what that sound was. I blinked. "No."

"No, what?" he grunted.

"They couldn't have underestimated me so much, could they?" I patted my pants pockets down and found...

Beyond insulted, I stomped my foot, immediately regretted it when more pain speared through my skull, then headed over to the door.

Aidan, well aware that my silence was seething, demanded, "What did they do now?"

"They didn't take my keys."

"Thank God for morons."

"I'm going to stab them in the eye with one," I vowed.

"I want us to get out of here without any bloodshed."

It was my turn to grumble, "Why?"

"Because you're here."

"So? Don't you underestimate me too!"

"I want you out of danger, Savannah," he snarled. "I told you earlier that you have no idea what I'm capable of where your safety is concerned. When you're out of the way, I'll start a war, but that's not going to happen while you're in the fray."

"And they said chivalry is dead," I said softly, tilting toward him rather than the door, wishing that I had the time to go over to him and kiss him for that alone.

Instead, I bit my lip, promised myself that I'd kiss him later, hell, that I'd tongue fuck him later, and I bent down and shot the flashlight onto the lock.

Aidan might think I was a master criminal, but that article had been a long time ago. It had been a series that recounted jobs that were traditionally handed down from father to son... and I'd gone in, proving that daughters could do it just as well as sons.

Sexism and feminism had been major themes in my writing back in college. That he'd read my rants and raves made me squirm with some embarrassment, and also delight that he'd taken such an interest in me.

He'd told me that he'd read everything I'd written, but I guessed I hadn't realized he'd truly meant *everything*.

Still, as I stared at the lock and tried to remember what to do, I unfolded the slimline pocketknife that Daddy had given each of his daughters and which I had hooked onto my keys. It looked like a regular old Swiss Army knife, but it was the size of my pinkie, as thin as a set of nail clippers, and was a weapon, not just a tool.

That was when I shook myself—my brain clearly wasn't working. I rushed over to him and with the scissor tool, carefully sawed through the nylon.

"They left you with a weapon?" he sputtered.

"They did," I said grimly. "Mr. Misogyny needs a Mobster 101 class. You really should get Mossad in to instruct them on how to be better criminals."

He grunted as he stood, then carefully started stretching his shoulder. "Are you complaining about their incompetence when it could save our lives?"

"You know I'm contrary," I retorted as I returned to the door and peered through the old-fashioned lock.

My eye watered at the spot-lit area but I caught a glimpse of a parking lot beyond the hut which fit the short journey from the truck to this hellhole.

That was when I saw someone sneaking toward us.

"Someone's coming!" I grated out at Aidan.

Even as he surged toward me, it was too late—the person was there.

I jolted back and straightened to a standing position just as a bullet popped through the lock.

How I didn't shriek, I'd never know because I'd almost fucking died via a bullet to my goddamn eye! But it all happened in such a flash that, instead, as the door jerked open, I raised my flashlight high, feeling the heavy weight in my biceps, and I brought it down.

Right on the bastard's head.

26

AIDAN

"SAVANNAH! NO!" I spat, getting there a scant second too late before the heavy-duty flashlight collided with Finn's temple.

I'd have laughed if we weren't in a hostage situation. Instead, I grimaced when Finn wobbled and sank to the ground, his knees thudding against the blood-soaked wooden boards.

"Finn?" Declan snapped. "What the fuck?"

"Finn?! Oh, shit! I thought—I..."

When she stopped talking, that was when I knew she was in shock.

Savvie was a talker, after all.

"The bullet!" she whispered before she groaned. "Our kidnappers would have had a key. I'm so sorry, Finn!"

How she wasn't a bubbling mass of panic was something I'd figure out later.

Instead, carefully grabbing her, I dragged her away from the door and tucked her behind me as Declan slipped into the shed with Brennan.

The spot-lit area behind them fucked with my eyes. We were in light and in shadow all at the same time.

"I'm never letting him live this down," Brennan drawled even as he was helping pick our brother up.

Declan's chuckle was low as he agreed, "Me either. Good aim, Savvie."

I grunted. "Less of the congratulations. What the fuck took you so long to get here?"

"Jesus, Aidan," Brennan grated out. "You've been gone like two hours."

My mouth worked. "Oh." Shit. "Sorry," was my sheepish retort.

"*Sorry* looks good on you," Savvie muttered at my back, especially when Brennan and Declan shot me astonished looks.

Yeah, I didn't say sorry often.

My bad.

"I thought we'd been gone longer. I don't have a clue what's happening."

"He was passed out for a while," Savvie told my brothers. "He probably has a concussion."

"Makes sense. That's why fuckface said sorry," Declan mumbled with a snort.

"Where are we?" I demanded, finally able to itemize the pain I was in and organize it so that I wasn't dealing with it right now.

The agony from my knee was one thing, but heroin withdrawals made that pain look like a walk in the park.

A concussion and a dislocated fucking shoulder were nothing by comparison.

"Docks by Coney Island Water Treatment Plant."

I frowned. "So we really are on Russian soil?"

"This wasn't approved by Lyanov," Brennan assured me. "I asked him straight if we were allowed to enter his territory."

"Good thinking." I reached up to rub my aching head. "Who's out there?"

"No one. Anthony was on guard duty but he's out cold now that Eoghan's treated his kneecaps to some pampering."

"He kneecapped him?" Savvie blurted out. "Fuck, and I missed it!"

Declan chuckled. "You're sick, Savvie."

"Watch it," I groused.

"Nah, there's no denying that I've got a skewed moral compass," was my wife's response. "Plus, I'm telling you, I will stab one of these fuckers in the eye. There were two of them who brought us here. Did you get the second guy?"

"Jonesy left for Hell's Kitchen as we infiltrated—"

"Jonesy," she shrieked. "That piece of shit betrayed the Five Points and then betrayed *us* too? What's he going to do as a hat trick?"

I had an idea... not that I was going to say it yet.

But the fuckers behind this ridiculous plot had made a massive mistake—taking me was one thing. Taking Savannah was another.

They'd rue the day they were fucking born for bringing her into this.

"The docks are empty?" I demanded, needing that reassurance before I could start to plan.

"They are. Hell, the whole place is a ghost town. But Conor got into the office; the boats are going out at four."

"So we're alone until then?"

"Or until Jonesy returns. We have no way of knowing when that might be."

"Are all of Da's detail in on this?"

"Conor says no. Their traces are showing the rest of them as being at home. He's working on figuring out which man in your crew gave them a key to your car."

My mind joined the dots. "Connolly's wife is Jonesy's uncle's great-niece."

"You guys need to spread out more, start marrying people who aren't related," Savannah muttered.

"You're preaching to the converted," Brennan retorted with a short laugh. "Apart from Dec here, of course."

"Fuck off."

I knew my brothers too well—they'd start bickering to help Savannah calm down, to help her relax, but we were in a hostile environment even if the place was currently unmanned.

That was when I heard the softest of noises beneath the usual city chaos, and the distinct creaking of some nearby gates.

"Conor says it's Lucas," Bren informed us.

"He's in your ear?" I asked.

"He is."

I held out a hand. "Give me the earpiece."

Brennan shrugged but did as I asked.

"Conor?"

"Oh, good, you're not dead."

"Not for another fifty fucking years at least," I told him.

"Poor Savannah," was Conor's droll rejoinder.

"You sure that's Lucas?"

"Of course I am," he sniped. "The place is dead. I have no idea what they were fucking planning, but it's a shitshow."

"They wanted to stage a coup without getting too many people involved."

"Why?"

I had my suspicions but it was likeliest that... "Because my little display the other day worked. Most of the Five Pointers recognize that sanity is far more terrifying than insanity," I said grimly.

"Anyone who's watched *Batman* knows that," Savannah muttered.

"That makes no sense," Declan answered. "Surely it's the opposite—"

Not about to get into it with either of them, I turned to her. "Lucas is here and I want him to take you home."

Her brow furrowed. "What? No! You told me you wouldn't—"

I didn't let her finish.

It was one thing for Conor to know what I'd had to do to earn her forgiveness, but I didn't want the rest of my brothers knowing as well.

If they did, they'd give me shit about it, and I had enough on my plate without that.

"Later, Savvie," I rasped. "I need you safe before I can do anything."

Finn came to my aid by groaning, "The fuck?"

Brennan's chuckle was the opposite of sympathetic. "Savvie clocked you on the head."

"Pistol-whipped?" Finn mumbled.

"Flashlight-whipped," Declan said helpfully.

"Fuck," he groaned again.

"Finn, do you want to go home?

"No, I'll be fine," he slurred. "Just gotta sit down."

"Okay. We need to deal with Anthony. I want to know who's behind this because it sure as hell isn't him. He ain't smart enough to make toast without electrocuting himself."

Declan demanded, "Think this is an ECD scheme, or someone else in the Five Points?"

"It's not the ECD," Savannah inserted. "This isn't their MO. They don't do abductions."

"I think you're right about it being an internal issue. That's why I want to know who's behind it. Fast." Mind racing, I asked, "Where's Anthony?"

"Tied up in my SUV," Declan informed me.

"Good. I'll ride with you, Bren, and we'll meet up at the cement factory." When I got their nods, I grabbed Savvie's hand. "Come on, Savannah, I need you to be anywhere but here."

I was surprised that she let me haul her out of there, but as I dragged her, with each step that separated us from my brothers, she drawled, "I know you have to play a part with them, Aidan, but you promised you wouldn't cut me out of the loop."

"And I won't. I'll tell you what happens." Goddamn, this was going to bite me in the ass. "But I don't want you involved."

"I got kidnapped too. Whatever you do to punish them, I want in on it."

"You just want to stab one of them in the eye."

"No one underestimates Savannah Daniels," she sniped.

"Savannah O'Donnelly."

I had no idea why that was what made me snap, but it did.

I grabbed her by the back of the neck and dragged her into me. Every fucking bone in my body jolted in response, but that didn't matter worth shit.

My mouth collided with hers as I speared my tongue between her lips.

When she gave me back as much as she got, something settled inside me.

Something that felt like relief and happiness.

She wasn't afraid. In shock, maybe. But not afraid.

Anger I could have dealt with, but her fear would have broken me.

Once the adrenaline dropped, true reaction would kick in, but that was okay—she'd be safe when that happened. She wouldn't be in danger, and she could cry without anyone seeing her. I knew my wife too well to know that tears and her weren't friends.

As I fucked her mouth, I didn't even draw back when Brennan sniffed. "Now ain't the time."

"You're saying that a lot tonight," Declan pointed out.

"Shut up, Dec," Brennan groused, the pair of them starting to bicker as they maneuvered Finn over to Declan's ride.

I ignored them all.

I carried on kissing her, letting her know she was my fucking oxygen as I imprinted my fear for her and rage at the world on her.

I only stopped when Conor murmured, "You two go any deeper, I think she'll be able to drag out your heart with her tongue. She got a fishhook on there or something?"

Jerking in response to his words, I slowly pulled back and pressed a final, gentle kiss to her pretty pink lips.

That was when I saw the state of her, and I got mad at myself for fucking her mouth like we were in our bedroom when she'd been goddamn injured.

Blood and all kinds of shit covered her face, never mind her clothes, but on her cheeks, and at her upper throat, beneath the grime and dirt, the baby soft skin was grazed with chemical burns.

She had bruises on her temple, too.

I reached up and carefully ran my thumb over one of the bruises.

"I'll make them pay for these, little one."

Her hand snapped around my wrist like the best cuff in the world. "I want you to stay safe, and I want you to kill whoever did this to us. Do you understand?"

Staring into her eyes, I rasped, "I understand you, Savannah O'Donnelly."

My filthy fucking queen.

Her nostrils flared as she leaned up on tiptoe and pressed a gentle kiss to my lips.

"You go home," I rumbled. "I'll be back soon and I'll tell you what you want to know."

"You'd better. And I'm not going home. I'm going to Conor's."

Despite myself, I had to grin. "You hear that, Con? You got company coming."

"Great," he griped.

"Says he can't wait for you to join him," I assured her.

She knew him too well, though, because she shot me a sheepish smile. "I'm sure." Her gaze darkened as she cupped my chin, and her thumb traced over the line of my jaw. That was when I realized she wasn't the only one with chemical burns. "Be safe for me," was all she said.

"Of course," I rasped, but I couldn't leave it like that so I pushed my forehead against hers. "I'm sorry for getting you into this, Savannah."

"Don't be. I prefer reading about it, but as long as you get the bastards, I'll forgive you for ruining our Sunday night."

"You're too kind." I found myself able to joke, kissing her smirk before I pulled back. "Go on, go. Let me get you the answers you need, hmm?"

Slowly, she nodded before she strode over to Lucas's car which was blocking the front gates.

Time wasn't our friend, but there was no way in fuck I could let her head home without that kiss.

I watched her go, our eyes entangled as Lucas reversed and pulled out. She stared at me until she couldn't anymore, and I knew that if Savannah cried later on, it wouldn't be for herself.

It'd be for me.

But I didn't need her tears even if she needed to shed them as she decompressed. My brothers were here, they'd saved our asses, and I was going to cement our family at the top of the tree so that no one dared question my leadership ever again.

I didn't know who was involved in this shitty attempt at a coup, and I didn't know what was planned so there was danger ahead, but she was right about one thing—this wasn't how we were going to go out.

With her gone, I turned and strode over to Brennan's SUV. My knee was weaker than I'd like from, I assumed, the crash, but it wasn't that bad as I made it over to the passenger door and jumped in.

We made quick work of getting the hell out of there, but at the next turn, I told Brennan, "Circle the block."

He cast me a look but did as I asked until he had to reverse because the riverbank was on the farthest side.

As he did, I held up a hand and climbed out so I could stare at the operation from the shore.

"Heard rumors about this place," Brennan muttered. "Didn't think it was true though."

I hummed. "Think Lyanov knows about it?"

It was only a minuscule operation. There were bigger marinas in the area, but this one was beyond simply small fry. Didn't mean a lot of shit couldn't go down here. Sometimes, the smallest of spots could house the most lucrative of businesses. Especially when twenty million dollars of product could fit in the palm of your hand.

"I'm not sure," Brennan admitted. "Lyanov was distracted when I called him, and afterward, he was cursing in Russian—"

"You have that effect on people, Bren."

"Fuck off," he groused.

As I lowered myself into the bucket seat, my smirk was absent as I said, "Thank you for coming for us."

He rolled his eyes as he reversed into the road so quickly the tires squealed. "What else was I supposed to do, dipshit?"

And that was the long and the short of it, I guessed.

We went to war for each other.

That was why there were no Five Points without the O'Donnellys.

My mind wandered as we drove over to the cement factory. I'd admit that though the pain was manageable, I'd knew I'd hit my fucking head somewhere along the way because it was difficult focusing on the task at hand and not those goddamn burns on Savannah's cheeks.

Thank Christ she'd been wearing a turtleneck that had covered half the skin there.

Whoever had been behind the wheel would pay for each of those fucking marks.

I just wished I'd seen who it was.

I could only remember twin bolts of light coming toward me, and as I attempted to evade a crash, it had been too late—collision was imminent.

Seconds later, Savannah's scream ringing in my ears, the airbag had deployed and my shoulder had snapped with the force of it. Just thinking about it had me wriggling it, stretching it.

"You hurt your shoulder?" Brennan asked, breaking into the silence.

"Dislocated it during the crash. Savannah popped it back in for me."

"Since when was she an EMT?"

"She's more capable than most know."

I knew he arched a brow at me, but I didn't say much else.

It was to my benefit that no one recognized what Savannah could do. People believed the ditzy news reporter act, and that was why Jonesy and Anthony had only duct-taped her hands and feet and hadn't zip-tied them.

If my brothers hadn't come, I had a feeling Savannah and I would have been just fine. Not that I was complaining. Especially as Eoghan had kneecapped that fucker Anthony.

"What's the plan, Aidan?" Bren asked, breaking into my thoughts.

In my ear, I could hear Conor talking to someone I thought was Paddy, but when it went abruptly quiet, I knew he'd put me on mute. Focusing wasn't easy at the moment so I appreciated the radio silence on his end.

I stared at the road ahead, unconsciously mapping the route Bren was taking to the factory as, slowly, I rumbled, "Torture Anthony, squirrel the details out of him, then make the fuckers pay."

"You got someone in mind? Someone you think is behind it?"

"Mark." When his hands tightened around the wheel, I knew why. *Guilt.* Worse than stomach acid for causing peptic ulcers. "You did what had to be done, Brennan. Callum was a traitor. Looks like he took after his father, but Da was just too blind to see it."

"I think Da had his eye off the ball for longer than we realized," Brennan rasped.

That was a fair point. "I agree. We can't rule like that."

"No?"

I heard the wary hope in his voice. "No. My head's on the chopping block; I'm fine with that. But we'll rule like we always should have done with Da—as a family. He let outsiders in. He should never have done that."

"He only let Mark, Tony, and Paul into the 'council' meetings after Frank and Paddy died."

I eyed his air quotes dubiously, but he wasn't wrong. "Guess that means that none of you fuckers can ever die."

Brennan snorted. "Camille wouldn't complain."

That reminded me... "Did Lyanov mention Victoria?"

He tensed. "Why would he? We were talking about business."

"You know full well that Victoria *is* Lyanov's business."

"Don't let Camille hear you say that. She's still got it in her head that he'll court her. Her words, not mine."

"Maybe he will. She's young."

"Don't I fucking know it." He rubbed the back of his neck. "She's trouble, and I can see it barreling our way, but she's..." He sighed. "I love her. She's the sister I never fucking had. I'm not happy about Lyanov getting his paws on her."

"Look at Savvie," was the only thing I could comfort him with. "Nowhere else she wants to be than in the lion's den." When Brennan just grunted, I murmured, "We have to get Anthony to talk fast. I want Jonesy and the ringleaders in our hold before dawn."

"Fucking slave driver. You're just like Da," he complained.

I thought about what Savvie had told me—that I was nothing like him—and I found comfort in that. Found comfort in her opinion because hers was the only one I really cared about.

"Yeah, where it matters, I am."

We made it to the cement factory where the gates were open for us.

Eoghan's Aston Martin was there, and he was helping Finn out of Declan's car, while Declan was dragging Anthony onto the floor.

We had about five guards on duty, and I knew they'd be working the perimeter and would have seen our arrival.

I had no choice but to say to Brennan, "Get the guards rounded up. Watch them until Lucas gets here. He can take over then."

"You think someone here might be involved?"

"We don't know who's behind this yet, do we? Could be anyone or everyone."

"You said—"

"I know what I said, but caution won't cost us anything."

Leaving him, I strolled over to Anthony, and letting my leg fly back, I kicked his knee.

That brought him back to consciousness nice and fast.

As he howled out his pain, I ducked down, grabbed his necktie, and started dragging him toward the factory entrance.

Behind me, my brothers followed, and though the night had proven that I wasn't untouchable, by the time morning broke, I knew one thing and one thing only—

I'd be unstoppable.

___

27

SAVANNAH

LEARN TO FLY - FOO FIGHTERS

LUCAS WAS all apologies on the ride home, but I didn't want or need apologies.

I wanted eyes on what was happening.

I wanted to know what was going down.

The craving for information had me in a chokehold. Curiosity had always been my weakness, but since I'd gotten with Aidan, it was as bad for me as opiates were for him.

Lucas followed me up to Conor's apartment and didn't leave me alone until Conor opened the door to let me in.

"Here you are, Conor."

That was when I saw Lucas hand over the laptop Star had left in my care.

Blinking, I muttered, "You think of everything, Con."

"Curse of the job," he grouched.

When Lucas gave me one more apology, I waved him off with a hand and headed straight for Conor's office.

I wasn't being a bitch, and I didn't blame Lucas, but I just...

I had a feeling that if I started talking, I'd explode. Or implode. I wasn't sure which was worse.

Before I could reach the office, a hand was on my arm and Conor was tugging me to a halt.

"Where do you think you're going?"

Because he was keeping me from what I craved most, I managed to choke out, "I want answers."

He scowled at me. "Savannah, you're covered in blood and you're injured. But mostly, you reek. You need a shower."

"You can't stop me—" I blinked again. Oh. He wasn't stopping me. And I *did* reek. "If I shower, you'll let me go in?"

"Of course. I just don't want you stinking up my place. What the hell have you been rolling in?"

"Fish guts."

"Great. You know where the guest room is. Shower first, then you need to apply some ointment to your cheeks, and..." He hesitated. "You know what Aidan's going to have to do, don't you, Savannah? You know that answers just don't grow on trees."

His concern on my behalf was kind, but I didn't need it. I needed no coddling.

"I'm a big girl, Conor. I know what he'll have to do, and—"

"You're okay with it?" he demanded before I could finish.

"We could have died tonight," I told him softly. "You can bet your ass that I'm okay with whatever he has to do to make people pay for that.

"And even if we hadn't almost died, I'd still be okay with it because I'm not a little girl and I don't wear blinders. I know exactly how big and bad the world is, and arming myself with the truth is my version of self-protection."

Though I could feel him analyzing my words, Conor merely cocked a brow at me. "Shower first, then answers."

"Agreed."

I ran over to the room where I'd slept last December when my apartment had been broken into, and I darted into the bathroom and tried to take the fastest shower in the world.

It didn't work.

I stank.

So bad.

Even after dousing myself in soap from top to toe, including the poor foot that had stood on that disgusting floor, I reeked of dead fish.

Every time I raised my arms to my nose and scented it, the need to retch grew stronger. Stronger. *Stronger.*

Until...

I puked.

Straight into the shower stall.

For a second, I remained leaning forward, hands on my knees to prop myself up as the shower spray beat down on my spine.

The angle didn't help with the blood rushing to my head but I just breathed through it until I was strong enough to straighten up. I pushed my back to the wall and stared blindly ahead.

"Aidan," I whispered miserably, wishing he were here but knowing that he couldn't be.

I thought about how he'd looked at me as Lucas drove away.

Men who went to war sometimes died in the process...

I swallowed down the urge to vomit again and forced myself to focus on what mattered here.

It was the intense scrubbing of my arms that had fed the frenzy of emotions, and I shoved them back down, packed them deep within me because I didn't have time for them right now.

Hell, I never had time for emotions.

My body tensed as I physically forced myself to think about something else, and mechanically, I grabbed the soap again, dragged the towel from the wall where I'd hung it, and I poured it liberally into the folds.

Using that to scrub at myself, I cleansed my body for what had to be the tenth time.

Only, when I raised my arm to my nose, the scent was still fucking there!

Another frenzied bout of rubbing my skin occurred, resulting in me puking once again.

"This is ridiculous," I snarled under my breath even as I was retching.

Forcing myself to recover, I ducked my head under the shower, and I decided that I'd run out of time.

Aidan could be arriving at the cement factory by now and I didn't want to miss that.

Soaked, I switched off the water at long last then stepped out. After, I draped a towel around me to dry off, then another around my hair. I grabbed the bathrobe on the back of the door, one that scented of detergent, and I shucked into it.

I'd prefer to be dressed, but beggars couldn't be choosers.

Covered enough for decency, I opened the vanity unit, found some alcohol pads in a well-stocked first aid kit, and swiped them over my wounds.

I'd been in a road traffic accident before so I knew the drill where chemical burns from airbag deployments were concerned.

There was grit in one of my cheeks and that hurt like a mother-fucker to dislodge, a splinter took too long to retrieve as well. Parts of my face were bright pink and oozing pinpricks of blood by the time I was done.

After going over my cheeks with another pad, I reached for the tube of antibiotic cream and dotted it over the tender flesh, finding myself grateful for the harsh scent as it overtook that disgusting smell of fish.

With the cuts on my fingers cleaned too now that chore was completed, I dosed myself up with a couple acetaminophen then gulped down some water.

Heading out of the bedroom, I stormed into the hall toward Conor's office.

The door opened easily.

So easily that I nearly fell through the opening.

"You've already fallen for my brother, Savannah. You don't need to do it for me too," Conor declared from somewhere in the space—he wasn't seated at his usual desk.

I frowned as I tried to find him, and when I did and saw that he was squatting beneath a different desk, I demanded, "What are you doing?"

"Hardware problem."

"Has Aidan arrived at the cement factory?"

"No. He and Brennan are still in the car."

Relief filtered through me to the point that I almost sagged with it.

Maybe I did; maybe I staggered backward or something because Conor was out from under the desk in a heartbeat, and he was at my side the next.

"Do I still stink of fish?"

He stared at me, those dark eyes of his somehow seeing too much and not enough all at the same time.

"Why would you stink of fish?"

I twisted around at the new voice and frowned. "Paddy? What are you doing here?"

"He just arrived from upstate. He was with Ma."

There was a soft lilt in Conor's voice at that. One I didn't understand.

Brow furrowing, I whispered, "We were taken to a...a shed, I guess you'd call it. They gut fish there. That's why I stink of it."

Paddy looked so much like his brother that it couldn't be good for Lena's heart to see him.

Well, he didn't have Aidan Sr.'s sharp edges. He was softer around the jaw, and he smiled more.

It was strange.

A smiling Aidan Sr.

Was hell freezing beneath our feet?

It was the first time I'd seen him since the funeral, and I assumed that, and the fact I'd hit my head harder than I realized, was the only reason I could think of for Paddy's appearance freaking me out.

Paddy's brow puckered at my words. "Conor was telling me

before his machine went on the fritz that someone dared take Aidan and you. I'm sorry, Savannah. You must have been terrified."

"I wasn't scared." I straightened up. "I'm pissed."

His lips twitched. "You told me," he said to Conor.

"I did. You owe me fifty bucks." Conor sniffed me. "It's there, but not as bad as before."

He had the worst timing.

The need to release a sob hit me at his words, but I contained that motherfucker and embraced the nervous breakdown it'd likely trigger in a decade's time because they'd made a bet on whether or not I'd lose my shit.

God damn them.

But it forced me to put on my mask. The mask I didn't have to wear around Aidan—fuck, I wanted him to be home—and I demanded, "I want to see where Aidan is."

Conor shrugged then waved a hand at a screen behind him. "I told you; he isn't there yet."

I pointed at his left ear which had an earpiece in. "Can he hear us?"

"No, I put him on mute. I don't want to distract him unless I have information for him."

"The hardware malfunction with your computer—does it affect what you have to do tonight?"

"No. I just underestimated the power of Star's gift, that's all."

"Her gift?" I asked warily.

"Yes. She gave me a worm."

My mouth rounded. "She *gave* you a worm."

"A powerful one." His lips twisted. "I'm pretty sure she wanted access to my files again but it's all good. It helped me out."

Brow furrowing, I asked, "When she was here last, did she take anything?"

"You asked me that before. And no. Nothing."

"Why didn't she leave the worm before?"

He jerked a shoulder. "Why does Star do anything?"

"True."

Movement behind him drew my attention, and spying Brennan's car pulling through some gates had me jerking away from Conor and rushing over to the screen.

I heard footsteps behind me, heavy set ones, and I knew it was Paddy.

"Are you all right?"

"No. But I will be once this is over with." I cast him a quick glance. "Is it true that it took Aidan Sr. two years to consolidate his position?"

If it took Aidan that long, I might need to schedule my nervous breakdown for five years in the future and not ten.

"It is," Paddy murmured. "The men didn't like him. Didn't trust him. They were partially right, of course. He was a headcase back then. Marriage settled him down in some ways if you can believe it."

My eyes bugged at that. "No, I really can't."

His chuckle was dark. "There's a reason he spent so much time on his knees in church, Savannah.

"Our da used to beat him for having the devil in him," he said thoughtfully. "Aidan heard it so often that he came to believe it."

"If he didn't like him, why didn't he pass on the Points to you or Frank?"

"Frank liked women too much to be the leader, and me? I'm a follower." He hitched a shoulder. "I don't mind admitting that. Aidan was the only one with the balls to do what had to be done. Da knew that."

"Junior is terrified that he's like his father," I rasped under my breath as I watched Aidan clamber out of the SUV.

He spoke with Brennan before heading over to Declan's car where he kicked Anthony in one of his injured knees then dragged him over to the factory entrance by his necktie.

"He certainly has his ingenuity," Paddy muttered as he cast me a look. "You aren't scared of him?"

"Was Lena scared of Senior?"

"At the start, sure. She was a smart girl," he mocked. "Funny how she became the only person who could control him in the end, no?"

I turned to look at him. "I doubt she controlled him."

"All she had to do was burst into tears and he'd have done anything to stop her sadness.

"If you cry, I wonder what Junior will do to stop your tears from falling..."

I wasn't sure why his questions agitated me.

I liked Paddy. Since his reincarnation, he'd attended many Sunday lunches and had even visited us for a few dinners because Aidan was his godson.

I hadn't seen him for a while before the funeral because he'd been in Canada with his son, Liam, during the NHL off-season.

But there was no reason for him to get under my skin. He was perfectly affable.

Maybe it was because I'd rubbed said skin raw in the shower so I was touchier than usual.

Turning my focus back to the screen, I watched as the cameras followed Aidan and his brothers through the factory.

"I think New York is in danger only if I am. He's not like his father. He does what he has to do, and he doesn't enjoy it."

Paddy hummed, but before I could snap at him to know what that meant because his hum sounded *dubious*, Conor hooted. "Yes! Fixed. Gotcha, you little bastard."

The screen's resolution cleared up dramatically and suddenly we were graced with Anthony's screaming in full surround sound.

"You sure he doesn't always enjoy it?" Paddy asked me dryly.

My lips pursed. "Like I said, Aidan responds to me being in danger. Why are you asking these goddamn questions anyway? I don't need a social commentary on my husband's nature."

"I want you to recognize what's about to happen. You shouldn't see this—"

I turned on him. "Anthony was involved in a plot that could have resulted in our deaths. I doubt they'd have let us die without some torture first, and let's face it, women always get raped, don't they? It's what men do to punish us." I sneered at him. "Anthony deserves what's coming to him."

"Is that why you want to watch?"

"No. I want to know what he confesses to."

"Why? Aidan will take care of it."

"Leave her alone, Paddy," Conor muttered, his fingers tapping now that he was back at his keyboard. "She ain't like Ma and she ain't like any of the other women, either. Savvie likes to be kept in the know."

Paddy shrugged. "Just trying to protect her."

"I don't need protecting," I sniped. Then, guilt hit me because he *was* family. It wasn't his fault that he was kind and I wasn't used to that coming without a price tag. "But thank you for trying."

His lips twisted, but he just shrugged again. "Don't say I didn't warn you."

My nails dug into my palms as I watched Aidan and Anthony, who left a trail of blood in his wake, while they entered a room that appeared to be set up for the explicit purpose of torture.

"God, it's been years since I saw that crucifix."

My eyes widened at Paddy's nostalgic tone. I didn't say anything, though, because I didn't need him asking me more questions.

I just fastened myself in for the most fucked-up ride of my life.

Did what happened next change how I viewed Aidan?

Maybe.

Watching him slice off Anthony's pants at the knees so that he could pack salt into the bullet wounds, salt that they appeared to keep in stock for this reason, watching him drag a knife through his flesh, watching him take skin with it...

Anthony's screams made me flinch, but I knew Paddy saw it, so I straightened up taller.

The brothers talked among themselves as they worked Anthony over, but it whispered in and out of my attention as I watched my husband torture the man who could have tortured us.

My pulse raced in my ears, my chest ached with how hard my heart pounded, and the urge to puke again was a raw need, but I fought it. Fought my natural inclinations to respond to what I was seeing.

That was when Aidan scraped a knife over Anthony's cheek.

As if he knew I was struggling, that was when he snarled, "My wife has burns because of you. Chemical burns. You should be thankful for that because if she was hurt more than that, you'd be feeling the consequences.

"Instead, let's see if you like how chemical burns feel."

Declan ambled over with a bottle in his hand.

Aidan unstoppered the glass top. "Couple drops of this in your eyes and they'll start melting. Acids are good for that, but bases are even better. I remember that you didn't like science in school, did you, Anthony? Unfortunately for you, I listened."

"What do you want to know?" Anthony screamed as Aidan moved the bottle, tipping it forward, making his eyes cross at the proximity of the liquid that promised his blindness.

That was when he talked.

As well as when he pissed himself.

He and Jonesy, he confessed around a sob, were working under orders from Mark, Tony, and Paul—men who I knew Senior had trusted.

Men who'd, originally, been on his crew back when he'd still had one. After he'd become the leader, I knew that had changed, and those three had become Generals, while Senior begun having a security detail.

The names had Paddy jerking in surprise. "Fuck. Their betrayal would kill Senior."

I focused on the screen again. "He's not around to deal with their betrayal anymore. We are."

Paddy didn't reply, just turned up the TV as Anthony started mumbling about the details of their plan.

"Some fucking plot," Conor groused. "Easy to see why Da was the brains of their crew."

Paddy snickered. "Your grandda called them Oompa Loompas."

I didn't have it in me to smile.

This betrayal would cut deep. Not just in our family, but in the Irish Mob too.

"How will this affect Aidan's standing with the Points?" I questioned.

"It won't," Conor dismissed. "A bunch of pricks who are clinging to their power while they have it—who gives a fuck about them?"

"What do you mean?" I asked.

"I mean Da listened to them, but Aidan won't," Conor said candidly. "Why would he? He has us to advise him."

That made sense.

"That's what this is about?"

"A power grab? Of course," Paddy answered. "Not just with them either. Jonesy should have been Senior's captain, but after he became the leader of the Points, everything changed. He probably thought he'd get to be the captain of Aidan's crew until—"

"What about the Russians?" I interrupted and turned to Conor. "Are they involved in this?"

"If you were listening," he said patiently, "you'd have heard Aidan send out men to grab the bastards and bring them back to the factory. We'll get more answers when they show up. For now, I need to make sure this isn't a trap."

"I'll let you work," I apologized.

"Good," Conor muttered. "You too, Paddy. I need peace."

Paddy returned his focus to the screen where Aidan hadn't let up with Anthony. "Fine."

"Why were you the only one at the docks?" my husband was demanding, that goddamn bottle of whatever looming over the bastard's face.

"They weren't sure if we'd be able to snatch you. We had to grab you then take you to the docks so we could rendezvous there later."

Aidan allowed a single droplet from the bottle to splash onto Anthony's face, on the upper curve of his cheek. As Anthony howled, as his flesh was eaten away, my husband demanded, "What was the end game?"

"Y-You," he screamed, body writhing as he tried to deal with the pain. "They were going to ransom you."

"What for? Money? Or power?"

Anthony cried, "Both."

"And if we gave it to you," Declan intoned, his voice darker than I'd ever heard it. "Would you have returned Aidan and Savannah to us?"

He closed his eyes which, I guessed, was his answer.

"Mark wants you dead," he rasped. "Callum—he's bitter about your da not investigating his kid's disappearance."

"An eye for an eye," Aidan said with a shake of his head. "Fitting considering what I'm going to do to those baby blues of yours."

Sniveling, he rasped, "Mark had a nice fat dose of heroin to jack you up—"

Aidan, on the move toward the other end of the room, froze in his steps. The purest rage flashed onto his face and Anthony released a whimper when each of the brothers leveled him with a glare worthy of Medusa.

He was seriously lucky that he hadn't been turned to stone.

With my fears realized, the idea that that had been their plan the whole time, I felt sick to my stomach.

It was a smart move. I couldn't fault them for that; it didn't mean I didn't want this Mark bastard to burn for it.

I backed away to one of Conor's desk chairs and sat down heavily in the seat.

"What happened to Mark's boy, Conor?" Paddy asked, inadvertently verbalizing the question that was at the forefront of my mind.

"Used to be one of my best friends," was Conor's grim retort. "He was a Sparrow."

"Shit," Paddy said with a hiss and, ignoring Conor's request for peace again, queried, "Mark doesn't know?"

"Da probably didn't want to hurt his feelings."

"Your father had skewed priorities," Paddy grumbled.

Was I the only one who noticed Conor didn't answer the question?

Conor harrumphed. "You don't have to tell me that. I already fucking know."

"This world ain't changed much," Paddy said on a sigh. "A man's weaknesses always come back and bite him in the ass."

I had no idea why Paddy drifted out of the room after making that declaration, leaving Conor and me alone, but I was grateful he had.

My mind was whirring, my heart was still pounding, and I thought about all those autopsy reports I'd read over the years and accepted that Aidan had gone easy on Anthony.

He'd broken easily.

Too easily?

Or was he just a wuss?

"Conor, Aidan barely touched him and he was spouting all that—"

"Savannah, if you let me fucking work, that's what I'm trying to figure out."

I kept my trap shut from that moment on, even when, in an aside, he said, "There's a doctor outside waiting to check you over. It pains me to utter these words, Savannah, but Aidan told me to tell you that if you don't agree to see him, he'll tie you to the bed again..." He arched a brow at me. "I'm asking you kindly to let the doctor tend to you so I don't have to hear anything else about your sex life."

Which was when I realized *why* Paddy had left—to bring in the doctor.

I shot them all a dirty look, but knowing it would put Aidan's mind at rest, and for that reason alone, I submitted to the checkup.

28

—————

AIDAN

IT WAS AMAZING what could be accomplished when every single Five Pointer was working to eradicate internal threats.

In less than an hour, Jonesy, Mark, Paul, Tony, and Connolly were all at the cement factory, as were the rest of their crews.

We didn't have the space to separate them, but I kept the ringleaders apart from the crews because, as far as I could tell, this was a small operation. Not just to keep the chance at success high, but because the majority of their men were loyal to me.

I needed that confirmation before anything else went down, though, so we got to work.

While Five Pointers weren't snitches, they were human.

When I used Anthony as an example of how I blinded men, they quickly spilled their guts.

A few hours in, and as I'd surmised, most of the crews were in the dark about their leaders' intentions, but they were sheep so I knew they'd have gone along with them anyway.

It was hard to torture a sheep for being a sheep when you wanted them to be a sheep so I cut my losses, warned them that they'd be on notice for the foreseeable future, and continued my hunt for a wolf among them.

One popped out.

Unsurprisingly, it was Paul's son, Hal. Middle-aged, soft around the gut, not that smart in the brain department, he kept to himself, did his job, but I knew he had a tendency to talk too much when he was drunk. Da had given Paul shit about that in the past.

What interested me the most was how the men naturally moved away from him as if they were trying to avoid his attention. Or was it that they were avoiding the wolf in the flock?

I didn't know him that well. Da hadn't liked him and who Da didn't like, we never hung out with. Callum, Mark's boy, Da had liked, and that was why he'd encouraged a friendship between Conor and Callum...

Hal was one of those kids who'd pulled off fly's wings for fun or who'd trained a magnifying glass onto an ant hill and let the sun's rays burn them.

Standard psychopath shit, but in a world of psychopaths, a man grew to be discerning.

Da was cruel, but nothing he did was pointless.

Hurting flies, burning ants, what was the use in that?

He was more likely to stomp on the ants and swat the fly then punch whoever had left food out that had attracted the bugs in the first place.

Psychopathy 101 from the master himself—was it any wonder I was fucked in the head?

Glancing over Paul's crew one final time, reading expressions and the minutiae that another could have missed, I informed them, "Hal, you're staying. The rest of you can follow Declan out of here."

The sense of relief was palpable. It was as if a massive set of bellows had triggered a gust of wind that wafted around the space, airing it.

Most of them sagged as I watched them trudge from the room,

muttering speculation under their breath, but I maintained my focus on Hal who Brennan sidled close to so he couldn't run off.

And he was showing signs of trying to—his eyes had gotten big, and they were flickering from left to right, quick enough that it could have given him motion sickness.

With Anthony still sobbing behind me until Declan returned and dragged him out, I headed over to a stool in one corner and I took a seat.

Resting my elbows on my knees, I stared at Hal and drawled, "Should have known you'd be in on this. You're too much of an idiot not to recognize when you should keep your nose out of things."

"Fuck you, Aidan," Hal snarled. "You ain't got the right to talk to me that way."

"He's got every fucking right," Brennan snapped, clipping him upside the head. "He's your goddamn boss."

"You ain't my fucking boss." Hal straightened. "If that soft piece of shit, Anthony, hadn't ratted us out, you'd never have known what was—"

His idiocy confirmed, as well as his treachery, I spat, "You asswipes had the subtlety of a nun in a whorehouse. You overplayed your hand, Hal. Far too early as well."

"Always were a moron. That's why you're still on your da's crew and never made anything of yourself," Brennan sneered.

Hal whipped around to glower at him. "Fuck you. If anyone can't talk about living under their father's thumb, it's the O'Donnelly boys.

"Look what happens the minute he dies—chaos."

"You're not wrong," I said smoothly. "But transition is always hard on everyone. You, however, made it easier on me, Hal. You did me a fucking favor by coming up with a useless plot to overthrow me.

"If anything, I'm reaping the benefits of my da's short-sightedness. He's the one who trusted those snakes in his crew, he's the one who brought them into the inner circle, and he's the reason I'm having a problem tonight."

"If you think there ain't deeper problems than that, you're a fucking idiot."

"Oh, I know we got issues, but I also know that after tonight, I'll have half-a-dozen fewer 'snags' to deal with.

"Unfortunately for you, you're the ones who brought yourself to the top of my list."

I withdrew a set of keys that Declan had given me earlier. He'd handed my cell and Da's back to me as well as the other shit that had been swiped from my pockets after the crash. These keys were proof of Mark's involvement as no one should possess them other than an O'Donnelly because they opened Da's office here.

Mark had been handling them like they belonged to him.

They didn't.

I'd never wanted this fucking throne of bones that my family had been dead set on leaving to me, but that didn't mean I was about to let it be taken from me either.

I thought about Savvie, I thought about what she was, who she was, and I thought about what she'd shown me tonight.

I'd married an equal.

But in my world, a wife would never be an equal. It just wasn't how we worked. We protected our women, we sheltered them, and we kept them safe. We often failed in those duties, but we had enemies, and that couldn't be helped.

But Savannah wasn't afraid.

Tonight, she'd acted with strength.

That was why I tucked the longest key between my pointer and middle finger, it was why I clutched the bundle of keys in my palm as I strolled over to Hal, and it was why I chose to gift her with her request.

When I was close enough to put a hand on his shoulder, Brennan was all that stopped him from bolting away.

I smiled at him, pleasantly, like we were about to have a chat, but the fucker surprised me.

Surging upward, using strength that was founded in desperation, he head-butted me. I didn't think he had more of a plan than that, but my already aching skull got a full-frontal hit, and though he dazed me, Brennan quickly grabbed him around the neck and hauled him down to his knees with a dull thud that had him shouting hoarsely in pain.

I had to laugh as I reached up and brushed a finger along my bleeding nose. "Nice try, Hal," I told him. "But all you've done is piss me the fuck off."

Pinching the tip, I winced as my eyes watered with pain, but one thing you got used to when you were raised by Da was a busted fucking nose.

Brennan shot me a look, but I dismissed his concern as I loomed over Hal, the side of my spare hand slamming into his throat.

While he choked, I informed him, "We might call our firm the Five Points, but the O'Donnellys is silent. There ain't no Five Points without the O'Donnellys, and there never fucking will be. Not as long as I have breath in my lungs."

I jabbed him.

Allowed the blunt tip of the key to penetrate the soft sclera of his eye.

Satisfaction filled me as he howled out his pain and his surprise. When he sagged over, I pulled my hand back and shoved the bloody keys into my pocket.

Blood spattered around him as he cupped his eye, his sniffles and wails merging into one long scream as he rocked himself.

Watching his suffering for a few moments, silently, I retrieved my cell from my other pocket, grabbed him by the back of the head, and tugged on his hair until I got a good shot of his face. He wriggled and writhed against my hold, my grip undoubtedly tugging on his new wound, but Brennan helped me by putting his foot between Hal's shoulders and forcing him to maintain his position.

With him shrieking like a banshee, I snapped a photo, moved away from him, and sent it to Savannah.

No caption.

Nothing.

I thought she'd be asleep, but she replied:

Savvie: *THANK YOU*

My lips twitched before I schooled my expression and turned around to face Hal once more.

Brennan's confusion was clear—why stab him in the eye with a key when I had a knife at hand?

I didn't bother explaining the imagery or why it was a reward. Brennan gifted Camille with diamonds and emeralds, not bloodied photos of torture victims. It wasn't like he'd get it even if I tried to make him understand.

Instead of explaining, over his incessant wails, I projected, "Now, Hal, you have a choice. I can pin you to that crucifix and you can bleed out slowly, or you can die with the rest of your conspirators. Quickly."

When he didn't reply, Brennan kicked him. "Answer him."

When a response wasn't imminent, he did it again. And again. Until Hal, his voice gruff from screaming, rasped, "What do you want from me?"

"Funny how all these soft fucks cave in so fast, isn't it?" Brennan mocked.

He wasn't wrong.

Conor had told me that the moment Anthony had confessed, he and Savannah had thought the admission spilled too easily, too quickly from his lips.

But that wasn't how dipshits like these worked.

They were sheep too.

They just thought they were wolves.

They weren't.

There were six wolves in the Five Points, and they were all goddamn O'Donnellys.

"It is," I concurred. "But, you see, that's what happens when you try to take something that you know will never belong to you."

"Sounds like idiocy to me."

I smiled at Brennan's objection. "Or faith. If anyone understands faith, it's us, isn't it?"

He rolled his eyes at that, but I just stared down at Hal and rumbled, "How many in the plot were in the ECD too?"

Hal's good eye flared wide. "N-No one."

More scared of the ECD than us...

Well, I couldn't allow that, could I?

I drew out my blade, ignoring the crusted edge of blood from its last victim, and crouched down in front of him.

Much as I'd done with Anthony, I let it scrape against his jaw, but this time, I burrowed in deep.

"My wife has burns here," I told him conversationally as Brennan grabbed his head and held him in place for me while he sobbed and snotted and cried out his agony. "Only fitting you should bear scars too." As blood seeped from the cuts I made, I rasped, "The ECD can't get to you here, Hal. But I can."

His good eye peered into mine and he blurted out, "J-Jonesy."

"Just him?"

He nodded within the constraints Brennan gave him.

I thought about his reaction. "Was Jonesy the ringleader behind this?"

"Mark was," he squeaked as I dragged my blade over the raw flesh on his jaw.

"Was this an ECD ploy or purely a Five Pointer coup?"

"Five Pointer."

I processed that, then I jabbed him in his bad eye with my fist. Brennan let go at the point of collision, so when Hal fell back, and his head hit the concrete floor, it was lights out for him.

"Tie him up," I ordered.

"Forrest," Brennan barked at one of his men.

"Coming, Bren," Forrest muttered, studying me warily as he dragged Hal away from us.

"What are you thinking?"

I allowed my mind to roam as I stared at him.

"We need a fall guy."

Brennan jolted at that. "What?"

"The Alphabets aren't going to stop until the First Lady's assassin is taken out."

Brennan frowned. "What does that have to do with this? Shouldn't we be focusing on what's happening here and now? Did that fucker rattle your brain or something?"

Grunting under my breath, I shoved a hand into my pocket while the other rubbed along my tender nose. "How many daughters does Jonesy have? Two, ain't it?"

"Yeah, but he let Samantha go because she was a lesbian."

I scowled at that. "'Let her go.' Like she's fucking trash. This goddamn toxicity has to end, Bren. Da treated Declan like he was a lesser son because he liked the ballet. He ain't even gay!"

Brennan slapped a hand to my shoulder. "One problem at a time, Aidan. Tell me what you want to happen."

My jaw worked as I stared at him. "I'm not used to saying this shit out loud."

"What shit?"

"My ideas. My opinions. Da wasn't interested in them."

"Da's dead. You ain't."

"Doesn't mean I don't feel the same way as when he was around." I slapped a hand to my throat. The side of it butted up against my Adam's apple. "Like he's got my vocal cords in a chokehold. He never trusted me, Bren. If he did, we wouldn't be in the state we are."

His eyes flared wide at that. "Because of the dyslexia? Is that where you're going with this?"

I dipped my chin. "He never said it, but I always knew I was a disappointment. Couldn't read, couldn't shoot in a straight line... I never fucking wanted this, Bren, but now I got it, I ain't about to throw it away."

His gaze narrowed as he stared right into mine. "You think you were alone in feeling like a useless piece of crap of a son, Aidan? I was the spare heir; Declan was the pansy because he liked art.

"The only ones he ever approved of were Eoghan and Conor. And why? Because they did what they wanted. They listened to their own heart and rebelled against him.

"He wanted our obedience, but he didn't respect us for giving it to him. Eoghan fucked off to the army because he didn't want to become a Five Pointer, and we all know Conor does as he's told but only because he wants to. Con can bitch about his workload, but you can't tell me that he don't get off on it too. As for Eoghan, he's the same.

"You, Declan, and me are the disappointments, Aidan. And we're the ones who are fucking interested in keeping this firm going. Not Eoghan, not Conor. They're interested in family. Not the business. But us...

"So, you take Da's foot off your throat, remember that you're not a useless fucker because you can't read easily, you goddamn remember that you beat an addiction without outside help, and you remember that you are my brother, and that I know how fucking smart you are even if Da didn't."

His words rattled me. Enough that I bowed my head for a second, enough that I had to process the truth in them.

He was right—Dec, Bren, and I had all been disappointments, and we were the only ones who'd ever obeyed.

Look where it had gotten us.

Peering up at him, I rumbled, "We can't keep second-guessing who is and who isn't a Sparrow or a *cheile*. It diminishes our power and our strength in the city, but it takes time and precious resources away from what matters the most.

"On top of that, we need a fall guy for the First Lady's assassin, and it can't be Eamonn Keegan—not only because he'll never hand himself in, but because we need him."

"Thought you wanted to take him down? Avenge Da?"

"I can do it Da's way or I can do it mine."

He narrowed his eyes on me. "Da's dead," he repeated. "You ain't. You're the leader now. We do what you think's right. I trust you, Aidan. I know you'll avenge Da. It just won't be how he'd like."

"With a bloodbath?" I asked with a smirk.

Bren dipped his chin. "Why do we need a fall guy?"

"Because the city's still on red alert, and the nation is too. That investigation isn't going to go away. It won't end until someone's sent up for her murder."

"That makes sense."

"If we want the city to open back up for real, we need to deal with that. And we don't want the alphabet agencies looking into Da's death, do we?"

"No," he agreed. "We don't. The investigations haven't caused too much of a problem with our business, though."

"The ports are still under scrutiny," I pointed out. "That'll affect product being shipped into the city."

"We use roads for that."

"Doesn't mean they're not being watched. Plus, the Armenians pay us to make sure their gear gets shipped in under the radar."

"So do the Albanians," he said, his eyes darkening. "Okay. I see where you're coming from. I wasn't thinking long-term. Everyone knows that the country's in uproar because of the assassination, but that won't stop business forever."

"No. It won't."

"So, tell me. What are you thinking?"

Taking a leap of faith, I released a breath. "Jonesy loves his wife, doesn't he?"

"Depends on who you ask. I'd say yeah, but that don't mean he ain't got a skirt he knocked up, living in an apartment off Midtown. And it don't mean his wife ain't resentful that her baby girl ain't welcome at home anymore because she prefers pussies to cocks."

"What's his weakness, Brennan?"

I watched his focus fade, shift, as he raced to give me the answer I needed. Brennan was good with shit like this. He didn't always see the bigger picture and could act prematurely, but he picked up details along the way and they always came in useful.

"The skirt. And the boy."

"Seriously?"

He nodded and clapped me hard enough on the shoulder to rattle my bones. As he called out, "Bagpipes!" I hid my wince.

Fuck, it had been nice to be without pain for a while. It was a shame it appeared to be my best friend.

"You barked," Bagpipes muttered as he drifted in, wiping his sweaty brow with the back of his hand—clearly, he'd been helping Forrest with Hal.

"Jonesy's sidepiece."

"What about her?"

"She got pregnant, didn't she?"

"Yup. Gave birth two months ago. A boy."

I smiled.

Bagpipes blanched.

I didn't see that though.

I was too busy thinking three steps ahead.

29

———————

TEXT CHAT

AIDAN: *I know I said this already, but after what we learned last night, THANK YOU. All of you.*

Eoghan: *You getting maudlin on us?*

Conor: *Eoghan, did you know that it's more difficult to get clean the second time around? Nothing maudlin about what could have gone down.*

Eoghan: *That would never have happened.*

Finn: *You don't know that. I'm thankful it didn't.*

Declan: *Agreed. I'm grateful they didn't fuck you up, Aidan.*

Brennan: *Me fucking too.*

Conor: *You heard Anthony, Eoghan. Mark was just waiting to dose him up with heroin.*

Aidan: *It was too close a call. Especially if Mark had given the task to Jonesy. They could have injected me with heroin at the site of the crash.*

Eoghan: *Unlikely. His job was to get you out of there and to move you to a secondary location. Plus, it was personal for Mark. It wasn't for Jonesy.*

Finn: *Jesus, we know to come to you for reassurance, don't we?*

Eoghan: *Just saying it how it is.*

Aidan: *That it didn't happen doesn't mean it couldn't happen in the future. It's a weakness our enemies will exploit. I'm sorry, dearthàirs.*

Declan: *They could jack anyone up on heroin, Aidan. It's not unique to you. You only think it is because of your past.*

Aidan: *The irony is that I thought I did a good job of hiding my addiction, but that bastard knew.*

Conor: *Any and all weaknesses can be exploited. There's no point in worrying about it. No point in regretting what's done. We just have to make sure that what happened can't happen again.*

Eoghan: *You're living in a fairy tale if you think that's easy to plan against. No one knows more than me how easy it is to take a life.*

Brennan: *Okay, you two, what the fuck's going on? Tell us before I ram your heads together.*

Eoghan: *I have no idea what you're talking about.*

Conor: *Dunno what you mean.*

Brennan: *Bullshit. Eoghan's been acting like he's quit sugar around you for what feels like months now, Conor. What the fuck have you done to piss him off?*

Declan: *You HAVE been a moody SOB, Eoghan.*

Eoghan: *Sometimes, the PTSD hits harder than others. Anyway, I'm gonna get some sleep before we have to get back to the factory. Glad you and Savannah are home and safe, Aidan.*

Conor: *Me too.*

Declan: *And me. Fuck, nearly took a couple years off my life when Conor called us.*

Finn: *Jesus, it was the same for me.*

Brennan: *Thought it was one of Kid's stupid jokes at first.*

Conor: *Charming.*

Aidan: *Well, whatever. But thank you. Knowing you guys have my back makes this shitshow I'm in charge of that much easier to handle. Get some rest, all of you.*

Declan: *Night, bro.*

Finn: *See you tomorrow.*

Brennan: *Sleep well.*

Conor: *You know if I'd needed to wean you off the heroin, Aidan, I'd have done it, don't you?*

Aidan: *Yeah, Kid. I know you would've. I'm a lucky fucker that you'd do that for me. Get some Zzzs.*

Conor : *Will do.*

30

———

SAVANNAH

I DRIFTED into awareness with the scent of musk, bergamot, and cedar in my nose.

Maybe because it wasn't fish, that was why I woke up.

Or maybe it had something to do with the fact that I was being carried... Last time, the pain... A stranger who wasn't a stranger...

I jolted awake.

Then sagged as I blinked up into Aidan's face.

Not a kidnapper.

"Go back to sleep," he rumbled, carrying me around like he hadn't just dislocated his shoulder and had spent an evening torturing men.

I wasn't sure which concerned me more, especially when I threw in his knee for good measure.

But cold logic told me that he knew what he was doing and that my best option was not to fidget and to stay deathly still so he wouldn't drop me.

"Where are we going?" I whispered sleepily.

"Home," was his answer, and I pressed my face into his throat, allowing him to take me downstairs when I had a set of legs that were in full working order.

The elevator cocooned us in a silence we didn't break, not even when I saw the bruising to his eyes, the cut on his nose, nor when I input the code into our door, or when he walked me over to the bedroom.

He placed me on the bed then spent the next minute shucking out of his clothes.

In the light from the moon, I watched him. "You have more bruises than earlier."

"One of the fuckers head-butted me."

He didn't sound angry, more amused.

Frowning, I asked, "Which one?"

"The guy whose eye I jabbed. Hal."

"You got him for both of us then."

"I did." He cast me a look. "The doctor said you have a mild concussion."

"I know. Conor set an alarm to wake me every hour," I groused before, arching a brow at him, I demanded, "Did you see a doctor?"

His hum told me everything.

Damn men.

Huffing, I asked, "What time is it anyway?"

"Nearly six AM."

I yawned and held out a hand for him. When he took it, I hid a grimace as the cuts on my fingers made themselves known.

"How bad are they cut up?" he asked, tracing the Band-Aids as he climbed into bed beside me.

"Not too bad. Just superficial."

He grunted his displeasure then proceeded to drag me out of my bathrobe.

Though I grumbled, I didn't stop him. "My phone's in the pocket. With the alarm on."

"Not like you to be so agreeable," he murmured wryly when he flung the bathrobe over to the other side of the room after he grabbed my cell and dumped it on the nightstand.

"I'm tired, you're home, you stabbed someone in the eye for me with a key like I wanted, which means I don't have to do it, so why would I be disagreeable?"

His lips curved, and because his face was a play of shadows and light, I sighed at his beauty, even though that beauty was busted up right now, and reached up to trace his mouth with my thumb.

"You'll never spill a drop of blood, Savannah. Ever. That's what I'm for."

While his words were sweet—for a mobster—I asked, "Do you guys use special soap?"

His head reared back at my question—clearly, it had come as a surprise. "What?"

"I nearly rubbed myself raw trying to get clean."

"You'd been rolling around in fish blood. We might have rats, but their blood smells just like ours."

His nose drifted down to my throat, and when he inhaled, I squirmed but not in a good way. I was half certain the reeking odor of putrefying fish was still the top note of 'Savannah perfume.'

"You smell like mine," he rasped.

"I am yours," I whispered back, liking his answer more than he could know.

"Then why were you wearing Conor's bathrobe?"

I had to grin. "You're jealous of a bathrobe? It wasn't Conor's. It was in his guest bath."

He huffed.

"Don't be a child, Aidan," I teased, leaning over to press a kiss to his lips. "Everything I am, is yours, husband." God, that sounded so formal. So Jane Austen. But damn if the words didn't resonate.

They did with him too.

He shuddered and his mouth fell onto mine. As he speared me with his tongue, I groaned and angled myself closer to him.

It was only when his wedding ring rubbed over my cheek that I yelped which had him jerking back like I'd stung him with a cattle prod.

I reached up and patted the tender flesh. "I should have gotten you one of those traditional rings, not a square-edge one."

Because, hell, that had stung, and he hadn't pressed down that hard.

"I'm so fucking sorry, little one," he rumbled, edging away. Farther and farther.

No way was I about to allow that to happen.

I snagged his arm and drew him back to me. I grabbed his hand, angled it, and pressed it to my throat where my turtleneck had protected the skin. "No burns there," I told him.

He growled. "There shouldn't be any anywhere."

"Gimme a week and they'll be gone."

A hiss escaped him. "I'll make them pay for this, Savannah."

"I know you will. I want a front row seat to whatever you're cooking up too."

He stilled. "What do you mean?"

"What do you mean 'what do I mean?'" I mocked. "You've got to have something planned. Something grand and elaborate. Something that'll cement who you are and what you are into the minds of the Five Points."

He was quiet. "Your brain is terrifying."

"Thank you," I told him, and I meant it.

Just as he'd meant his compliment.

He let go of my throat and flopped down onto the bed. "I hadn't gotten that far yet. I dealt with what I had to tonight and then I came home. My head is killing me, or I'd still be out. My goddamn alarm is set for two hours' time. I shouldn't have bothered disturbing you upstairs."

I heard what he wasn't going to say, and I was fine with that—he'd needed to reconnect with me. Aidan always rambled when he was feeling defensive.

I rewarded him by turning onto my side and hooking one of my thighs over his. My hand went to his cock and I angled us so that the tip was rubbing up against my clit.

"Savannah," he warned tiredly. "Not now, little one."

"I know, I know," I muttered. "I'm going somewhere with this, I promise."

He heard my teasing tone because he snorted his amusement.

I wasn't lying though. Every part of me was aching. Every. Single. Part. Orgasms might help with pain relief, but I wasn't doing this for that.

When I was wet enough to accept him into me, not drenched like usual, but enough for my purpose, I slipped him inside with a sigh.

He hauled an arm around my shoulder and tucked me into him, exhaling deeply with the relief of our re-connection.

"You could have died tonight," I whispered.

"You could have too, baby girl." His mouth pressed against my temple, and he rubbed his lips back and forth, back and forth. "You could have been raped; you could have been hurt." He let loose another heavy exhalation. "This fucking world."

He was right, but... "It isn't the world, Aidan. It's humans. It's people. People make up the world. Don't forget that," I warned.

When he didn't answer, I squeezed his cock to keep him hard inside me, gently pulsing my pussy just to maintain the link.

For the first time in a long while, I truly didn't want sex. I just wanted to connect. I just wanted to feel him inside me.

I wanted to know he was home.

"There were..." I swallowed. "I thought you were dead in the truck. You weren't moving, and I didn't dare check if you were alive or not. I knew that if they thought I was conscious, they might try to torture me for information. So I stayed still, and I tried to figure out what was happening and..."

He pressed his mouth to mine to still the words.

"If I could have spared you from that, I would have."

"You can't 'spare' me from life," I quoted him. "This is reality, Aidan. Our reality. I came into it with my eyes open, and sure, I got a dose of it tonight that came out of the blue, but we're here. We survived. We will live to see another day, and we will thrive. Won't we?"

He didn't answer my question, but his fingers entwined in my hair, gently stroking it in a way that soothed as he muttered, "When the Aryans took Ma, Da blamed Brennan. He said he was the one who should have been guarding her. He was a kid, Savvie. A fucking kid. But he blamed Bren, and when he captured the Aryans, Brennan was the one who hit the kill switch."

I'd heard the tale. I wasn't sure anyone in the underworld, or anyone who was curious about it, hadn't heard what Aidan Sr. had done to the men who'd dared take his wife, who'd raped her and abused her...

"The car crusher?" I whispered.

"Yeah. Bren told me once that Da had the Aryans lined up in concrete boots, strung up above the jaws of the crusher. Bren hit the switch that released 'em into its maw.

"For months afterward, I'd hear him screaming in his sleep. We ignored it. That was what you were supposed to do. If Da could have stopped him having nightmares, he would have.

"Instead, we just pretended it wasn't happening, and Da was so fucking focused on Ma anyway because she was a wreck that Bren's trauma got forgotten about. We pulled together; that's what we do. Bren was never the same after, though.

"That's the kind of man my father was, Savvie. Those were the shows he put on for the world, and the aftermath wasn't only felt by the city, but by us too."

"Like it or not, that story resonated within New York's underbelly, Aidan." Even as my heart ached for the teenaged Brennan, even as my soul wept for what Aidan was going to have to do, I told him, "You don't have to be like your da, you don't have to make the same choices he did, but you have to follow his path to some extent.

"Your da knew how to make memories last. His reputation made him the city's boogeyman. You need to do that if you want to survive this, Aidan, baby."

"If we have a kid, I'll never put him or her through what Da put us through. I promise—"

"You don't have to promise me that," I assured him. "Because I will make damn sure that you don't."

A soft breath had him sagging against me. "You mean that."

I snorted. "Of course I do. My mom and dad made a lot of mistakes, and they did weird shit that I wish I could unsee because, *gross*, but... they were good parents.

"They let us get away with too much, and we weren't on a tight enough leash, but that doesn't take away from the fact that I know what good parents look like.

"I can fangirl over your family, Aidan, but I can say, *categorically*, you had folks who deserved to go to jail for child abuse and child neglect." He stilled at that. "They fucked with your heads, they tore you down, and they broke you so that they could shape you into the image they wanted you to be. Then, when you were how they wanted, they punished you for that too.

"So, no, if we do have a child, I'll never let you do that. And if I ever think you are starting to go down that path, I will take that child and I will leave your ass because that kid is me and you together. Before life and the firm and everything else got in the way.

"That kid will be our love. A union of us. Pure and perfect and exactly how it was supposed to be.

"The other night, I told you that lying to me was my hard limit. But that's the current Savannah. Not the 'mother' Savannah. Remember that, sweetheart. Your ma didn't go to war for you, but I sure as fuck will go to war for your child. Do you hear me?"

I wasn't sure why I expected recriminations. He'd already told me at the start of our relationship that there would never be a divorce for us. That we were it. And it had nothing to do with him being 'semi' Catholic.

So I expected a negative response to my stark warning.

Something that'd tell me I was his woman and that nothing

would tear us apart... Not even a child. That he was the he-man and I was the woman and I should listen, blah, blah, blah.

What I didn't anticipate was for him to roll us over so that I was on my back and for his dick to turn to steel inside me without me having to clutch at it to hold him there.

He pumped into me, his hands snagging mine as he drew them over my head and pinned them to the pillows. Using that as the fulcrum for the slow thrusts that he tormented me with, he breathed into my mouth, "My fucking queen."

I shuddered at that. His words, not at what his cock was doing to me.

Not at what he was making me feel.

But at his respect.

His appreciation.

He didn't take offense at my words; he gloried in them.

His tongue thrust between my lips with as much force as his dick slid into my pussy, and I let him. I let his stroke against mine, let him devour me, let him bask in the things this mouth had told him.

Hard truths, but loving ones.

Protective ones.

Assertive ones.

For a kid we might never have.

As he drove his cock into me, his pelvis did most of the heavy lifting as he ground into my clit, and while the spikes of pleasure were there, it wasn't the desperate need that I'd come to associate with sex with him.

It was loving and needy and clingy and wanting. It was love made real. It was everything I'd never known I'd needed because Aidan had already given me so much in the bedroom.

He swallowed my air and I took his. He cherished me and worshiped me all because he'd accepted the truth—I wasn't like any woman he'd ever known.

I wasn't supposed to be.

I *was* his queen.

Maybe it made sense that those thoughts were what made me come.

As I cried out, my lips tore away from his, and his mouth drifted down the length of my jaw, bringing sensitive nerve endings to life, before he sucked on my earlobe. And as he impaled me on his cock, over and over, chasing his own release, in my ear, he whispered, "Mine, mine, mine."

And I was that.

In all the ways under the sun.

Strong enough to stand up to him. To stand up for him.

Strong enough to melt under his intensity.

Strong enough to endure.

Strong enough to fight, to be at his side with no doubts between us.

I was his equal and, I knew, this moment was the first time he registered that.

So maybe I needed to thank our kidnappers for showing him a hard truth so early on in our marriage...

As he pumped his seed into me, I almost hoped we'd made a kid together even though I knew it wasn't possible. It just felt fitting.

But... no.

We weren't ready for that yet.

The world wasn't ready for that yet.

Because New York wasn't ready for Savannah O'Donnelly to be a mother, and the East Coast sure as fuck wasn't prepared for Aidan to be a dad.

I sighed at the thought and tugged at his grip on my arms. Not to dislodge them, but to shift them. I twisted us over, well aware that he let me, and I settled on him, clinging to him as much as I blanketed him.

Tucking my face into his throat, I nuzzled into him. "I love you."

He kissed my temple. "And I fucking love you, little one."

I released a breath at that and settled deeper into him.

We were safe, and we were together.

We might not always be the former, but we would always be the latter...

31

AIDAN

"YOU WON'T HURT MY FAMILY," Jonesy sneered, but I saw the fear in his eyes. Saw it, embraced it.

I wasn't Da—that didn't mean I couldn't be me.

That didn't mean I wasn't aware of what needed to be done to secure my family, to protect us and keep us safe from pricks like this one.

"Won't I?" I mused, staring at his half-naked body with a displeased glance.

All the traitors had been stripped to the waist so we could check for ink.

Hal, no surprise, had proven himself to be a fucking liar—Mark shared the same phoenix tattoo on his shoulder as Jonesy did.

Mark was a goddamn *cheile* too.

Still annoyed by the discovery, I clicked my fingers. The door opened and Lucas walked in with Jonesy's side piece and his son on his hip.

The woman was terrified. I couldn't blame her. She kept eying her son then darting her focus to the floor. Her fear was palpable, and the kid responded to that by bawling and slapping his hands against Lucas's chest.

Jonesy blanched the second he saw them, then he snarled, "You piece of shit."

For the first time, his control was ruptured. He jerked his seat upwards by the bindings on his wrists which only resulted in the piece of crap falling forward because gravity wasn't kind to a man whose beer gut was as big as a pregnant mother's belly.

As he collided with the floor, the woman started sniffling.

"You better not have fucking hurt him," Jonesy howled, trying to scramble onto his back, proving that he was a moron because he was literally a tortoise with a chair-shaped shell, and there was no way in fuck he was going to do anything other than look like a fool.

"Jonesy," I murmured as he carried on scrabbling around, ignoring the fact that his wrists and ankles were bleeding from the tight bindings. "I told you what would happen if you didn't listen to me. Now, I'm *showing* you what'll happen."

My gaze caught the woman's, and though her bottom lip trembled, she kept her mouth shut.

Exactly like I was paying her to.

Jonesy sagged against the floor. "You fucking bastard," he sobbed. "You can't threaten a man's child—"

"Didn't realize that was the rule of the game," was all I said as I grabbed his chair and hauled his deadweight into an upright position.

I moved over to my captain, and though she tensed, Jonesy's side piece, Rebecca, didn't argue when I took their boy, Richie, from Lucas and propped him on my hip. The kid stunned me by falling quiet as I held him against me. He smelled of soap and baby wipes. I recognized both because of Cameron.

As I moved over to Jonesy, I saw the longing and the love in his eyes for his son, and it sickened me. Not because it was wrong to want to protect your kid, or to love them, but because this child was cherished because it was a 'he.'

The man had two daughters: one he'd thrown away like she was trash, and the other was a Five Pointer's wife with kids of her own, but what really got to him was me holding his son.

Because he was a boy.

Like daughters didn't matter.

Still, I couldn't complain. Not when this was his pressure point to gain his obedience.

I narrowed my eyes on him as I asked, "If you do as you're told, Jonesy, nothing will happen to them. I'll watch over them, make sure they have enough money. Which, to be frank, seeing as you're old and unhealthy as fuck, is more than they could hope for if you died of a heart attack. This way, you can make sure they're cared for when you're worm food."

Jonesy's eyes leaked as he rasped, "Your da would never have threatened a baby."

I smiled at him. "Ain't I told you fuckers enough? I ain't my da."

Jonesy gulped, but his mouth wobbled as he dipped his chin. "I'll do it. For him."

I moved away from him and handed the kid back to Rebecca. She clung to him the second I handed him over.

"I made you a promise," I whispered to her, soft enough for Jonesy not to hear, tutting as her lips trembled.

She sniffled and stepped back.

"Take her home, Lucas," I drawled, twisting around to face Jonesy again, who snarled:

"What did you fucking say to her? Leave her alone, do you hear me? Leave her the fuck alone."

I didn't bother gracing him with an answer, just told Brennan, "Get him cleaned up. We got work to do."

32

AIDAN

CHANGE (IN THE HOUSE OF FLIES) - DEFTONES

A COUPLE HOURS LATER

"REMEMBER, Jonesy, you make one wrong move, Lucas has his orders."

Jonesy staggered up the staircase to the security door and pressed the intercom. Within seconds, the door buzzed and he pushed it open.

He could have rushed inside and locked us out, but he didn't.

Brennan, noticing this, muttered, "He was right when he said Da would never have threatened a kid. Why doesn't he know that you wouldn't hurt a baby either?"

"Because he would and if he's capable of it, then everyone is."

Weighing into the conversation, Declan grunted. "Sick fuck."

"Not going to argue," I murmured as I climbed the staircase to the building's entrance and moved inside the foyer.

I got my bearings as Jonesy led us to an elevator, and we all packed inside as we raced to Keegan's floor.

"Just show your face, and we'll deal with the rest," I told Jonesy.

"I know what I have to do," he snapped, glowering at each of my brothers and me. "Do I have your fucking word that you'll never touch Richie?"

"If you do as you're told. The moment you're about to get a lethal injection, my man, is the moment you have my promise no harm will come to Richie."

He gritted his teeth and turned his face away from us.

The elevator doors opened, and he stepped out into the hall. This was another part of today's play that could go belly up, but I had high hopes. Jonesy's concern for Richie was palpable, and I wasn't above using that against him. Just like he'd have used my pressure points against me.

I knew men like Jonesy. Savannah would have been raped, assaulted, and abused, all to get to me.

But what Jonesy didn't understand, and what I hadn't either until last night, was that Savannah wasn't my weakness. My vulnerability. She was a source of strength. A solid counsel that I'd need in the days ahead.

In my ear, Conor broke into my thoughts by murmuring, "Got eyes on Keegan through the window. He's acting naturally."

"Good," I said under my breath.

Keegan opened the door when Jonesy knocked on it, and when we surged in behind him, his reaction time was impressive. The door hadn't even closed before he'd grabbed a hold of Jonesy and had his throat tucked into the bend of his arm.

A man like Keegan knew how to go for the jugular too.

"You fucking traitor," he spat in Jonesy's ear while the bastard squawked and groaned as his oxygen supply was slowly cut off from him.

With the snap of the door closing, and with each of my brothers now in the room with us, I remarked, "You don't want to kill him, Keegan."

"I don't? The fucker betrayed me."

Keegan, for all Eoghan had painted the renowned 'Dagda' as a legend, wasn't as impressive as I'd imagined. He was a man. A resourceful one, a clever one, but not unstoppable.

"He's betrayed a lot of people," was my answer. "He tried to kidnap my wife and me, so I think if anyone has the bigger grudge, it's me, and I let the bastard live."

"Well, you and me ain't the same person," Keegan sneered, his arm turning white from the force he exerted upon Jonesy's throat.

"No, we're not, but I'm here to talk. I'm not here to fight. I'm not here to kill you. I'm here to make a deal."

Keegan reared back at that, taking Jonesy with him. In the blink of an eye, Jonesy's arm was up in the air and he was collapsing to the ground as Keegan cut off the blood supply to his head. Jonesy released a low groan, letting me know he wasn't dead, which I was thankful for.

I had plans for him, after all.

Stepping over the huddled pile of arms and legs, Keegan approached me, demanding, "You bring your brothers with you every time you choose to make a deal? Need them to hold your hand?"

I smiled at him, his mockery failing to find its target. "Some business transcends dollars and cents. This is blood. You took my father's life—"

"And he took my sister's," Keegan snarled, getting in my space.

My brothers tensed up around me, but I didn't flinch.

I'd been doing my due diligence on Eamonn Keegan ever since I'd heard his name for the first time.

I knew what he was, knew what he was capable of.

Much like Da, his weakness was family.

So, with his face so close that his hissed words had saliva flecking my chin, I told him, "You'd be dead already if I were here for you."

"More powerful men than you have tried," he sneered.

I graced him with a soft smile. "You'd be surprised how powerful I am."

"So powerful that a fucker like Jonesy can take you unawares? Look at the state of your fucking face—"

"We all make miscalculations," I told him simply. "You trusted him too, didn't you?"

His nostrils flared at the direct hit.

I stepped away from him and headed over to the fireplace that was the focal point of the room.

As I looked around, I mused, "Not a bad place to hole up in."

The building was old, but the post-modern interior reminded me of a supermax cell.

To each their own, I guessed.

"You here to talk interior design?" Keegan sneered.

"Maybe. Seeing as you clearly liked your time in a high security prison." I focused on him. "Why haven't you left New York? Why aren't you back in Ireland?"

His jaw worked. Then, he surprised me by flicking the quickest of looks at Finn.

I clicked my fingers. "What was that about? Why did you look at Finn?"

"He's my family, isn't he?" was Keegan's reply.

"You're here because of Aoife?" Finn demanded.

Keegan didn't reply, but that he tipped up his chin gave me all the answer I needed.

Contemplatively, I swiped at my jaw. Knowing he was a family man was one thing, but it had never occurred to me that was why he'd remained in the city. I just thought he was still here either on unfinished business or because he couldn't get out yet.

Conor had told me the man never left his apartment...

"This place is just around the block from Aoife's bakery," I deliberated. Turning to Finn, I asked, "Did you know about this?"

Finn's shoulders straightened. "Of course I fucking didn't. Aoife hasn't—"

"Aoife doesn't even goddamn know I'm here," Keegan growled. "Don't bring her into this. She's already gone through enough this year."

"What do you know about my wife?" Finn snapped, lurching

forward and only stopping when Brennan grabbed him by the arm and hauled him back when I shot him a pointed look.

"I know she lost your baby. I know she figured out that you've been fucking lying to her for your whole marriage. I know that she's split a chasm down the O'Donnelly clan because she wouldn't forgive your bastard father for what he did to her mother." He sneered at Finn. "I don't know the girl, not really, and I'm already fucking proud of her."

Eoghan and I shared a glance.

Ma had made many mistakes, but... Da's gamble had worked.

Keegan believed Da was the one behind his sister's death.

Relieved despite myself, I moved over to the sofa and took a seat. As I stared up at him, I murmured, "Your death would cause more problems than solutions."

He blinked then settled heavily on the sofa opposite me. "What?"

"You heard me. I don't believe in an eye for an eye. Clearly, you do, and we both know my father did, but I don't. It'll serve no purpose for us to tear each other to shreds, but that doesn't mean I won't do it."

He crossed his legs, settling his ankle onto his knee. "That's assuming you can kill me. I got more weapons in this room than you have brothers."

"I'm sure you do," I mused. "Doesn't mean one of us won't get to you first. As I said, your death causes more problems than solutions.

"When our father died in our arms, I vowed that I'd bring you down, tear you apart. But I was thinking about our current situation, and I realized that if I do that, I'll make a martyr out of you.

"My father's killer will never be a martyr. But, I know what you want, Keegan. I know what your end game is, and I know that you won't get that by blowing up buildings."

He sneered at me. "And what do I want, Junior? Seeing as you know me so well."

"You want a unified Ireland and, for whatever reason, you also want to take the Sparrows down." I shot him a smirk. "I'm the closest you'll ever get to achieving both, Keegan.

"On your own, you're a renegade. A tool that's used by governments around the world. You're a cog in a machine that's bigger than you." I leaned forward. "I own this city, and by the time I'm done, I'll own the East Coast and I'll have a sitting president on my side.

"If you want to annihilate the Sparrows and marry the Republic to Northern Ireland, I'm your best bet."

The silence that settled among us was so thick that we could have choked on it, but as he looked at me, as he studied me and tried to find my tells, as he tried to read me and discern my truths from my lies, I watched as reality sank home.

"And what do you want for all that?"

"I want the ECD. It's mine by birthright anyway. But I want you, the sitting leader, to show me loyalty. I want you to sit on the council, and I want you to be seen supporting me." My lips curved. "And if you ever want to know your niece and your great-nephew, then this is the only path where you'll be able to carve that out for yourself because Finn will never let an enemy of the family anywhere near his wife and son."

Straightening, Keegan got to his feet. I felt Eoghan tense up behind me, literally felt the air around him vibrate as he leached a warning into it, but I didn't ignore it, just knew that Keegan needed room to think.

He wanted to maneuver.

But I was good with negotiations.

Better than they realized because Da had never utilized me as a negotiator.

Da had never let me fucking do anything other than be his heir in name only.

Eventually, he said, "I want immunity."

"Why do you think Jonesy is still alive?" I knew exactly what he was talking about.

Keegan turned to me. "He won't cop for the assassination charge."

"He will if I threaten his family."

"His boy? Richie?"

I nodded.

"You'd kill a kid?"

No.

He didn't need to know that though.

"I'd do whatever it takes to get what I want."

His eyes narrowed with... Jesus. Respect.

"If he cops to the charges," I told him, "you won't need anything else. Your freedom is yours."

"I want to see Aoife."

"That isn't down to either of you," Finn snarled.

I cast him a look but agreed, "It's down to Aoife."

Finn gritted his teeth. "One false move, Keegan, and I'll turn her against you faster than you can take your next breath."

Keegan scoffed, "Blood is thicker than water."

Finn scowled at him, but it was Eoghan who drawled, "The Dagda I heard about wouldn't let anyone talk to him that way."

"The Dagda you heard about hadn't spent decades in prison being passed around like a fucking pawn at the whim of any government who paid the goddamn English enough money to use me. I'd have stayed in the army if that was what I wanted.

"Even in prison, they didn't leave me the fuck alone." He pointed his thumb at himself. "I'm tired and I'm old. I want to get to know my family, and I want to be my own man at long last. I want Ireland to be one. And I want those Sparrows taken down. That's my grocery list.

"I'm not an idiot, Junior. The chances of Ireland being unified are small, and it won't happen in my lifetime, but decimating the Sparrows is within reach.

"You give me that, you give me my freedom, and you give me the opportunity of having a relationship with the only family I have left... then I'll give you the ECD."

My smile was cold. "We have a deal."

33

TEXT CHAT

AIDAN

REX: *Haven't heard from you since Sunday, but my eyes and ears in the city have told me you're causing chaos…*

Rex: *Glad to hear you got home safely.*

Me: *Conor told me he keyed you into the situation. Thank you for helping out.*

Rex: *No problem. You need anything, anything at all, you can depend on the Sinners.*

Me: *You mean that, don't you?*

Rex: *Not in the habit of saying shit I don't mean.*

Me: *Appreciate that. More than you fucking know.*

Me: *And I'll bear it in mind. I think we're good, but thank you.*

Rex: *We're allies.*

Me: *Allies don't make offers like that.*

Me: *I won't forget it.*

34

———

SAVANNAH

THE DEVIL'S TEARS - ANGUS & JULIA STONE

THE FOLLOWING DAY

AROUND A YAWN, I checked my watch for the third time, annoyed at myself, more than my sisters, for their chronic inability to be punctual.

Why did I ever believe them when they scheduled anything with me? Why did I bother wasting my time?

Paris was usually better than Aspen with timekeeping, but ten minutes was one thing, an hour was beyond a joke.

Huffing, I shoved my phone back into my purse and hesitated over my next move. I was still exhausted from Sunday night and my entire torso was aching like a bitch.

I'd spent most of yesterday in bed, sleeping, and I'd only dragged myself off my damn mattress because Paris had confirmed she wanted to catch up late last night plus I needed to buy stuff for the cat Lucas had dropped off yesterday afternoon.

Because ibuprofen and bed beckoned, I started to gather my things together, my intention to head over to the cashier to pay so I could return home and rest up some more once my errands were complete, but when I saw a face from my past standing in front of the display cases, my plans were whipped away by my surprise.

Cassie Rundel.

There was no missing that head of hair—it was like silk. It gleamed in the lights above the counter. As purely golden as it had been the last time we'd met.

Taken aback, but in a good way, I left my shit at the table and moved over to the line. When she didn't turn to look at me, I grabbed her by the elbow.

"Cassie?!"

She jumped a foot in the air from the tug on her arm, and her eyes were shadowed and haunted as she shot a terrified look at me.

Her brow puckered, but she stopped dragging away from my hold as, confusedly, she murmured, "Savannah?"

Though I knew something was very, very wrong, I beamed a grin at her. "It's me, Cass. It's me! How are you? Oh, my God, it's been so fucking long since we caught up."

She shot me a wan smile, one that packed half the punch of her old megawatt one, and that was when my surprise downshifted to outright concern.

"Are you okay?" I asked softly.

She shot me a tired smile. "I'm just working on a deadline."

She was lying.

And were those...

Shit.

They were.

Bruises.

Around her eyes.

"Do you come here often?" I questioned. "I'd love to catch up when you have some spare time." I slipped my hand into my pocket and withdrew one of my cards from the holder I always carried around with me. "Call me if you'd like that too."

I backed off rather than cause her any more discomfort and watched as she pocketed my card without looking at it.

Our eyes lingered on each other until I turned away and retreated to the table I'd been on the brink of vacating because I'd given up on my sisters ever arriving.

As I plunked my ass down, I stared at the back of Cassie's head as she purposely kept her gaze averted from me, wondering what was going on with her.

We'd met in school; I wanted to be a journalist who took on the world and needed to make it a better place. Or, at least, to shine a light on the darker parts and to bring some truths out of the shadows.

Cassie wanted to be a food journalist. She'd started college with me then had transferred out a year before graduation to head into a culinary school.

She'd become a trained chef the last I'd heard.

The investigator in me took note of the brittle way she held herself, the slight tremor in her hand as she held out some bills to pay; then, I watched as the server packed her order.

Aoife's bakery was my go-to place now to meet with people, so I knew her menu inside and out.

Was it a coincidence that a woman I knew to be a food journalist was here trying all of Aoife's new items?

Since she'd gone viral, interest in the bakery had increased to the point where I knew Aoife wanted to expand the business.

Was Cassie here to write an article on the place?

Or did she just want lunch?

Before I could let my thoughts run away from themselves, a large crowd of twelve or so students drifted away from a table.

In the mire, and quite by chance, I saw one of the staff head into the backroom.

As the door drifted to a close, my eyes widened when I saw Aidan sitting there with—

Shit.

I couldn't make out who it was.

I tried my best to catch a glimpse of his lunch partner, angling around in my seat to figure out who his meeting was with, but the door closed before I had a chance.

Cursing my bad luck, I grumbled under my breath but didn't have long to complain because my sisters finally showed up.

I only realized because they sat down beside me, and it drew me out of my irritation.

"You're late," I sniped at them, reaching for my coffee to take a sip.

"Why do you always have to focus on the negative?" Paris groused. "We're here, aren't we?"

"Don't make out like I asked to meet up with you and that you're gifting me with your precious time," I mocked. "If you're going to be the one who instigates the arrangements, at least have the decency to show the fuck up." I stared at my watch. "I don't have long anymore. What do you want?"

"Maybe we don't want anything," Aspen argued.

"You always want something. It's what you do."

"Savannah!" Paris hissed. "There's no need to be mean."

I scowled at her. "I've had a long weekend, Paris. A really fucking long one. I'm tired, I'm aching, you haven't asked after the burns on my cheeks, and I'm not in the best mood but, somehow, I still managed to be punctual. I didn't cancel or try to reschedule. I'm here."

Aspen squinted at my burns. "What are they from?"

"Aidan and I were involved in a car crash. It's from the airbags."

"You didn't tell Mom and Dad!" Paris reprimanded. "If you did, they'd have let us know you were injured."

"I saw no reason to concern them. We're alive and well, just a little sore.

"And I *would* have told them, but it happened Sunday evening and I've been sleeping a lot ever since. I prioritized lunch with you today over the call I'll have with them later on," I said pointedly.

"God, you're such a pain. We get it, don't we, Aspen? We're terrible people for being late all the damn time."

Aspen didn't answer, just started delving through her purse. "I think I have some concealer that will cover that up if you want."

"I'm not putting make-up on it." I resisted the urge to check my compact. "I just need it to heal."

"It's ugly."

"So are you," I retorted, much as I'd done when we were younger. Her face puckered up like before, but this time, she couldn't cry and tell Dad that I was being mean to her.

I hid my grin behind my coffee cup.

"Anyway, at the risk of more insults about things I can't help, what did you want to meet up for?"

"It was Paris's idea," Aspen sniped. "I told her you'd never want to help because you're such a bitch."

My lips curved. "I mean, I really try to live up to your expectations, Aspen. You're who I aspire to be."

She glowered at me, but it was Paris who reached over and tapped her hand. "Stop it, Aspen."

I arched a brow when Aspen pouted but shut the hell up.

A server appeared and took their orders as well as mine, and all the while I kept trying to peer through the backroom door as if I had X-ray vision.

"Do you have fleas or something?" Aspen complained. "Why can't you sit still?"

I ignored her and, to Paris, asked, "What do you want? I thought this was supposed to be about Mom."

"It is, but I asked Daddy and he told me that I needed to stop projecting."

"Projecting what?"

She wriggled her shoulders. "We've been stressed, you know, about the show. He said that I was reading into things that weren't there."

Whoa, way to gaslight, Dad.

Still, I kept my mouth shut on that topic. "Okay, so, what, then?"

Just her mention of the show told me that was her reason for not canceling.

"We're having a problem with the thirty-five to forty-five demographics."

I played it dumb. "Huh?"

Paris frowned. "You heard me. We're falling short on viewers in that age range."

"So? What do you want me to do about it?"

"We'd like you to come on our show. We'd love you to talk about what you're doing. There's no reason it has to just be about Paris and me. We could expand for you and Camden to be featured as well," Aspen said brightly.

"Wait a minute, are you hitting me up for a guest appearance?"

Paris shot me a smile that I knew she thought was winsome but just looked desperate. "I think it would be great exposure for you. It's a completely different platform. You could hit home with some of your opinions, and you could spread the word about your articles and things."

I tipped my head to the side. "Paris, what articles am I writing at the moment?"

She blinked at me. "Umm, you know, about, like, sexism and stuff."

I groaned under my breath. "You don't even know what I'm working on right now! What's really going on here? Why are you so interested in getting me and Camden on there—" My words waned as realization struck. "The network wants to cancel your show?"

Aspen squinted at me. "No. Of course they don't."

"Yeah, they do. Let me guess, you got Daddy to agree to go in front of the camera, but you'd like a triple whammy." Or... "Did offering Daddy up stop them from canceling, but did they offer big money if you got Camden on there too?"

"You're no way near as famous as he and Camden are," Aspen grouched. "We just don't want to be mean and cut you out."

"Nice try, baby sis; you feel free to be mean. Because, let me guess, Camden said he won't do it unless I do."

When she scowled at me, I knew I was right.

Daddy was Daddy, and he was famous and rich and definitely a coup. But Camden? Camden was massive. And he was everyone and their mother's idea of a dreamboat.

Camden was the real tour de force. He hit more demographics than Adele, and each year, he was beating his own records at the Grammys.

I leaned forward and murmured, "If you wanted me to work on convincing Camden to be on your show, you should probably have turned up on time. I might have been more amenable."

Amenable...

The word triggered a whirlwind of thoughts and had me shooting out a message to Conor.

Me: *Conor, could you do a background check on a Cassiopeia Rundel, please?*

Conor: *What's with the name?*

Me: *Her parents were star gazers. Will you look into her for me?*

Conor: *Sure. She's a Sparrow?*

Me: *No, she's someone I know from school. I just bumped into her, and, I don't know, I feel like she's in some kind of trouble.*

Conor: *I'll send you what I find.*

Me: *Thank you so much xo*

Conor: *You owe me.*

Me: *What do you want?*

Conor: *You're at Aoife's bakery, aren't you?*

Me: *I won't disrespect either of us by pretending that I'm not. Stalker.*

Conor: *Bring me one of her apple pies and I'll do whatever you want.*

Me: *Will do. :P*

"You're not listening. So rude," Aspen bit off.

"I have business of my own to attend to, Aspen. My day isn't dedicated to you and your whining." I scowled at her. "You really need to have an attitude check, and I'm saying that. Me. I have a shitty attitude too. If I think you're a pain in the ass when I am one, then you're screwed."

Paris snorted. "You won't make her listen. Her new boyfriend likes her being a brat." She leaned forward. "You should hear them. They fuck all night long."

I grimaced. "You two need to get places of your own."

"Just because I have a sex life and you don't because you're boring and married," Aspen sniped.

Chuckling, I told her, "You're right. I need to live vicariously through you, Aspen."

With a sniff, she got to her feet. "I'm going to the bathroom."

"She isn't," Paris muttered, pointing to a man who was heading to the back of the coffee shop. "That's her boyfriend."

My brow furrowed. "Huh? What's he doing here?"

The guy was tall, beefy, and he was stacked with ink. He even had something above his brow. With a ring in his nose and a full beard, he wasn't Aspen's type at all.

Paris shrugged. "Dunno. I can read her texts upside down though. Yours too. Who's Cassiopeia?"

"You're a little shit, you know that?"

She beamed a grin at me. "I do. But I embrace it."

"She's a friend from school. I think she was... She had bruises on her eyes, and she held herself as if she were sore."

I was holding myself like that at the moment, so I recognized the signs.

Paris frowned. "Oh! You think someone's hurting her?"

"It's only an idea. I just wanted to check in; that's all." Casting a glance from the corner of my eye, I asked, "Why did Aspen come? From your message last night, I thought it was just you."

"I didn't know until she sent Misha a message." She huffed. "She's driving me crazy."

That had me frowning—these two never talked smack about each other.

"Ever since they got together, it's Misha that, and Misha this. From her text, I think he didn't intend for them to meet up."

Confused, I asked, "What do you mean?"

"Knowing Aspen, she followed him here. You know how she gets when there's something she wants."

Possessive wasn't the word. Spoiled brat were two more.

Bewildered by the conversation, I asked, "Are you okay, Paris?"

"Of course."

"Do you think Misha is bad for her? You don't look happy that she's found someone."

She hitched a shoulder. "You know what Aspen is like."

"A bitch?" I queried helpfully.

Paris shot me a small smile. "She isn't really. It's just when you two are together, you bring out the worst in each other."

I shrugged because she was probably right.

"Will you come on the show, Savvie, please?"

"What would I talk about on there?" I groused. "I'm not famous, Paris, and I have no desire to be famous either."

"You're notorious in certain circles."

"In the thirty-five to forty-five demographics?" I mocked.

She smirked. "Yup."

"You're incorrigible."

"Maybe." We thanked the server who showed up with our drinks before she rounded in on me again. "It'd really help us out, Savvie. Camden said he'd do it if you suffered too."

"I bet he phrased it exactly like that as well," I grouched.

"Of course. It wouldn't be for long. It'd take maybe a day of your time."

I heaved a sigh. "You'll have to tell me when. I don't know what's going on with my schedule yet."

Paris nodded eagerly. "That's so awesome."

"What is?"

I blinked at Aspen who'd sneaked back and was peering into a mirror and touching up her lipstick.

Glancing around the bakery, I saw the guy who'd followed her to the bathroom and frowned when he went into the backroom.

As the door closed, I finally saw who my husband was sitting with —Maxim Lyanov.

My mouth rounded, and I turned on Aspen. "Misha's Russian?"

She put down her lip pencil to demand, "What are you talking about?"

"Misha's Russian," Paris confirmed.

"Shut up, Paris."

I turned on Aspen once more. "Do you know who he is?"

She hitched a shoulder. "He runs Silk in Tribeca."

That had to mean Silk was a Bratva front.

I gaped at her, unable to get my brain around what was happening here.

My sister was fucking someone in the Bratva.

And she'd come for lunch because she'd sneakily found out where he was and she'd wanted to check up on him?

She wanted to check up on a Bratva brother!

I snagged her wrist in my hand. "Aspen, he's a dangerous man."

Paris frowned. "Don't be silly, Savvie. He owns one of the hottest clubs in Tribeca."

"So do most factions of the mafia in the city. It's a front," I hissed.

"A front?" Aspen queried.

"Yes. For the Bratva. You can't be following him around town, Aspen. If you do, God only knows what'll happen."

She smirked at me. "I bet it ends with me getting off."

"Either that or getting shot."

Paris gasped. "You can't be serious, Savvie?"

"I am, deadly."

"You can't say anything," Aspen sneered. "Not when Aidan does what he does."

Curious, I inquired, "What exactly does Aidan do?"

"You and the family treat us like we're still fourteen. Everyone knows who the O'Donnellys are. They're the city's worst kept secret."

"Yes, well, they wouldn't appreciate being followed around either. This won't end well, Aspen. You need to watch your back."

She took a sip of her coffee. "Shut up, Savvie. You have no right to make any judgments about my love life."

"I never said that I did, but I have to warn you about who he is. You don't mess around with the mob, Aspen. Their nationality doesn't matter."

Though she bit her lip, she returned her attention to her makeup.

As she primped, I shook my head at her. "You have no idea what you're getting mixed up in."

Aspen narrowed her eyes at me. "Like you, you mean? Did Aidan do that to you?" She wafted her blusher brush at my face.

I had to laugh. "No, Aspen. We got into a crash. You say you know who he is. You say you know what he is." My chin angled upward slightly. "His universe is a crazy place to be, and trust me when I tell you that you aren't ready for it. Especially if you're just messing around."

"Who said I'm messing around?" She glared at Paris. "Did you say that?"

"No!" she retorted, mumbling the answer around a spoonful of foam from her latte. It was clear she'd have preferred to be anywhere else but here. "You two, I swear. You're so alike and it's crazy that you don't see it."

"Shut up, Paris," I grumbled.

"Fuck off, Paris," Aspen ground out.

She just rolled her eyes.

"If you're not all in," I warned, "then you're in danger. You don't mess around with guys like that. Trust me, if anyone would know, it's me."

Aspen tipped up her chin. "I love him."

"Do you love the club businessman, PenPen?" I asked, using the name Paris had called her when she couldn't pronounce all her letters. "Or do you love who he really is?"

Her expression revealed two things. The slight tightening around her eyes told me she didn't have a clue what I was talking about. The curl to her top lip told me she was going to fake it until she made it.

Before she could answer, I said, "Don't dive face-first into something that you're not ready for. We argue like we're cats and dogs, but that's just how we are. You have to trust me when I tell you that he's a dangerous man. Take that from someone who knows what it's like to be married to one." I got to my feet before an argument could be triggered between us, and I pressed a kiss to Paris's cheek, then to Aspen's temple, surprised, in all honesty, that she let me. "Give me the dates for your show, and I'll try to work it in. If I can't, I'll convince Camden that he needs to help you.

"Stay safe, the pair of you. New York is a dangerous place to wear blinders."

I didn't wait for a response because I knew my sister too well—any more from me and I'd shove her straight into Misha's arms.

Whoever the hell this Misha was, that is.

Ducking over to the counter, I put in a request to have a pie delivered to Conor's penthouse then headed out.

When I made it onto the sidewalk, Lucas at my back, I arched a brow when I saw Cade standing by a car.

I walked over to him, twisting around to toss Lucas my keys, and I opened the back door to Aidan's ride and jumped in.

"You should go home," Lucas told me as he caught the door before I closed it.

I stared at him. "Is he meeting with the Bratva leadership?"

Lucas stonewalled me. "He's not on my detail today."

"Then, I'll just have to stay here, won't I?"

"Naturally, after this weekend, a conversation was necessary..." Lucas sounded like he was choking on his words.

I narrowed my eyes at him. "Was that so hard?"

"If it gets me killed, yes."

"Aidan won't kill you, Lucas. Not unless you're a *cheile*. Or a Sparrow. Are you either?"

"No," he muttered crossly. "But you have to be as much trouble as them."

"You're full of compliments today," I drawled, but I shuffled out of the car as easily as I'd climbed in.

He frowned at me as he backed up. "What are you doing?"

"You told me what I wanted to know so we're going to see my sister-in-law."

Relief lit his eyes. Honestly, he'd be a handsome bastard if he'd just chill out. I'd never seen a more stressed-out man in my life.

Before I left, I turned to Cade. "Glad to see you back on your feet."

His ears turned pink.

Literally, pink.

That was the cutest shit I'd seen in my life. And coming from a man that fine, it was even fucking cuter.

"Thank you. I'm sorry about Sunday."

I shrugged. "Not your fault you had an allergy to whatever bit you."

He swallowed but dipped his chin in silent farewell.

Tucking my arm into Lucas's, who tensed up the second I did it, I murmured, "You two need to find ways to relax."

"These aren't relaxing times, Savannah. Men on our crew, brothers we trusted, have betrayed us. Your husband is on the loose, hunting down enemies and spies and..." He released a breath. "No, these aren't relaxing times."

He had a point.

I peered up at him as we walked around the block where my car was waiting for me, Mickey, standing much as Cade had, at its side.

Lucas opened the door for me and I climbed in. He clambered onto the seat beside me.

"Take me to Inessa's place," I ordered, tacking on, "please," when I realized how bullish I sounded.

Goddamn Aspen. She always made me act like such a bitch.

I grabbed my cellphone as Mickey obeyed and pulled us out into traffic.

Seeing Conor had been a busy boy, I pulled up the file on Cassie and started reading through it.

Because he'd seen I'd read his message, he bumped it:

Conor: *Trust you to know the blogger everyone's talking about.*

I stared at the certificate of the domain name listing he'd sent me over.

Me: *I live to make mischief. Keep it quiet though, yes?*

Conor: *I'm the soul of discretion.*

Me: *Ha. I'm sure.*

He was right, though.

Cassie *did* run *We Cream For Ice Scream*. It wasn't simply Aoife who'd gone viral; it was Cassie too.

The anonymous food blogger who could go into any eatery and make it light up with dollar bills with one of their reviews...

That was Cassie. Only, it wasn't the one I'd known, but this new version. This sadder version.

I stared at the wedding photos that Conor had included and I peered at the man who was her husband.

My mouth tightened as I studied the clasp he had on her hand. His fingers were taut, and hers bled white from the pressure.

It was a controlling hold.

He beamed a bright smile at the camera, whereas her posture was cowed, her shoulders faintly hunched.

Hadn't her family seen what was going on?

By the time we made it to Inessa's building, I was both outraged and *en*raged.

Conor, clearly intrigued, had sent me more information. I'd received private medical notes from several ERs and had looked at too many X-rays of broken ribs and fractured ulnas—both were proof of Cassie's husband's brutality.

That photos had been taken gave me hope that she was trying to fight her way out of the marriage, but there wasn't a single DV charge on Harvey Rundel's record, for fuck's sake.

Had Cassie never reported him?

As I tried to figure out if I had any means of helping her, I recognized that I could do more harm than good by intruding on this situation. It killed me to leave her in that toxic environment, but I didn't have a choice.

If she needed me, she had my number.

I had to hope that she remembered how close we'd been before our careers had taken us in different directions, and I had to hope that, from my articles and rep alone, she'd know I was a safe place to land.

Angry and hurt, sorrowful and grieving for the woman Cassie had been and what she'd been reduced to, I was shaking when I stepped out of the car and was still trembling when I made it into the elevator.

Aidan might think that Inessa had all the personality of white paint, but when she saw the state of me, her arms immediately opened and she tugged me into a hug.

"Are you okay? I know it's terrifying when these things happen. But you're safe and Aidan protected you and everything will be okay."

My lips had to twitch.

Here she was, thinking I was crying because of Sunday, and instead, I was here for an entirely different reason.

Maybe Lucas was right—I *was* more trouble than the Sparrows and the ECD.

I pressed a kiss to her cheek and, as I pulled back, told her, "Never change, Inessa. You're far too sweet for this world of ours."

She blinked at me. "Thank you... I think."

"I definitely meant it as a compliment."

Her hand hovered by my cheek. "The burns look sore."

"They are." I grimaced. "They won't take long to heal."

"Eoghan told me what happened."

"He did?"

She shot me a smile as she grabbed my hand and pulled me into the kitchen with her. "He tells me some things. Things I probably shouldn't know."

"Color me intrigued," I teased.

She snorted. "You probably know a lot more than me."

"Maybe. Not about Eoghan..."

Though she caught my eye, when she shook her head, I knew I'd catch none of his secrets today.

Pity.

Although, maybe not.

It wasn't like I'd be sharing Aidan's secrets over coffee.

"Tea? Coffee? Wine? It looks like it's been one of those days and it isn't even three yet."

"Wine," I said with a stout nod. "A large glass, please."

Smiling, she headed into the fridge and pulled out a bottle of white.

"I wasn't sure if you'd be in until Lucas called ahead."

She shrugged. "Day off."

"On a Tuesday?"

"College is..."

"Boring? Fun? Exciting? Stressful?" I prompted when she fell silent.

"Mostly stressful." As she poured wine into a glass, she admitted, "When I was growing up, I was told and taught that I'd be one thing. Well, two, I guess."

"A wife and a mother?"

"Yes. They were my future careers. Then, I met Eoghan, and he tells me, 'Inessa, you can have the world if you want it.'"

"Discordant," I agreed as she handed me the glass.

"Very."

Before I took a sip, I told her, "College will be good for you. It'll help spread your wings, grow your horizons."

"It's already causing problems." She heaved a sigh. "Eoghan is going crazy right now."

"Why?"

"There was an issue. He can't get over it."

"What kind of issue?"

"You know he has PTSD, don't you?"

"No, but I'm not surprised. I've seen his service record."

Interest gleamed in her eyes. "You have?"

"Of course. I know everything there is to know about the O'Donnellys. I stopped when I got with Aidan though."

"Because it was okay to be a stalker before you were a part of the family? Then it changed when you were inducted into the O'Donnellys?"

My lips twitched. "Something like that."

She chuckled. "I wish I had your balls, Savannah. Truly, I do."

"These balls were earned."

"No, I think you were... cultivated that way. Just like I was cultivated another. It's okay. I can accept that." She bit her lip. "Eoghan's—"

"Eoghan's, what?"

"When we were on our honeymoon, he did a job." She laughed at me as my only reaction was to take another sip of wine. "Don't pretend you're not dying to know who, what, and when."

Sheepishly, I shrugged. "I wanted to be polite."

"You're not a polite person, Savannah. You should embrace your flaws as well as your strengths."

I laughed. "That might be one of the wisest things anyone has ever said to me."

"Happy to be of service," she drawled with a crinkle of her nose. "He gave me some details, not many, but it led to some... issues.

"He's crazy protective anyway, and he's only gotten worse, then Conor comes around one day, tells me that Eoghan wants him to fix something on his computer. He asks me to make him a smoothie, and the next thing I know, the window he's standing in front of has spiderweb cracks..."

My mouth gaped—whatever I'd expected from my visit today, it definitely wasn't this conversation. "It was fired at?" I sputtered.

"I'm going to assume so. Neither Conor nor Eoghan would tell me anything. But ever since, he's been furious with Conor. To the point where they're barely speaking.

"From that alone, I know they *were* bullets, and I know that Eoghan would only be so angry if he believed Conor put me in danger.

"How he'd think I was considering the glass didn't break, and I was in another room, and Conor was clearly the one putting himself in danger, I don't know."

"PTSD paranoia for you."

"Exactly." She placed the bottle back in the fridge now that she'd poured herself a glass, then she turned around, took a sip of her own, and asked, "Have you heard of Kembesh?"

"Yes and no."

"Meaning?"

"Meaning I've never been, don't particularly want to go, but I know there was a battle there that the government had to do a clean-up job on."

"Eoghan was there."

My eyes widened. "Really?" Shit, that must have been in the redacted parts of his record.

"He has nightmares about it. They come and go depending on his stress levels, but they're back. With a vengeance."

"Off the top of my head, there was a battalion of soldiers stranded at a station. They were surrounded by the enemy, and the US left them to their fate. If Eoghan *was* there, then I'm not certain if that story is even true."

"Ever since the honeymoon, and that thing with Conor, he's terrified for my safety. I was late back from college a week ago and when I got home—"

My hand snatched at hers. "He didn't hurt you?"

Inessa derided, "No, he'd never hurt me. *Himself?* Sure. He didn't eat for two days, didn't sleep. Insisted on escorting me to school. We're having some work done on Victoria's bathroom, and he watched the workmen like they were self-confessed rapists. Wouldn't utter a word about what was going on." She sighed. "Don't they understand that we worry about them as much as they worry about us?"

"They're men, Inessa. So, no."

"It's very annoying," she sniped.

"Tell me about it. But, and I'm not excusing him or your concerns for his well-being, after what happened this weekend, can you blame him for being scared for you?" I reasoned.

The exhalation she released was heavy. "And there's the bitch of it. College is a party for most people in my year. It isn't like that for me."

"Do you like learning?"

"I don't know. I think I do, but I think I'm jealous," she admitted on a rush. Then, her hand clapped to her face. "I'm so sorry to be whining about this after everything you've been through."

"Hey, you're not whining! It's good that you have someone to share this with.

"I can't say that I know how you feel entirely, Inessa, because I can't. I wasn't the initial bridge between two enemies becoming allies," I said dryly. "But my dad was rich, and we had enemies of our own, and college wasn't freedom for me either. I had guards and they cramped my style, let me tell you."

"I'm used to the guards. I can deal with them. I just... Every time I go out, I know Eoghan is going crazy with fear. And now this place isn't even a haven for him. He has no peace, whatsoever."

"That's no reason for you to become a prisoner in your home, Inessa. You can't stay inside 24/7 to make him feel better.

"His PTSD is his problem, and it's yours too, as his wife, but it isn't a burden that you need to shoulder entirely. If Eoghan makes you feel that way, then he's a jackass."

"No, you don't understand. He wants me to live, Savannah." She rubbed her brow. "He wants me to learn things and meet people and... Just, maybe now isn't the right time."

She wasn't stubborn like my sisters, but that didn't mean she couldn't dig her heels in and do whatever she wanted.

And, to be frank, like it was with Aspen, I could advise but I couldn't force.

"You need to live your life, Inessa," I told her kindly. "No one else will do it for you. There will always be constraints, there will always be a war that's brewing, and there will always be people out there who want to hurt us. Don't let your decision to pull out be about them. Hmm?"

Her nod was jerky, but she said, "I know where you're coming from. Sorry, Savvie. You didn't come here for this."

"Maybe I did." I winked at her. "Maybe I knew you needed to talk."

She stuck her tongue in her cheek. "Are you a psychic now?"

"That would be cool, wouldn't it? I always wished I was special like that. Too many paranormal romances when I was a kid. Plus, my sisters have this weird twin thing going on and I was always jealous."

She laughed. "I thought you'd be all about the romantic suspense, not the PNR romance."

"Nothing like a vampire who's three thousand years old to get the juices flowing," I teased. "But, you're right in a sense. I did come here for a particular reason."

"What is it?"

"Aidan would never ask you. Maybe Eoghan would, but I don't know if he'd want to draw you into these politics."

At my words, she straightened against the counter. "Now I'm the one who's intrigued. What are you talking about, Savannah?"

Where to start?

"I saw Aidan meeting with Maxim Lyanov at Aoife's bakery

today." I peered down into the golden-hued liquid in my glass. "There was a man there with him."

Never let it be said she wasn't quick off the mark…

Tilting her head to the side, she asked, "Blond hair? Tattoos all over his hands?"

"No. Brown. Tattoos up his throat."

"Not uncommon descriptors for the Bratva," she teased but her eyes narrowed contemplatively. "Compass here or here?" she asked, motioning to separate parts of her neck.

I thought back to the man I'd seen in the coffee shop and pointed to the center of my throat. "But it was, I don't know, it had some kind of leaf detail around it. Oh, and I think he had ink above his eyebrow."

When I gestured at its location on my forehead, she swallowed. "Misha."

"My sister called him that but I wasn't sure if she was lying. Or," I admitted with a grimace, "if it was a pet name."

"Why would she lie?"

"To get under my skin."

"She's seeing him?"

"Apparently." I pursed my lips. "She followed him to the bakery and forced a meeting."

Inessa's eyes flared wide. "Are you being serious?"

"Yes. Sadly."

"Jesus." She whistled under her breath. "He's not good people, Savannah."

"We're married to men who aren't good people, Inessa. I'm not worried about his job. Well, I *am*. Partly. But mostly, I'm worried about the man. Who is he?"

She chewed on the inside of her cheek before admitting, "Some say he's Maxim's brother."

"'Some?' It isn't a fact?"

"I don't think even Maxim knows the truth. Or maybe he does now. Maybe he had a DNA test done." She hitched a shoulder.

"Maxim was a street rat. Born and bred in Moscow. I don't know how he got to the US. I just know that he showed up one day and Misha was with him."

"He isn't his Obschak or his Sovietnik," I pointed out.

"No. Misha is... reckless." She leaned into the counter then whispered, "They say he suffocates his victims and sits with them as they die."

"Charming habit," I groused, rubbing tiredly at my eyes. "But it isn't like I can judge, not considering Aidan's job."

Was skinning people alive better than suffocating them to death?

What a fucking question.

Though she chuckled at my words, the chuckle broke off halfway through. "Oh."

"What is it?"

"I just remembered something... Misha and Maxim are massive *noxxious* fans. When he used to drive me around, *noxxious* would always be on the stereo when I got into the car."

Unease slithered down my spine.

"It isn't unusual for us to be collected," I said, fully aware that my tone had turned cold. Bitter.

"You know, your life is fascinating to me," Inessa mused. "So different than mine, so much safer and so much cleaner, but still so dangerous. You're still a target; you still have enemies. Only, you didn't do anything wrong. Neither did your dad. He just made music that's beloved." Her brow puckered. "It isn't fair, really."

"And your path was fair?"

She shot me a weary smile. "My burden is a husband who loves me too much, Savannah. I wouldn't pity me."

"Would you pity Aspen?"

She took a deep sip of wine. "Maybe. It depends on how they met."

I grabbed my cell, and as my screen unlocked, I was faced with the graphic photos of Cassie's brutal marriage.

Spying them, Inessa demanded, "Who's that?"

"Someone I used to know."

Me: *How did Aspen meet Misha?*

Paris: *You're not going to interfere, are you, Savvie?*

Me: *No. I just want to know how they met.*

Paris: *Backstage at one of Daddy's concerts. He was a VIP.*

Me: *Thank you xo*

"At a concert. They met at a concert," I rasped. "The trouble is—"

"If you try to push them apart, she'll want to be closer to him?"

"She's a brat."

She snorted.

My lips twitched. "Yes, my parents reared a bunch of brats but she makes me look like a good girl."

"Jesus."

"Yes. Jesus," I drawled with a sigh. "God, as if things weren't complicated enough."

"Maybe it's a blessing in disguise."

"What do you mean?"

"Family and blood—they're the only markers of trust, aren't they? For the O'Donnellys, at any rate."

"I'm not selling my sister out so Aidan can have faith in the Bratva!"

"Does she know what he is?"

"After our conversation, yes, but she probably doesn't understand it in its entirety."

Even after all my research, Sunday's events had shaken me.

If, God forbid, something similar were to happen to her because of Misha's business, how would she react? With her past and everything?

She shrugged. "Then if she stays with him, you know she wants him. Maybe you're more alike than you realize."

"I hope not."

"No," she agreed, shooting me a worried glance. "It *is* like jumping from the frying pan into the fire."

"Speaking of... what do you know of a Stepanov? Aidan never

mentioned a first name." Sheepishly, I said, "That's probably more important than what's going on with my sister."

"Stepanov's the little shit who's bullying Victoria."

I straightened. "What?"

"You heard me. They're at the same school. He's making her life hell. I'm thinking of transferring her to St. Lawrence's."

"If you move her, you should shift her to the one where Shay is."

"Yeah, you might be right. She likes Shay. He'd be good for her. Her studies have started to suffer because of that little bastard."

"What else do you know about the family?"

"They were suck ups. Always trying to eat at our table."

"That's weird."

Inessa smirked at me. "Not really. Each faction has its ways. Every third Friday, Papa would hold a meal. He invited those who'd pleased him to it. Stepanov had ambitions."

"Funny you should say that..." I pointed at my face.

She gaped at me. "He was involved in what happened on Sunday?"

"We were taken to Bratva territory, Inessa. And it wasn't with Lyanov's approval."

"Stepanov is trying to take over the Bratva?"

"I think so."

Her brow furrowed as she stared at me, but the doorbell rang. "Just give me a minute, Savvie."

"Of course."

I stared down at my wine, trying to piece all the parts of the puzzle together. Not really listening to Inessa, absently I heard her say, "Thank you for bringing it up, John."

When she stepped back into the kitchen, however, for all that her voice had been calm and steady, she was as white as a sheet.

"Nessa?" I queried, straightening up with concern. "What is it?"

She swallowed as she stared at the box in her hands. "I've seen this packaging before."

"Eoghan?"

Her head whipped from side to side. "No. Maxim. Lyanov," she corrected with a croak.

"Why would he be sending you gifts? Jesus, don't tell Eoghan. He'll go crazy."

"It isn't for me," she admitted heavily.

"Who's it for then?" I asked in confusion.

"Victoria." She placed the box on the counter and stared at it like it contained a ticking time bomb.

"Why would he be sending gifts to Victoria? That's kind of creepy."

She shot me a glance. "There's a lot you don't know, Savannah. After Camille married, there was a lot of bad blood... Camille came home after Papa's knees were shot out. He was going to marry her to his Sovietnik, but Camille... Brennan." She shrugged helplessly. "To get to Brennan—" Somehow, I knew she'd skipped a ton of information. "—she killed Papa."

My eyes flared. "Camille? Camille killed your father?"

"He was a brute, Savvie. He was behind our mother's death because she couldn't give him anymore children and he needed a son to leave everything to." She clenched her fists at her sides. "I don't blame her for doing it. I wish I'd been there. But afterward, his Sovietnik and his Obschak tried to take over the gang—"

"They're the ones Lyanov beat to take the role of Pakhan?"

"Yes. But they also tried to kidnap us. The Sovietnik, Abramovicz, he tried to, well, he wanted to marry Victoria."

"But she's a baby!"

"He didn't care about that. He'd have kept her with him until she was of legal age, so Camille stopped him too."

"That's when she bit off his dick?" I whispered, well aware of that story.

"Yes." Inessa swallowed. "Maxim took the head of the Obschak—"

"Why do I think you're being literal there?"

"Because I am. He packaged it like this, all pretty, and he had it delivered to us."

My eyes bugged. "He had a head overnighted to you?"

"To Victoria. What the hell has he done now?"

My hands curled into fists before I forced my fingers to relax. "There's only one way to find out." I dragged the box over to me and unfastened it.

The stench of blood was strong. The moment I unraveled the ribbons, it hit me straight in the face like a soaked rag that someone was shoving over my nose and into my mouth.

On a bed of velvet, wrapped in plastic, rested a severed hand.

Both of us stared at it, but I was the one who broke the silence, "Who does it belong to?"

My whisper had her tensing. "Victoria must be talking to him."

I stared at her. "You think it's the boy—the Stepanov bully?"

She hugged herself. "I need to call Eoghan."

Nodding, I wrapped up the box again and muttered, "I'll leave you alone for that conversation."

35

AIDAN

A RUSH OF BLOOD TO THE HEAD - COLDPLAY

LATER THAT EVENING

"DIDN'T EXPECT to hear from you this soon," I drawled as I stepped out of Brennan's ride. Peering around the place that could have been the site of mine and Savvie's deaths, I murmured, "And definitely didn't expect to be meeting you here."

"There's a symmetry to it that I appreciate," Lyanov retorted.

"Stepanov's here?"

"He's incoming." He cast Brennan a look. "I appreciate the trust you're showing me, O'Donnelly. I'm well aware that you don't owe it to me. Not after everything that's happened."

"We both have had troubles in the ranks," I demurred. "I appreciate the rapidity with which you're willing to work."

He arched a brow. "The rapidity, hmm?" He shoved his hands into his pockets. "Fancy words."

"Fancy occasion. Not often an Irish mobster gets together with a Bratva brother on their turf to dispose of a mutual enemy together."

"Very true," he agreed.

I looked past him and saw the men I'd met last Christmas as well as the guy who'd hung around at the meeting I'd had with Maxim earlier.

Discussing business at Aoife's bakery had felt like a smart way to conduct our affairs in private.

Neither of us wanted the city to know that we were dealing with dissent, after all—I just hadn't anticipated that Lyanov would deal with Stepanov within hours of our meeting.

"It's been a long fucking day," Brennan complained.

Lyanov replied, "He has reason to want to be here. The wait won't be a long one."

"What reason? A gun shoved at the back of his neck?"

Lyanov's teeth gleamed in the streetlights as he smirked at me. "No. More sentimental reasons. He won't cut out and run."

"You don't have guards on him?"

"*Niet*," was his reply.

A guard shouted something I didn't catch, but it had Maxim nodding. The gates pulled inward and thirty seconds later, an expensive Bentley rolled in.

The door opened the moment the car came to a halt, and a man burst out of the backseat, hurling what sounded like Russian insults at Lyanov.

He didn't appear offended. If anything, his grin widened with whatever bullshit Stepanov was saying.

"English, please," Lyanov directed. "So our guests can understand."

"I'm here. Give me back my son," Stepanov rasped, his accent pure Brooklyn.

"His son?" I asked Lyanov.

"Timofai has trouble understanding the word 'no.' Especially when it comes to a woman under my protection."

"He's a boy. He makes foolish mistakes," Stepanov snarled. "You can't just take him because some little whore said he assaulted her."

"Some little whore?" Maxim's voice was soft, so soft that it made the sudden flurry of action all the more surprising.

One second he was standing beside me, and the next, he had Stepanov by the throat and was shoving the barrel of a gun between his lips.

"What little whore?" Brennan rumbled, the words dripping slowly from his tongue.

"He's talking about Victoria," Lyanov ground out.

I tensed. "His son touched her?"

"*Da*. She called me in fucking tears because she knew this had nothing to do with her and everything to do with Bratva business," Lyanov spat. "So I made it true Bratva business, Stepanov. Would you like to see what I did to your precious son?"

Stepanov's eyes flared wide as he choked on the gun, his hands raised in a surrender that would get him nowhere.

"I think you would. I think you'd like to know what I did to him to punish him. You're a man who believes in punishments, aren't you?" Maxim hollered a Russian command, and the guy I'd met earlier, Misha, dragged out a bag.

Stepanov shrieked around the gun as Misha pulled down the zipper and out dropped a bunch of body parts.

The other man sagged as he stared at what had once been his child.

That was when I got a text.

Eoghan: *Lyanov's up to his usual tricks. Victoria received a severed hand today.*

I snorted and showed the screen to Brennan whose scowl darkened.

"I should let you live. Should let you suffer with the knowledge that your fucking son died at my hands, that he was alive when I made the first cuts." Lyanov smirked at him. "Instead, you went too far. Mutiny is one thing, but you could have brought more war to our doors."

He pulled the trigger.

The noise ricocheted around the yard, and Stepanov's brains splattered the Bentley and part of the asphalt in the vicinity.

Maxim let go of the body, turned to me, and as if he didn't have specks of blood on his face, shirt, and hands, questioned, "We will return to business as usual?"

I nodded, but it was Brennan who demanded, "His kid hurt Victoria?"

"She said he touched her. I made him pay."

"It isn't your fucking right to make him pay," Brennan snapped. "She's my sister-in-law. She's my blood."

"And she'll be my bride. It's good that she knows to come to me for these matters."

"You know the score, Lyanov. She ain't yours until you make her fall for you."

"That will not be a problem," he said coldly. "Now, gentlemen, with that business concluded, I will have to leave you."

Behind us, Misha started collecting the body parts he'd dumped on the floor.

"Lyanov," I called out as he started to walk over toward a car whose headlights flashed on.

"What?"

"You know what this place is?"

Maxim sneered, "A disgusting excuse for a fish merchant?"

"No." I stepped over to him. "There's long been a rumor that blood diamonds are coming through the docks. Smuggled inside fish. The exchange supposedly happens in the Atlantic, on fish trawlers.

"This is Bratva territory, and Stepanov gave my men leave to use this place for their plot... Maybe the talk of blood diamonds isn't a rumor at all?"

Anger flashed in his eyes. "I appreciate the intel."

"We're allies, Lyanov. It will be good for us to work closer together in the future."

He stared over my shoulder at Brennan who was undoubtedly glowering at him. "Will your brother be a problem? It's clear that he has an issue with me."

"Do you mean to do right by Victoria?"

"Of course. She's the jewel in my crown. There are not many like Stepanov. Their numbers die out and those who screech loudest are deafened by the roars of many.

"Victoria's father ruled like a king of old. He left many men short to pay for his lavish lifestyle. Men like Lukov and Abramovicz, Stepanov too, they liked the status quo.

"But there are more foot soldiers than generals. I speak for the foot soldiers, and it is they who give me my power.

"To have a bride like Victoria is to cement my position all round. It satisfies the old guard, the new, and Moscow itself."

"Treat her like a chess piece, and you'll never get her down the aisle. She's family, Lyanov," I warned. "You want her to be your wife, I'll back Brennan to the hilt—you won't force her into anything."

He flashed a grin at me. "Nothing that is taken by force is worth keeping."

"That's bizarre logic for a man who stole his way to the top of the Bratva tree."

"Nothing lasts forever." He ducked into the car and seated himself. "Until next time, O'Donnelly."

As he closed the door, I backed off, retreating to Brennan who snapped at me, "If she doesn't want him, I won't make her marry him, Aidan."

Pursing my lips, I studied him. "She told him, not you or Eoghan, about Stepanov's boy, Brennan. I don't think her consent will be a problem, do you?"

That he didn't reply, only clenched his jaw, told me he knew I was right.

He just didn't want to admit it.

36

SAVANNAH

"I NEED CHAMPAGNE. FUCK THE MIMOSAS."

Aoife chuckled. "Tell us how you really feel, Savannah."

I glowered at her as I slammed my ass down on the seat and held out a hand. Though she rolled her eyes at me, she poured me a glass and passed it over.

Taking a deep drink, I sighed as the fizz hit my veins.

"What's wrong with you, anyway?" Aela groused as Cameron gnawed on her boob.

"He can't understand me yet, can he?"

"I think it's too late to wonder about that," Aoife drawled.

I flipped her the bird. "I'm horny."

Inessa snorted then clapped her nose as she managed to swallow bubbles up her nose; as she choked, Camille asked, "How can you be horny?"

"Aidan won't fuck me until the burns have healed." I pouted. "He's cockblocking me, ladies. *Cockblocking* me. And he's doing it by avoiding me. The jerk-off."

"Cameron, welcome to the world of Auntie Savannah," Aela

crooned. "You do something nice for your wife, let her heal up, and she still gives you shit for it."

"I got it at first, but this is the fifth day. It's a good thing we're having this impromptu afternoon tea because I'd have lost my shit otherwise."

Aela cast me a look. "I think you need to record the things you say and listen back to them."

Inessa chuckled. "Like in *Arrested Development*."

"I'm not as bad as Tobias," I grumbled.

"You almost are," Inessa teased with a grin.

I huffed. "You'd think he'd realize how great sex is as a distraction."

"Maybe that's why he doesn't want to do it. They're dealing with a lot right now. That's why we're here and not having dinner at my place this evening," Aoife pointed out.

"Well, *I* want to be distracted."

"Ever heard of B.O.B."

"No, what's his number?" I mocked before I cast a glance around the suite we were in. "Surprised they let us in just for the afternoon."

Aoife picked up a finger sandwich. "I learned something about the hotel while I was living here."

"What?"

"Have you seen *John Wick*?"

"Of course she has," Aela retorted, which had me grinning.

"You know me so well, Aela."

"Too well for such a short length of time," she complained.

"There's a special hotel in the movie," Aoife continued before the conversation could derail.

Eyes twinkling, I replied, "I remember, Aoife. You're talking about the hotel where there are fines if crimes happen on its grounds?"

"Yup. The Victoria is that."

"No way."

"Way."

I gaped at her. "How did you find that out?"

"My next-door neighbor shot at one of my guards. The management sent me a bouquet of flowers, apologized, and told me a fine had been administered.

"When I asked Finn what kind of fine they were talking about, he explained it to me."

I snagged a piece of cake from one of the plates. "I'm in a murder hotel."

"I think the point is for there to be no murders," Camille teased.

"You know what I mean." I wafted my fork in the air. "What does that have to do with using the suite for the afternoon?"

"The management is well aware of our current familial situation. I don't think they want a shoot-out in the main dining hall."

"Good point." I frowned. "Aidan's quelled most of the 'rebellion.'"

"Think they're erring on the side of caution." She hitched a shoulder. "Whatever, when I booked a table, they informed me the suite was available."

"Do you miss it?"

After Aoife's miscarriage, the family had moved out of their penthouse and into the hotel. Paddy was using their old place as his digs when he was in the city, and they'd been in this suite until their move to the brownstone.

"I miss room service," she admitted dryly. "But no. I didn't mean to stay so long, but the more we were here, the tougher it was to move out.

"Finn hated it. Security reasons. I think..."

"You think?" Camille queried with a raised brow.

"I think that I might have been channeling Savannah."

I blinked. "Me?"

"Yes. You know, being a brat?" Though I pulled a face, I didn't interrupt as she said, "I might have been trying to punish him.

"You owe me an apology, by the way."

"Why? What have I done now?"

"Finn's been butt-hurt ever since you clocked him on the head on Sunday."

My lips twitched. "It was by accident."

"I'm sure it was. Doesn't take away his headache," she grouched.

Nose crinkling, I admitted, "If it makes it any better, he could have shot me in the head."

Aela blurted out, "Jesus, Savannah! How does that make it better?"

Aoife's eyes were wide. "Are you being serious?"

I shrugged. "Yes."

"You need to tell us what happened," Inessa insisted. "I think we've been very patient."

"Have you?" I mocked, but I winked at her.

"Finn won't tell me anything," Aoife said with a sigh.

"Eoghan won't either."

"Nor Brennan."

"Declan told me that it was a close won thing but little else."

I knew they were kept in the dark, and I didn't need to hear their admissions to appreciate my husband, but God, I was so glad Aidan had begun sharing things with me.

Over the past ten months of our relationship, he'd been like trying to break into a walnut with a pipe cleaner, beyond impossible getting him to open up; but gradually, if I asked questions, he'd answer now. That was without his apology and his promise to be more open with me.

"We were in the car and this truck came out of nowhere. T-boned us. I don't really remember much about the crash. Just that I woke up in the bed of the truck, and Aidan was there.

"We got dragged out and dumped in this shed in Bratva territory. It reeked." I shuddered and dumped my fork on my plate. "I swear, I can still smell fish on my hair."

"Fish? They held you at a dock?"

I hummed. "My hands and feet were duct-taped. Aidan's were zip-tied."

Aela whistled. "You gotta appreciate the Five Points and their sexism."

"Yes, the feminine revolution hasn't hit Hell's Kitchen yet," Camille said with a snort.

"Exactly," I growled. "I was so stinking mad. Plus, they left me with my keys! Can you imagine?"

"Too stupid to live," Aela agreed. "But we should be grateful they were morons because you're safe and not fish food."

"That's a fair assessment," I concurred. "They definitely wouldn't win a place at Mensa."

"They're still alive?" Aoife questioned.

"Yes. I made Aidan promise that when he killed them, I could be there."

Inessa's eyes bugged. "You'd want to be?"

"Of course. They would have killed me, Inessa. Not before they did a lot of other shit to me first."

"Bloodthirsty bitch," Aela commented, but she didn't sound as if she disapproved.

"Are you okay now?"

I nodded at Camille then turned my palm over. "Seems crazy but these were the biggest pain in the ass."

They peered at my hands and the various cuts into the flesh. They were mostly healed, thank God, but they were at that itching phase that was driving me nuts.

"What caused those?"

"If I tell you, you can't ever make fun of me for it." I thought about what the doctor had told me on Sunday night. "I had a concussion and I was in shock. At least, those are the only reasons I can think of for me being that stupid."

Inessa touched my arm. "We won't mock you for it."

"I know how scary it can be in those situations," Camille soothed.

Yeah, I guessed if anyone did get me, it was Camille.

I shot her a sheepish smile. "I should have checked my pockets first but I just... I didn't. Anyway, I found this flashlight. It was old-fashioned and had this glass plate. I smashed it with my heel, broke the glass, and used it to cut through Aidan's zip ties."

"That Jungle Jane training of your dad's worked, didn't it?"

"Apparently," I said with a laugh as Aela smirked at me.

Aoife took a sip of coffee. "How did you fuck up?"

I shoved a hand into my pocket and pulled out my dad's gift to me.

"Nail clippers?" Aoife asked when she took them from me.

"Nah. Open it up."

She frowned but started tugging on the sides, pulling out the attachments.

"My dad had them custom made for my sisters and me. He gave them to us when we hit eighteen."

Aela took it from Aoife. "It's really light."

I nodded. "Strong though. I should thank him for saving my ass, but if I tell him that his gift came in handy, he'll need to know what happened and I don't want to scare them."

Which, of course, was when I understood my mom's dilemma.

Sometimes, you kept things from the people you loved. Not to be selfish, not to hide, but to protect them. The truth didn't always serve a purpose.

Just because I'd spent most of my life seeking it out didn't mean that it was everyone's friend.

"I think we can forgive you for not realizing you were carrying this with you," Camille said, as kind as ever. "In the fray, you wouldn't have noticed it. It's too lightweight."

Grimacing, I muttered, "I have to admit, for my first true glimpse at the Five Points in action, I was woefully inadequate."

"Meaning?" Aela asked.

"Meaning that I almost got shot by friendly fire and I hit Finn over the head with a flashlight." I rolled my eyes. "I acted like a moron."

"I think you're being hard on yourself," Camille chided.

"Maybe." I shrugged. "I mean, Finn was the one who blew out the lock. If he'd been one of our captors—"

Aela grinned. "He'd have had a key."

"Exactly." I scrunched up my face as I grabbed my glass of champagne. Lifting it in a toast, I declared, "To it never happening again, but if it does, I channel my inner superheroine and singlehandedly get us out of there."

Chuckling, they joined me in the toast, Aela too, but she subbed the mimosa for orange juice.

It felt good to hang out with them. Better when I realized it might never have happened.

Accepting my mortality triggered predictable responses that were, nevertheless, aggravating.

I was spending most of my time in bed, slept a lot, and had brought Star's research into the bedroom where I was reading up on how the Sparrows selected their newest members.

In between, I cried, ate too much chocolate, thought about how Aidan could have died, and then ate cake before my new cat let me snuggle it to sleep—the tiny beast recognized a woman on the edge.

Today was the first day I'd actually wanted to get out of bed.

If Aidan had spent more than an hour beside me on the mattress, I was pretty damn sure getting laid would have gotten me out of my funk sooner.

I wasn't saying that he had a wonder dick or anything, but it was a better wand than Harry Potter's... That was for damn sure.

Aoife reached over and gently clasped my hand. "I'm glad you're here, Savvie."

My smile was sheepish. "Even if I'm a brat?"

"It's part of your charm," she teased back, her gaze drifting to my cheek.

The burns were the only visible sign of what I'd gone through. The bruises at my hip and shoulder were still there, but I'd covered them with my long-sleeved tee, and my fingertips were starting to scab over.

"Not long for the burns to heal," Inessa comforted. "I'm sure Aidan will have you back in the saddle soon enough."

I snorted. "That's Camille's kink." Seeing her cheeks bloom with color, I crowed, "You still haven't gotten him to fuck you on a horse?"

"When would he have been able to do that, Savvie? Aidan and Brennan have been thick as thieves this week. I barely see him."

I grimaced. "True."

It wasn't like I'd seen a lot of Aidan.

He crept into the apartment at odd hours, jostling the bed so that I stirred in my nap, then when I woke up again, he'd be gone.

He was busy.

We talked on the phone, and he answered questions I asked, but those were few and far between this week.

My questions weren't for a phone call.

I wanted to look into his eyes as he explained what was going on.

"Are you okay, Savvie?" Camille asked.

"I'm fine," I dismissed.

"You don't have to put on a brave face for us."

My smile quivered. "It's dumb."

"Nothing you feel is dumb," Aoife reprimanded me. Her fingers squeezed carefully around mine.

"I think it's... I'm not scared. I'm not worried about it happening again either."

"Then, what is it? You look like you could cry."

"Isn't it stupid?" I whispered to Aela.

"No, it isn't. You went through something traumatic."

Camille stood up and moved over to me. As she crouched at my side, she said, "It's one thing to read about what happened to you, but experiencing it is something else, Savannah.

"You're a tough cookie, but every cookie crumbles sometimes."

Sniffling out a laugh at her analogy, I muttered, "I think it's just everything." I explained about my mom and begged them to keep it quiet. Then, I said, "It's ridiculous but I kind of miss Aidan Sr. too."

"That definitely *is* stupid."

"No, it isn't, Aela." Aoife shot her a dark look. "It makes sense. Now, all the responsibility is on Aidan's shoulders. It means your whole lives have been shaken up."

"So have yours," I pointed out.

"Not like with Aidan. Even if he rules differently, which I think he is, because Aidan and Brennan haven't been the only ones MIA this week—"

"I've barely seen Eoghan," Inessa admitted. When I shot her a look, she moved her head a fraction to the left...

Hadn't she told him about the hand?

Or did she just not want me to mention it here?

Aela nodded too. "Declan's been out a lot, and he's only put Cameron down to bed once this week and eaten breakfast with Shay twice. He always tries to make it home for those."

"Finn has hardly been home as well. He made it to a couple of dinners before Jake's bedtime, but that's it."

"Everything's changing," Camille agreed. "We have to adapt to the new order."

"Aidan told me some of the horrible things Senior did—"

Before I could finish my sentence, Aela demanded, "Why do you think I give you shit for hero-worshiping him? I hope to God Aidan isn't anything like him."

"He has to make a stand," I rasped. "He doesn't have to do it like his father did, but this is his first challenge and he has to show up. How he reacts to this will affect how the city responds to him."

Inessa bit her lip. "What's his game plan? Do you know?"

"No. I know it's happening tomorrow though."

"On a Sunday?"

"It's Halloween."

"So?" Aela queried.

"I only know that's when it is."

"Does that mean Sunday lunch is canceled?" she asked hopefully.

"I think so," I said with a laugh as I mopped at my eyes with a napkin. "Sorry for crying. The past couple weeks have been intense."

Aoife patted my hand. "That's what we're here for. No one can ever understand what we're going through outside of this room. We're in this together."

She was right.

"When I find out what's happening, I'll let you know, okay?" I cast each of them a look. "I know you're not like me. I know you don't want details, but I think we need to break glass ceilings, ladies.

"They want to protect us and shield us from the world, but keeping us in the dark just means we'll fall over more."

"I want to stay out of the business," Aela admitted.

"I want to know enough to be kept apprised of any danger," Aoife said eventually. "I've experienced the 'dark,' and Savvie's right—it just makes the fall all the more brutal."

"I feel the same way," Inessa concurred.

Camille shrugged. "I don't mind knowing details. Brennan is very protective. He forgets that I was raised with a father like mine."

"I was too," Inessa argued.

"I saw things I'm grateful you never did," Camille said sadly. "It isn't a competition, Inessa. I know Papa was as much of a brute to you as he was to me. I just... I was old enough to be aware of things you weren't."

Inessa frowned, but she didn't argue.

"I'll bear your wishes in mind," I told them. "And I'll let you know what's going on."

"Do you really think if Aidan doesn't make... I don't know, enough of a splash, it'll affect us?"

I shot Aela a glance. "Yes."

My answer was stark, but so was the truth.

We fell silent after that and drowned ourselves in cake, coffee, and champagne.

Aware that because in this patriarchal society in which we found ourselves, we were our men's weaknesses. That meant, as had been proven time and time again, we had nice, fat targets on our foreheads.

Whether they liked it or not, Aidan's next steps and the seeds of the legacy he sowed in the upcoming days directly affected them. They just wouldn't know *how* until it was too late.

37

TEXT CHAT

SAVANNAH

ME: *You didn't tell Eoghan about the hand?*

Inessa: *Of course I did. I just didn't tell Victoria.*

Me: *Why didn't you? She might want to know.*

Inessa: *Savannah, she isn't you, lol. You might think a severed limb is a suitable courting gift, but I don't.*

Me: *I'd feel safer knowing I had someone around who was willing to cut people up for me.*

Inessa: *Again, only you.*

Me: *Not only me. My sister's just as bad, apparently.*

Inessa: *Apples don't fall far from the tree.*

Me: *I know that Eoghan blasted your father's kneecaps, Inessa. That had to make you feel better, knowing he'd take care of your boogeymen for you.*

Inessa: *It did help.*

Me: *Well, then?*

Inessa: *She's still a child.*

Me: *Babe, I'm a LOT older than you. I say this with all the love in my goddamn heart, but to me, YOU are a kid. You're closer to her* *age than I am, and I know for a fact that I wouldn't want to be called a child at 16. So you definitely have to know that.*

Me: *Haven't we learned this year that secrets get us nowhere?*

Inessa: *Dammit.*

Me: *:P I can be logical sometimes, you know?*

Inessa: *I'm flipping you the bird. Just so you're aware.*

Me: *Flip me a hundred of them if you want, lol.*

Me: *What was with the head shake at afternoon tea, then?*

Inessa: *I haven't told Camille either.*

Me: *Ohhh. You going to rectify that too?*

Inessa: *Yes, Mom.*

Me: *:P*

Inessa: *Eoghan was pissed about not being the one to deal with Stepanov Jr. So was Brennan. He came around to talk about the situation.*

Me: *Oh, to be a fly on the wall for that conversation, lol.*

Me: *Did neither of them think that talking about it with Victoria was a wise move?*

Inessa: *They're trying to protect her.*

Me: *Protect her when she clearly spoke to Maxim about this situation and not them? Isn't it obvious that keeping her in the dark does nothing apart from make her seek outside help?*

Inessa: *Shit.*

Me: *It sucks when I'm right, doesn't it?*

Inessa: **sighs**

Me: *See you next Saturday?*

Inessa: *Yeah, yeah.*

38

AIDAN

LEANING against the railing that fenced off the park outside Jonesy's building, I watched as kids trick or treated.

It was Saturday night, the day before Halloween, but there were still mini-Elsas and *Minecraft* characters darting here and there, collecting as much candy as they could.

They didn't appear to notice how the cops had cordoned off the entrance to Jonesy's building.

Or, if they did notice it, they were more interested in getting to the people who *could* give them candy.

New York never ceased to amaze me sometimes.

A man's life was in the balance, his world teetering on the brink of implosion, but did his neighbors care?

No.

Over the next forty minutes, evidence was retrieved from Jonesy's property. Bagged up and tagged, it was slotted into one of the many vehicles that were taking up space on the street, until eventually, finally, Jonesy left the building.

Though I kept my features expressionless, I watched as Jonesy was taken to a nondescript black SUV. I hoped that he'd see me, that he could see the threat that was my presence here, and he did.

As our gazes collided, he swallowed, nodded, then focused on the SUV as if that were his salvation.

Ironically enough, it was.

When he was taken away, slowly but surely, Maria, Jonesy's wife, was left alone. The cavalcade of black SUVs made their retreat, as did the forensics van, until I was the only one in a suit remaining.

Well, except for one car and the two agents who wandered over to me in the aftermath.

In the dark, with their black suits, they almost blended into the shadows.

Unfortunately for them, the only boogeyman hanging around this area was me.

The thought made my lips twitch as Reeve lit himself a cigarette, the glow of the lighter blossoming against his palm as he shielded the tip so it would light, as he confirmed, "He confessed."

"Copped to all of it?"

"Every last bit, and the rifle was where you said it would be," Palinsky crowed. "Director Eric told us to thank you for the tip, Mr. O'Donnelly."

Dismissing the gratitude, I tucked my hands into my pockets. "What happens now?"

"We break him down, make sure that nothing stops a conviction, and we get him on death row."

"I like how the Secret Service works." I pursed my lips. "Jurisdiction going to be a problem?"

"Maybe. We're not worried. We're overseen by Homeland, and if it gets tossed out of our hands, they'll snatch it up."

And if that failed, and it fell to the FBI, we had the director in our pocket.

I didn't bother with a farewell, just strode away from them. "Keep me in the loop as much as you're able."

When I was at the corner of the block, Palinsky called out, "You think he'll change his mind?"

I turned back to face him. "Wouldn't you in his position? But the evidence says it all, doesn't it?"

Reeve took a deep drag on his cigarette. "It does."

"Then that's the only thing that matters, isn't it?"

Palinsky nodded. "Evidence is king."

I merely quirked a brow at them then headed around the corner.

Seeing my approach, Lucas jumped out and opened the door.

"You're not a servant, Lucas," I objected as I took a seat. "I can open my own damn door."

"Your father—"

"My father did things his way. I do them mine. The only door you open is for Savannah. Understood?"

"Yes, sir."

I grunted as he folded himself behind the wheel.

"Everything work out, sir?"

"Aidan, Lucas. My name's Aidan."

He cut me a look in the mirror. "Aidan."

"What's with all the subservience?"

"I think you know, Aidan."

"Wouldn't have asked if I did," I grumbled, turning to face the street.

"Do you still want to go to your building?"

"Yes."

Silence fell between us until my da's cell buzzed.

Spying Grainne's name, I frowned and dragged my thumb over the blood-soaked cracks in the screen.

It was dumb that I wasn't ready to let go of it—I knew that. Didn't mean I was going to toss it in the trash any time soon.

"Please tell me there aren't a bunch of Five Pointers causing trouble at Queens of Heart."

"No," she drawled. "No trouble. Not tonight, anyway."

I grunted. "What's the reason for your call, then?"

"You didn't inherit you da's ability for small talk, did you?"

"No."

"Even though he didn't give a shit, he often found a way to ask about the little things."

"There's the difference. I already know about the little things. I don't need to ask about them."

She fell silent. "What does that mean?"

"It means I already know you have a son who's in the Midtown Mental Health Facility. I already know that half of your place flooded two nights ago, and that it's affecting the electrics in your office."

"You can't know everything."

"With my resources, I can make sure I'm kept in the loop about most matters."

"That's how you're going to lead?"

"For the moment. Until the city's used to me."

She hummed. "Your da wasn't smart enough to remember all that stuff."

"No. He wasn't." The cracks in the glass on the phone rubbed against my cheek as my arm jolted when we went over a grate. "Plus, he relied on the wrong men."

"And you won't?"

"I have my brothers. They aren't the wrong men."

"I'm sure your father felt the same about his generals."

"I'm sure that he did. I'm dealing with the proof that he was wrong. What's with the call?"

"I was pondering your wife's request."

My brow furrowed. "Savannah's request?" It took a second for me to catch up. "Oh. For an interview?"

"Yes."

I rubbed my brow.

Of course, Savannah would be the wild card.

Here I was, spouting BS about knowing fucking everything about the people who mattered, and my wife was the one to prove me a liar.

But Conor had taught me a lesson. One I doubted he'd realized he'd been teaching.

Doubt was a powerful motivator.

Doubt made people forget what was real and could encourage them to believe the impossible was true.

"Your father would never have allowed me to have an interview with her."

"Before or after she became his daughter-in-law?"

"Both. He liked me to remain in the shadows."

"And you're wanting to know if I'll let you give the interview?"

"I am."

"When was the last time she emailed you?"

"Last October."

This request was out of the blue then.

"Her interests have shifted since last October."

"I know."

I thought about how Savvie had been cooping herself up this week.

She was a closet hermit by nature. Always reading and writing. But she inhabited different parts of the apartment.

I hadn't been home that much, but it hadn't stopped me from checking in with her via our security system, and I'd noticed that she rarely left our bed. Except for when it came time to hunt down chocolate.

I'd seen her crying herself to sleep, had watched it and felt like my heart was being shattered by a sledgehammer, and that was when I went home.

Even if it was just for a sixty-minute power nap.

It was also why I'd encouraged Aoife to call her to get her out of the apartment today.

Savvie was strong, but the strongest faltered from time to time too. I'd long since come to terms with my mortality, and I knew last December had helped her embrace the fact she wouldn't live forever, but throw in Da's death, her mom's health issues, plus Star's disappearance, and it was no wonder she was up in her head about these things.

Breaking off from her Sparrow investigation—read obsession—might do her some good.

Though this was perfect timing, that didn't alleviate my suspicions.

"Why now, Grainne?"

"Have you heard of a man called Miles Monroe?"

I scrubbed a hand over my jaw.

"And this is where your omnipotent act falters, Aidan. You can't know everything," she drawled. "It's impossible."

"I never pretended to know everything about the world," I snapped. "There are billions of fucking people that I don't have a connection with. I'm just saying that the ones who matter to me are of adequate interest for me to keep tabs on."

She sniffed her disdain of my argument. "Miles Monroe used to live in the city before he headed for greener pastures in Jersey."

"Okay, what about him?"

"He became a church deacon, which, trust me, is insane considering the shit he's into—"

"He was a client?"

"He was. A personal one. Back before I stopped all that and began running Queens of Heart."

As her words waned, her silence told a tale of its own. "He's the bastard who beat you and left you for dead?"

"Where you found me," she concurred. "It's always interesting to me how you saved me, and you didn't even know it. You had no idea how you shaped my life without realizing what you did that night."

"What did I do?" I asked cautiously.

"You took a hooker and made her into the city's madam. That might not seem like a graduation for some, but trust me, I never expected to get this far.

"Aidan Sr. might have built this club for me, and he might have used it for his own gains, but my loyalty wasn't aimed at him."

"It wasn't?" I queried warily.

"No. It was for you. The kid who didn't know who the fuck I was, who acted against explicit instructions, and who helped me anyway." She hummed again. "I heard him tell you to get away from me. I heard him order you back to the car.

"But you, and it was Conor, I think, you insisted, and you shamed him."

"I think you're wrong," I said gruffly. "I think realizing you were Frank's..."

She snorted. "No. He didn't like me when I was with Frank, and he sure as hell wouldn't have liked finding me naked in a back alley.

"If you hadn't been there, I'm pretty sure he'd have shot me and would have considered it an act of mercy." Her laughter was cold. "But I have to admit, the old bastard still managed to surprise me."

Uncertain where she was going with this, I asked, "What did he do?"

"Before he died, he left me a gift. I only got it today."

"What was it?"

"I'll take a picture so you can see for yourself."

I pulled back and clicked through to the photo she'd sent.

It was a newspaper—*The West Orange Record*.

Goddamn West Orange.

Why did all roads seem to fucking lead there?

I squinted at the screen as I read the headline:

LOCAL DEACON FOUND GUILTY OF MURDER

"Da arranged that?" I questioned.

"I'm going to assume so."

"You can assume nothing where he's concerned." I pursed my lips. "That's why you want to speak with Savannah? About Monroe?"

"Yes."

"Are you going to jeopardize—"

"Aidan, I told you that you had my loyalty, not your father, for a reason. I will not do anything to hurt you or your wife, and I sure as hell won't do anything to jeopardize the case against Monroe.

"He'll be appealing the verdict, and if you read the article, you'll see he was arrested earlier this year—"

Knowing I wouldn't be able to read it easily, I reached up and rubbed my temple. "Da had the trial expedited?"

"He must have. No way in hell would his case have been sent to trial this quickly otherwise."

"Savannah's been through a lot the last couple weeks, Grainne. This might cheer her up. But if you do anything to upset her, I'll make you regret giving me your loyalty."

She released a soft laugh. "You sound just like Frank."

I frowned. "He loved you?"

"He did. Not that your father accepted it."

The lack of bitterness to her words told me she'd long since grieved her loss.

"I'm sorry, Grainne."

"Not your fault. Your father's, sure. But you're the only reason I'm here.

"I know something's in the works, Aidan. I'm not a fool, and I know how the Five Points function. You'll be getting your men to swear their loyalty to you.

"I want you to know that you have mine. Women might not be foot soldiers, but I've provided your father with enough intel over the years that I should have been made an honorary one."

"I appreciate that, Grainne," I rasped, knowing she meant it, even if I didn't really fucking deserve it.

"So, I can agree to the interview with Savannah?"

"Yes."

"Thank you."

She hung up the phone, leaving me with dead air in my ear.

As I tucked Da's away into my inside pocket, Lucas asked, "Everything okay, boss?"

I scratched my jaw. "Yeah."

Rocking my head back against the rest, I closed my eyes as he drove us to my building.

I might have looked like I was zoning out, but mostly, I was thinking about what Grainne had said.

Someone had sent her a newspaper.

Someone on Da's detail?

Another fucking leak I needed to plug?

I narrowed my eyes as a thought occurred to me.

Occam's Razor... Conor was the one who'd taught me about that.

Me: *Have you been fucking around in West Orange?*

Conor: *Be more specific.*

Me: *Jesus H. Christ. Don't we have enough shit to be dealing with?*

Conor: *I'm better at multitasking than you.*

Me: *You're behind the Miles Monroe murder trial, yes? Please tell me you are.*

Conor: *Of course.*

Me: *What else are you fucking around with in West Orange?*

Conor: *It's more of a long-term project.*

Me: *Meaning?*

Conor: *Da set me the task of finding pedophiles for the Sinners' VP to kill. I've been busy though.*

Me: *Can you get someone else on the job? That's a worthy cause and I don't want Da's death to hinder it.*

Conor: *I'll figure something out.*

Me: *Great. So, no more leaks to plug?*

Conor: *Well, not in this instance.*

Me: *I'm surprised Da cared about Miles Monroe...*

Conor: *He didn't. I did.*

Me: *Wait, you're the reason he's in jail now?*

Conor: *I used to have nightmares about Grainne, Aidan. Bet your ass I wanted a resolution.*

Me: *How did you find out who her attacker was?*

Conor: *I asked her. When we visited Ma the next day, I said I needed the restroom but went and found her in one of the wards. It took me a fucking lifetime to track her down, but I did it.*

Me: *You've always been a stubborn PITA.*

Conor: *Yup. Anyway, she was out of it on pain meds. I doubt she even remembered talking to me.*

Me: *You framed him for the murder, right? Or was he really guilty?*

Conor: *Framed him. Da had a bag of bones just lying around... Seemed dumb not to make use of them.*

Me: *You've always been annoying, haven't you?*

Conor: *It's a talent.*

It sure as fuck was.

Still, at least justice of a sort had been granted, and it was Conor's doing, not another rat in our midst.

When I made it home, I was surprised to find Savannah walking the length of the living room.

Her hair was wild, she had chocolate spread stains on her cheek, and she was wearing one of my T-shirts which looked better on her than it did on me.

Like a madwoman, she was pacing back and forth, and the cat was following her. It'd have been funny if her appearance didn't have me concerned. Then, she spun on her heel and proved she'd known I was watching her by declaring, "This is the answer."

Tiredly, I dragged off my jacket and let loose a yawn as I tumbled onto the sofa. The sudden movement had the cat racing off, hopefully to its bed and not to be sick on the bathroom rug like this morning.

Staring up at her, I asked, "What's the answer, babe? In fact, what's the question?"

She moved over to me, straddling my lap with the ease of someone who was very accustomed to getting in my space, and shoved some papers at me.

"The answers are here."

"Dyslexic, remember?"

"You don't need to read them," she said with a sniff. "I'm just saying, 'Ta-dah.'"

My lips quirked despite myself. "Ta-dah?"

She grinned. "Yeah. Or 'abracadabra,' if you prefer."

Snorting, I reached out and cupped her side with one hand. She squirmed against me as I traced one of her burns with the other, monitoring how much longer the healing process would take.

"How much champagne did you have today?"

"An adequate amount."

I laughed. "You're such a pain in my ass, do you know that?" I was pretty fucking certain that she and Conor had been heaven-sent to keep me on the straight and narrow.

Well, as straight and narrow as it got for a leader of the Irish Mob.

"Better the ass than the heart," she said piously. "Anyway, stop distracting me. Star sent me a bunch of information on how Sparrows are inducted."

"I remember. So?"

"So?!" Savvie shrieked. "So?! She gave us the key to their door. You plant someone in there, several someones, and you use them to dismantle it from the inside out.

"We've only met Sparrows who were bribed into being a part of their organization. Five Pointers who were faced with a choice to obey or go to jail for a crime they didn't commit.

"We've put away men and women who were Sparrows because their crimes caught up with them.

"But we've never been there from the ground up."

I blinked at her. "You're right."

"Of course I am," she said with a sniff. "And to be frank, it took me goddamn long enough to figure it out. I was looking in the wrong place. Star sends me a bunch of shit all the time. Why she can't just annotate a document with 'this is the key to dismantling the organization,' I'll never know."

"She likes to keep you on your toes," was all I said as my mind raced.

"She likes to keep me dangling," she griped. "But I should have seen it sooner. I'm sorry for being slow."

"The last month hasn't been easy, Savvie," I told her calmly. "And this isn't easy either. This route is the dictionary definition of slow."

"It is," she agreed. "But... it's also a way for you to get what you want. If you still want it, that is."

"I don't want to be the leader of the NWS, Savvie," I said gruffly. "Hell, I don't want to lead the Five fucking Points. But... this seems like the best option."

"You get people positioned in the organization first, then you make your moves," she agreed.

"A takeover would be hostile," I warned her.

She shrugged. "You're a new leader. Your ties aren't as set in stone as your da's were. And... if I stopped releasing articles about them, if it looked as if you had me under your thumb, you could say that you married me to shut me up.

"I haven't released an article since Lodestar went missing. Not about the Sparrows. It could look like it was timed with you becoming the leader."

"You'd be prepared to do that?"

"I'll play the long game, willingly, if it takes the motherfuckers down."

"You think that would work?"

"I think you're clever enough to make them think whatever you want.

"They had the *Famiglia* as a front for decades, Aidan. Their business will have suffered without them as the face of their dirty deeds."

I pondered her words. "Jonesy was arrested tonight."

"Why?"

My lips twitched. "Framed him for the First Lady's assassination."

She whacked me in the arm. "You jackass. You didn't think to tell me that before?"

Because I knew she was pissed about missing out on the scoop, I smirked at her. "It's been a busy couple days, and I wasn't sure if I had the right leverage."

I'd admit that to no one but her.

She squinted at me, her displeasure clear. "What leverage?"

"He had a girlfriend who gave him a son."

"And?"

I snorted. "You forget the antiquated world you've entered, Savvie. A son is worth three daughters."

Her scowl told me what she thought about *that*.

"I'm not saying I agree."

"Good. You better fucking not. I hope if we do have a kid and she's a girl, then she'll take these fuckers and bring them into the twenty-first century."

"Jesus, don't say that," I rasped, feeling myself blanch. "I don't want her involved in any of this at all."

She patted my arm. "It'll happen. I practically willed it into being. These jackasses need to know what a woman can do. I swear, you think we stay at home and make doilies and shit."

"I don't think that."

"Yes, well, you're surprisingly evolved."

"Good to know," I mocked, but I laughed at her umbrage.

"Okay, what about the kid? You threatened to kill him?"

"I wouldn't have," I assured her.

She rolled her eyes. "Duh."

"He didn't know that though."

"Of course not. And that worked?"

I shrugged. "Yup."

"He confessed and everything?"

"Told him I'd look after the kid and the girlfriend, make sure they had whatever they needed."

"Huh." She arched a brow at me. "You didn't tell me because you thought I'd judge you for using the kid as a pawn?"

"Maybe."

"Maybe. Huh," she said again. "I told you I understand that you have to do some shitty things to take charge of the city, Aidan."

"Some shit goes below the belt."

"I know it does. I won't judge you for it."

"Why won't you?" I demanded, frowning at her. "You should, Savvie. You fucking should. I'm turning into a monster and all for a business that I don't goddamn want."

"Our safety, your family's safety, is tangled up in that business. Nothing could have proven that like last Sunday."

I clutched at her ass and sighed. "Da actually wanted to be the head of this fucking mess, can you imagine?"

"Your heart isn't in it, and I get that, but it needs to be. Now, what else haven't you told me?"

"Used Jonesy to get to Eamonn Keegan."

"Dagda," she breathed, her eyes lighting up.

"A lesser man would be jealous," I grumbled.

"I'm married to a sensible creature who knows his wife's pussy creams only for him," she teased.

My lips twitched. "Got him on our side. He agreed to step down as leader."

"No fucking way! And you didn't tell me?!"

"I'm telling you now," I drawled, aware I was getting a hard-on from how she was rocking around and squirming.

"Don't you dare get an erection, Aidan O'Donnelly. Not now, not when I've been waiting all week and you've managed to annoy me out of being horny."

"That's not going to make it go down."

"You told me you'd keep me in the loop."

"And I have. Telling you now, ain't I? I never said it would be a play by play of whatever went down any given day," I retorted. "Anyway, I have a gift for you."

"I don't want a gift."

"You'll like this one..."

"What is it?" she asked suspiciously.

"Grainne Ledger."

Her brow furrowed. "The madam?"

"Yup."

"What about her?"

"She'll be contacting you regarding setting up an interview."

Her eyes bugged. "Are you shitting me?"

"Nah."

"Manhattan's Madam wants to talk to me?" She grabbed my collar and jerked me forward. "What did you do? Bribe her?"

"No. She has an ulterior motive." Understatement.

"Everyone does," she dismissed, but there were stars in her eyes again. Stars I was happy to see.

I didn't tell her that I'd been worried about her this week.

Mostly because I knew she wouldn't want to hear it. She'd think I was taking her meltdown as a sign of weakness, and that I'd use it as leverage to keep things from her.

But I'd used drugs to medicate myself and my pain. Now I was using stress to shove shit aside.

This wasn't Savvie's first exposure to danger, but it was as my wife, as the bride of the Five Points' leader.

It was the first time we could have both died.

It was the first time we'd almost lost everything.

It fit that, amid that meltdown, she'd come across a way to bring down the Sparrows.

My wife would always, *always*, surprise me.

Her fingers clutched at my collar again. "This could be good timing."

"What for?"

"The Sparrows. Making it look as if I'm shifting tracks. Let's face it, the whole fucking underworld seems to think that wives always listen to their husbands and obey them," she scoffed. "I bet if I started writing about alternative themes, they'd accept it better that I was leaving them alone."

"We still don't know if that's feasible."

"I bet it is though. You need to work on getting some law enforcement agents in your pocket. Sliding them into the Sparrows." She reached for the packet of papers she'd dumped at my side. "Getting in takes time, but with Amara's help, we could get more names, and we could position whoever you use to infiltrate the organization beside those Sparrows.

"Maybe we could even use the fact that the Sparrow in question is in danger of exposure as a method of getting our inside man close to them."

As I watched the ideas slip and slide behind her eyes, I dragged my hands up her arms as I reminded her, "Tomorrow, I'm dealing with the traitors."

She blinked at me, jolting herself from where her mind had taken her. "What are you going to do?"

"I don't want to spoil the surprise," I teased, enjoying how she switched gears and glared at me. "You can be there. If you want to be."

"Of course I do. I told you I did."

"Wanted to check in. Make sure you hadn't changed your mind."

"Nope. I'll be there."

I just grunted. "You might not like what you see."

"Maybe I will, maybe I won't. Maybe I shouldn't. But I want to be there." She cupped my cheek. "What's the next move, baby?"

"Brothers loyal to me will get tagged."

Her brow puckered. "Tagged?"

"Ink. Da never really went that far. Men chose to get branded if they wanted, but he didn't insist on it. Most of the runners have some tattoo on them somewhere, but none of the higher-ups. Declan might —I never asked. His crew was on the ground so if he did, it'd have been to fit in with them."

"Are you getting ink?" she asked, her eyes gleaming.

I laughed at her. "Do you want me to?"

She wiggled her eyebrows. "I wouldn't say no. Savannah's husband. That sounds like a good tattoo to me."

I reached up to run my thumb along her brow. "'Property of Aidan.' Right there."

"How very MC of you. They all have them, you know? The Old Ladies. 'Property of' tats. Before you, I'd never have gotten ink for a man, but..." She shrugged. "When you know it's forever, it doesn't seem that much of a sacrifice."

I hummed. "I don't need ink. Everyone else does. But... you could try to convince me."

"Oooh," she breathed, her lips brushing against mine. "How could I do that?"

I slid my hands up to her hips and encouraged her to rock against my erection. "Why are you wearing panties?"

"Because I'm not a heathen."

"I like it when you're a heathen." I drew her panties to the side and let my fingers slide down to her slit. "How's your face? How are you feeling? Still sore?"

"If you stop, I *will* kill you, Aidan," she groused, arching against me as I slipped the tip of one digit inside her.

"That's not an answer."

"Just don't give me beard rash and my cheeks will be fine." She smoothed the backs of her fingers against my jaw. "Shave and you'll be able to kiss me."

I smiled as I used the flat of my tongue to smooth over the smudges of chocolate spread on her cheek. She jolted in surprise then melted into me, breath shivering from her parted lips.

"Delicious," I whispered under my breath before straightening up and taking her with me as I launched off the sofa.

She clung tighter to me but I wasn't going far. I took her to the dining table and, kicking out the closest chair, I rested her ass on there.

Reaching for the hem of her shirt, I drew it over her head and bared her to my ravenous gaze.

It had been almost a week since I'd slid inside her, and it felt like a fucking lifetime.

I traced a revering hand along her throat, down her chest to her tits, over the curve of her waist, and to her hips.

She wasn't as thin as she'd been back when we first got married, but I loved her new softness.

When we fucked, it was like she was stronger. Not as brittle. I didn't have to worry about breaking her anymore.

Her hands moved to my arms in a silent entreaty, and it was only because of the past week that I didn't stop her.

We'd almost lost each other.

It took longer than six days to get over that.

I rubbed my fingers along the crotch of her panties from the front, while, with the other, I traced her nipple.

"You are so fucking beautiful, Savannah. Do you know that?"

She shot me a sheepish look. "I know that you make me feel beautiful."

"I'm glad that I do. Because to me, you are perfection, little one. Everything about you, from that brain I'll never understand, to this pussy that is my home, is beautiful and perfect and *mine*. Do you understand me?"

She shivered. "I do." Leaning forward, she moved her arms around my waist. "I love you, Aidan."

"Love isn't a fierce enough word to describe my feelings for you, Savannah. I thought I knew what love was, thought I could figure it out, but it's a shadow of what you inspire in me.

"The words don't exist for what I feel for you, Savannah O'Donnelly." I rubbed my lips against hers, softly because I didn't want to irritate her burns. "I want to worship you and wreck you all at the same time.

"You're on my fucking mind constantly. You're the reason I'm doing this, and the reason I want to stop. You're my nightmare and a dream come true.

"I'm blessed to have you, and I'm not worthy of you, little one. But I'll spend the rest of my life making sure you know that, to me, you are every-fucking-thing. Do you understand?"

She swallowed and pressed her forehead to mine. "I just need to be yours. Nothing more, nothing less."

"Always," I rumbled, shifting so that I could lay kisses to her throat. "No matter what."

My fingers tugged on her panties again, and I slid beneath them to find her soaking core.

"You're always so fucking wet for me, Savannah. So fucking perfect for me."

She squirmed against me, one leg kicking onto the table, her toes curving around the edge, the other spreading wide. She reached between us and unfastened my fly before she delved between the tines and pulled out my cock.

"You're too far away," she muttered as she tugged me by my dick into moving closer to her.

The moment the tip collided with the slick folds of her cunt, we both groaned, but I let her slot my shaft into her.

As her body accepted me, welcomed me, I drew her nearer. Her ass squeaked against the shiny wood, and she chuckled at the noise, but it didn't stop her from settling her heels against my ass.

Looming over her, I slowly started to buck my hips.

Nothing fast, nothing heavy, just wanting her to know that I meant every fucking word I said.

"Tell me you love me," I commanded.

"You know I do." The words broke on a pleasure-soaked sigh. "I love that you trust me. I love that you believe in me. I love that you know I'm smart, and that you're not afraid of what I can do. I love that you don't judge me for the weird way my mind ticks, and I love that you accept who I am, Aidan.

"You accept *me*, all my flaws, all my bratty, bitchy ways. You accept them and embrace them, and you make me feel whole." Her cunt clutched at my cock. "Not because you fill me just right, not because my pussy was made for your cock, but because you were made for me.

"We were born to rule over this hellhole together, Aidan. No matter what comes, we'll do it together. Always together."

"Always," I whispered, breathing the word onto her lips as I sped up.

I didn't fuck her. I made love to her. Not just because the

moment needed that, but because she was still sore—Savvie hadn't said she wasn't, so I knew to trust in her omissions rather than what she said outright.

I gave her myself, and she gave me herself.

It was an exchange.

A mutual agreement.

That we were it for each other.

The worst shit I could do, she'd forgive me for.

The worst shit she could do, I'd forgive her for.

We were an open book.

Pages still to be written on.

And the ink?

The slick juices that drenched her cunt and the seed that spilled from me as we came.

TEXT CHAT
SAVANNAH

SAVANNAH*: Star?*
   Unread Message From 5 Weeks Ago
   Savannah*: Please answer.*

SAVANNAH

NEVER STAY DOWN - UNSECRET, SAM TINNESZ

I KNEW I WAS WEIRD. Hadn't I said it last night? Hadn't I told Aidan that I loved him for loving me even though I *was* weird?

But seeing him standing on a platform in the cement factory yard, wearing a goddamn leather jacket, jeans, and a black tee, bruises finally beginning to fade but doing nothing to detract from his powerful aura, watching him command the fear and respect of the hundreds of men here, it got to me.

God, it did.

It was like a liquid aphrodisiac.

I was used to sex being on tap, so my body hadn't appreciated being starved of it for a week, but last night had been beautiful.

Slow, loving, *cherishing*.

Today, when this was over, I needed to be fucked.

I needed that more than I needed what was going to happen.

As I walked through the crowd, the need for vengeance burning a hole in my soul, whispers followed me.

Mutters of surprise and shock, of disapproval and curiosity.

Eventually, they didn't just follow me, they outpaced me, pushing me onward like the tide was forcing me toward the shore.

I reveled in the attention, knowing that this would only add to the day's spectacle; that whatever he had planned would never be forgotten. That, today, he'd cement the foundations for his legacy into the Five Points' memory banks.

When I made it to the front, Aidan was there, his hand outstretched for me as he hauled me onto the platform.

I appeared to be what he'd been waiting for because after I was tucked at his side, he ground out, "Last Sunday, some of my people, brothers, my so-called *family*, T-boned my vehicle.

"They snatched Savannah and me from the wreckage, and they took us to Bratva territory. Even better than working with a faction within the Bratva who oppose the leader we support, one of these bastards decided that they were going to dose me with heroin—bring me to my knees that way.

"Now, my brothers wouldn't have me tell you this story. They think I'm letting you in on a weakness. But my weaknesses are my greatest strengths.

"The moment they dragged Savannah into this, those responsible were always going to die. Always. I was their end game, their target, and I would have killed them for that alone, but instead, they went for my throat, so I'm sending them a message.

"I'm pounding it into your minds because you are my foot soldiers. You do what I say, you do what I tell you to do because I will keep your asses out of jail, I will protect your families, and I will line your pockets with enough wealth to make you happy men. In return, I expect loyalty and obedience.

"After today, I will expect you to present yourselves at one of four tattoo studios on our territory where you will be inked with a new insignia. We aren't a gang, we're a firm, but whenever you look at that fucking tattoo, you'll know what it is, what it represents—*ownership*. You belong to me.

"Your sins are my sins, your weaknesses are my weaknesses, and your crimes are my crimes. Every one of you here plays a role in my organization, whether it's small or large." He let the whispers stir among the crowd. "Anyone who has a problem with that," he slipped in calmly, "you know where the front door is."

Those softly uttered words landed with all the weight of a wrecking ball into a wall.

The men looked at each other for back up, outrage slithering between them like dozens of snakes, but no one spoke up.

Not a single man.

Stepping away from me, he shoved his hands in his pockets and moved to face the contraption at his back.

The noise from a motor turning over ricocheted around the lot, and a buzzing sound came next as a crane stirred into motion, its arm swinging around, bringing with it a large boulder of rebar, which hung suspended in mid-air. Tied around the rebar were several lengths of rope—nooses.

Jesus.

He was going old school.

As it hovered about ten feet from the ground, it came to a halt and his crew—Lucas, Cade, and Mickey—as well as a few of Lena's guards appeared, lugging wooden crates about four feet tall with them which they proceeded to position beneath a noose. These crates had clearly been custom-made for this purpose, though, because there was a step on each.

The crew moved over toward either end of the rebar, where two longer lengths of rope hung.

Metal fixtures were screwed into every corner of the platform we were standing on, and a man took one of the ropes and slotted them through a loop. The rebar was stabilized to a certain extent, and it stopped swaying.

With all the choreography of a show on Broadway, my brothers-in-law appeared next, as well as some guys I didn't recognize, each one dragging a traitor to their doom.

When their eyes clashed with their fate, a surge of bitter satisfaction filled me, something that was only impacted by Aidan gifting them all with the coldest, most terrifying smile I'd ever seen him grace upon anyone.

I froze at the sight, semi-terrified and semi-awed by that malevolent curve of his lips.

It spoke a thousand words, yet it boiled down to seven—*you came for me, and you lost.*

More whispers stirred among the crowd.

The six traitors trudged onto the platform, most of them being shoved along by an O'Donnelly. Conor was here as well—that surprised me more than anything.

When I caught his eye, he shot me a wink, which had me hiding a smile.

The traitors had been battered. There was no other way to describe it. Each was naked from the waist up, allowing me to see that there were more bruises than clean flesh visible amid their filth, and each was crusted with blood and God only knew what else.

It'd have been a solace to go to prison, but the Five Points weren't kind.

And that was another point Aidan was ramming home.

They weren't kind even if you were family.

The men behind each traitor grabbed the noose and tucked it over their head.

As they did, Aidan replied, "There's a science to hanging. Each rope is the specific length to break your neck. But only *if* you stand on the box. If you don't, you'll be strangled to death."

He said it so calmly, so coldly, that it sent a shudder down my spine, but of course, there had to be one.

I didn't know who it was, but he appeared younger than most of the old men whose shoulders were hunched in on themselves and who, frankly, looked to be relieved that their days were coming to an end.

I recognized this guy, though—he was the one Aidan had stabbed in the eye, the one who'd dared head-butt him.

The moron tried to shove Declan aside but Brennan was there in an instant, his knife pressing against the underside of his chin as Dec finished looping the noose around his neck.

While the others climbed onto their crates, Brennan dug his knife harder into the guy's chin when he tried to step onto the box too, but my brother-in-law drawled, "It's too late for that, Hal. You made your decision when you tried to run."

Hal spat, "You're a fucking bastard, O'Donnelly."

Brennan smirked, and before he could dole out an insult in return, Aidan declared, "Remember today. Remember this moment." His voice was barely above a conversational tone, but somehow, it slipped over the murmurs from the crowd like a scream. "Remember that whenever a Five Pointer betrays me, *betrays us,* this is how it'll end."

Interrupting him, I demanded, "Who was driving?"

He studied me for so long that I didn't think he'd tell me. Then, he rumbled, "Anthony."

He pointed to him and, as cool as a cucumber when my heart was pounding like crazy, I moved over to the bastard who'd mowed into us.

With my back to the crowd, my gaze locked on the blind man's face which had burn spatters from the base Aidan had used to destroy his eyes.

He didn't sway his head from side to side as if trying to understand what was going on. No, if anything, he kept his chin angled down, his shoulders rounded, his stance one of utter defeat.

He wanted this to be over with.

When Aidan clicked his fingers and the men kicked the boxes out from under the traitors' feet, I did the same.

I put the flat of my sole against the crate and I shoved it backward. The guys had made it look easy, and it wasn't, but I didn't stop until the fucker was paying for what he did to us.

As they swung in place, the noises that escaped them heinous, the sounds of their deaths gruesome and all the more fascinating for it,

Cade, Lucas, Jamie, and Mickey unfastened the ropes that held the rebar in place.

A moment later, the crane moved higher, higher. Fifteen feet, twenty, twenty-five... It stopped there, not allowing a single man to hide from what their fate would be if they betrayed Aidan.

A point that was rammed home as the others swung in place, their necks breaking cleanly, whereas Hal wriggled and writhed, his face turning puce as he was slowly strangled to death by his own body weight, his bound hands trying to loosen the rope around his throat.

I tilted my head back to watch them swaying, struggling, *dying,* then I sucked in a sharp breath as relief and delight and vengeance swirled around inside me.

That was when I retreated to Aidan's side—when he'd fulfilled his part of the deal, and those bastards who'd have forced their way into my body, who'd have used and abused me for information, who'd have tortured him, gotten him hooked on heroin, ransomed him, who'd have killed us, swung above me.

As he held out his hand, I entangled my fingers with his.

Without looking at me, he gave them a quick squeeze. "I can give mercy or I can repay your treachery in kind.

"You're *my* men. You're *my* family. But *we* are the Five Fucking Points!"

I didn't expect his words to make the hairs at my nape stand on end, but they did. Bewildering tingles hit various parts of my body as if he were pressing kisses to my flesh.

I wasn't alone in reacting to Aidan's call—a cheer surged among the men.

It was bizarre and obscene but a hauntingly powerful moment, nonetheless, as the Five Points accepted him as their leader.

I should have known that was when he'd strike again.

Having lulled them into a false sense of security, what better moment was there to hit them where it hurt?

He let go of my hand and stepped in front of the crowd, moving away from me to stand beneath the swinging bodies.

This was clearly organized because the crane lowered the rebar and he climbed onto the box beside Hal.

The cheers died abruptly.

A knife was in his hand.

Hal, still struggling, his eyes bulging in a way I knew I'd never forget, his face—

I didn't focus on that. Couldn't.

Instead, I watched as Brennan and Declan came to hold him still. Somehow, that made it worse. The noises escaping him were exacerbated before he garbled his pain as Aidan tucked the tip of the blade into his shoulder.

Swallowing as I watched him slice off a piece of flesh, I watched as, once his task was complete, the crane surged high again.

Aidan held up the skin in his hand. "You see this phoenix?"

A stillness overcame the crowd.

"This is a calling card. It means your loyalties aren't solely to the Five Points where they belong. It means you're a part of the ECD." He jabbed the knife in front of him. "Each of you is going to take your shirt off. No bullshitting me on this, no arguing. You're going to strip to the waist, and my men are going to check you for this ink.

"If you have one, you have a choice to make." He jerked the knife at the swaying corpses. "You can end up like them, or you can ally yourself to me."

"How do we do that?" someone called out.

"It starts with keeping your mouths fucking shut," he said easily, lifting the patch of flesh and studying the phoenix as if it were the most fascinating thing in the world. "Not a word. Not to the ECD, not to your families, to no one. Anyone talks about this, I'll find out who the rat was and I'll make Hal's death look pleasant in comparison to what I do to them.

"As for the rest, you'll have to wait and see what the future brings. Trust is an expensive commodity to lose in our family," he rasped, his gaze reverting to the crowd. "You *cheiles* are about to learn just how costly it is."

There was deadly silence, then:

"Is it true what they're saying, boss?"

Aidan frowned down into the crowd. "Depends on who is saying what, Darragh."

"About Jonesy. That he was behind the First Lady's assassination."

He hurled the flap of skin into the crowd. "We have the ECD to thank for that plot." His mouth curved into a sneer. "Now, strip. I ain't got all day and I need to know which of you fuckers believes a phoenix trumps the Five Points."

41

AIDAN

SHE WAS quiet as we drove home, her gaze introspective as she stared out onto the road.

I didn't break into her thoughts, not when Cade and Lucas were sitting in the front seat, able to listen to everything we had to say, but I made sure that I kept her fingers tucked into mine.

She didn't pull back.

I considered that a good sign.

I'd intended to jump back into work; there was shit to be done, after all. But it *was* Sunday, and we didn't have to go to Ma's for Sunday lunch, so I intended to spend the day with my wife. Hopefully trying to bring her out of whatever mood she'd sunk into upon witnessing six brutal deaths.

Well, *one* brutal death. The others had been relatively peaceful all told.

As peaceful as a hanging could be...

And she'd surprised me by taking care of Anthony.

Was she regretting that now?

Would she blame me for what happened back at the cement factory?

When we were finally alone in the elevator, as the door drifted to a close, I turned to her and began, "Sav—"

That was when she was on me.

Her hands scrabbled at the hem of my tee, dragging it halfway up my chest. She was on her knees before I even had a chance to finish her name, and her fingers were on my fly as she pulled the zipper down and grabbed my cock, drawing it out of the confines of my pants.

A grin curved my mouth as she drew her tongue along the quickly thickening length of my shaft, her lips slipping around the tip as she bobbed her head, accepting a couple more inches of me into her.

She pressed it against my abs and slid her tongue down the thick vein at the back before curling her hand around the base as she began jacking me off.

"Come on, come on, come on," she whispered, her gaze magnetized toward my shaft until she'd sucked it and jerked it into a full-blown erection.

In my defense, I'd been half certain she was going to ask for a fucking divorce, and even if my reaction time was fast, my dick was clearly wary.

When it was hard enough, she leaped upward, her gaze pinned on mine, and she demanded, "Talk after, fuck first."

I knew Savvie was technically insane, but I'd never embraced that insanity wholeheartedly until this moment.

If, after what she'd just seen, she wasn't asking to separate and wanted me inside her, I could more than handle that.

I knew why as well.

Something about me being the boss got her hot so, to reward her, I grabbed her by the nape, dragged her into me, and bit her bottom lip.

As she whimpered, I twisted her around and shoved her toward the glass. Her hands clapped against it and I said, "Look at me in the reflection."

My command had her wilting, her head bowing as she watched me in the mirror.

I let go of her and reached down to unfasten the fly on her slacks.

Shucking them down, I dragged off her panties next, kicking them to the ground too, then I widened her stance.

Slipping my dick against her slick folds, I thrust into her, and that was when I grabbed a hold of her hair. Her keening wail lit me up from the inside out, and I dragged her head back so it was butting up against my shoulder, twisting it slightly to the side so that she could look at me.

"You want my dick, little one?" I growled against her temple.

"Yes, yes, yes," she whispered, her words almost a mantra.

"Open your mouth."

She obeyed.

I let saliva drip from my lips and watched as she swallowed it.

"Nothing comes between us, Savvie, *nothing*, ever again."

She bobbed her head eagerly as I urged her back toward the mirror and burrowed my face in her throat.

Fucking her hard and fast, giving her what she needed, I bit down with my teeth and held on for the ride.

I let go of her hair and reached down to tear at the buttons on her shirt. Dragging off the cups of her bra, I grabbed her tits and squeezed them in my grasp, using my hold on them to keep her pinned to me.

"Oh, my God," she screamed as I drove my cock into her, over and over, deep and wet.

The sound of her cunt, so juicy for me, was as sweet a sound as her cries and sobs.

When she bucked in my hold, her cunt clamping around my dick, I sucked down on the area I'd been biting.

Her whimpers turned into a long scream, and I thrust into her, pumping every drop of my cum inside. Not stopping until she'd milked me dry.

We collapsed against the mirror, her face smushing up against it as her breath came hot and heavy, fogging up the glass.

When the doors opened a second later, I laughed in her ear.

"Conor just got an eyeful," she drawled on a rasp.

My laughter turned sour, and I grunted, reaching over to press the button that'd close the doors.

"What is it about you and elevators, hmm?" I asked her, sucking on her earlobe as I thrust my slowly softening dick into her.

Her sigh was broken. "It's the first ounce of privacy we get."

She had a point.

Nothing about that car journey home had been private, and that was the future for the next short while. No traveling anywhere without guards for both of us.

Slowly, I pulled out of her, aware that gravity had worked its wiles as our juices slipped out with me.

I thrust two fingers into her, plugged our release back inside, and whispered, "Clench down."

Groaning, she did.

"When I pull out my fingers, I want you to clamp down even harder. I want back in this pussy, and I want it wet and warm when I do."

She sagged against me, her head lolling back on my shoulder. After a couple panting breaths, she whimpered, "Okay."

I released my hold on her only to swoop down so I could draw her pants back up, making her decent for the hallway, and then proceeded to pick her up in a bridal hold.

She squeaked but didn't complain as she pushed the button to let us out, then after we walked to the door, she entered the keycode.

I moved us over to the kitchen because the counter was at the perfect height for me to look at her, and I propped her on there.

Unhooking her shoes then dragging off her pants and panties only to toss them on the floor, I spread her legs. "Let me see."

Cum oozed from her folds, so purely white that it seemed to gleam against the bright red of her pussy.

I thrust two fingers into her again then retreated and raised them to her lips.

"Taste us, little one."

She hummed as she sucked down around them. "Like us."

I nodded, watching as she curled her tongue around the digits, slurping up our release as if it were the best thing she'd ever eaten.

"That got you hot today?"

It should have been a rhetorical question...

Or maybe it shouldn't have been.

I never fucking knew with Savvie.

A mewl escaped her as she flopped back against the counter. Her fingers went between her legs, but I didn't stop her. Instead, I watched as she rubbed my cum into her pussy as if it were lube.

"You were so fucking hot," she moaned. "They were scared shitless of you. I've never seen anything like it in my life."

"I have your seal of approval for my grand gesture, then?"

Her fingers pumped into her slit. "Yessss," she hissed, elongating the 's' sound. "They were terrified, but they respected you." Her voice turned thick. "And you're mine. I don't have to be scared of you. You're mine."

She drifted upward, not stopping until her mouth was on me. I'd been trying to be careful because of her burns, but she wasn't having any of it.

As she groaned, her fingers still pumping into her slit, she thrust her tongue into my mouth until my dick was getting hard.

"So fucking wet for you, baby," she cried, pulling back. "I need your cock, please, please."

Growling against her mouth, I ground out, "What my little one wants, she gets."

I spread her legs again, drove my dick between her folds as she pulled her fingers away, and I sank home.

It was wet and creamy and fucking heaven.

My wife's cunt was perfection, but when it was loaded with our release?

This went beyond paradise, and it might be the only kind I'd ever experience because no way in fuck was St. Peter letting me through his gates.

But I had her.

I had Savvie.

She'd make this life memorable, that was for sure.

Then, she wiped my thoughts away. Wiped my worries away too.

As I fucked her, she screamed, her arms clamping around my neck as I took over rubbing her clit. I laved her bottom lip with my tongue before I bit down again, loving her hoarse shout of, "Oh, God, Aidan. Please, please."

I fucked her, then slowing down when her pussy clutched at me, I kept her on the edge, hovering, waiting, until I rimmed her slit with my fingers then reached down to slip a single digit into her ass.

Thrusting up against my dick, faster, faster, I waited for her screech and was graced with that delicious moment when she squirted.

Liquid seeped from her in a high pressure burst that drenched my shirt and hers.

She writhed against me, working herself on me as much as I thrust into her, and when her head fell back, the endless whimpers morphing into a ceaseless cry, I gave myself up to her and filled her full of my seed.

Again.

42

SAVANNAH

POISON - RITA ORA

WHEN AIDAN PLACED his hand at the bottom of my back as we walked into Glas, the whole room fell silent.

This had happened to me before—not in reaction to my presence, of course. But this kind of thing wasn't unusual when my dad and the band were around.

All eyes were on us.

I was pretty certain that if I sneezed, everyone would react as if a gun had been fired.

The notion amused me, but I could sense Aidan's surprise as the maître d' shuffled us over to the table in the center of the restaurant that was on a kind of dais.

It seated six, but there were only two chairs which were clustered beside each other at one of the corners; I had a feeling that that was at Aidan's request.

As we reached the raised platform, the air changed again.

Aidan naturally commanded attention, but this was definitely different.

Charged.

Anticipatory, almost.

Were they expecting a floor show?

The maître d' held out a hand for us to take our places at the table, and as Aidan dragged out the chair for me and tucked me in once I was seated, low level conversation slowly started back up again.

My lips curved as Aidan sat down beside me, and I listened with half an ear as the maître d' prattled on about the specials of the day and the wine list.

When I accidentally knocked my napkin onto the ground, I leaned over to pick it up which was when I noticed him put his hand on the edge of the table as I straightened.

My insides were already melting, but that slight act, so small, put me in major trouble.

Especially when I saw that it was absentmindedly done.

His focus was on the maître d', not me.

But his awareness was such that he didn't want me to knock myself on the table and had taken steps to prevent that from happening.

Inwardly, I preened then returned my attention to the menu before I transmogrified into a complete and utter bowl of mush at the table.

I let Aidan pick the wine because I was a heathen and didn't really care about pairing fish with red wine instead of white, and I made my choice so that when he returned to uncork the bottle, I'd know what I wanted.

As he rushed away, and having selected my meal, I turned into Aidan and remarked, "I didn't expect to see you today."

He arched a brow. "Why not?"

"Thought you'd be busy." I peeped a smile at him as I grabbed his hand. "I'm not complaining. Feel free to torment me any time."

His laughter, when it came, was light and free; more silence spilled into the restaurant.

I had my confirmation that rumors had spread about O'Donnelly Jr.'s methods of retribution.

The quiet filled me with relief in all honesty.

It meant that the message had been rammed home, and that, for the moment, we were safe.

Until the next time someone tested him.

I knew, over the course of our lifetime together, that would happen repeatedly.

For now, I was intending on enjoying the lull.

Especially when people were reacting as if he'd withdrawn a tommy gun and was pumping them full of lead *Peaky Blinders*-style.

"Speaking of torment," he drawled once chatter recommenced, the soft clinking of cutlery drifting with it, and he brought out his phone and placed it in front of us.

I bit my lip at the sight of the controls to the vibrator I was wearing as his screen lit up once he'd unlocked his cell.

His tone was dark, deep as he rumbled, "You keep yourself under control throughout lunch..."

"I get a reward?" I queried, curiosity spiking at that rumble.

"You can do whatever you want to me tonight."

Interest gleamed in my eyes, but I pointed out, "You already owe me for tying me to the bed the night you had to go to Queens of Heart."

"I'm sure I paid you back for that."

"No," I sniped. "You didn't. I'd remember."

His lips twitched. "It's in your best interests to keep it cool, then, isn't it?"

"Why? So I can pack more of a punch in one go?"

"Exactly."

That gleam made another appearance in his eyes as he set the vibrator on medium.

I'd endured worse at his hands. At least this one didn't thrust.

I pursed my lips as I determined to settle down and to wait it out.

The only problem was solving how to eat when my appetite was at a zero. I hadn't been hungry when he'd come home, intent on surprising me with a meal at one of the restaurants in our building.

Now, I was hungry for his dick—I didn't think that counted as one of the food groups.

The maître d' appeared with our bottle of wine just as a shiver brushed down my spine when Aidan settled his hand between my shoulders.

Glad that I'd settled on a silky camisole above a pair of high-waisted pants, I took full advantage of not wearing a bra to mess with my husband's head as he stared down at me.

My smile taunted him as he traced his fingers around the nodules of my spine, sending whispers of pleasure throughout my nervous system.

"Don't take your eyes off me, Savannah. I want them on me or your food. Do you understand?"

I bit my lip. "I understand."

The restaurant was clearly intent on impressing us because the maître d', not a server, went through the whole tedious process of opening the wine with Aidan. He gave him a taste, and I watched as Aidan swirled it around the bottom of his glass, raising it to his nose before he sampled it.

His hum would have felt better against my clit than the vibrator.

Once the maître d' had earned his approval, finally, he poured some wine into my glass too.

Aidan snagged it for me and raised it to my mouth.

Eyes on him, I sighed as he tilted it against my parted lips. He didn't let me swallow too much before he was pulling back, holding it out for me.

There was the faintest tremor in my hand as I reached for it, the cool glass comforting against the tips of my fingers which were still sensitive from the healing cuts.

Sipping the wine, I savored the fruity notes—Aidan always knew what I liked best—and I tapped the menu so he'd know what I wanted.

All the while, I kept my gaze locked on him as he dealt with the intruder and gave him my order of deconstructed shepherd's pie. Aidan requested a steak.

"I like having all your attention," he rumbled, turning to me once we were alone.

"In a room full of people? Or just in general?"

He snagged his own glass and drank. "In general, but mostly, here. Especially when I know what your body is going through."

"Experienced a vibrator against your clit, have you?" I teased, enjoying his husky laughter. Before he could joke with me, I leaned into him and, knowing his guard was down and that his gaze was on my tits, questioned, "Is this a front?"

"Perhaps." He grinned at me, well aware of my game. His fingers tangled with mine, the tips rubbing down my digits. The simple act, so unsexual, had my heart pounding as if he'd slipped his hand between my thighs. "Who else would back an Irish chef with his eyes on a Michelin star that served grub from the Old Country?"

"Only your da," I said with a shake of my head.

"Exactly." His disapproval was clear. But he didn't comment on that, just took another sip of his own wine. "Do you like it?"

"The restaurant or the wine?"

"Both."

"The wine is good. You know I'll drink it from a box though."

"Heathen."

I liked that he used the same word I had to describe myself.

"As for the restaurant—" I hesitated. "It's very gray."

"That's what *glas* means in Irish Gaelic."

"Gray?"

He nodded.

I peered around the gray-on-gray-on-gray decor. "It reminds me of those prison cells. Either that or as if a Scandinavian designer came in here and vomited."

"Those cells are white."

That he knew what I was talking about didn't come as a surprise.

"How do you know that? Are you a mind reader?"

Aidan shot me an amused glance. "I guess. Only where you're concerned, unfortunately."

"Those prisons are illegal, aren't they?"

"Yes. Doesn't mean they don't exist."

"White cells, white food, white clothes, white everything. It's no wonder people go crazy."

"I'm not sure you comparing this restaurant to a prison dedicated to white torture bodes well for the chef's hopes and dreams."

His mocking tone had me snorting into my glass. "No, I suppose not."

His head tipped to the side as he studied me. "How are you doing?"

"I'm fine."

"Still not freaking out about what happened last Sunday?"

I rolled my eyes. "No, Aidan. I'd do it again."

He hadn't stopped me from kicking Anthony's crate over, but he regretted me doing the deed.

I damn well didn't.

My neck had been twinging like crazy from that goddamn crash for the last few days.

I squeezed his fingers. "Thank you for caring."

"Of course I care," he said gruffly. "I wanted to take your mind off things today anyway."

When he said stuff like that, he reminded me of who I was married to.

He owned the city, sure, but he owned my heart first and foremost. Just as I owned his.

"I should be at the hospital with Mom."

Today was the day of her surgery, and I'd only gotten it out of Dad by promising to keep my mouth shut to my brother and sisters.

"You should," he agreed. "But she didn't want that."

I heaved a sigh. "It'll be okay, won't it, Aidan?"

"Of course it will, little one."

I turned to him and rested my hand on his thigh as he pressed a kiss to my forehead. He breathed in, sucking in my scent as much as I sucked in his. "Can we spend Thanksgiving with them this year?"

He nodded. "I intended to. Do you know where they'll be?"

"Hawaii, at the moment. But if that makes things difficult with the security... I could convince them to stay in New York."

"It'd be easier," he admitted. "How about they come to our estate?"

"I like it when you use that word."

"Which one? *Our?*" He shook his head. "You're too easy to please, sweetheart." He rubbed the silk cuffs on my wrists that I wore for him, part of a gift he'd brought home for me, then tangled his fingers with my charm bracelet. "Haven't seen you wear this for a while."

I shrugged. "No, I didn't feel like wearing it."

"I like it on you. Almost as much as I love my ring on your finger." He ran his fingertips over the wedding band before, with his free hand, he delved into his pocket and pulled out a small box. "It's perfect timing for you to wear it today. I saw this and thought of you."

Surprised that he'd gotten me another gift, I reached for it. "You didn't have to. *Thank you.*"

He cocked a brow at me, and as I palmed the box, the intensity of the vibrator sped up a notch.

It was probably a testament to how often we played with toys that that medium-level buzz had been something I'd easily acclimated to. What had affected me more was the freedom with which he touched me in public.

The new vibration was deeper, however. It settled in my core and sent shards of heat soaring through my abdomen.

I sucked in a breath as I bowed my head, trying to get myself under control. He didn't help by placing his hand back on my knee. The heat of it made me want the heat of *him* between my thighs.

Still, he'd told me about a flogger, and I wanted him to use that on me tonight, so I behaved, got myself under control, and distracted myself with his gift.

When I opened the small box, I had to laugh.

"You just happened to see this, huh?" I mocked, loving his grin.

"Yeah. It was just sitting in the jeweler's window, waiting for me."

I held out my wrist. "Put it on for me?"

He picked up the 'Property of Aidan' charm and slotted it onto the bracelet. "I don't want any ink marring your skin. This'll have to do."

I peered at the tiny details, the engraving on each letter, as well as the inlaid gems on the medallion. "You must have had that poor jeweler working double fast to get this ready in time." We'd only been talking about ink on Saturday, and it was Thursday afternoon.

"My name comes with perks."

"You don't say," I drawled. But I swiftly admitted, "I love it.

Before I could thank him again, a server was there with our dishes.

Aidan's phone slid into his pocket, and as he tucked it away, the jerk slammed on the tempo so the vibrator tortured me further.

Though I glowered at him, he kept his focus on the server, thanking her until she departed with a flush.

I stared down at my meal which, to be fair, looked tasty, but it might as well have been a plate of crackers for all my stomach was engaged.

"When you said you wanted to distract me, did you have to distract me from the food?" I whined, which made him snort.

"It serves a purpose."

I rocked my hips a touch, trying to stop myself from getting riled up.

Having long since learned that it was easier to control my need by not getting overwhelmed by it, I picked up my knife and fork and took minuscule bites of the shepherd's pie. I'd had it before at Lena's, but this was different.

I wouldn't tell her that this was better—I knew that without even being interested in what I was eating.

As Aidan tucked into his steak, he informed me, "Do we start with the Feds or do we head for a different agency entirely—somewhere like Interpol?"

I stared at him blankly. "What for?"

"Your plan."

"You expect me to talk strategy?" I squeaked.

"You claimed to be good at multitasking."

I squinted at him. "I'll get you back later on."

"Looking forward to it," he teased, but his gaze was dark as he leaned into me and brushed a kiss over my still tender cheek.

One of his hands returned to my goddamn lap, and he stroked his fingers along the length of my thigh once more.

My heart stuttered when he rumbled, "Spread them for me, little one."

With a combination of a gasp and a gulp, I obeyed and nearly melted into the chair when he rubbed the seam of my crotch.

"You're better than the vibrator," I whimpered.

"Good to know, baby girl." He graced me with another kiss. "Now, Interpol?"

I sucked in a breath as I felt his hand rubbing up against the crotch again, pressing down harder on the vibrator.

My eyes fluttered closed until he murmured, "Gaze on me, Savannah."

Another breath whispered from my lips as I stared at him. Just him. Only him.

A piercing laugh broke into the daze around me, and I blinked, jolted back to the moment, aware that we weren't sitting in our dining room but were in a restaurant.

This was why I hated eating in public now.

"Savannah?"

I swallowed. "We have Feds in our pockets already—"

Something snapped to life in his eyes.

It didn't take much to figure it out—*we*.

I'd said 'we.'

I wasn't the only one who liked personal pronouns.

"Yes, but not from the ground up," was his rasped reply. "Caroline

Dunbar hasn't burned her bridges, but I heard she was passed over for a promotion. That means she's on the way out."

"How did you hear that?"

He dug his fork into some steak he'd pre-cut—he'd planned eating and tormenting me at the same time. Fucker. "How do you think?"

"If you have someone in there already, then why do you want another inside man in the Feds?"

"Because he's focused on switching attention from the Points and onto other people."

"Who is he?"

His lips twitched. "The director."

A gasp escaped me and it had nothing to do with the sex toy intent on driving me mad.

"When—" I gaped at him. "Wait, no. How? No. What?!"

He laughed. "Eat your lunch."

"That's impressive." I meant it too. The Director of the FBI was one of the longest serving in the bureau's history.

"Not really." He shrugged. "This will be a much more complex task."

He wasn't wrong. Especially if the director had been on the Five Points' payroll since the start of his career.

"Do you know anyone at Interpol?"

"I know of people," he said with a nod. "But I'd set Conor onto finding the appropriate candidates."

"Plural?"

He gave me another nod. Somehow, he managed to imbue his desire into that simple gesture.

"You really want this, don't you?"

My whisper had him gracing me with his focus. "I do."

"Why?"

"Because Da would never have tackled the Sparrows this way, and taking them down can be my legacy.

"If we have a kid, I want them to be proud of me, Savannah. I don't want them just to think of me as a Five Points' butcher. I want them to know I'm more than what he made me."

My heart turned to goop. "They *will* be proud of you, baby."

"Not if I don't make things right. The NWS are a plague, and they need eradicating. We're not saints, but by comparison, we're angels." He shook his head. "I don't want my kid growing up in a world where they rule the roost."

I leaned over and pressed a kiss to his cheek. "I love you."

"I love you too."

The ease in which he uttered those words made my pussy flutter.

I looked into his eyes. "We'll make it happen."

He squeezed my thigh, this time with the intention to show gratitude, not to tease.

It was oddly impactful to have my body on red alert while my brain was focused on what he wanted. It was like looking in two different directions with each eye—should've been impossible, but the impossible was possible around this man.

I moved my chair closer to him, needing to be nearer even if it was only a difference of a couple inches, and he rumbled, "I should have ordered take-out."

"What? Why?"

"Then we'd be in our dining room and you'd be naked and sitting on my knee."

A blush turned my face pink as I admitted, "I'd have preferred that."

He replaced his knife on the dish and raised a hand.

The maître d' made short work of arriving at our table, squawking, "Is everything okay, Mrs. O'Donnelly? Sir?"

"It's lovely," I assured him, appreciating that he asked me first.

"We'd like this to go," Aidan ordered.

As he retreated with the dishes himself, I murmured to my husband, "I don't think he's used to serving."

Aidan just snorted. "With the amount of money we invested in this place, the chef himself should be bringing out our plates."

43

AIDAN

I THANKED God that we didn't have to travel to Glas because it was in our building.

As I paid, I ordered the guy at the desk to bring it to our floor so I'd recognize his face when he rang the bell. Though it went above and beyond his job description, no one made a peep of complaint.

It was good to be king sometimes.

With my hand folded around Savannah's as I tugged her into the elevator, I asked, "Which do you prefer? The 68? Or here?"

"Here. The food's better," she admitted easily, her words dismissive as she wiggled in place.

I smirked at the realization she was having to cling to the vibrator now that gravity was working against her, and I murmured, "You did good, baby."

Savannah wasn't well versed in denying herself.

She liked to glut herself on pleasure, and because I was a soft touch around her, I usually conceded.

Why wouldn't I want my wife to drown in orgasms? Why wouldn't her desire and passion spike my own?

A man who failed to give his wife pleasure was half a man in my eyes. A fool, too.

But on occasions like these, it was good to remind her that I was benevolent, and that I didn't always have to be.

She squirmed against the wall. "I won our bet." Her fingers tugged at my shirt, and I felt the soft pressure of the fabric conceding to the bite of her nails.

"You half-won. We left before we finished," I retorted, reaching up and pressing a hand to the glass behind her head.

"*I* was finished," she asserted.

"I wasn't. You barely had more than three bites. Plus, we didn't order dessert. I know that's your favorite part of the meal anyway."

Her lips twitched. "I'll be your dessert."

I hummed under my breath. "I prefer your cunt to chocolate anyway."

The elevator came to a halt, and an elderly couple stepped inside.

I realized we'd hit the restaurant floor for The 68, and these must be our neighbors.

That was the joy of New York. You didn't have to know who lived beside you... But this was a special elevator, reserved for the upper floors, and few had access to it.

I didn't bother with politeness, just kept my back to them and stayed looming over her. The fruity notes of the wine were strong on her breath, clueing me into the fact that she'd barely eaten, but my focus was on her tits.

God damn her for not wearing a bra.

Her nipples had been taunting me since we'd stepped out of the apartment earlier.

We both jolted when the man whispered in a hushed voice, "Can you hear buzzing, Eloise?"

I almost laughed out loud when he reached up and played with his ear, making me realize he wore a hearing aid.

Watching as Savvie's cheeks turned a hot pink, I ran my nose against hers.

Eloise shook her head. "I can't hear anything."

"It's loud," he argued. His gaze caught mine in the reflection, and I just arched a brow at him.

He frowned. "Can you hear buzzing?"

Savvie choked out, "I think it's the elevator. Maybe it needs servicing?"

"Maybe *you* need servicing," I rumbled, nostrils flaring as I attempted to contain my laughter. My lips twisted as I bit the insides of my cheek, and I waited and waited for the doors to open again.

When Eloise and her husband stepped off, I let them turn toward their door before I tugged her out.

She blew out a breath. "I'm not going to make it."

I picked her up in a fireman's lift, one of my favorites since my knee had healed, and I carried her down the hallway toward our door.

It was easy to key in the code, and it was easier still in this position to spank her ass as I walked us over to the bedroom.

"No fair!" she sniped, wriggling so much that I almost dropped her.

When I slapped her ass again, she yelped, which had the cat darting from out of nowhere and knocking over a goddamn vase.

Neither of us cared about the vase. Savvie was too busy moaning as I dug my fingers against the seam of her crotch, pushing against the vibrator until I felt the heavy vibrations against the tips.

"Oh, fuck," she mewled, the deep thudding sensation not seeming to be diminished by her still wearing underwear and pants.

"That's what I want to hear," I growled then tossed her onto the bed, letting her bounce a couple times.

Following her descent onto the mattress, I grabbed the neckline of her camisole and I tore it off her. She shrieked, but I just snarled, "After teasing me with those fucking tits of yours, what do you expect?"

A lustful groan escaped her as she scrabbled at her fly, and I helped her drag her pants down even as I took one of her nipples into my mouth. I bit her there, hard enough to make her squeal before I slapped the inside of her thigh, ordering, "Over."

She obeyed, rolling over and holding her arms back for my attention.

On her wrists, she wore her charm bracelet, but a pair of dainty cuffs graced them too. They had small loops on them which hooked to her crotchless panties. Panties I'd brought with me as another gift today.

I dragged off the remains of the camisole then restrained her with her arms behind her back, murmuring, "Roll onto your knees."

Savannah and grace didn't go together in the bedroom on a regular day, never mind when her hands were restrained—she was much too eager for that. But seeing her scramble into position made my dick ache.

"What do you want me to do, little one?"

She froze. "Huh?"

"I'll let you be boss today."

With her weight on her shoulders, and the position shoving her face into the covers, she twisted around and stared at me with gluttonously large pupils.

"You said you had a flogger."

"For punishments." My lips curved. "You've behaved. For once."

She groaned, her breathing coming hot and heavy as she shoved her face back into the duvet.

I dragged my hands over the curve of her ass, short, blunt nails scoring lines into her flesh. I knew what that groan meant, knew why she'd hidden her expression from me.

"Have you been bad, Savvie?"

She groaned again. "Maybe."

"What did you do?"

A heavy sigh whispered from her lips. "I told the others what happened on Sunday."

I frowned. "Which others?"

"Camille, Aoife, Inessa, and Aela."

That she wanted to be punished didn't come as that much of a surprise—Savvie liked to be taken in hand.

I figured it was from a childhood of being allowed to run off to the goddamn circus without much more than being grounded for a couple days as punishment.

Dragging my blunt nails over the curve of her ass again, digging deeper this time, I rumbled, "That's for their men to tell them. Not you."

"I didn't want them to be in the dark. I promised I'd keep them in the loop."

"That isn't our business."

"They're our family!" she argued, twisting around to glower at me. Her face was already pink, and whorls of hair clung to her forehead. The battle in her eyes made my dick ache. It was that fire, that fight, that always reminded me of why we were perfect for each other.

"They are, but we keep our noses out of their business, and they do the same for us."

"They should know if they want to know. Aela requested to stay out of it, but the others wanted minimal details."

"It isn't your place to make those decisions, Savannah." I spanked her ass, making sure I caught her sit spot. She howled as I ground out, "The way our marriage works isn't how theirs work. I'm very permissive with you."

"It really feels like that," she said with a huff, trying to wriggle so that her ass was no longer in my direct line of fire.

"Who just confessed to something I didn't even know about?" I grumbled.

"Me," she said with a pout.

"Just to feel the lick of the flogger."

Despite my irritation with her, I chuckled under my breath as I reached down and tugged at the vibrator.

I could have pulled it out and away from the panties, but I didn't. I thrust it in a couple times, watching her back bow and arch as she released a shrill cry.

"I got a special flogger for you, Savannah," I rasped in time to my thrusts.

"Y-You did?"

I heard the raw need in her voice and felt it slice into my marrow.

When she got like this, it went beyond her fangirling over my position.

This was us.

Raw and rough.

Hungry, always hungry, for what the other could give.

A wife responding to her husband. A husband responding to his wife.

"How are your shoulders?"

"They're okay."

"Are you sure?"

"I'll tell you if they hurt."

I knew she was still sore from the accident. I had my own twinges, but the pain was manageable for me. By comparison to what I'd been dealing with for the previous five years, it was a walk in the fucking park.

I also wasn't the one tied with my hands behind my back, so checking in was imperative.

I retreated to the closet and pulled out my latest toy.

This one was something I'd bought online.

It was made from a rich leather, the color of oiled walnuts, and it served two purposes.

Unboxing it, I sprayed it with the alcohol I stored with our toys, then I headed into the bedroom.

Seeing Savvie hump the air had me reaching down and liberating my dick.

I pulled out the vibrator which had her groaning, and instead, I thrust the handle of the flogger into her.

She shrieked at the sudden cold, twisting around to see what I'd done.

At the sight of it stuck in her pussy, she released a sob. "That shouldn't be so hot."

"Nothing we do together isn't hot," I mocked, twisting the flogger a couple counterturns to make her squirm.

Her butt arched, legs spreading wider as she angled low onto the bed so that her chest was against the duvet.

"Such a brat, little one," I growled before I started fucking her with the flogger.

Soft cries drifted from her parted lips; the noises were hardwired to my heart.

That was, of course, when the buzzer rang.

I released a hissed exhalation and ordered, "Stay exactly like that. Do not move, Savannah. I mean it."

Self-sabotage was her kink, I was sure of it. Maybe it was why we got along so goddamn well.

It was painful to shove my cock back inside my fly, but I managed it as I retreated to the door.

A quick glance through the peephole confirmed it was the guy from Glas. Didn't stop me from palming my knife as I opened the door.

When he stared at me wide-eyed, I told him, "Wait."

He swallowed hard.

I stopped palming my knife, and instead reached for my wallet.

Handing him a hundred-dollar bill, I told him, "Thank you for bringing it up."

He gaped at me, then the tip, and quickly backed off with a, "You're more than welcome."

I closed the door after I grabbed the bag he'd placed on the ground, then I retreated, taking the food to the kitchen.

I was hungry, not just for Savvie's pussy, so I drew out my steak and ate a few bites as I shoved the rest of the containers in the fridge.

I poured myself a glass of the wine they'd re-corked and took a deep sip.

Working out a couple kinks in my neck, I stretched it from side to side, then I heard her wail, "AIDAN!"

Smiling, I checked my cell phone to make sure the city hadn't started burning down while I was out for lunch.

I had a couple of messages from my brothers—no fucking change there—but New York was still in one piece.

"Please!" she screamed, which had me shaking my head.

Grabbing my glass, I toed out of my shoes and left them in the kitchen as I stepped over to the bedroom.

"You'd think I dosed you with Viagra with how you act, Savannah," I rumbled, watching the way she was wriggling against the sheets.

She hadn't dropped out of the position I'd ordered her to stay in though.

I took a sip of my wine. "Roll over."

She did as requested then twisted around to look at me.

Her cheeks were bright pink, her hair already sticking to her forehead.

I sighed just looking at her—tits shaking, her entire being so focused on pleasure no one else in the city existed apart from me.

Escape—that was what she was to me.

The rest of the world wanted a piece of me; Savannah just wanted my heart, my soul, and my dick. The order depended on what was happening at any given moment.

Carefully tugging her arm, I supported her as she straightened, rolling neatly onto her knees so she was kneeling on the mattress.

"Crawl to the edge of the bed," I requested, watching as she scrambled nearer.

I couldn't stop myself from reaching behind her back and snapping the silken restraints that linked the cuffs on her wrists to her panties.

Though she yelped, she didn't complain about me destroying an expensive pair of lingerie. Instead, she moaned, those pupils of hers bloated once more as she kneeled there, quivering, the flogger hanging down between her thighs as she hovered by the edge.

I pressed my hand between her shoulders, encouraging her to lean against me as, knotting my fist in her hair, I tilted her head back, directing, "Open up."

Blinking, she obeyed as I took another sip of wine then, hovering my face above hers, carefully poured it between her lips.

She swallowed what I gave her, making me hum, "Good girl."

Her eyes sparkled as she leaned into me. "I can be sometimes."

I grinned at her. "Only sometimes. Why did you tell the others what happened on Sunday, Savvie?"

The daze of pleasure faded from her eyes as temper overtook it. "Just because they have uteruses doesn't mean they shouldn't know what's going on in the city."

"That isn't your decision to make. It's theirs and their husbands'. The last thing I need is my brothers heading over here to kick my ass because their wives are sobbing at night in fear."

Her scowl would have felled a lesser man. "You do know they didn't marry pussies, don't you?"

"Well, technically..."

She sniffed. "We've all been through stuff that has made us strong. You think we're weak—"

"I don't," I countered immediately. "You're not. I'm not in a position to say whether they are or not. I know, for a while, Camille had nightmares after she was kidnapped, Savvie. Did *you* know that? Did she tell you?"

"No."

"Well, then..." I quirked a brow at her. "Don't presume they're like you. They have their moments, and I'm proud to call them family, but it isn't *your* choice." Though I knew I was playing a broken record, I repeated, "It's theirs and their husbands'."

She huffed.

"Do you know how it fucking terrifies me whenever you see a side of my world that's cruel or wicked?"

"Scares you? I doubt it," she scoffed.

I grabbed her chin and held it in place. She squirmed against the firm pinch but I didn't release her.

"Yes, *scares me*, Savannah. You keep saying that nothing will push you away, but I know that's a lie. There'll come a day where something happens that's too much for you, and I'll fucking lose you. You don't have to leave the apartment for me to lose you, Savannah. Trust me, I know that. I lived through it with Ma."

"I'm not her."

"No, thank Christ you haven't gone through what she has, and I pray you never goddamn do because I will devolve into my father if anyone dares hurt you.

"I'm torn between wanting you close and wanting to push you away because these last couple weeks are a reminder of how things can roll, and we haven't even been attacked by outsiders. These were men who were supposed to be loyal to us." I sucked in a breath. "Though you told me you wanted to be at the hanging, you still stunned the fuck out of me by kicking Anthony's step over. Even *then*, I was concerned when you went quiet.

"I thought you had regrets."

"I regret very little." The simple answer had me blinking but she shrugged off my bewilderment. "You can't regret what you want at the time. If I have regrets, it's that we wasted five years apart. It's that you and I didn't have more time as a couple before this crap came down around us.

"It's that to your men, I'll always be a weakness, when I want you to know that I have your back, no matter what.

"I will never judge you. If you go crazy like your da, I won't then either. Because I love you and this kind of love doesn't go away. If those five years proved anything, it's that."

My lips curved as I looked down at her. Gently, I pressed a kiss to her mouth and I rumbled, "How am I supposed to flog you now?"

She pulled back but her fingers clung to my shoulders. "You do it with a smile."

I couldn't stop myself from snickering if I tried.

Shaking my head, I told her, "Pass it to me then."

"It'll be wet," she warned.

"Lick it clean first."

A mewl escaped her and her eyes fluttered closed.

She inhaled, slowly exhaled, then reached down and tugged it free. Her throat bobbed as she did so, then she drew it to her lips and started to clean the handle.

"It's nine inches," I informed her. "Custom made for you."

She swallowed as she sucked it between her lips. The sight made me reach down and unfasten my fly again.

I strode away from her to place the glass of wine on the dresser before I returned to watch her.

"You're fucking gorgeous, Savannah. Turn around and present that beautiful ass of yours to me. Legs spread wide. I want your pussy to feel the licks."

I snatched the flogger as she obeyed and retreated to her earlier position, but her legs were wider this time.

As I spun the flogger in an arc, letting the tips dance over her curves, I moved it along the length of her inner thighs then over her ass and up to her hips. She wasn't used to being flogged, so I kept it light, enough to get her blood flowing, her heart pumping.

She squirmed and writhed, soft noises escaping her, ones that turned into hard shrieks whenever I concentrated on one area.

When her ass was burning a bright red, I slotted the tip of my cock into her cunt and I thrust it back and forth, getting it slick with her juices, then I notched it against the pucker of her ass.

She groaned into the sheets, her hands clutching at them as I thrust inside her.

"Take it, Savannah," I growled, watching as she forced herself to relax.

I grabbed her by the hips and thrust the handle into her drenched pussy, tipping the tails so that they danced between her legs.

As I plowed into her, she screamed as I tugged on the flogger, twisting it, gently moving it back and forth so that it rubbed against my dick with every driving thrust of my hips.

Her fingers dragged the sheets off the corners of the bed as she screamed, bucking back against me, fucking me as much as I fucked her.

When I felt her inner muscles clamp down around the handle, I angled my cock down against her happy spot and felt the ramification of that ricochet through her body.

She froze.

She fell silent.

She didn't even breathe.

Then, as I fucked that spot, arching back onto my heels to hit it from both angles, she exploded around me.

Coming so hard that her cunt and ass nearly pushed me and the flogger out.

As she soaked my pants with her cum, I smirked at the mess as I let myself fall.

Free, in a way that only Savannah would let me experience.

44

TEXT CHAT

SAVANNAH

LATER THAT NIGHT

Me: *Any news, Daddy?*

Daddy: *She's doing well, sweetheart. I'm sticking close to her side—you don't have to worry.*

Me: *Has she woken up yet?*

Daddy: *No. She's still out of it.*

Me: *Text me when she does?*

Daddy: *I will. She won't want to speak with you, baby.*

Me: *I know. Daddy?*

Daddy: *Yes, honey.*

Me: *Did we do something wrong? For her to react like this, I mean?*

Daddy: *No! This isn't on you. It's on your mom and her odd family.*

Me: *What do you mean?*

Daddy: *Your grandparents were weird about illnesses. I think it* *was the hippy in them. Why take a pill when you could smoke an herb? They made her the same.*

Daddy: *Remember that time she told everyone she sprained her ankle and hobbled around for weeks with a broken toe?*

Me: *Oh... yeah! I remember that. God, that was years ago.*

Daddy: *She hates canes, casts, bandages. If you ask her, she'll tell you they make her physically sick.*

Me: *Jesus! How didn't I know that?*

Daddy: *Well, she knows it's irrational and didn't want you to be the same. Just like how she hates elevators and enclosed spaces but never let on that she did with you kids so you wouldn't be scared of them too.*

Daddy: *This is just her way of trying to protect everyone. She doesn't want to look weak or frail, and she doesn't want to put herself on you either.*

Me: *But she wouldn't be. I'd prefer to be there than sitting here, wondering what was happening.*

Daddy: *She'd have preferred the opposite when her mom was ill. That's why she's trying to save you from it.*

Me: *Isn't that our decision to make?*

Daddy: *Yup. Don't worry, honey. When I'm sick, I totally expect all my spawn to haunt the hospital.*

Me: *:P I know. You milked the hell out of that knee replacement surgery two years ago.*

Daddy: *A father's right. I'll make up for her being a weirdo.*

Me: *LMAO. Thanks for putting a smile on my face.*

Daddy: *;) You're welcome, baby. Get some rest. It's gonna be a long night, but the doctors are hopeful. This was totally a preventative measure. She's going to be fine. Xo*

Me: *Thank you, Daddy. Love you xo*

Daddy: *Love you too, pumpkin. xo*

45

SAVANNAH

"I THINK AURORA IS A SUBMISSIVE."

"And you're not?" I scoffed at Jen as I stared at the grounds of the O'Donnelly estate.

She scoffed back before she began doing this humming thing as Saverina started to fuss. Thirty seconds later, she complained, "I'm not talking about me taking it up the ass because Luc gets hot and heavy—"

"It's illegal to talk about that stuff when you're holding a baby—"

"—I mean like a proper submissive. I saw her coming out of that strip club, you know, the Queens of Heart?" she asked, totally ignoring my earlier comment.

"I know it."

"Well, Luc said it's a sex club too."

My brows rose. "It is?"

Aidan hadn't told me that.

Dammit, now I really had to know what it looked like on the inside. Especially if Luc had taken Jen to the club. No way was she going to hold that over me.

She just hummed again, more at me this time, and not my namesake.

"And you saw Aurora leaving there?" I prompted.

"Yeah. With that guy who showed up on our wedding day. He arrived late to the reception."

"He was hot."

"He is," she agreed. "His name's Hunter. But how they were kissing..." She clucked her tongue. "I'm telling you that was no ordinary kiss."

"What did he do? Stuff a ball gag between her lips?" I teased.

"Might as well have. Trust me, Aurora was *not* in the building."

"You mean... sub space?"

"Well, I think so. I've only read about it."

"He's a shitty Dom if that's the case. Isn't that the whole point of aftercare? To bring them back down to earth before they part?"

"How much BDSM romance have you read?"

"More than you," I joked.

She pshawed, "Doubt it. Maybe she's a Dominatrix."

"Well, that was a fast graduation."

"I could see her using a whip in court. Getting everyone in line, you know? Head to toe in latex."

I grinned. "Make up your mind. Is she the one being tied to a St. Andrew's cross or is he?"

She sniffed. "I'm telling you that wasn't an ordinary dynamic."

"Babe, I trust you with my life, but you don't know shit about D/s relationships."

"And you do?!"

"Aidan's got his quirks."

"No way he's a fucking Dom."

"I never said he was! I'm just saying that there's more nuance to that kind of relationship than a scorching hot kiss outside a sex club." Before we could get into an argument, I asked, "What were you doing at Queens of Heart, anyway?" I tried to keep my tone light. The last thing I needed was to make this into a competition between us.

"Nothing fun, sadly," she drawled, which perked me up to no end. "I was just stopping by Aoife's for some hibiscus tea and that new Bundt cake of hers—have you tried it yet?"

"No." My ears pricked up. "Like boring Bundt?"

"Nah. When does Aoife make anything boring?"

"True. I need to try that."

"You do," she agreed. "Whatever, I was heading home—have you noticed the police blockades have finally gone, by the way?"

The capture of the First Lady's murderer had been all over the news...

"Yeah, thank God. They were a major pain in the ass," was all I said to that. I shared a lot with her, had even told her about the kidnapping, but I didn't want to fuck up Aidan's plans.

"They were. Anyway, that was when I saw them. It had to be, like, an afternoon quickie or something. They were kissing and pulling away then went back to kissing. It was pretty sweet. If anything about that viper could be considered sweet."

"Does it matter?"

"Not really. I just... She's such a cunt."

I burst out laughing. "Does it make it better you knowing that about her?"

"Maybe. Fucking bitch."

"What has she done now?"

She huffed. "Nothing in particular. She just looks at me and I feel like a piece of crap."

"I think you're projecting."

"I doubt it."

"I don't. Luciu wouldn't allow her to get away with that. He's too protective."

A sigh whistled in my ear. "True."

"Maybe she doesn't know how to get close to you. It's not like her life has been easy the past couple years, is it?"

"Stop being logical. And rational."

"Let me guess, Aoife told you the same thing?" I tried not to be petty, but... Who was I trying to kid? I was no angel.

"No. I haven't spoken about this with her."

That petty part of me preened that she'd come to me about this first.

"Why not?" I asked as I watched Declan, Shay, Brennan, and Eoghan start bouncing a basketball and shooting hoops.

Attention pricked when Aidan walked onto the court too, I released a soft groan when he took off his jacket and snagged the ball out of Eoghan's hands.

"Savannah? Are you even listening to me?"

"Aidan started playing basketball with his brothers."

"So?"

"So?! Have you seen my man?"

"He's not as hot as Luciu."

I pshawed. "Suck on my donkey dick, bitch."

"Nah, I'd prefer to suck Luc's."

"Sucking more would have stopped you getting pregnant again so fast."

She blew a raspberry in my ear.

"I thought I'd stop feeling like this after a while." I whistled.

"I did too. Luc can still take my breath away."

"I almost don't want it to stop, but I can't cope with lady boners when I'm about to sit down for dinner with his ma."

"Is it dinner or lunch?"

"You mean, what time do we eat?"

"Yeah, everyone calls it something different."

I blinked. She had a point. "It's neither, so I guess that's why it's interchangeable. We eat between two and three."

"That's some fucking logic there." She snorted. "Anyway, how is the bitch?"

"Jen," I chided.

"Just because you don't hate her, doesn't mean I like her. After what she did to Aoife and her mom..."

"I know." I sighed. "Right now, she's sad. Medicated up to her eyeballs. Wearing full-out black. I'm talking every-frickin-thing. Scarf, blouse, skirt, shoes, stockings. It's like looking at Morticia."

"Dude, don't ruin Morticia for me."

My lips twisted. "The bittersweet truth is I think she misses Aoife. If anyone could get her through this, it'd be her. They used to always be in the kitchen together."

"Life's a bitch."

"It really is."

"Maybe she'll die soon and then it won't be a problem."

"Jen," I grumbled.

"What? She knocked down Aoife's mom with a car and drove off like nothing happened, Savvie. Jeez."

"I know." And I did. It didn't stop me from feeling sad about the chasm that had torn the family apart. "Saverina doing okay?"

"She's perfect."

My lips twitched. Jen coming out with dopey words like that, in that dreamy voice, was still hard to acclimate to.

"And the baby?"

"Making me puke all the time."

"They do that," I mused.

"Have you and Aidan started thinking about kids yet?"

"Nothing's changed since the last time we had this conversation." I chuckled at the idea. "I'm too much of a kid myself, and he's focused on securing his position."

"Thought a life-and-death situation like the kidnapping might have changed that."

Had it?

"No. It could have. But we haven't talked about it."

I sighed when he dribbled the ball and managed to dart around Brennan. As he scored, he punched Eoghan in the shoulder then slipped Shay a high five—clearly they were on the same team.

"I think you should be nice to Aurora. The next time you see her, I mean."

"In like forty minutes? She's coming around to eat. Unfortunately."

"Well, that's perfect timing."

Jen griped under her breath, making me smile.

"She'll be one of the kid's godparents, won't she?"

Jen sniffed. "No, she fucking won't. You will be this one's. Stan can be again—"

"I get to be godmother this time?" I squealed, stunning myself by how happy her declaration made me.

And it *was* a declaration. Definitely not a request.

Typical Jen.

"Yes, babe. Of course. But not her. Not as things are."

It wasn't in my best interest but I couldn't stop myself from chiding, "Jen, she *is* Luc's twin."

"I don't give a damn. She has to suck up to me big time before I'll even think about it."

"I didn't think you'd pick me over Aoife. I know I'm not overly maternal."

"Nah, but you're my best friend, and you'll be a great mom when you have a kid of your own. You just need to be less pussy-centric."

I snorted out a laugh. "Like you don't get horny."

"I never said that," she teased. "Anyway, I'd better go. I have to get changed before Aurora turns up."

"Why?"

"Well, I had a real low-cut shirt on."

"Why?!"

"My tits are bangin' right now. I felt like showing them off and it would have the added benefit of annoying the living fuck out of her."

"What are you? Five? I'm not the only one who needs to grow up in this conversation."

She blew another raspberry in my ear.

"Let me know how you all get along."

"Will do," she grumbled.

"Tell Luc he can thank me for sowing the seeds of peace another time."

"Don't get ahead of yourself," she grouched.

"Give Savvie a kiss from me."

"Saverina," she corrected with a laugh. "But I will. Speak later, babe."

"Yep. Laters."

After I cut the call, I opened the window and leaned on the sill so I could throw down a wolf whistle.

It had the brothers turning to face me, but I only had eyes for Aidan who grinned at me.

He dribbled the ball over to the window where I was standing then made his shot...

He scored.

Whooping, I told him, "I didn't know you played basketball."

Shay would often shoot hoops by the garage, and one of his uncles would join him, but Aidan hadn't thus far.

Turning around to face me, he said, "My knee's good enough to let me."

I eyed him, saw the slight gleam of sweat on his brow, and murmured, "You look hot. And I don't just mean sexy either."

He chuckled. "You and balls, Savvie."

I winked at him then grabbed his hand. "You ready for food?"

"As ready as I'll ever be. Ma's out of it."

"Meds will do that to a person. I just got off the phone with Jen."

He arched a brow. "What did she do?"

"Nothing. She told me that Queens of Heart is a sex club?"

"It is."

"You didn't tell me that before. You said it was a brothel."

"Stop pouting. We're not going there."

"Why not?"

"Because no one will see your pleasure apart from me," he groused, his tone dark enough to make me sigh.

"Okay."

"Okay?"

"Yeah. Just talk that kind of dirty to me and I'll forget," I goaded.

"Food's ready."

The announcement came from the door, and the tone was flat.

I turned to face Conor who didn't look to be in the best of moods.

"You okay, Con?"

"Been better. I'm hungry."

"More like hangry. I feel your pain."

"You're always hungry," Aidan mocked.

"What can I say? I burn a lot of calories." I winked at him again then jumped when he kicked his leg over the sill and climbed in through the window.

Immediately, his hand found mine and he tugged me into him. With one arm going around my shoulder, his heat sank into me, and I let him guide us out of the small sitting room and toward the dinner table.

As we made our approach, I saw that a place had been set at the head.

Though I frowned, and I knew it gave Aidan pause, he went to his usual seat, but Lena, her voice weird, spaced out, commanded, "Head of the table, Junior. That's your place now."

"I'd prefer not to, Ma."

"Sit where you're told," she grated out.

Aidan clenched his jaw, but I tugged on his hand as she retreated to the kitchen to collect more dishes. "Do it. Just to keep the peace."

He rolled his eyes and took the seat where his da used to sit, but I knew his irritation belied his unease.

I sat at his side, to the left, and Aela found her place to his right.

Everyone lined in, and they all shot a surprised glance at Aidan.

"I didn't suggest this," he grumbled.

Conor drawled, "Ma's in self-destruction mode."

"I heard that, son."

"I meant for you to," he retorted. "I was thinking that this house isn't good for you, and I reckon you just gave me the proof I needed."

"I agree," Paddy said as he sidled in and sat beside Lena. "It's fucking massive, and you rattle around the place."

"This is my home," Lena grunted as she took a seat, snapping out a white napkin that practically glowed against all the black she was wearing.

As usual, she reached for the first dish, the silent catalyst for everyone else to pick up the dishes in front of them and to serve themselves then to circulate each bowl around the table.

"I think you should move in with Uncle Paddy for a while." A dull thud sounded from under the table, and Conor laughed. "Did you just kick me, Paddy?"

"Yeah, I did." He glowered at Con. "Don't be forcing nothing on your ma. She can stay wherever the fuck she wants, but I agree, she needs to be in the city. Not out here on her own."

"Maybe I want to be alone."

"Nah, Lena, you're not meant for solitude. Six fucking kids, noisy little bastards, then Aidan and me and Frank... plus all your brothers. Nope. It's not right. You need the chaos."

Lena wriggled her shoulders. "What I need is a vacation."

Aidan nodded as he served himself mashed potatoes. "I think you're right. You do. Take a cruise to the Caribbean, Ma. It's nice and hot. Get some sun."

She hummed. "Maybe."

Eoghan commented, "You ain't been on vacation in years, Ma."

"Years? More like decades." She straightened her shoulders. "Your da never felt safe enough to leave the city."

"Then you definitely deserve a break."

She shot Paddy a look. "Do you want to come with me, Padraig?"

"Can do, Lena. I don't wanna go to the Caribbean though."

"No?"

"Nah. Been there a couple times. Not my thing. Beautiful islands, don't get me wrong, but I'm not a rum man. Always tastes like suntan oil to me."

Conor retorted, "How much suntan oil have you been drinking?"

Before they could start bickering, Lena asked Paddy, "You want to go to Europe?"

"Yeah."

"I want to go back to Europe," Shay said on a sigh. "Mom took us all over the world, but that's my favorite place. You can't imagine seeing an opera in the original opera house it was meant for; the acoustics are heavenly."

Victoria laughed. "I'm not sure that's everyone's dream."

"I agree, Shay," Aela said with a nod as she loaded her fork with chicken and potatoes two ways. "We should go back to Europe. Your dad's never left the States. We need to show him the sights."

"What? Ever?" Shay's eyes bugged. "Europe is awesome. Never mind the museums, but the streets... just everything. It's so old."

Declan curved his arm around the back of Aela's chair as he took a sip of beer. "Not right now, Shay. It's not the time to leave the city."

"Maybe for your birthday," Aidan murmured. "That'd be cool, right? Family vacation to Europe, Shay?"

He shot his dad a look. "That *would* be cool."

Declan cocked a brow at Aidan. "You'd be okay with that?"

"There are six of us. The city can cope with there only being five O'Donnellys in residence. Each of us should go at some point this year. We're all newlyweds, apart from Con, of course."

"My time's coming."

My lips twitched at Conor's droll rejoinder.

"No one's gone on a honeymoon apart from Eoghan," Aidan continued as if Conor hadn't spoken. "Speaking of going away, Ma, this year, we'll be spending Thanksgiving with Savannah's family."

"Invite them here," Lena said with a frown.

"No," Aidan dismissed. Though his declaration came as a surprise, especially after we'd agreed to invite them to our estate, his consideration made me reach over and squeeze his knee in thanks.

"She's got her own traditions, and I don't want her to miss out on that."

"I'd love to eat Thanksgiving with Dagger Daniels," Conor muttered, shooting Aidan a glower.

"Yeah, well, tough shit." He huffed. "You'll have everyone else here, Ma; it'll just be us missing."

"It's not right," Lena declared, her hands tightening into fists around her knife and fork.

That was when everyone started darting looks between them as if we were at a game in Arthur Ashe Stadium.

"I don't care if it is or it ain't," Aidan stated, lobbing a serve. "Savvie's got family she cares about. She's entitled to do her thing as much as I am." His words were weighed down with a warning. "We'll alternate holidays so she doesn't miss out too."

"Savannah, surely you can see how unfair it is after Senior—"

"Don't, Ma," Aidan growled. "Don't guilt trip her into something that ain't even her idea in the first place. They spend time in Hawaii for the holidays, and you know what? I want a break too."

"Maybe I should just go on a cruise for Thanksgiving," Lena sniped, slamming the butts of the handles on her cutlery down against the table. "Save myself the back ache of making a feast for you ungrateful—"

"Do what you want," Aidan grumbled before she could finish her sentence. "If that makes you feel better, do it. I won't stop you."

His defense of me felt good, particularly when it wasn't something I'd asked for. But then, if a man knew the importance of family, it was Aidan.

I bit my lip as chatter was slow to stir around the table in the aftermath.

It figured that no one had expected Aidan to put his foot down about this, not at the moment, and the tone was definitely different than when Senior had been at the head of the table.

But as families usually did, especially ones as close as the O'Donnellys, they brushed over it, and the meal carried on like there hadn't just been an almost argument over the roasted chicken.

It *would* be good to head to Hawaii. And I hadn't spoken about Thanksgiving with Mom yet, but it'd be better for her to spend some time there, to get away from the city to recuperate properly.

Appreciation for my husband and his care filled me once again, as well as gratitude. Something that was only rammed home the following day when I received an out of the blue phone call...

46

SAVANNAH

"SAVANNAH?"

Having scheduled to meet with Grainne Ledger for a preliminary interview tomorrow afternoon, my mind wasn't exactly where it should be.

I'd been trying for three years to get in with Grainne, so I was beyond excited over meeting with her.

And maybe she'd show me the sex club part of Queens of Heart without me having to ask Aidan...

"Savannah?"

"Yes?" I asked absently as I stroked Bupkis. The name was official now; she had a name tag and everything.

"It's me. Cassie."

I blinked. "Cassie? Oh, why are you whispering?"

"I-I need your help."

Not every woman daydreamed about meeting with Manhattan's Madam, but I wasn't every woman. And those daydreams were blown to smithereens at Cassie's words which triggered a waterfall of memories.

All those goddamn snapshots of her beaten up, the domestic violence charges never filed...

"Are you in danger?"

"I'm always in danger," she whispered. "But Harvey just left. I-I know it's an imposition—"

"An imposition? Are you crazy? Cassie, I saw the state of those bruises on your face last week." I knew I had to be careful here. She couldn't know I'd looked into her. "How can I help? Please, tell me."

"I'm tied to the bed. H-He didn't realize I had a spare cell phone tucked down the back of the mattress if he did this again."

Having been tied to the bed by my husband, but with a more pleasurable end in mind, it was somehow all the more obscene that she was being restrained there with a different intention.

I bit my lip and, though I already knew, demanded, "Where do you live?"

"I'm in New Jersey. Caldwell." She rattled off the rest of her address. "I know you're in Manhattan. God, I should never have called you. He just... He's really mad, Savvie." She started sobbing, and her sobs damn near broke my heart. "He's so mad. So mad. I didn't mean to smile at the delivery guy, I swear!"

Sucking in a breath, I rasped, "I know you didn't, Cassie. I know you didn't. This isn't on you; it's on him.

"I have friends in West Orange. They could get to you before me. Would you be okay with me calling them?"

"Please." She swallowed audibly. "He's going to kill me, Savvie. I know he is. I think that's why he went out."

"We should call the cops," I started, but her sobs increased.

"No! They don't listen. He'll say I'm sick again. They'll lock me away. I can't go back to that place—"

Horror filled me. Her husband had had her committed? Why wasn't that in the notes Conor had sent to me? "Okay, I won't call the cops, I promise."

"I don't know who else to call, Savvie. I-I don't want to die. I don't want to die."

"You won't die, honey," I said fiercely as I jumped to my feet and I rushed over to the landline in the kitchen. "Stay on the line with me. Understood?"

"I will. I will."

Her whimpers sounded in my ear, and each one was like a nail in my coffin. My heart started racing as I dialed Conor's number.

"Savannah?"

"Conor, I need someone to go to this address."

After I recounted it, he pointed out, "That's the address of the chick you had me investigate."

"Yes, it is. She's scared for her life, Conor. I'm on my way but I don't know if I'll get there in time."

"Savannah, don't you dare leave the apartment. Not unless you want to give Aidan a coronary. Stay put, I'll have someone bring her to you."

"She's scared, Conor. Hell, she thinks she's going to die."

"I'll get one of the Sinners to take their woman along. Okay?"

"Fine. But hurry!!"

"I will. Stay on the line."

It was weird being the piggy in the middle of two conversations, but Cassie's weeping made it so much worse.

I heard Conor on the other line, demanding, "Rex, I need a favor."

As he detailed what was happening, I could tell that there wasn't a problem on the MC's end in helping out.

Her sobs broke me and I rasped, "Cassie, help's coming, honey. Just bear with me."

A couple minutes later, the address shared, Conor reappeared in my ear, saying, "Nyx and Giulia live near her. They're en route."

I grimaced, wishing it'd been Lily and Link who lived nearby, but beggars couldn't be choosers. I'd just have to warn Cassie that both her saviors might look like they were hell-sent, not heaven.

"Thanks so much, Conor."

"You're welcome. Let me know when she arrives."

"Why?"

"So we can deal with her husband and get her into a safe house. Rachel Laker, she's the MC's attorney—"

"She's the Sicilian's lawyer as well."

"Jen has a big mouth."

"Mine isn't small."

"Don't I know it. Anyway, Rachel will help. She takes on cases like this *pro bono*."

"Okay, I'll let Cassie know. But she might not want to press charges." From her terror of before, I wouldn't blame her if she didn't.

"Let's see if we can change her mind. I fucking hate these bastards who think they can treat women like their punching bags." He growled under his breath. "Call me."

When dead air sounded in my ear, I said to Cassie, "Honey, two of my friends are on their way. I need you to be prepared for the sight of them."

"W-Why?"

"Well, one of them is a biker, and he's a pretty big guy. His wife will be with him. She's got a more corrosive tongue than sulfuric acid, but I promise you her heart is in the right place. His name's Nyx and she's Giulia.

"They're going to get you out of there and bring you to me, okay?"

"I don't want to be a burden."

I heard the rattle of cuffs against the railing, and I winced.

I wasn't sure if Aidan would ever be able to tie me to the damn bed again, not without making me think of Cassie.

"You're not a burden. Please, don't say that."

"Of course I am. You haven't heard from me in years, Savannah. Years. But I call you out of the blue to ask for your help?" The tears in her voice broke me. "I'm just as awful as Harvey says I am."

"You're not! Maybe if you'd known my number before, you'd have called me sooner."

"He isolated me, Savannah. I don't talk to my mom anymore, I barely have any friends left, and he slept with my sister..." She sniffled. "I should have left him then, but I was too scared to go."

"I'm so sorry, sweetheart. We'll get you away from him. I promise."

Another rattle of the cuffs against the bed echoed in my ears.

I sucked in a breath. "I live with my husband, Cassie."

"I know. I read about your marriage to Aidan O'Donnelly. I thought it was funny."

"You did? Why?" I asked dryly.

"Because you always had such a lady boner for the old mob families. It was fitting that you ended up with him." Her laughter was tear-soaked. "Wouldn't it be hilarious if he was less dangerous than my husband?"

"He is, honey. Aidan would never hurt a woman."

"Why don't I believe that?"

"It's the truth. Now, your husband, sure. He'll hurt the fuck out of him. Especially if I ask him to."

"No. I just want to get away. Please, please, Savannah. Don't get him involved. I don't want any trouble." She sucked in such a swathe of air that it was a surprise she didn't choke on it. "Savannah, there's someone at the door."

My cell rang.

"There's someone on the other line."

"Please, don't leave me alone!" Cassie pleaded.

"Two minutes, let me call you on the landline." As I dialed her number from my cell, I connected with the unknown number a moment later.

In one ear, I heard Cassie panting through her fear and I told her, "I'm back. I'm here. You don't have to be scared."

Then, in the other, I heard Giulia demand, "We're here, Savannah. What's going on?"

"You'll have to break down the door, Giulia. She's cuffed to the bed. Her name's Cassie. She's terrified."

A grimness overcame the other woman's tone. "We'll deal with this. Don't you worry."

A second later, in both ears, I heard a door being kicked in. Cassie started sobbing while Giulia ground out, "Well done, baby."

Stomping footsteps came next, and then there was a whispered, "Are you Nyx?"

"I am, and you're safe now. I promise."

Giulia chimed in, "You have no reason to worry, honey. Nyx will keep the motherfucker who hurt you away."

"They mean it, Cassie," I told her, trying to affirm that she was in safe hands.

It was frustrating hearing everything secondhand, but I was just grateful Nyx and Giulia had managed to get to her so quickly.

"Do you know where the key is? Or did he take it with him when he left?"

Cassie's gulp was audible. "It's over there."

"The bastard," Giulia hissed in my ear.

"Where was it?"

"Close enough to be torturous, far away enough that she'd never reach it."

"Prick," I snapped. "But at least she can get out easily enough."

Of course, that was when all hell broke loose.

"Who the fuck are you?" someone, I assumed her fucking husband, roared. "Cassie? What's going on here?"

Cassie started sobbing, and my anxiety levels shot through the roof.

"You're safe," I chanted in her ear. "You're safe, I promise. Nyx is..." How did I use his reputation as a killer of pedophiles to reassure her?

Jesus Christ.

Then, I didn't need to.

Because there was a dull thud, a couple more, then Giulia hooted, "Nice hit, baby." She rounded that off with, "You take that, prick. And that."

I heard some thuds and asked Cassie, "Is she kicking him?"

"She is," was her response, and I could sense how close to hysteria she was because her breathing was so loud in my ear that I knew if she didn't control herself, she'd trigger a panic attack.

There was a metallic click, then I heard Nyx say, "You're free now. You should put your head between your legs so you can regulate your breathing."

To me, Giulia demanded, "Tell her to calm her breathing, Savannah. She's going to have a panic attack if she's not careful, and we need to get her out of here."

"You do, but..." My mind raced. Things were different now that her husband had returned to find two strangers in their apartment. Especially after Nyx had kicked the door in. "Think about how it will look. He could call in a charge of kidnapping or something."

Giulia grunted. "We've dealt with worse charges."

"No, Giulia. I won't let this be a problem for you, not when you're doing me a favor."

To Cassie, I urged, "I need you to listen to me. I know you don't want to go to the cops over this, but if Nyx and Giulia take you away, then you have to understand that your husband could say they were kidnapping you."

In my ear, her breathing practically rattled. Worse than the echoing clink of the cuffs against the headboard. I was sure she wouldn't answer, then she breathed, "What do I do?"

"You need to listen to Giulia and Nyx." To Giulia, I remarked, "Put me on speaker."

"We can hear you."

As I hung up the landline, I asked, "Do you have a cop in your pocket?"

"West Orange's sheriff," Nyx rumbled.

"Call him in."

"Will do," Giulia replied. "Thank you for giving a damn."

"Of course. You're only there because I asked, and, hey, we're allies, aren't we?"

Giulia laughed. "Guess we are. We can get this creep locked up by the night's end. Do you still want her brought to your place?"

"Cassie? What do you want? Do you want to stay there?"

"No!" she cried. "I want to get away from here. He'll come looking for me, Savannah. He always does."

I narrowed my eyes. "You can stay with us, Cassie. Please, don't worry."

"Savannah?"

"Yes, Giulia."

"She's bleeding and she's half-naked."

"He raped her?"

"I think that was his end goal. It looks like he tried to cut off her clothes." There was another thud, and I knew she was kicking the bastard. "Cassie, shall we get you washed up?"

"No," I told Giulia. "It's horrible, but she needs to stay like that. The sheriff needs to see the state she's in." To Cassie, I said, "I'm so sorry, honey, but please, just bear with us."

"Sheriff's ETA is five minutes," Nyx rumbled in my ear.

"Five minutes, Cassie. That's it. I know it's a lifetime, but let's get you safely out of there, yeah?"

She didn't answer, but her breathing sounded loud in the room again.

I swore those five minutes were as long for them as they were for me.

I was just thankful as hell that Cassie lived in goddamn Jersey, in a town near enough to where Giulia and Nyx had been when they'd gotten the call.

"His jurisdiction isn't here," Giulia commented. I knew that wasn't to me, but to Nyx.

"Doesn't matter. We need him to smooth things over," was all her Old Man said.

I stayed on the line with them, even though no one spoke to me for the next forty-five minutes.

I was there when her husband was arrested, and I was there when Giulia helped her into the bathroom.

I was there as Giulia promised they were safe now and when Cassie broke down, I was there too.

I listened to it all, wishing like hell I could be with her and not Giulia, and I whispered, "I'm so sorry, Cassie. So sorry."

I didn't expect her to answer, but she did. "You saved my life, Savannah. You have nothing to be sorry for."

47

AIDAN

WHEN CONOR BROKE off to take a call and uttered Savvie's name, I was prepared for the ensuing chaos.

Not that it really hit us.

He contacted Rex, the Prez of the Satan's Sinners' MC, while we watched on.

Fifteen minutes later, he turned back to me with a nod. "Handled."

I scrubbed my chin. "What's she done now?"

"Saved a friend."

I blinked. "Savvie?"

"Yes."

Declan muttered, "Is it a state secret or something?"

"No. But we should get back to business. This is our first council meeting, and we need to get our shit together."

"Nothing's going to get done if you don't tell us what that was about," Finn drawled.

Conor huffed. "You're worse gossips than a bunch of housewives."

My lips curved. "It'll be over faster if you just explain."

"Savannah met an old friend at Aoife's bakery. She was badly beaten. She asked me to investigate her; I did. It wasn't the first time she'd been abused. That friend just called her and asked for help. You heard the rest."

Eoghan whistled under his breath. "You know, I really fucking hate men sometimes."

"I hate people," Brennan agreed.

"Meaning you hate everyone?" Finn mocked.

"Why not? Pussy or dick, they're all fucking asswipes."

I snorted. "You including us in that mix?"

"Most definitely." Brennan remarked. "I have to deal with you fuckers, though, so I'm immune to you. My trigger finger stopped twitching back in my teens."

"Good to know," Finn joked, but he turned to Conor. "Rex didn't mind helping out?"

"No."

"I'm not surprised," I admitted. "The Sinners seem to be good people."

"Don't fucking talk to me about them," Brennan growled. "I still owe that bastard Enforcer a beating."

"If you're talking about Nyx, he isn't the Enforcer anymore," Conor muttered. "He's VP."

"Well, I owe the Vice fucking President then."

"Why? If it wasn't for him being a jackass, you wouldn't have met Camille," Conor pointed out. "Don't you think some shit happens for a reason?"

"He treated her like crap."

"You ain't exactly been a gentleman with your exes," Finn retorted. "None of us have been." He grimaced as he swiped his hand across his chin. "Fuck."

"Is now really the moment for this conversation?" Eoghan grumbled.

"Not particularly." Trust Savvie to derail things when she wasn't even in the room.

Still, I sent her a text:

Me: *If you need me, let me know. I can be home in twenty.*

It didn't come as a surprise that she didn't answer, but I knew from Conor's end of the call that she was at the apartment, i.e., safe, so I didn't worry too much.

"I like Savannah's idea to be honest," Conor mused. "Infiltrating the Sparrows, getting those inside men close to key members, draining the swamp from the inside out—sounds like a great plan."

Declan nodded. "Otherwise, how the hell else do we take down an organization of this size?"

"It's one thing to say that leading it is how you steer it toward an iceberg, but this ain't the Titanic, Aidan," Brennan argued.

I scowled at him. "Did I say it was?"

"No. But you ain't the type to be a savior."

"Never said I was."

Bren just arched a brow at me, and I could sense his disbelief from all the way across the room.

"You told me we were going to war for Da," Eoghan rumbled.

"And we are. But wars don't always have to be fought how he tackled them," I sniped, rubbing a hand over the back of my neck, digging my thumb into the nape where a tension headache was brewing. "I meant it when I said I wasn't about to have Da's killer be a martyr for the cause."

Eoghan pulled a face. "I don't see no war."

"Didn't think you'd want one," Declan pointed out. "Thought you'd dealt with enough of that bullshit."

His tone was uneasy as Eoghan said, "I have but, I don't know, the ECD are... dangerous."

"Why do you think I want to lead them?"

"Clearly you're a headcase," Finn mocked.

I rolled my eyes at him. "To use the Titanic analogy, if I captain the ship, I can decide when it sails and where it goes."

"You have no intention of unifying Ireland," Eoghan retorted.

"No, but I have every intention of bleeding Eamonn Keegan dry. I have every intention of using the ECD for our gain."

"Do you intend on eradicating the ECD at some point?"

"Eventually," I told my youngest brother. "Give me time."

"When's the first meeting?"

"Keegan said he'd introduce me to the ECD before Thanksgiving."

"Why so late?"

"Because the ECD don't get together every fucking week. The Five Points haven't gotten together this much in fucking decades. It's not unusual for a bunch of criminals to not meet up weekly for a sleepover," I snarled at him.

Eoghan raised his hands. "Calm down, Aidan. We're just pointing shit out to you. What use would we be if we only kissed your ass?"

"Savannah does that enough for you," Finn joked.

My lips twitched the barest fraction of an inch. "She might still fangirl over me, but she holds her own."

"She stunned the fuck out of me when she kicked over Anthony's crate," Declan offered, scratching his jaw. "Didn't think she had that in her."

"She's stronger than she looks."

Finn rubbed his head where she'd clocked him that night at the docks. "Tell me about it."

"So, the next couple weeks," Conor remarked, getting us back on track, "we look into law enforcement who fit our bill, correct?"

"Correct. I know someone at Interpol."

"Me too," Conor agreed.

Finn drummed his fingers against the table. "I know someone at the IRS who'd be perfect for this."

"The IRS as in the Internal Revenue Service?" Declan's eyes bugged.

Finn nodded. "She's got a thing with numbers. Only fitting. She's unusual; I think she'd fit in well."

"We'll meet next week with suggestions, and we'll pin down if we can get them to infiltrate."

"Ain't the last couple weeks proven that we can't trust outsiders?" Eoghan muttered.

I rocked back in my chair. "I know we can't." *Talk about stating the fucking obvious.*

"Then aren't we putting all our eggs in one basket?"

"Nope." I smirked at Eoghan. "We ain't."

Con's words came slow as he stared at me, his eyes narrowing as he said, "We're reverse-flipping the Sparrows?"

I shot Con a grin. "That we are."

"Reverse-flipping? What are you talking about?" Brennan demanded.

"They got to our guys by getting them to take the fall for crimes they didn't commit. They framed them for the job and bribed them into compliance through jail sentences. We do the same. Just with law enforcement."

"And how the hell do we do that? Do we really want dirty cops on our side in this?" Declan grated out with a scowl.

"We use drugs. I reckon I can get Valentini to help us out with that. Red is popular for a reason. It's exclusive too. Big price tag."

"You want us to get them hooked?" Eoghan asked with a frown.

"For fuck's sake, do you have no imagination? We plant it on them, Eoghan. We make it look like they're users. We reverse engineer this so they look like they're addicts."

"So, get the men more aggressive and reacting badly at shit to work?" Brennan queried.

"Yeah. Doesn't have to be drugs; they just come with the worse prison sentences. It can be gambling, women, whatever. Debts via a loan shark mean broken bones if they don't repay them. We spread the net wide, see what we can bring back in the trawl."

"Even when we torture Five Pointers, we can't trust them to speak the fucking truth. Look at Hal," Eoghan growled. "You mean to tell me you want us to trust in shady law enforcement agents, the ECD, and the Sparrows as well? That's only going to fuck us over in the long run."

"The end will justify the means," I told him, keeping calm because I knew his trust issues went deeper than mine.

PTSD did that to a man.

"This is a leap of faith," Declan mused. "But if we don't do something, we won't get anywhere."

"The risk/reward ratio is high," Conor agreed.

"We're talking about destroying people's lives."

"You really got a problem with that, *Whistler?*" I retorted, watching as Eoghan's cheeks flushed at my use of his handle. "Destroying their lives means more leverage over them. That won't buy trust, but it exerts pressure. That should let you sleep easier at night." Grateful that that shut him up, I continued, "In the meantime, look through the notes Savannah and Conor have made for us about how they induct new members."

"Do you think they're still working the same pattern when everything has changed?" Declan asked.

"I think where there's a vacuum, something will always try to fall into that empty space. It's how nature works."

"Plus, the NWS is a massive business. There's a lot of money depending on them staying afloat."

I nodded at Conor. "Once we get into the NWS, that's when we figure out how to take down the others."

"We need a backup plan," Brennan muttered. "It ain't enough to go into this with just the one strategy in motion."

"I have one. We use the ECD for that."

"How?" Finn asked.

"I want the ECD to be our sledgehammers where the Sparrows are concerned. Keegan has a grudge against them. I want to know what that grudge is.

"Whatever it might be, we use them as the force, not the Five Points, so that we look clean when we take over from the *Famiglia* as their front."

"How can you use a sledgehammer against a secret society?" Declan asked. "It's not like they gather together often."

"We have to dig into the NWS one by one. Prison ain't enough. Death is. We get them running scared, and that's how we swoop in. I offer the Sparrows safety. I offer them the Points as a front, all the while, the ECD are taking them out. That's how *we* infiltrate."

"That shouldn't be a backup plan," Conor argued. "That should be something we're working on at the same time."

"Fine. I just need to get a handle on the ECD."

"When are you meeting with them again?" Finn inquired. "Or hasn't he given you any specifics other than 'before Thanksgiving?'"

"Whenever it is, I'll be there," Brennan intoned, shooting me a warning glance before I could answer. "Don't even try to stop me."

"I wasn't going to," I bit out. "Keegan said they're meeting a couple days before Thanksgiving. A church hall over on 9th Avenue."

"The fuckers were meeting on our turf?"

I understood Dec's irritation. "They got big balls; that's all I can say."

"Half of their numbers are Five Points." Eoghan's declaration had all of us scowling as we thought about the many goddamn phoenix tattoos we'd come across the day of the hanging. "Meeting in Hell's Kitchen would make sense because it wouldn't raise any brows."

Declan leaned forward. "You decided what we're going to do with the Pointers who betrayed us?"

"We use them harder than the others. They want to play on both teams, then they get double the workload." *Double the risk too.*

My brothers nodded their agreement at me, and that was when I decided to come clean about some other shit I'd been plotting.

Knowing it was a long shot, and knowing that I had to sell it, I blew out a breath. "You guys are going to have to help me figure this out, but I want Shay in the White House."

Declan snorted. "The kid can't even put his socks away, Aidan, and you want him in the Oval Office? He'll change his fucking mind about the president being his dream job. That's what kids do."

"Well, we need to make sure that doesn't happen, and between now and then, we need to figure out how to make ourselves look as respectable as possible."

"Why do you want him to be president?" Declan demanded, sitting up straighter when he realized I wasn't pissing around.

"Isn't that obvious?" Brennan retorted, to which Declan flipped him the bird.

"Because I don't want him in the Five Points. He ain't made for this life, and I don't want him to think he has to wade into this bullshit—"

Declan slumped back in his seat. "Oh. "

"Yeah. Oh. I'm protecting him. But also, it'll come in useful to have his influence where we need it."

"He's too proper for that," Brennan argued. "You won't get him to do anything he doesn't agree with."

"Good. But where family is concerned, he'll learn that some rules are meant to be broken." I arched a brow. "So, I want to work toward a path of respectability, you hear me?"

Silence fell at my declaration, but Finn was the first to say, "Aoife's bakery might be one way of achieving that."

"Why?"

"We associate good things with bakeries," he rumbled. "Warm memories. It's a nice front. It's Aoife's baby right now, but I know she has plans for the business. She's more goal-oriented than you think.

"When Shay's old enough, you get him on the board as well as a bunch of us, and we finance a nationwide expansion. All of a sudden, the O'Donnellys aren't associated with Acuig but with blondies and brownies."

I grinned at him. "I like it."

"Thought you might. I'll have to plan it out; I'll probably need your help with that, Con."

"Whatever," he said dismissively. "But if you think Aoife won't mind, you're whacked."

"Why would she care so long as the quality is there? I think she'd like it. Don't think she ever thought she'd be doing so well on her own anyway; I figure getting a couple bakeries statewide will be a dream come true, never mind the nation.

"With our financial backing, the sky's the fucking limit. Everyone in the country could be creaming themselves over her brownies—"

"Doesn't she get Jen to do her books?" Conor interrupted.

"So?"

Kid snorted. "If she isn't going to relinquish control on the books, what the hell makes you think she'll let her *young* teenage nephew and brothers-in-law take control?"

"I'll work on it."

"Please, do," Kid hooted. "Just don't come around to my place when she kicks your audacious ass out."

Brennan shook his head. "I think it's a good idea. But, Aoife aside, it's if you can get Shay on board. You forget, I'm the one who hangs out with him the most apart from Declan. He's not as malleable as you think."

"I don't think he's malleable," I argued, rocking back in my seat. "I think he's loyal, and it's his loyalty that will be tested when he wins because he *will* win.

"Da wanted a president in his lineage. That's something I'm going to give him."

Conor frowned at me. "Why that? In particular, I mean."

Wriggling my shoulders, I admitted, "I don't know. Just because he ain't around doesn't stop this stupid, pathetic need I have to impress him."

Brennan whistled between his teeth. "Can't lie, I feel that."

Eoghan tipped his head forward. "He fucked us up real good."

"Agreed. I owe that man dick, but it never stopped me from trying to earn his approval," Declan admitted.

Conor's gaze was firm as he looked at me. "We'll get you what you need, Aidan."

My lips quirked up at the corner. "We can but try, Kid." I shot Brennan a look. "We need to address the abilities of the men."

"You mean that they're fucking useless?" Brennan questioned drolly.

"We need someone to train them or something. Get their skills up there with the best. Savannah mentioned that her father's guards are trained by ex-Mossad agents. Maybe we could get them in to cut ours into shape."

Brennan frowned. "More outsiders."

"You want to add that to your to-do list?" I grated out.

"No," he admitted with a grumble.

"Fuckers like Jonesy ain't got no place on the street," Declan said with a nod. "He couldn't run around the room without having a heart attack."

"You have a point. So we need to shift the older guys into different positions—"

"Or retire them out," Finn commented.

"Da didn't like doing that," Declan pointed out.

"Aidan's doing nothing like Da did," Finn countered with a choked laugh. "He's already got the men shitting themselves. Maybe they'll be grateful to be made redundant."

My lips twitched. "I don't want to weed people out just because they're old. Old is experience and wisdom. They just need to not be working the streets anymore."

"They're not desk jockeys," Declan retorted.

"Then they have a choice. Redundancy or helping us where it counts." I hummed under my breath. "Speaking of choices, what's going on with the families of the traitors?"

Brennan stretched his hands out in front of him, cracking his knuckles as he said, "Priestley and Callum's kid have moved in with Mark's wife. Neither of them are going to say anything, not with the money they're on."

"They been inducted into the Old Wives' Club?" Finn asked.

"Nope. They won't let them in. Not yet, at any rate. Their men betrayed the Points. You know how they roll. They think they should have keyed us in to what their men were doing."

Declan frowned. "That's not fair. It's not like we tell our wives everything."

Well, he was wrong about that, wasn't he?

Not that I bothered arguing with him.

"Isolating them won't achieve anything other than allowing more bitterness to fester." I turned to Finn. "You're charming—"

Conor cackled. "Since when?"

"Fuck off," Finn groused.

Brennan grinned. "Anyone's the charmer, it's you, Aidan."

"I'm not charming."

"I think charismatic is the word they used in that 'bachelor of the year' article they printed on you last year," Eoghan said with a chuckle.

"Fuck." I rubbed the bridge of my nose. "Brennan, I ain't got the patience, so you'll have to do it."

"Me?! Since when was I fucking charming?"

"You'll just have to learn. Or, I don't know, get Camille to do it. Hell, get the wives in on it for all I care. We isolate those women, we isolate their families, and it'll make resentment fester. That's not what we're about."

Brennan folded his arms against his chest. "I ain't getting Camille involved."

"I don't give a fuck. Just sort it out."

"I was already watching over Priestley and Callum's kid," he complained. "I don't need this shit."

"Well, now you're looking after a bunch of traitors' families too."

"It looks good on you, Bren," Conor offered. "You're always the one who bats for the underdog. It's why Ma's still got you hooked up to her apron strings."

Temper flashed in Brennan's eyes. "You want to say that when we're in the ring tomorrow? I'll show you what I fucking think of that."

Kid's lips curved. "Don't worry. I'll show Shay how to take a fucker like you down."

Before this could get into much more of a pissing contest than it already was, I retorted, "Duke it out however you want, just do as I ask with the families. They've all got sons and daughters in the ranks. We fuck this up, we're as big a dipshit as Da was."

Finn scrubbed a hand over his jaw. "I was looking up ALS."

I frowned at him. "Why?"

"I wanted to know what was going on. Recent studies are saying that ALS is behind a lot of cognitive malfunctioning."

Declan reached for his glass of water. "Meaning Da's judgment was impaired?"

"It was impaired without the ALS," Bren muttered.

"True that," I said on a sigh, but guilt and hurt and bitterness and a whole host of emotions choked me.

He'd gone through that alone.

He hadn't come to us with it.

Hadn't trusted us.

That need to prove myself hit me again.

For us all to prove our worth.

We were more than the sons of our father.

New York City needed to learn that.

And though that father had fucked us up, his legacy was one that I wanted to outlive us.

48

SAVANNAH

"NO, I DON'T WANT TO."

My brow puckered as I stared at the other woman who was clinging to Bupkis and who, surprisingly enough, wasn't trying to scratch her to get free. "Cassie, I understand that you don't want to, but surely you see that you *need* to? He won't stay in jail if you don't press charges."

"Especially as he's claiming he restrained you as part of a consensual sex act," Rachel Laker murmured, her expression calm where I felt anything but. "Harvey will be out the day after tomorrow, Cassie, if you don't make a stand."

The meeting went from bad to worse as Cassie pretty much turned into a mute from there on out.

My temper kept trying to surge and flare, but Cassie's despondency was what broke my heart. I remembered her passion from before, and she was so *un*passionate now. The bastard had taken so much from her, and she was still allowing him to steal more of her spirit away.

Twenty minutes later, as I walked Rachel out of the apartment after a thoroughly pointless meeting, I muttered, "I'm so sorry for wasting your time, Rachel. Thank you for coming to see us here and for fitting us in."

It had been a nightmare on my schedule, but I'd snapped up her offer to come visit us at my apartment.

She shook her head. "You don't have to thank me or apologize. When Giulia told me the state of her when she and Nyx brought her here, I had to act."

"I run charity foundations, Savannah, for this explicit purpose. I know you talked about them with Lily at the BBQ."

"We did. We need to confer; I'd like to help spread the word. My star's never been higher, so now's the time."

Her smile was loaded with gratitude. "I'd appreciate that." The smile faded as she pulled her bottom lip between her teeth. "Cassie knows he'll come after her, but she's trying to minimize his anger."

"Let him try to get into this building," I seethed.

"You can't protect her forever," Rachel pointed out. "You're already going above and beyond for a friend."

"Hardly," I dismissed. "She's only staying with us. It's not like I'm giving her a kidney."

Rachel snorted. "Is that how you compare everything? To organ donation?"

My eyes twinkled. "Only with friends."

The other woman laughed. "Good to know."

"What's our next move?"

"I'm not sure," she admitted grimly, her laughter fading. "I can put out a restraining order on him, but even then, there's no just cause if she won't press charges. Maybe work on her?"

"I'll try. Cassie's pretty damn stubborn." I thought about her career, a career I was supposed to be in the dark about. "She can work from home, so I have a feeling she'll just stay in all the time."

"And you'd be okay with that?"

"Not really, but what else can I do? Mostly, I feel like I let her down," I admitted, rubbing my tired eyes.

"Forgive me, Savannah, but how did you let her down? You

haven't spoken for almost a decade, and it seemed as if the only reason you stopped talking was because life got in the way. It isn't like you had a falling out."

I shrugged. "I'm not that good with people who aren't family." There was a reason only Jen, a self-confessed bitch, put up with me. "I should have made more of an effort. Cassie really liked me. I know she did. And there aren't that many people who want to get to know me just for me and not because I'm Dad's daughter."

"Maybe if we'd stayed friends, she wouldn't have fallen for that bastard."

Rachel pursed her lips. "You don't know that, and that you can suggest it at all tells me you have an ego problem."

My nose crinkled. "Charming."

"I try." She quirked a brow at me in a silent prompt.

"Okay, okay. It's not my fault."

"Nice to know you're not an egomaniac."

"Aidan wouldn't agree."

"He's your husband. Of course he wouldn't."

Amused, I let loose a chuckle, but when I thought about the woman in my kitchen, it softened into a sad sigh. "I'll do what I can."

Rachel nodded. "Let me know what's going on."

"How long until he's out?"

"Less than fifty hours."

"I'm on the clock." I dragged open the front door and said, "Appreciate the home visit."

"My pleasure. Hopefully, we'll speak soon."

As I closed the door, I twisted around and checked my watch. Not long until I had to go out... Damn.

I retreated to the kitchen where Cassie was sitting, and I said, "You and my sister-in-law would get along great. I barely use this room, and you haven't left it since you arrived."

She shot me a tired look. "The kitchen is the heart of the home. Or, at least, it should be."

I shrugged. "Whatever floats your boat."

It was weird because she was the same woman I'd always known, and yet, I didn't really know her anymore. We'd both gotten married in the time that separated us, and her marriage had ended badly, and mine was only just starting...

But, once upon a time, she'd been interested in journalism. Maybe that was something that could fill the void between us.

"I have to go out. Would you like to come with me?"

Her lashes fluttered. "I-I shouldn't."

"Why not? He's in jail. This is the only time where you'll definitely be safe from his reach."

Her cheeks blanched.

"Sorry," I offered, feeling bad when I realized that might have been a low blow.

"Don't say that if you don't mean it," was her sharp retort. "I've had more sorries over the last five years than I've had punches to the gut. Sorry doesn't mean anything without action behind it."

"Won't hear me arguing. And I *am* sorry. I didn't mean to hurt your feelings. I was just being honest."

She pursed her lips. "I know you think I'm stupid."

"I think you shouldn't put words in my mouth. I know you're scared. In fact, I can pretty much feel it from across the room. You vibrate with it. But the only way to stay safe from him is to put his ass in jail long term. I, however, can't make you do dick.

"I have to go out. I have an appointment, and I don't want to leave you alone, so that's why I invited you to come with me."

"What kind of appointment could a friend tag along to?"

"The kind that's an interview." Excitement flushed through me. "You heard of Grainne Ledger?"

She snorted. "Who hasn't heard of Manhattan's Madam?"

I peeped a smile at her.

Her eyes bugged. "You got an interview with her?"

"I do. In an hour. Want to come with me?"

She gusted a breath into her cheeks. "I'm a food journalist now, not—"

"You're still a journalist. Don't you want to hear some juicy details?"

Though she bit her lip, I knew I had her.

Everyone and their dog was curious about Grainne Ledger. She didn't crop up in the news that often, but when she did, it was because she was associated with some fancy schmancy celeb or politician.

"I'll come with. I just need to get changed."

"You and me both. I'm wearing smart casual."

She nodded. "I have something I can wear. I didn't bring all my clothes with me, but I should have something suitable."

"If you want to borrow anything, just ask."

"Thanks."

I shot her a grin then darted off to my room to get changed.

I wore one of my power suits: stark black, tailored to my curves, creases so sharp you could cut through butter with them.

I paired the outfit with a set of red heels and a bright-red patent leather purse.

Slipping on my charm bracelet, I tied my hair back in a taut bun, oiled it down so it gleamed, and because I looked hot, I took a picture and sent it to Aidan.

Aidan: *Someone's ready for war.*

Me: *Don't you know it.*

Aidan: *Or bed. Do I mean bed?*

Me: *:P You're not here, so it's definitely war.*

Aidan: *You look hot. Don't change until I get home.*

I laughed.

Me: *Sure.*

Aidan: *You taking Cassie with you?*

I knew Aidan didn't like having Cassie in our space, and I got it. It wasn't ideal having an almost-stranger-cum-old-friend hanging around, but I wasn't going to let her be on her own. Not now that she was back in my life.

Me: *I am.*

Aidan: *I'll inform Grainne of the change in plan just so she knows and is prepared for a guest.*

Me: *Thank you. <3 I didn't think about that.*

Aidan: *It's okay. I'll deal with it. Have fun, little one.*

Me: *I will <3 Love you xo*

Aidan: *Love you too xo*

My smile refused to die as I headed into the living room where I found Cassie waiting for me. She wore a smart black and white chevron shirt dress with an oversized electric blue purse. Matching pumps peeped out from the long hem.

"Will I do?"

"You will. Come on, let's go."

I'd cut it tight, but Queens of Heart wasn't that far away.

"Probably be quicker to walk it if that's fine with you?" I asked her as we made it out of the elevator and into the lobby.

"Whatever."

Seeing them appear from out of nowhere, I cast Cade and Lucas a glance, watching from the corner of my eye as they followed us out of the building.

It was an unseasonably warm day, and we were quiet as we walked, so I kept an eye on my phone, making sure Aidan didn't send me a message appertaining to my meeting with Grainne, but we were halfway there when Cassie sucked in a deep breath.

I turned to glance at her and saw she'd stopped on the sidewalk. "You okay, Cass?"

Swallowing, she straightened her shoulders and took another deep breath. "It just hit me."

"What did?" I asked warily.

"I could have died yesterday."

Grimacing, I muttered, "Happy thoughts, then, huh?"

Not that I could blame her; I'd been in her shoes.

"That *is* a happy thought," she retorted. "I could be dead. Instead, I'm alive. I'm with an old friend who saved me by reaching out at a time when I thought I was totally isolated. I'm in the city and I don't have to be nervous."

"Nervous?"

"He timed me," she admitted, her gaze darting to the sidewalk. "H-He knew I *had* to come to the city for work because, when he lost his job, I covered our bills.

"But even after he started waiting tables at a restaurant nearby, he wanted an itinerary of where I was going, and if I didn't get back in time, there'd be repercussions."

My throat felt as if someone had it in their grip. "How did you live like that, Cassie?" I whispered, my hand reaching out to clasp hers.

"I don't know. I just did. It got to be normal." She shook her head. "*Normal.* Can you imagine?"

"No. I can't," I admitted gruffly.

"Me either." She sucked in a breath. "I don't want to see him again, Savannah."

"You don't have to," I told her immediately.

"He'll come for me."

The stark answer made me swallow. "Not if you put his ass in jail."

"I'd see him in court."

"Rachel could make it so that you go via video conference."

She reached up and rubbed her brow. "Do you think she'd be able to do that?"

"I do. I think she'll make it so that you never have to see the bastard again." And if that wasn't possible, well, I knew people...

Aidan would help; I was sure.

"I'm making us late." She started to walk, shuffling forward through the crowd, but I hauled her back.

"No. This is important."

"It isn't. You're already going above and beyond for me, Savannah. Getting me out of my apartment, letting me stay with you. I'd never be able to afford a lawyer like Rachel Laker."

"She's working *pro bono*," I argued.

"I would never have thought to get in contact with her." She squeezed my hand. "Thank you. For everything, Savannah."

"You don't have to thank me. I'm sorry we lost touch." Her tone set me on edge. "We can call Rachel now. Tell her to press charges."

"No." She shot me a hesitant smile. "We'll head to your meeting first. That's important."

"Not more important than this," I tried to argue.

She hustled me forward. "Anyway, I'm curious about Manhattan's Madam. I don't want to be late."

Though I frowned at her, my eagerness got the better of me.

As we rushed through the crowds toward Queens of Heart, Aidan called me: "All set."

"Thanks for checking, babe."

"My pleasure. I wanted to ask her something anyway."

"What?"

"Grainne said she'll show you around."

A squeal of surprise escaped me. "No!! You asked?"

"I'm not going with you, and this is the only way your curiosity will ever be quenched," he teased.

"You're the best husband in Hell's Kitchen."

"Not the world?"

"Maybe the city."

"At least the country, surely?"

"The state."

He laughed. "I'll definitely need to work up to the world, then, huh?"

"For sure." I twisted around to face Cassie, to tell her the weird news, only...

She wasn't there.

My heart sank.

I stood on tiptoe, trying to see over the crowd, but the only people I noticed were Cade and Lucas who were a couple steps behind me.

"Did you see where she went?" I called out, knowing they had to have. I might be their target, but they couldn't have failed to spot her drifting away.

In my ear, Aidan demanded, "Where who went?"

"Cassie. She's..."

Lucas pointed across the street where I saw the chevron pattern on her dress whipping against her body in the wind.

I sagged. "I think she's running away."

"From whom? It's not like you're holding her hostage," he drawled.

I bit my lip. "She doesn't want to press charges."

"Why the hell not?" he groused, and I heard papers shuffling in the background, his fingers clicking against a keyboard.

"She's scared."

"So why is she running away?"

"I think she thinks she has a head start." I hovered, unsure what to do. I had guards who could chase after her, who could bring her back. But... "I need to go," I told him slowly.

"Yeah, your appointment starts soon."

"I'm just a block away."

"You shouldn't even be walking. I got a notification from Lucas that you were."

"It'd take longer in the car," I grumbled. "And most of the threats are neutral right now. Plus, I'm in our territory."

He grunted. "I'd prefer you in a car."

"I wish we'd taken the car too now. She wouldn't have run off."

"What do you think she's going to do?"

"I don't know. Am I helping by letting her go? Or am I making things worse?"

"You're letting her exercise her free will. After a marriage like hers, that's priceless."

I cleared my throat. "Do you think Conor would keep an eye on her for me?"

"I think if you asked him nicely, he'd do anything you wanted him to."

That had me arching a brow. "We talking about the same brother?"

"You have to know he has a soft spot for you."

"Who? Me?" I squeaked. "Nuh-uh."

"Uh-huh," he retorted with a laugh.

"She didn't take any of her things with her—" *The oversized purse.* Did that have all her worldly goods tucked inside? My voice broke as I said, "I wanted to help her, Aidan."

"I know you did, baby. Some people don't want to be helped though."

I thought about her appreciation, and I shook my head. Not that he could see me.

"You need to get moving, little one."

He wasn't wrong.

"I'll speak to you later, Aidan."

"A car will be waiting to pick you up."

When we ended the call, I took another look in Cassie's direction, indecision still filling me.

"Less than ten minutes until the interview starts, Savannah," Lucas prompted.

His words stirred me into action, but as I rushed over to Queens of Heart, my excitement had definitely waned.

I just hoped she'd be able to stay safe... and if not...

Pausing on the sidewalk outside Queens of Heart, I called Conor.

"Conor, can you find Cassie's bank account?"

His tone was derisive as he muttered, "I found that during my initial sweep."

"You didn't know that that prick of a husband had her committed the last time she tried to escape his clutches, did you?"

"I did actually. Just didn't send you the files."

"Why not?"

"A woman's allowed some dignity."

The simple answer immediately soothed my irritation and I

switched gears to the matter at hand. "Can you transfer ten thousand dollars into her account?"

"Why?"

"She's taken off."

"Want me to find her?"

I hesitated because I wanted to say yes. It was on the tip of my tongue, but... "No. She wants to do this, and I have to respect her wishes. But I want to help her. The first thing she'll do is clear out her bank accounts, so this way, she'll have enough cash."

He grunted. "That makes no sense. She'd be safer with us."

"I know."

"Rachel sent me an email and told me that she doesn't want to press charges."

"She's too scared."

"Illogical, but I get it. Does she know we can have him killed in jail?"

Annoyed, I sniped, "No, Conor, I didn't tell my friend who's been a victim of domestic abuse that we can do things like that. I didn't feel like terrifying her even more."

Not yet, anyway.

When I'd mentioned that Aidan would hurt Harvey if I asked, she'd pleaded with me so I'd been building up to having that conversation again.

"Maybe if you had, she wouldn't have run."

"Not helping."

He sniffed. "I think it's dumb you let her run."

"I can't imprison her at the apartment," I rejoindered. "She could have run at any time. At least now she has a head start. Her husband is locked up for the next two days. She could leave the country by the time he's out."

"True."

"I hate to ask because I know how busy you are, only... I can't stop her from running, and I can't stop her from doing what she thinks is right for her, but—"

"I'll check in with her every now and then."

"Would you?" Gratitude flooded me. "Thank you, Con. Truly."

He hummed. "No problem. Transfer sent."

"I'll pay you back later."

"Don't worry about it. You stopping by Aoife's place?"

I thought about the extra workload I'd put on his shoulders and offered, "Want some apple pie?"

"Please."

"Consider it done."

It was the least I could do.

49

AIDAN

"COME IN, COME IN!" Savannah chirped, leaning up on tiptoe to graze the cheeks of the men looming in the doorway in welcome.

Mickey, Lucas, Cade, and the new guy who'd replaced Connolly stepped into my apartment with a wariness that wouldn't be conducive to a fun evening.

Connolly's replacement, Findley, was one of Tony's younger sons. His being transferred to my crew was a politically smart move, so long as he didn't try to stab me in the back for what I'd done to his father.

I couldn't exactly spread the word that the traitors' families weren't to be isolated if I didn't turn the other cheek myself, so, here I was. *Trying*.

Trying fucking sucked.

Standing by the table Savannah had set up with new decks of cards, brand new rolls of poker chips, and bowls of snacks, I dug my hands into my pockets as the guys traipsed in.

I felt like Ma had forced me to attend a birthday party of the kid I hated most in class—I guessed this situation was kind of like that.

This was Savannah's idea.

It wasn't a totally shitty one, but fuck if I'd have preferred to be doing anything but this.

"This wasn't my intention when I bought you this table," I groused at her as she moved toward me, curling her arm around my waist.

"We can play strip poker another time," she hissed in my ear with a smile. "In fact, we can play as a reward for tonight. You have to be nice. These guys are your crew. You want them to trust you, and you need to trust them. You can't do that if you don't try."

Though I rolled my eyes, I knew she had a point.

With a grunt, I asked, "Who wants beers?"

Mickey, Lucas, Cade, and Findley nodded.

Immediately.

Seemed like they wanted to be here as much as I did.

My lips curved into a grin as I pulled out some bottles from the fridge that was inbuilt into the new table.

As I handed them out, Savannah, as bright and bubbly as she only ever was when she was trying to get her own way, declared, "I don't like playing poker without high stakes."

"How high are your stakes?" Cade asked warily.

I knew him from back in the day. Cade had been in Eoghan's class at school.

If Da had treated Eoghan like the rest of us, I knew he'd have forced them to be friends, but Eoghan had always gotten away with shit his older brothers didn't.

When Lucas had told me he needed help with Savannah's detail, Cade had been an obvious choice.

Ironically, Lucas and Cade were the brothers of that aforementioned kid I'd hated most in my class. I'd drunk champagne when that piece-of-shit Allan had gotten his head blown off in an armed robbery gone wrong twenty years back.

"Fifty bucks," she declared, breaking into my thoughts.

Allan had always played up my dyslexia, calling me out for being a dumb ass.

Almost the whole fucking class had joined in.

Was it any wonder I didn't play nice with my peers?

Lucas snorted. "Fifty bucks? Those are hardly high stakes, Savannah."

She grinned at him, and though a burr of jealousy flickered through me, I set Lucas on her the most. It was only natural she'd get friendly with her guards, and Lucas was so unlike his brother it was unreal.

Both of us had dyslexia, and both of us had been tormented by that fucker.

The rule of 'the enemy of my enemy is my friend' was pretty much why I'd picked him as captain of my crew.

"What do you want to go up to?" she grouched. "Five thousand?"

Findley whistled under his breath. "That's too high for me."

"You just got a promotion," Cade retorted.

"I got expenses, bud. I have a kid."

Findley's son was one of the reasons Savannah had suggested him as a new member of my crew.

I had to assume she knew as much of the shit she did about my men because she'd asked Conor. Even I didn't fucking know Findley had a kid until Savannah had come to me with the information.

I was coming to learn that having a wife involved in the business both saved and drained time.

"Can you spare fifty bucks?" Savannah asked, her concern clear.

Findley's cheeks burned. "Yeah, fifty's okay. I could go up to two-hundred."

"You sure? I know it's tough being a single parent."

"How do you know it is?" Cade asked her.

I made a mental note to give Findley a raise—if money was that tight for him, his kid didn't deserve to be brought up on the poverty line. Not when Findley's wife had died of cancer a year back as well.

Did he have insurance bills to pay that he hadn't told me about?

She huffed. "I just know. It's obvious. No help with the bills, duh."

"Okay, two hundred it is," I stated, trying to get things on track even as I made a mental note to get Conor to look into him. Financial weaknesses could be exploited by enemies, after all. Taking a seat, I asked, "Who wants to deal first?"

After Cade tossed a couple hundred bucks onto the center of the table, he raised a hand. While Savannah doled out poker chips, I threw him the new pack of cards and watched as he started shuffling them.

Savannah eyed his abilities with the deck, and I could see her interest flickering to life when he made two equal halves with the pack, squared the bottom half on top of the other, then interwove both of them before performing a bridge shuffle.

"A Faro shuffle," Savannah mused. "Interesting choice."

Cade smirked at her. "I used to date a dealer at a casino."

"And you wasted time getting her to teach you how to shuffle cards?" Findley mocked.

I chuckled which made each of them, aside from Savannah, freeze like I'd withdrawn a weapon.

"Come on, guys," my wife said lightly. "Aidan's here for poker, not as your boss."

I cocked a brow at her but didn't correct her.

Each of us knew I'd always be the boss, and each of us knew they'd always treat me like the boss—no matter what she said.

None of us had the heart to point that out though.

"Findley's right," Lucas said after he took a sip of beer. "You're talking about Lacey, aren't you?"

"Yup," his brother said.

"Lacey had tits bigger than a couple cantaloupes. You need some charm tips, Cade, if all you got her to do was teach you how to shuffle cards."

I wasn't sure how Savannah would react to the sudden downshift in conversation, but she just hooted out a laugh. "I'll help, Cade. I know how to charm a woman."

"You really don't." I accepted my cards once Cade had dealt

them. Peering at the Jack of Spades and Hearts in my hand, I flicked a glance at her. "All I had to do was be a mobster."

Cade blinked. "You liked that about him?"

Savannah wafted a hand after she peered at her cards. "It's an attractive quality in a man."

Findley's brows rose. "I'd have thought it was the opposite."

"I'm a lucky man," was all I said to that, and it had each of them laughing.

"Apparently," Lucas agreed.

Savvie huffed. "It's not that weird."

"It kind of is. Most women don't like knowing their men kill people for a living," I drawled.

"You don't kill everyone," she retorted.

"Just the ones who need it." That those words came from Findley had me arching a brow at him. His gaze was calm, resolved, as he stated, "You did me a favor."

There was no mistaking what he was talking about.

"Tony was a jackass," Mickey agreed after he made a bet. "Complete twenty-four-carat bastard."

"You knew him well?" I queried.

Mickey shrugged. "Me and Findley are tight."

"Didn't know that," I admitted.

"Plenty you don't know about us," Mickey countered. "Seems like that's going to change if we're having poker nights and shit."

Lips twitching, I tipped my beer bottle at him. Savvie beamed a smile at me, her pride shining through loud and clear that I was doing as she wanted—*playing nice.* I fully intended on tongue-fucking her for that smile later.

Christ, she was beautiful when she was like this.

"You got rid of the poison in the ranks," Findley muttered, "that's for sure. I owe you for dealing with my dad."

"That bad?"

We shared another glance.

"The worst."

My brow furrowed, but he retreated to his cards as he made a bet.

When Mickey called his cards out, I scraped a hand over my jaw.

I didn't think I'd be so lucky that every kid and spouse of the traitors would be grateful I took out the trash on their behalf, but Savannah had clearly picked wisely.

We shared a glance, and she mouthed, "I got your back. Always."

In all honesty, I'd already known that.

She'd just rammed that home—without really trying.

Just like she cleaned us out and took home every cent in the pot.

50

AIDAN

COUNTING STARS - ONEREPUBLIC

AS A GREETING, arriving to find a knife being held against your throat wasn't the most cordial way to start any meeting, but I didn't mind.

I expected a show of force, even if it was pure fiction, and I was prepared for it.

Keegan's eyes flashed a warning as he drew me into the church hall, where dozens of faces I recognized greeted me.

I grabbed his forearm, scraped the blade against my throat, uncaring if I bled, then I twisted his arm up and back and darted out of his hold.

Straightening and smoothing down my sports coat, I turned to Brennan. "What a welcome."

His knife was in his fist and he thrust it in Keegan's face. "Watch your-fucking-self."

Keegan only sneered at him before he drew us through the crowd of silent watchers. Just before heading for the door, I'd heard the noise in here, the chaos of the crowd, so the dead silence was telling.

They had no idea I'd be here.

Keegan had kept them in the dark about the upcoming change in leadership.

Much as I'd kept him in the dark about knowing which of his *cheiles* were also Five Pointers.

Jerking my chin up as I headed for the front of the hall, knowingly giving them my back, I followed Keegan to the stage where a table stood, taking note of the faces turned to look at me as I walked.

The only one I tipped my head to was the Director of the Secret Service.

As I climbed the few stairs to reach the hall's stage, I cast a glance at Brennan, taking note of his position at the back of the room where he was watching over the situation, and noticed that Keegan, in that short time, had already taken the only seat at the table.

Smug as fuck, evidently hoping that I was destroyed by the Five Pointers' betrayal, he declared, "Brothers, two faces are here today who are not *cheiles*, but that doesn't mean they won't be embraced as such. The time has come for me to step down, and Aidan O'Donnelly will be your new leader."

The men shot each other wary looks, but no one argued.

Not a single goddamn one of them.

Satisfaction filled me—their fear wasn't something I craved, but that they knew they'd fucked with me would instill compliance in them.

"We've lost several brothers these past few months, but with this new merger, with a head who reigns over both the Five Points and the *Éire le chéile go deo*, there's safety to be had and a brighter, more powerful future ahead of us."

As Keegan moved out of the chair and held out a hand for me to take a seat, I dipped my chin in thanks.

To me, quietly, he questioned, "Was it really necessary to kill Mark?"

I arched a brow at him. "He was complicit in the kidnapping plot. Jonesy answered to him."

He heaved a sigh. "What *eejits*."

"You had nothing to do with it, I suppose?" I drawled.

His lips twitched. "You'd be dead if I had."

"Reassuring," I retorted.

"I try my best."

Ignoring him, I faced an audience of brothers who knew what I was capable of, and a group of two dozen or so who didn't understand the lengths I'd go to to consolidate my position.

It was time to ram that lesson home.

"To the Five Pointers here today, you ought to know you're only alive by my mercy. I warned you last month what I'd do to traitors, and I consider each of you to be one of those." Sitting down, I allowed that to settle among them: the threat, the dread. I let it fester. Let it rot. Then, I continued, "Letting you live is an act of benevolence, and I will expect twice as much from you as I do a regular Five Pointer."

"I think that's fair," Keegan rumbled.

"I don't care if it's fair or not," I snarled, jerking to my feet and knocking my fists against the table. "However, we have work to do and I need all hands on deck."

Keegan clapped me on the back. "He's promised us Sparrow blood, my fellow *cheiles*."

"I have," I agreed. "But first, I want to know *why* you're anti-NWS, and I want to know what plans you have in motion."

"All in good time," Keegan intoned calmly. "Before any of that, there's the initiation. No brother can be a *cheile* without it."

I tipped up my chin. "As you wish."

He smirked. "Oh, I do wish it, O'Donnelly. I do."

51

SAVANNAH

THAT SAME EVENING

"WHY ARE we going to Florida and not Hawaii?" Aidan asked around a yawn as he dragged off his necktie and settled back in the bucket seat.

"Dad said he didn't want to put Mom through a longer flight."

"Makes sense." He grimaced. "I'd have preferred Hawaii."

"Why? Because you want to see me in a grass skirt?"

He snorted. "Always. But no, got three agents we're trying to turn in Florida."

"Three?" I asked, brow puckered.

"Unfortunately. Florida, California, New York, and Chicago—they're the states where we're targeting high-ranking Sparrows."

"You never told me that."

"Telling you now, aren't I? When it becomes pertinent, that's when I loop you in."

"Such a cop out," I said with a sniff. "You cut it close getting here."

Aidan had just headed from his first meeting with the ECD to the airport so we could take off in time for Thanksgiving.

"The joy of chartering your own jet," he countered, "is that you can leave whenever you fucking want."

I didn't bother arguing. "What happened at the meeting?"

"Keegan didn't tell them what was going on until I stepped into the room. They just thought it was a regular meeting."

My eyes flared wide in surprise. "What was their reaction to you becoming the leader?"

"They were bricking themselves. But Keegan had no idea I knew how many *cheiles* were Five Pointers. At least I had that over the smug bastard," he muttered, nodding his thanks at the flight attendant who poured him a couple fingers of whiskey.

I knew the meeting must have been rough for him to have ordered whiskey.

When he took a deep sip and sighed, I asked, "Were there any problems?"

"No more than anticipated."

He surprised me by placing his glass down and unbuttoning his shirt. I wasn't going to complain, but he looked too tired to get his next words out, never mind make us permanent members of the Mile High Club.

Frowning, I asked, "Were there many members who weren't Five Pointers?"

"Couple dozen. There were around eighty men there." He dipped one arm out of his shirt and dragged the silk away from his chest. "You got your wish."

I gasped as I saw the initial layout of a tattoo that would eventually be beautiful. Right above his heart, it looked like a tear in his chest, as if a knife had sliced him open, and beneath it, there was a harp in the center, around which the words *Éire le chéile go deo* encircled it.

"This is the leader's ink."

"It's beautiful." Even half-complete, it oozed talent. "Who did it?"

"A *cheile.*"

It made sense that they'd have a tattoo artist in the ranks. "When will you have it completed?"

"When I get back." He showed me the one on his shoulder. "Brennan got one of these too."

I recognized the phoenix with its wings spread wide, a white flag with a shamrock in the center clutched between its talons.

"Do you think Keegan backed down too easily?" I asked, my tone cautious.

Ever since he'd told me he'd gotten Keegan under his thumb, I'd been concerned about that, just hadn't wanted to add to his workload.

"I know why he capitulated," he said with a growl. "Fucker's given me the headache of overseeing the brotherhood because he's running his own end game."

"Which is?" I asked carefully.

"Fucker had a daughter in the Sparrows' system somewhere. Been trying to get her out ever since he found out about her."

"Eamonn has a child? One who's been trafficked?"

Aidan nodded.

"That's insane."

"Tell me about it. He doesn't know if she's dead or alive. Doesn't even know if she got out or is still in their system. Just knows that he wants to take the fuckers down who sold her like a piece of meat."

I whistled under my breath. "That's some motivation."

"I should have fucking known there was blood involved. It all boils down to family, Savannah. It always goddamn does." When I didn't disagree, he reached up and rubbed at his eyes. "Past couple weeks have been fucking hard, Savvie."

I nuzzled into him. "I know, baby." I pressed a kiss to his temple. "Do you want to chill out and get some sleep so when we land you have some energy?"

"Sure." He pressed his lips to mine. "Sorry I haven't been around as much."

"You've been around plenty," I argued, even though, in truth, I *had* missed him.

I didn't just love Aidan; I liked him. Slowly but surely, he was becoming a best friend as well as my husband.

I never really thought that was how marriage worked; although, looking back, maybe that made me a moron for not having figured that the fuck out.

Especially with an example like I had with my parents.

I'd been feeling on edge since Cassie had left as well, and though I'd been focused on perfecting my editorial piece on Grainne Ledger, I kept feeling as if I were waiting for the other shoe to drop.

Aidan's presence would have helped with that, but I knew what he was doing, and I knew it was important—shoring up our defenses, making us impenetrable.

He angled his seat back. "You get some sleep too. Camden will probably piss you off so you need to conserve your energy."

"He will because I need to ask him about those tickets for Katina."

"Think he'll give you shit?"

"I know he will."

"I can buy the tickets," he offered.

"Nah. The bastard can do me a favor this once. Plus, I need to get him to go on Paris and Aspen's show.

"I said I'd do it and they want to schedule something this December. He's saying he can't because he never thought I'd agree, so they want me to convince him, i.e, shame him, into doing it," I grumbled, though my lips twitched before I turned my face toward the window to watch us take off.

His fingers stroked my chin as he turned me back to face him. "What was that smile about?"

"Nothing," I said innocently.

He narrowed his eyes at me. "Savannah."

"Ugh, do you know what that tone does to me?"

"Don't distract me."

"You're the one being distracting. You tell men to kill with that tone of voice."

He blinked. "I don't!"

"You do." I sighed. "It's so hot."

"Jesus, little one."

Now that he was well and truly distracted from that smirk that spoke of the petty joy I found in going head-to-head with my brother, I reached over and bopped a kiss to his cheek and nuzzled my head against his shoulder.

"Let's sleep. It's not a long flight, and I know Mom will have dinner ready for us when we get there."

His hand stroked over my hair as he rasped, "How don't I scare you?"

"Because I know you'll never hurt me. In fact, I know you'll hurt yourself before you hurt me. I'm, like, the most dangerous woman in New York because of you."

He snickered. "You're probably right. Did you get the interview sent off?"

"I did."

There'd been a bidding war over my interview with Grainne, and I'd cleaned out.

I fully expected to be on TV again this Christmas, but not discussing the holidays or the Sparrows, just my meeting with the most notorious madam in New York's history.

People were ready for a 'tell all' accounting on who her clients were; they didn't realize that A, she was using a pseudonym so she didn't end up getting Caponed like Heidi Fleiss, and B, it was more of a tell all on the realities of being a hooker in Manhattan.

"'Topic aside, I had fun writing that," I told him. "It sharpened my skills because I had to write it without getting her into trouble." Plus, I'd gotten to look around Queens of Heart. That had been an eye-opening tour.

"Rex's Old Lady is her lawyer, isn't she?"

"Yup. I had everything triple checked with Rachel."

"Grainne won't be in trouble with the law?"

"Nah. I call her 'The Madam' and no names are mentioned. It's all very cleverly written, if I do say so myself."

"Bupkis settle in okay with Bren and Camille?"

"Yup. She scratched him twice and adores Camille."

He chuckled. "Sounds about right."

I nuzzled into him for the last time, directing, "Sleep. We'll feel better."

He kissed my temple and relaxed into the seat. Surprisingly, I did too, and both of us were woken up by the attendant hours later, just in time for landing.

I yawned throughout the process, but it felt good to get out of the cold New York winter and to head into the warmer climes of the Florida Keys.

A limo waited for us on the tarmac of the private airport, and I stepped down the stairs, knowing my stuff would be dealt with by the flight attendants and our guards.

Cade climbed into the front seat of our limo, and Mickey got into the car behind us.

As I settled in the backseat, Aidan slipped in beside me, and I murmured, "Feel better after your nap?"

He still looked exhausted.

"Not really," he admitted with a dopey grin. A yawn escaped him as we settled in for the ride to my parents' house in the Keys.

The silence was comfortable, so I relaxed and spent most of the journey just texting both sides of the family to tell them that we'd arrived safely.

By the time we were pulling up to the house, Mom and Dad were sitting on the front veranda, waiting for us.

I didn't wait for Cade to open the door for me, just clambered out and rushed over to see them both.

As I slipped my arms around Mom, Dad hugged me from the back, and I squealed with delight to be here.

She pulled back to study me, and her fingers moved over to the patches on my cheeks where the skin was pink and new from the burns.

"Tender?" she asked when I cringed.

"Just a touch." I arched my throat so she could see the one there. It was redder. That one pissed Aidan off whenever he saw it.

"I guess I can't tell you off for not telling us about the crash after..." She grimaced.

"Nope, you can't."

"Still, we shouldn't have had to find out via your sisters."

"I didn't think they'd tell you immediately. I told you on the same day." Before Daddy could get involved, I studied her color and her features for fatigue, taking in the fact her short curls were on full display—no wig. "You look great, Mom."

She shoved my shoulder. "Oh, don't you start. Your father's been hovering like crazy. He's driving me mad."

"That's my job," he retorted before he turned around and reached over to shake Aidan's hand. "Good to see you, Aidan. You look exhausted."

His smile was sheepish. "It's been crazy since Da's death."

Dad clapped him on the shoulder. "Getting everything under control while you're grieving must be hell."

"It is." His smile turned tight. "It's good to be here."

"How long can you stay?" Mom asked.

"We can stay until Monday," I told her. Aidan arched a brow at me, but I just grinned. "I told Aidan Saturday, but we both could do with a break. I squared it with Finn and Conor," I informed him.

He rolled his eyes. "Of course they kept it from me."

"They'd be fools to get on my bad side."

"Speaking of..." Mom started worriedly. "Aspen brought a guest with her."

"Who's the guest?"

"A boyfriend. His name's Misha."

"Misha," I repeated dumbly.

It wasn't like that was a common name...

Paris hadn't said if Aspen and the guy I'd seen at Aoife's bakery were still dating, but I hadn't heard from her outside of the arrangements for the show.

"Misha?" Aidan asked, clearly sensing that I knew something he didn't.

I cleared my throat. "He's friends with Maxim."

His eyes flared wide. "Are you kidding me?"

"No, I'm not."

"You know him?" Dad asked carefully.

"I do," Aidan growled, storming forward without waiting for an invitation into the house.

My husband was oddly polite, and beyond respectful with my parents, so his behavior was out of character and definitely protective.

Touched that he was trying to defend Aspen, I rushed after him and found him calling out, "Misha, where the fuck are you?"

The brown head I'd seen back at Aoife's bakery poked out of a room.

He frowned at Aidan. "I mean no harm."

"What the hell does that mean?" I grumbled. What kind of a greeting was that?

"How dare you talk to my boyfriend that way?" Aspen was sniping, darting around Aidan like a pesky poodle intent on biting his ankles.

Aidan ignored her, so did I, and he stalked over, grabbed Misha by the collar, and shoved him into the wall.

As Aspen squeaked and squawked, my parents watched on in bewilderment as Aidan snarled, "You fucking hurt her, I'll bring the might of the Points down on your head. Do you hear me? She's goddamn family."

Trying not to shiver, I shot Mom and Dad a look. Both of them looked a combination of amused and concerned, whereas Paris, who was leaning over the railing, drawled, "I can see why you like him, Savvie. You always did get boners for power."

"Do you remember when she had a crush on Gorbachev?" Mom inquired with a soft chuckle.

Misha and Aidan didn't hear me whine, "Shut up, Mom!" They were, thank God, both in a world of their own.

"I mean her no harm," Misha was telling my husband on repeat while Aspen was dragging on Aidan's sleeve like she could get him off her boyfriend.

I could have told her that there was no moving Aidan unless he wanted to be moved.

When she shot me a pleading glance, it resonated with me.

More than I'd like.

I'd been second-guessing myself since Cassie had left, a lot on edge, and that resulted in me questioning my reactions and interactions with people.

Namely, what had I said or done to make Cassie run away? If anything happened to her, it was my fault. So, softly, *doubtfully*, I said, "Aidan, maybe he means well."

Aspen, for the first time in fucking years, shot me a grateful look.

"You can kill him if he fucks up," I offered next, earning myself a glower from my sister.

"What a promise," Camden taunted, stepping into the room with a bottle of milk in his hand. "Hey, sis. Hey, insane brother-in-law."

"Aidan isn't insane," I argued before, deciding to change the topic and, hoping to calm Aidan down, I pointed my finger at him. "I need you to do me a favor."

"Me? What do you want?"

"I need backstage passes for your next concert in New York."

Warily, he asked, "Is that all?"

"Well, that and something else. But we can talk about that later."

Though he narrowed his eyes at me in suspicion, he just drank some more milk. "Okay, I'm going to the recording studio, Dad. Want to come strum some tunes with me and escape..." He glanced over at Misha and Aidan and waggled the bottle. "...whatever this is?"

Dad nodded but asked Mom, "Everything okay here?"

Her gaze on Aidan who was still holding Misha against the wall, Mom shot a smile at him and patted his chest. "I think we'll be fine."

52

AIDAN

"IT REALLY IS YOU."

She snorted as I showed her the meme with Michael Scott from *The Office* pissing himself with laughter over a photo that said, 'Pump gently, I squirt.'

She shoved me in the side. "Hush."

"That makes me want to do the opposite."

"That's because you're difficult."

I grabbed the pillow and rearranged it under my head just as a knock sounded at the door.

"Who is it?" Savvie called out.

"It is I. Misha."

"Do you think he knows he sounds like a thousand-year-old vampire?"

I couldn't deny, the Russian asshole did sound like he came from another era.

Maxim had lost the accent. He'd picked up the vernacular, but Misha hadn't.

Since I'd first met him at Aoife's bakery, I'd done my due diligence. What I'd learned hadn't disturbed me, not until I realized he was dating my sister-in-law...

I got to my feet and moved over to the door.

After the initial greeting, I hadn't exactly lowered my walls around the Bratva brother and had been monitoring him ever since.

Once I opened the door, I leaned against it. "What do you want?"

"Here."

He passed me his cell phone and I lifted it to my ear.

"Who is this?"

"It's Maxim."

"What do you want?" I groused.

"I wanted to tell you that Misha is on his best behavior."

I turned my back on Misha and strolled deeper into my bedroom.

"How can you give me that assurance? Is he brain dead and you order him around?"

"No, but I have him on a short leash."

"How short?"

"Very short." He grunted. "He is not a bad man, Aidan."

"I don't care if he's good or bad. He's Bratva, and he's dating my sister-in-law who has to be ten or so years younger than him."

"Eight years," Misha called out.

"What's your game, Maxim?" I demanded, ignoring Aspen's boyfriend.

"Misha met Aspen at a backstage party. There's nothing more or less innocent than that."

"The very fact you're calling me tells me something shady is going on."

"He wished you to know he has good intentions."

"The marrying kind?"

"Yes."

My brows rose as I turned to look at the Bratva brother who was staring at me, his gaze stony, but his eye level just at the line of respectability—at my chin height.

"How long have they been dating?"

"Not long enough for Aspen to understand what he does for a living. Not long enough to understand that Misha is not like every other man. But I trust him with my life. You might not, and you don't have to, but you should know, from one ally to another, that I would discourage this match if I thought there was danger to our friendship."

Despite the situation, I had to admit that I appreciated his reassurance.

"If he hurts her, betrays her, does anything to impact her life, I will consider him an enemy of the Five Points." My gaze was fixed on him as I said that. At last, our eyes met. "Does he understand that?"

"I'm sure he does," Maxim drawled in my ear.

Misha nodded.

I grunted. "And do you understand the ramifications of that?"

"I'm certain you'll choose an appropriately medieval way of punishing him," he concurred.

"It will not affect our alliance," I said, making it more of a statement than a question.

"It will not. I informed him of the stakes of this relationship, and he agreed that he understood the damage he could cause to our business association."

"As long as that's understood... Happy Thanksgiving, Maxim."

"And to you."

We cut the call, and I handed Misha his cell back.

"I meant it, Misha. You hurt her; I'll hurt you."

He dipped his chin. "I have no desire to hurt her. I have every intention of making her happy."

I knew how the Bratva made their women happy.

For some men, that might have eased their concern. For me, I thought about the goddamn body parts Maxim had gifted Victoria.

"What have you done?" I demanded.

A soft smile graced his lips. "Nothing." He withdrew from the doorway.

As I closed the door behind him, jaw clenched, I called out, "Remember what I said, Misha."

He didn't look back, so I turned to Savvie who was staring at me bug-eyed.

"Was that Maxim Lyanov?"

"It was."

"Did he say that Misha was an okay guy?"

I scoffed, "He's Bratva, baby. He's not a good guy. Just like an Irish mobster ain't a good guy. I already told you that I didn't want you in this world; if I could save you from myself, I fucking would. Never mind Aspen.

"Jesus, she's a baby. More interested in fashion than good sense. At least you knew what you were diving into."

"You're the only person I don't want to be saved from."

Her genuine earnestness softened some of my tension and stopped me from pacing.

"I like that you care about my sisters," she told me as I clambered into bed beside her.

"They're family," I said dismissively.

"I know, but it's still sweet." She tucked herself beside me, and her fingers twirled in the meager hair on my pecs. "We have a safe room."

"I'm not fucking you in your parents' safe room, little one," I said around a yawn. "You'll just have to contain yourself until we get back."

"Meanie."

"Your meanie," I said with a grin.

"Is Misha serious?"

"Sounds like it."

"Aspen can't get serious about anything other than whether the Kardashians are going to make a new season."

"I wonder what she sees in him. Anyone with eyes can tell he isn't an Instagram boyfriend."

"You know what one of those is?"

"Of course."

"What are they?" she asked suspiciously.

"Oh, ye of little faith. It's a boyfriend who takes photos of his girlfriend who puts them on Instagram. They spend their whole day taking photos of them in different poses."

She hummed. "I'll give you a gold star."

"You do that," I teased, "and you can put it on my cock."

"Now who's making it about sex?" was her waspish retort. "Paris and Aspen are weird with men."

"Because of the kidnapping?"

She nodded, her face tucking into my throat as she curled around me like a spider monkey.

It never stopped surprising me that I loved how up in my space she was.

Something about climbing into bed with her every night, and her being all over me like this, rammed home just what we were to each other—man and wife.

At the end of the day, no matter how shitty it had been, this was how I started the next one, and that made it infinitely better than yesterday.

"You'd think they'd want someone safer," I mused as I played with a strand of her hair.

"I bet Paris ends up with a cop."

"Great. A pig in the family," I said with a snort. "I think I'd prefer a fucking Bratva brother."

Her laughter tinkled in my ear. "Be careful what you wish for."

Though I rolled my eyes, I knew she wasn't wrong.

Family—even when they weren't yours by blood—were still a goddamn pain in the ass.

"You still owe me, by the way. Don't think I've forgotten."

I frowned down at her. "What for?"

"The night you tied me to the bed and left me to go to Queens of Heart."

My lips twitched. "You're a brat, do you know that?"

"Hasn't that long been established?" she teased, batting her eyelashes as she looked at me.

"What do you want?"

She reached up and ran a finger across my bottom lip. "This mouth."

"You know it's yours." I tapped her on the ass. "You wanna use it to get off, baby girl?"

"Do you know how hot you were today?" She scrambled onto her knees. "You owe me an orgasm."

"If we're talking about debts..."

She slapped my pec then scrambled to straddle my waist. "One," she wheedled. "I'll be quiet."

"You're incapable of being quiet," I derided. But my tone darkened as I told her, "I don't share the sounds of your pleasure with anyone." And sure as fuck not with a Bratva brother in the house.

"You can gag me," she pleaded.

Unable to deny her, I narrowed my eyes on her. "One sound, just one fucking sound, Savannah, and we stop. Do you hear me?"

Swallowing, she nodded. "I hear you."

"Go and get one of my neckties."

Showing more obedience than usual, she practically leaped off the bed and hurried over to the closet.

Hearing rustling sounds, I reached down and pulled out my dick from my boxers. As I fisted my fingers around it, I jacked off. Her nostrils flared at the sight of me upon her return, and she stilled as she tied the gag around herself.

"So eager," I rumbled, watching her walk toward me, her gaze locked on my dick. "Eyes on me, little one. Not my cock. Just me. You said you wanted my mouth, not my dick."

Her brow furrowed, and I almost smiled.

I loved painting her into a corner. I just wished I could see her pout.

"Take off your sleep-shorts," I ordered. After she dragged them off, she reached up to grab the hem of her sleep-shirt, but I shook my head. "Keep it on." I moved further down the bed then drawled, "Come on then. Sit on my face, little one. Seeing as my mouth, and only my mouth, are what you want."

I saw the despair etched in her expression at my cockblocking her as she hovered there.

Denying her shouldn't have gotten me so fucking hard, but it did. Fuck, it did.

She wanted to renege.

Wanted to make a sound of complaint.

But she didn't dare.

She knew I'd stop this before it had a chance to begin.

"Come and use my mouth, baby girl," I directed, watching her pupils dilate.

My words had her finally jerking into action.

She started by straddling my waist, but I tutted and told her to sit with her back to me. Once she was in position, I quickly dragged her higher up so that her knees were on either side of my head.

"No hovering," I said gutturally. "You take your pleasure, Savannah. Do you hear me?"

Her nails dug into my chest as she obeyed.

The fucking scent of her got to me more than anything else.

As I jacked off, I sucked on her clit, humming around the nub as I flicked it with my tongue before sliding it down her pussy, through her folds and to her slit.

Thrusting into her made her grind against me and her fingernails dig into my stomach.

I didn't give her my fingers because she'd set the terms of this, but I tugged on her pussy lips with my teeth, pulling back to slurp my way up to her clit.

She was drenched, so fucking wet that my mouth and nose were soaked with her juices almost immediately, and I lapped it up. Lapped *her* up.

And she creamed even harder with every stroke and every flutter of my tongue.

Nipping her clit made her scratch her nails against my abs, and she worked herself higher, grinding into me as I used the flat of the muscle to rub around the nub.

When her hand reached for my cock, I grabbed her wrist, squeezed it in a punishing warning, and mumbled against her cunt, "No dick. You didn't ask for dick."

Her nails scratched down my leg in silent protest, but I just smiled against her sodden folds and went back to my work.

Stunned that she'd remained silent for this long, I decided to stop teasing her.

Instead, I sucked down on her clit, *suckling* it, giving her the pressure I knew she needed until she was bucking against my face, using it to get off.

I fucking loved how she owned her pleasure, how she wasn't ashamed to go after what she wanted.

When she grabbed my hips and squeezed down, I muttered against her sex, "Come for me, little one. Come now."

She tensed.

Turning rigid above me, she squeezed my face between her thighs.

The softest, most guttural of groans escaped her, and though I stopped like I'd said I would the moment she made a sound, she finally sagged against me, still using my face as a seat, and I jacked off faster than before. Harder. Rougher.

When I came, I knew my cum splattered back against my abs.

I didn't complain when she lapped it up like a kitten who'd gotten the cream.

Not having realized I needed that to get to sleep after the clusterfuck of a day, when she was done cleaning me up, I rearranged her on the bed because she was limper than overcooked spaghetti, and we huddled closer to each other while I stripped off the necktie and tossed it on the ground.

"Feel better, little one?" I rumbled, dragging my nose down her cheek.

I was still faintly wet from her juices, but she didn't care.

Yawning, she nuzzled into me, mumbling, "Uh-huh."

When she drifted off, so did I, and I finally managed to rest, proving her right when she said I needed a break.

At three AM, however, a scream sounded through the house, jarring me awake.

On red alert, I reached for my gun, but Savannah smushed her face into my throat and drew me back down to the mattress.

"It's Aspen," she said sleepily, as if this were a common occurrence.

Maybe it was.

"Shouldn't we check on her?"

"She has nightmares. Go to sleep," she whispered.

My hands tightened into fists at the scream that twisted into heart-wrenching sobs, and the promise I'd made Misha morphed into a vow—if he hurt her, I'd do more than *just* hurt him.

In my life, I'd ignored too many of my loved ones' nightmares.

Not anymore.

53

SAVANNAH

"*DIE HARD* IS A CHRISTMAS MOVIE."

Aidan nodded at Camden. "I agree."

"How is that a Christmas movie?" I groused.

"It takes place at Christmas."

"So do bank heists, but that doesn't mean that armed robbers are spreading festive cheer among men," I sniped as I cut into my turkey.

"While you have a point," Camden agreed, "you also don't."

"Like usual then," Paris mocked as she posed with a glass of wine and took a snapshot for Instagram.

Aspen ignored us all, utterly wrapped up in Misha who, clearly, had never eaten Thanksgiving food before.

The prospect of corn with gravy had him stumped.

It was strange seeing my sister actually be okay with disconnecting from her phone and existing in a world of her own with the guy.

Aidan's call with Maxim had given me some ease, but not a lot.

My sisters, though pains in my butt, were sensitive.

More sensitive than the world could imagine.

Probably more than I knew too.

"Put him down, dear," Mom chided Aspen who'd started kissing Misha. "Let him eat his turkey."

"Mom," Aspen mumbled.

"She has a point. I don't need to see your tonsils, Aspen," Dad chided as he grabbed his beer and took a deep sip.

I watched him peer around the table, spying his grin grow.

Dad, for all that he was a rockstar, for all that he was a rock legend, loved being with his family.

"Next year, we'll stay in New York," he declared.

Mom arched a brow. "You got confirmation?"

"I did. Frankie—" His agent. "—sent it through to me last night."

"Sent what through to you?"

"*noxxious* is playing at the Macy's Thanksgiving Day Parade next year."

Aidan chuckled. "Conor will die if that happens."

Dad laughed. "I hope not. I don't want his death on my conscience."

"I'm sure he'll resurrect in time for the first song," Aidan drawled. "He's still in awe of the fact we're related."

"You should have brought him with you for Thanksgiving," Mom chided.

"Us coming here was enough of a battle. Never mind breaking away Conor too."

Mom winced. "Lena wasn't happy about you coming to us for Thanksgiving?"

"Not really," he said lightly. "But she was being selfish."

"That's harsh." Dad took another sip of beer.

"No, it isn't. Savannah has family too. They matter to her, as much as my family does to me, and we have to compromise."

"That's so kind of you, Aidan," Mom said, her smile almost beaming from her. "I wasn't sure if we'd lost Savannah for the holidays, in all honesty."

"No. I wouldn't do that."

"Maybe, sometimes, we could go to our estate in New York?" I suggested. "Aidan could have the best of both worlds. We could drop in with his mom for breakfast and then have a meal in the evening together."

Dad surprised me by nodding. "It's funny you should say that, but I was looking at real estate close to your place."

"You were?" I asked, loading stuffing onto my fork. "Why?"

"To be nearer to you, silly," Mom teased.

"Really?" I knew my eyes were wide. "I'd love that. We're not spending that much time there right now though. We're mostly in the city for Aidan's work."

"Speaking of, did you finish that interview with Grainne Ledger?" Camden queried.

"I did. It was awesome, if I do say so myself."

Camden chuckled. "Your ego, Savannah, is bigger than mine."

"Yours is larger than Texas, so I don't think you can judge me for having an ego the size of Connecticut."

"It's a well-rounded piece."

"You read it, Aidan?" Dad asked, lifting his brows. "Savvie never lets us see pieces before they go live."

Aidan smiled. "I only read it this morning."

"So I couldn't tweak it. I was nervous. It's the first time in a long while that I'm writing about non-Sparrow stuff," I admitted after I took another bite of Mom's yams.

"Are you not going to write about the Sparrows anymore?" Dad asked as he loaded his plate with green bean casserole.

"Just for the moment." Aidan and I glanced at one another. "Until Star gets back."

Mom huffed. "*If* she gets back."

"Don't start, Mom." Aspen surprised me by stating, "You don't know what she's been through to get to where she is today. Just because you think she's a bitch for walking out and forging her own path doesn't mean she is. It means she did what she had to to survive."

I reached for my glass of water. "I didn't think you even liked her."

"I don't. But I don't have to. You like her, and you wouldn't like her if she was a bitch."

"Didn't know you valued my opinion so much," I admitted.

"Only where it matters," she said pointedly before she scooped up some food onto her fork and ate.

She was doing that thing people with eating disorders did so it looked as if they were eating.

Each forkful was minute, and she moved half her food around the plate.

Misha whispered something to her, something low enough that I couldn't hear, but Aspen took a larger mouthful.

Had he noticed?

We shared a look, and he simply blinked at me and turned his attention back to my sister.

Over the remainder of the meal, I took note of their interactions and had to admit that I could understand why Aspen was enamored.

She had his focus.

All of it.

It would have been intimidating for some, but she was a rockstar's daughter, and she was used to people wanting a piece of her—not for herself, not because she was Aspen and because she was a great person, but because she was Dagger Daniels's kid.

If it had started out as a crush because he wanted to get closer to Dad, I thought that had long since faded.

As we watched the game afterward, Aidan kissed my ear. "Should I start getting jealous?"

My lips twitched. "About what?"

"How hard you're studying Misha."

I grinned. "Nah. My pussy's all yours."

"Ewww." Paris cringed. "I did not just hear you say that."

"You shouldn't be listening to private conversations."

Camden chuckled. "What did she say?"

"I can't say it without gagging," Paris declared dramatically.

I reached over to the bowl on the coffee table and popped an M&M into my mouth, telling Camden, "I said, 'My pussy is Aidan's.'"

Camden crinkled his nose. "TMI, Vana."

"You know it." I winked at him. "I'm the Queen of TMI, haven't you learned that already?"

"You're *my* queen," Aidan rumbled in my ear as he nipped my earlobe.

I shuddered at the gesture and cuddled into him as the Dolphins scored a touchdown.

"Thank you for giving me this," I said softly.

He angled his head so I could see his scowl. "I'd give you the world, Savannah. Thanksgiving with your family is nothing."

I brushed my lips against his, well aware that this was only the first of many holidays we'd share as a married couple.

The future might be crazy, it might be dangerous, but we'd get through it.

Together.

54

MISHA

LATER THAT NIGHT

ASPEN'S SCREAMS stirred me from sleep like usual, so I curled her against my chest and started stroking her hair.

My *zaychonuk* had worse nightmares than I did, and after a childhood on the streets of Moskva, with only Maxim and Nikolai at my back, I knew what it was to suffer.

Knew how fear could fill the belly as much as food could.

She settled under my care, my fingers tracing the bony sections of her shoulders as I attempted to soothe her while I let my mind race.

This was complicated.

More complicated than I'd intended.

I hated complications.

Here I was, sharing a roof with a Five Pointer, his death threats still ringing in my ears from the night before. In fact, I wasn't just sharing a roof with him; I was directly below him in the mansion.

Always a light sleeper, his presence only exacerbated that trait.

Every single one of my instincts declared that I was in danger. Yet those same clamoring instincts were at peace with Aspen around.

I'd never been this torn before, couldn't afford to be now, but here I was—sleeping in the home of one of my idols, sharing a bed with his daughter, finding peace with her, wanting more, craving a future when I'd only ever been concerned about the present...

Da, I was in danger. It just wasn't the kind that came with a knife to the throat.

Although, Aidan O'Donnelly would probably disagree with that belief.

Gradually, I became aware of the thudding upstairs.

At first, I thought they were fucking. Then, I realized it was more like pacing.

Curious, I tucked Aspen on her side and climbed out of bed.

A light flickered on in the hall, and as I reached the door and pulled it open, I saw the guards Aidan had brought with him storming toward the staircase that led to the upper floor.

Concerned now, I followed them, which was when I heard Savannah shrieking, "You have to do something, Aidan! Cassie wouldn't send me a goddamn text message saying she feared for her fucking life if she didn't mean it. You need to kill him. You need to take him out."

"I have no ties down here, Savannah," I heard Aidan growl. "If we were in New York, you think I'd fucking hesitate?"

"So you're just going to let him get her?"

"Of course not," he snapped.

With the silence I was known for, I climbed the stairs and headed down the hall. As I peered into their room, I watched Savannah throw a cell at Aidan and demand, "Conor needs to find her."

"The second you got that message, he was on it. Conor will find her and we'll go to her. I just have to be careful. You know what shit we're pulling down here. There are bigger games at play in Florida—"

"We can't let her get hurt."

"And I won't allow that to happen, little one. I just need time."

"She doesn't have time."

When Savannah started sobbing, much as Aspen's tears always kicked me in the gut, I could no more hold my tongue than I could leave Aspen to cry herself silently to sleep:

"Bratva ties in Florida are strong. I have a man I could send in."

Aidan twisted around to glower at me. "This is none of your fucking business, Misha. It's sure as fuck none of the Bratva's business. I'm dealing with this."

Savannah turned to me. "You can really help my friend?"

I shrugged. "If you wish."

She turned a pleading look at her husband. "Aidan, please."

His nostrils flared as he pointed at me. "You fuck this up, I fuck you up."

That was when I knew whatever score they were pulling down in Florida was big.

If he was willing to rely on me, then I couldn't even imagine what the fuck was going on here.

"I have no intention of fucking up. Not when a friend of the woman who will one day be my sister-in-law needs help from my brothers and me.

"Please, send any information you have of her whereabouts to me. I'll have Aspen text you my number."

Not letting them reply, I retreated as silently as I'd entered.

Whoever this Cassie was, she was a Bratva problem now, and I had just the man for the job—*Nikolai.*

TEXT CHAT
SAVANNAH

THREE WEEKS LATER

SAVANNAH*: Star?*
>   ***Unread Message From 11 Weeks Ago***
>   **Savannah:** *Please answer.*
>   ***Unread Message From 7 Weeks Ago***
>   **Savannah:** *Stay safe. I love you.*

AIDAN

THREE WEEKS LATER

IN MY LINE OF WORK, I was the one who made people's skin crawl. But Dr. Donald Davis, for all that he knew how to handle a scalpel, had the bedside manner of Chucky. That he could freak me out was a feat in its fucking self.

"Your knee has healed like a champ. Now, that doesn't mean go run a marathon," he told me with a chuckle as I pulled my pants on and began to step off the exam table.

The fact that I could move around without my knee buckling was proof that the man knew what he was doing. Liking him wasn't a necessity.

"After the farce of the last knee replacement, and what happened beyond that, I didn't think I'd feel good ever again. I have you to thank for that."

He looked up at me with a smile, one that told me he knew his worth, before he returned to his notes.

When he'd finished, he set his computer onto the counter and asked, "How's your exquisite wife doing? Be sure to say hello from me."

Every possessive bone in my body cringed at his mention of

Savannah, but she was how I knew of this guy—Dagger was an ex-patient.

Though unease throttled me at his mention of her, I said, "She's good, and I will."

It was only because of Savannah that I was standing here today. That I was clean. That I was goddamn whole again. But Davis had played a massive part in that too. I barely had any pain anymore. Even after this last couple disastrous months, the once weak joint had held up.

"It's crazy how time flies," he was saying, shaking his head as he continued, "Never could get Dagger to listen to me about jumping off the stage."

"You should have spoken to Lorelei. You know she's the only one who can make Dagger Daniels listen," I drawled as I reached out to shake his hand. When he took it, a slight pissing contest went down between us, but upon his concession, I let my gratitude toward him overflow as I told him, "You need anything, you let me know."

In my world, you didn't say shit like that easily, and it was clear to see that he knew what I was offering—a favor. But he deserved one. I didn't have time to be on my ass, resting my knee, and he'd spared me from that.

Still, he stunned me by starting to cry. I expected many things out of people when I was offering them a favor, but not tears. Not unless I was torturing them, at any rate. "There is something I'm actually concerned about, well, terrified, to be frank."

Frowning, I asked, "How can I help?"

"My daughter." He sighed and looked up at the ceiling. "The reason I dye my hair is because of her. She's like her mother. I barely survived losing her. I don't think I can survive another loss. I just can't lose hope.

"We all deal with grief differently and Isabelle, that's my daughter, is delicate. Her mind's fragile, which is why I need her back, so at least I can make sure she takes her medication."

Until this moment in our professional relationship, Davis had been a man of few words. I'd appreciated that about him. This flowery turn of phrase set me on edge, but...

"You know where she is?" I queried calmly, slipping my hands into my pockets as I straightened to my full height, something that was only possible because of his skills.

If it weren't for him, I'd still be limping, would still be relying on drugs to manage my pain—I owed him.

When he closed his eyes, warily, I questioned, "Dr. Davis?"

They darted open. *Weird.* "Yes, sorry."

I frowned and placed a hand on his shoulder. "You know my reputation, doctor. Family *is* everything to the O'Donnellys. You don't need to apologize for worrying about your daughter."

He nodded. "I was going to retire but, to be honest, work has kept me sane."

"Well, I'm grateful you didn't. Where would I be without you?" I squeezed his shoulder. "Where is she?"

"She's gotten caught up with some motorcycle gang in Los Angeles."

I quirked a brow. "Which club?"

"The Disciples."

"They've been in the press recently," was all I said because I'd been keeping a watch over them.

I was pretty sure they weren't involved in the Sparrows, but only time would tell.

"I went to the police and FBI. I mean, how could I not? Especially with that one being on trial for triple murder."

"Ryder. He was acquitted," I said slowly. "Isabelle is with them?"

"She was. The sad fact is she's sick, mentally. She got that from my late wife. I'm convinced they've brainwashed her and are forcing her to... My worry is that she's being..."

When he started to cry again, I didn't know where to fucking look. Just to get out of there, I told him, "You don't need to say another word. It'll be my pleasure to untangle this situation for you."

"Thank you. You have no idea what this means."

I nodded. "Consider it done."

When we finished up, it was with relief that I got the hell out of there. But a favor owed was a favor owed, so I grabbed my cellphone.

"Cade?"

"Yes, boss."

His tone was always a combination of wary and eager—wary because he knew that I could send him out on a shitty job, eager because he still felt guilty about that mess back in Jersey.

Regular poker nights were making my crew adapt to me, but they were still cautious.

I couldn't blame them. Not with the rep I'd earned since Da's death.

Slice first, ask questions later.

That was goddamn MacMurray's fault. Brennan's too, come to think of it. He'd been the one bitching about having to get that fucker to jot down the answers to whatever questions Bren had given him.

Only in my world would that whole situation not be viewed as an incompetent mess. Instead, people were scared of me. Terrified I'd cut *their* tongues out first then worry about questions later.

They weren't wrong—the best defense was offense.

"Got a job for you," I told my man as I headed into the elevator to get out of the clinic.

I hated hospitals, even fancy as fuck ones like this. Of course, when I saw Savannah waiting for me in the lobby in the glass elevator, the place got a damn sight better.

"Sure," he answered easily. "Where do you need me?"

"On a plane to LAX before the day's out."

EPILOGUES

STAR

CRYSTALISED - THE XX

The Russians knew how to do fancy houses.

I'd been in a few in my time, but these were closer to a palace than a mansion.

The homes of *noxxious's* band members had been something special, and Lily's place was a rich man's wet dream, but this was a king's.

Maybe, at one time, it *had* been a palace. Maybe it had housed a prince and a bunch of baby princes and they'd ruled over Moscow while peering through the many trees in Petrovsky Park until the Bolsheviks had ruled them.

All I knew was that now, it housed an answer to a question I'd been asking myself since Bear, the ex-Prez of the Satan's Sinners' MC, had died.

I stared up at a ceiling that a Renaissance master had undoubtedly painted. "Fancy."

Maxim grunted. "Painted with money stolen from the people."

"Didn't picture you as a communist, Lyanov."

"I grew up on these streets without a ruble to my name," he said as he took my coat off my shoulders and handed it to a waiting attendant. "The government nourishes the rich and lets the poor suffer."

I couldn't argue when I knew that to be a fact.

"Why do we have to be here again?"

I arched a brow at him. "You're not supposed to ask questions."

He huffed and dragged me deeper down the hall. "Let's get this over with. Kuznetsov puts me on edge."

"He should. He's a dangerous man."

"I knew that without you telling me," he grumbled, and I couldn't blame him for his shitty attitude.

This palace wasn't simply an oligarch's home—it was the headquarters of a group I'd never even heard of until Bear had died.

The United Brotherhood.

Upon Bear's death when I'd been invited to his base, when I'd seen what he'd learned, when I'd read his intel on the Sparrows, one question had been driving me: *who was his source?*

I'd been certain he didn't know who fed him the intel.

I'd been even more certain that the information he'd left behind as an inheritance to his son should never have been for anyone's eyes but his own.

That was the thing about bikers—you couldn't trust them not to betray you.

They were loyal only to the club.

And thank fuck for that.

Every piece of information his source had handed him, Bear had kept and stored in his 'murder room.' A motel bedroom that was filled with papers and photos and string that ran across the room in a web that he'd pegged more information to.

Digging and digging and digging, using the worm Maverick had created, I'd managed to find my way in by going back to the beginning. Bear had sent photos loaded down with data to himself—huge files that had once helped me crack the nut that was the Sparrows.

There'd been nothing to trace in those files.

So clean.

Too clean.

Until Maverick's worm tore the code to shreds.

Until it had ripped my world apart as well and had sent me spiraling, changing endgame plans, pushing me onto a plane to Russia.

Which was when I realized Bear *had* known who his source was—that was why he'd been researching the United Brotherhood.

And that was why I was here tonight.

It was why I drifted into a ballroom on Maxim Lyanov's arm.

Every step had led me to this moment in time, to this *location.*

The United Brotherhood's HQ.

After a glance around the grandeur, Maxim didn't ask if I wanted to dance, just led me onto the floor. He was a surprisingly adept partner, generous and polite, respectful, good at dancing, clean manners at the table.

He knew when to step in and when to butt out.

As was the case now.

When the host of this party, Anton Kuznetsov, drifted over to me in the middle of a waltz and asked, "May I cut in?" Maxim didn't argue. He just nodded at Anton and smiled.

Anton was nearly eighty, but he had the face of a sixty-year-old thanks to plastic surgery.

His smile was tight whenever he graced me with it, but I didn't think that had anything to do with Botox.

This was not my first party where the man had attended.

Intentionally so.

This man was the head of the United Brotherhood.

This man, somehow, amid this palace, had been the one to send Bear the information that had been crucial in tearing down the Sparrows' walls.

"You dance just like your mother."

At first, I thought I hadn't heard him.

At first, I thought someone else had uttered those words and, in the whirl of dancing, I'd inadvertently eavesdropped into another conversation.

But when I stared at him, shock in my eyes, he graced me with that tight smile again.

"Would you care to step into my office, Ms. Sullivan?"

He'd earned the full throttle of my attention. No man ever wanted that. But Kuznetsov was a fool.

I'd only met one man who wasn't a fool, who never underestimated me.

Guilt hit me, sorrow too, but I shoved them aside.

I wanted answers. I needed them. I couldn't think about who I'd left behind, not when I'd been seeking understanding for decades now.

"How do you know my mother?" I rasped, not answering his earlier question.

"Do you want to step into my office?" he repeated, clearly not willing to be drawn.

My jaw clenched, but in my flawless Russian, I told him, "Will you answer my questions if I do?"

"Of course. I wouldn't invite you in there otherwise."

He gripped my elbow in his and led me off the dance floor.

As we meandered across the ballroom that was pure Renaissance elegance, something that Catherine the Great herself might have danced in, he murmured, "You are with Lyanov?"

"I'm with no one."

He clucked his tongue. "So like your mother."

I didn't reply because the desperation for answers was a toxic mass leaking cancerous cells into my bones.

If I blew this, I'd get nothing other than a burial in a mass grave.

I knew that.

I was here for this purpose.

I'd identified this man's IP address.

I'd identified, through investigation, that he was the head of a brotherhood I'd never even heard of, not outside the murder room Bear had left behind.

And as a result, I knew what the United Brotherhood could do and what this man was capable of.

Embracing my death as I headed to his office, I accepted that I'd come so far in my search for answers that I couldn't stop.

Why had Eamonn Keegan killed my mom?

The question drove everything I did.

The silence of Anton's study was immediate. A stark contrast to the band out in the ballroom that graced the party with modern and classic music.

More like a library than a study, the walls were lined with books, and they ranged from floor to ceiling, with those special stepladders perched in different corners to access the books that were hard to reach.

Above the fireplace, there was a wall of photographs of Anton shaking hands with everyone from celebrities to presidents.

The fire bloomed with heat as if he'd been sitting in here all evening and hadn't been playing host to a party beyond these doors.

In the center, which would put his back to the windows, his desk sat pride of place.

He ushered me over to the chairs in front of it then retreated to the fireplace.

When he returned to my side, he was carrying two photo frames.

My brow furrowed as I realized he was shaking my dad's hand in one. Mom was at his side, smiling that smile every spouse of a celebrity learned to use—apathetic interest.

In another photo, she was there too. Younger, this time. Dressed in a dark suit, boxy, little tailoring, lined against a wall, watching as Kuznetsov shook hands with Clinton.

The problem was... she wasn't standing *near* Clinton.

She wasn't *his* protective detail.

She was Kuznetsov's.

"I knew you'd come to us, Star," Kuznetsov mused as he studied the photo of my parents. "I knew you'd find us. It was just a matter of patience."

My throat felt as if I'd swallowed an apple whole. "Who are you?"

He smiled as he leaned against his desk. "We are everything, and we are nothing. We were there before the Masons began, and we will be here when one superpower decides to blow up the world with a click of the leader's fingers."

That didn't help.

He knew it.

Impossible, but... "Was my mom one of you?"

"Of course. Born and bred—"

"That can't be." I knew my voice was hoarse with desperation. "She was with the CIA. She was American."

He smiled at me, but it wasn't that tight one he'd been gracing me with since we'd met. It was sly.

Cunning.

"Was she?"

"Yes," I hissed. "She was American. Born and bred."

"As much as I regret it, she's dead and has been for a long time. My interest is in you, Star. You, not she, are the reason I brought you in here.

"I've watched you, cultivated you, seen you grow and blossom until you're the perfect vision sitting before me.

"You're a weapon. Honed and precise in a way that your mother could never be—"

"I don't believe you," I whispered, clinging to one solid truth: "Mom was American."

"Your mother was whatever I wanted her to be."

My nostrils flared as I jerked to my feet.

The desire to flee was strong, but the urge to know more was stronger.

I stood there, hovering in place, trying to decide what to do.

Was the truth that unpalatable that I couldn't withstand it?

After everything that had been done to me?

"There's nowhere to run and there's nowhere to hide that I can't find you, Star Sullivan. There never has been, and there never will be."

Feeling invisible cuffs tighten around my wrists, shackles tying me in place, I clenched my hands into fists as I rasped, "You lured me here?"

"Naturally."

"What are your intentions?" Before he could answer, I tipped up my chin. "I was a sex slave before. I will never be that again."

"That was the CIA's desire, not mine. How do you think you were liberated? You think that was just pure luck? You don't think it was engineered." He pshawed as he got to his feet, moving to stand in front of me. "It is your past that makes you deadlier than your mother."

"Don't pretend to know her. If she was..." I couldn't get the words out. "If she was who you think... then she was just a soldier."

Kuznetsov smiled at me again, but this time, it sent a cold bitter chill through my veins, one that was more devastating than the winter night outside. "That's where you're wrong, granddaughter."

"Here's the latest news about yesterday's explosion in Petrovsky Park. The Kremlin claims to have made an arrest while eyewitness reports say—"

When the buzzer sounded at the door, I frowned at the TV, turned down the volume, and trudged over to the screen to see who was there, only...

No one was.

Not at the intercom, at any rate.

"Who is it?" I questioned, on edge and not in the mood to be messed around.

Bombs didn't just go off in one of Moscow's most popular parks for no reason. Ever since the news had hit, I'd been trying to find more information about who the target had been.

My gut didn't lie to me, and right now, it was screaming.

I just didn't know *what* it was screaming.

Before my temper could blow, a small body jumped into the camera's spectrum. It reminded me of Tigger from *Winnie the Pooh*.

"Conor? Is that you?"

I recognized the voice. "Katina?"

"Yes! It's me! Can I come in?"

My heart tumbled down into my stomach.

"I need to talk to you," she cried as I fell silent, my tongue on lock-down as I tried to figure out how the hell she'd gotten here.

I hit the buzzer and let her in even as I was heading toward the elevator.

Was she alone?

How had she gotten to Manhattan on her own without someone from the Sinners realizing she'd run away?

There were a dozen implications that set my nerves on edge, but I knew she'd only come here for one reason—Star.

As the doors to the elevator opened, she was there, waiting to step in. Only, when she saw me, she did the damnedest thing, and she broke my fucking heart.

She burst into tears.

I wasn't great with tears, but I immediately crouched down onto my knees and held out my arms. She rushed into them, and all the questions I had about how she got here, about what she was doing running away, faded into inconsequence.

She sniffled and sobbed and wept in my embrace as the elevator doors rumbled to a close and I held her through the storm.

Then, in my ear, her cheeks drenched with tears, her nose snotty, she sniffled, "You have to bring her back to me, Conor. You have to. She promised she'd call, she promised. Why didn't she call me yesterday? Why didn't she? Star never makes promises she can't keep."

My stomach twisted.

My palms started sweating.

Coincidences—I didn't believe in them. And I sure as fuck didn't when Star was around.

That bomb in Moscow—was that Star's work?

If it was, she'd have been able to make that call though, wouldn't she?

Terror made my voice harder than I'd like as I demanded, "What happened, Katina?"

Her arms clutched at me. "You have to bring her back to me."

That was all she said.

Over.

And over.

And again and again.

Her devastation triggered the impossible because Star and I were the same regarding promises, but I made her daughter one anyway: "I'll bring her back to you, Katina. I swear."

I just didn't know whether I'd be bringing her home in a body bag, or at my side...

To be continued in FILTHY FECK
www.books2read.com/FilthyFeck

AUTHOR NOTE

Conor O'Donnelly
THE FIVE POINTS'
MOB COLLECTION
FILTHY
FECK
SERENA AKEROYD

He's about to get his woman...

But, before he does, Hunter & Aurora are going to get their story.

You can check that out here: www.books2read.com/Valentini Three

And... I'm sure you'll be happy to hear that the Bratva are coming to get you!!

You can preorder the first in the Bratva series here: www.book s2read.com/BratvaOneSerenaAkeroyd And no, I'm not telling you who the hero or heroine are. :P

Hope you're excited!!

Don't forget the second FILTHY KING hits 500 reviews, I'll be dropping a bonus scene in my Diva reader group!

You can join here to read it when it happens: www.facebook. com/groups/SerenaAkeroydsDivas

AND...

I'm so pleased to announce that I'll be co-authoring a project with Cassandra Robbins!! A character from her Disciples will be falling for a Fecker!! Can you guess who?!

You can preorder here: www.books2read.com/FilthyDisciple

Published stories outside of the Feckers' universe include:

Luciu & Jen - **THE DON** - www.books2read.com/ValentiniOne

Amara & Quin & Hawk - **HAWK** - www.books2read.com/ HawkSerenaAkeroyd

Nyx & Giulia - **NYX** - www.books2read.com/Nyx

Rex & Rachel - **REX & RACHEL** - www.books2read.com/ RexSerenaAkeroyd www.books2read.com/RachelSerenaAkeroyd

Much love to you all,

Serena

xoxo

THE CROSSOVER READING ORDER
WITH THE SINNERS & VALENTINIS

<u>FILTHY</u>
<u>FILTHY SINNER</u>
<u>NYX</u>
<u>LINK</u>
<u>FILTHY RICH</u>
<u>SIN</u>
<u>STEEL</u>
<u>FILTHY DARK</u>
<u>CRUZ</u>
<u>MAVERICK</u>
<u>FILTHY SEX</u>
<u>HAWK</u>
<u>FILTHY HOT</u>
<u>STORM</u>
<u>THE DON</u>
<u>THE LADY</u>
<u>FILTHY SECRET</u>
<u>REX</u>
<u>RACHEL</u>

<u>FILTHY KING</u>
<u>FILTHY DISCIPLE</u>
<u>THE CONSIGLIERE</u>
<u>THE ORACLE</u>
<u>LODESTAR</u>
<u>SILENCED</u>
<u>END GAME</u>
<u>FILTHY RICHER</u>

This story features orgasm control in a BDSM setting.
Secrets & Lies is now free!

CONNECT WITH SERENA

For the latest updates, be sure to check out my website!
But if you'd like to hang out with me and get to know me better, then
I'd love to see you in my Diva reader's group where you can find out
all the gossip on new releases as and when they happen. You can join
here: www.facebook.com/groups/SerenaAkeroydsDivas. Or you can
always PM or email me. I love to hear from you guys:
serenaakeroyd@gmail.com.

ABOUT THE AUTHOR

I'm a romance novelaholic and I won't touch a book unless I know there's a happy ending. This addiction is what made me craft stories that suit my voracious need for raunchy romance. I love twists and unexpected turns, and my novels all contain sexy guys, dark humor, and hot AF love scenes.

I write MF, menage, and reverse harem (also known as why choose romance,) in both contemporary and paranormal. Some of my stories are darker than others, but I can promise you one thing, you will always get the happy ending your heart needs!